MARK W. TIEDEMANN

REALTIME

Mark W. Tiedemann's love for science fiction and writing started at an early age, although it was momentarily side-tracked—for over twenty years—by his career as a professional photographer. After attending a Clarion Science Fiction & Fantasy Writers Workshop held at Michigan State University in 1988, he rediscovered his lost love and focused his talents once more on attaining his dream of becoming a professional writer. With the publication of "Targets" in the December 1990 issue of *Asimov's Science Fiction Magazine*, he began selling short stories to various markets; his work has since appeared in *Magazine of Fantasy & Science Fiction, Science Fiction Age, Tomorrow SF*, and a number of anthologies. His bestselling novel *Mirage*, the first entry in the *Isaac Asimov's Robot Mysteries* series, was released in April 2000; its follow-up, *Chimera*, was published in April 2001. His most recent novel, *Compass Reach*, was published in June 2001 by Meisha Merlin Publishing, Inc. Currently, he is working on the third book in the *Robot Mysteries* series, to be published in 2002. Tiedemann lives in St. Louis, Missouri, with his companion, Donna, and their resident alien life form—a dog named Kory.

AVAILABLE NOW

THE ALFRED BESTER COLLECTION
The Deceivers
The Computer Connection
re: demolished

THE ARTHUR C. CLARKE COLLECTION
The Sentinel
Tales from Planet Earth

THE HARRY HARRISON COLLECTION
Bill, the Galactic Hero
THE EDEN TRILOGY
West of Eden
Winter in Eden
Return to Eden

THE ROBERT SILVERBERG COLLECTION
Sailing to Byzantium
Science Fiction 101: Robert Silverberg's Worlds of Wonder

ISAAC ASIMOV'S ROBOT CITY
Volume 1
by Michael P. Kube-McDowell and Mike McQuay

Volume 2
by William F. Wu and Arthur Byron Cover

Volume 3
by Rob Chilson and William F. Wu

ISAAC ASIMOV'S ROBOTS AND ALIENS
Volume 1 by Stephen Leigh and Cordell Scotten

ISAAC ASIMOV ROBOT MYSTERIES
by Mark W. Tiedemann
Mirage
Chimera

WILD CARDS
Edited by George R.R. Martin
Wild Cards
Wild Cards II: Aces High

The Alien Factor
by Stan Lee with Stan Timmons

Arthur C. Clarke's Venus Prime: Volumes 1, 2, 3, and 4
by Paul Preuss

Battlestar Galactica: Resurrection
by Richard Hatch and Stan Timmons

REALTIME

MARK W. TIEDEMANN

ibooks
new york
www.ibooksinc.com

DISTRIBUTED BY SIMON & SCHUSTER, INC

An Original Publication of ibooks, inc.

Copyright © 2001 by Mark W. Tiedemann.

An ibooks, inc. Book

Distributed by Simon & Schuster, Inc.
1230 Avenue of the Americas, New York, NY 10020

ibooks, inc.
24 West 25th Street
New York, NY 10010

The ibooks World Wide Web Site Address is:
http://www.ibooksinc.com

ISBN 0-7434-2393-3
First ibooks inc. printing October 2001
10 9 8 7 6 5 4 3 2 1

Edited by Steven A. Roman

Cover design by J. Vita
Interior design by Westchester Book Composition

Printed in the U.S.A.

For Allen and Linda Steele
Thanks.

PROLOGUE

Three A.M. passed quietly in St. Louis alleys. A peaceful city. Foot patrols, neighborhood walking parties, City Hall's curfew, the general prosperity combined into subtle and not-so-subtle inducements to social conformity. Even in areas where most people expected a certain level of criminal activity—and, indeed, found enough to validate common prejudices—three on a Monday morning was usually quiet and uneventful. Alleys ran throughout the warehouse district like narrow canyons. Sodium vapor lamps brilliantly bathed them in sepia and gold. Empty at three A.M., they looked like something from a Romanian surrealist vid. Endless turns down identical paths, and above, an all-seeing intelligence watching as the typecast hero runs the maze to an insistent pulse reminiscent of late-twentieth century electronic music.

Time, though, in Romanian surrealist vids did not exist; there was no three A.M.

At three A.M. in empty St. Louis alleys there was no all-seeing intelligence. . . only a small group of people gathered around a bound woman.

Her breath came hard, as if a short string held the insides of her chest together. Each inhalation tightened the string, preventing her from getting enough air; if she did not move, she could control it. They had already moved her a lot, but now she knelt on the pavement under yellow-orange lamps, and the pain receded a little.

Her hands were cuffed behind her back. They had not bothered to bind her legs—her left ankle was broken, but they had not done that, not directly; she had stepped off a truck dock and come down on it, which was how they had caught her—nor had they gagged her. They had been polite until the interrogation began. One of the men even apologized after he knocked out the first tooth.

The van in which they had brought her waited at the end of the alley. She ached, sharply and dully, all over. She wondered if they intended to stand there till dawn, wordless, watching her suffer.

She looked at the stark walls of the buildings on either side. Unremarkable metal shells leached of color by the nightlights, nothing that told her where she was: an alley in the production district, near the locks along the Mississippi. She knew that, but it was far from where she had been caught. How she had gotten here, like this, was another matter.

A crazy path, she thought, one staggered and stubborn, shifting and turning, appearing and vanishing. Often it had seemed a different trail entirely, until a detail emerged—a name, a fact, a puzzle-part that reminded her of what she had been working on before and what she would continue to work on after . . . if there was an after. Finding that path in St. Louis had surprised her. Her mission here concerned another matter entirely. She almost laughed at the irony, till the string in her chest tugged and she coughed instead.

Time skipped a city, she thought caustically, stopping in one place, resuming in another, different threads . . .

Right now, however, time was a force she wished to stop. What did the gypsies call it? *Realtime.* The time for accounting. The time that cannot be ignored, bypassed, avoided, or bartered away.

Three of the people around her fidgeted. Amateurs, she thought, temporary help. Their speech was rougher, less polite than the others. They telegraphed their intentions constantly. She knew when one would pace, another light a cigarette, still another make a sarcastic remark. She knew they would kill her, but she carefully evaded that thought, habit reinforcing a belief that she might yet survive, based partly on the alleged fear that killing a federal agent supposedly generated in people. Experience told her that fear was mythic, an illusion, at least in the case of a certain class of people, but it was a handy crutch. It might even be true for the three amateurs. They clearly did not like the situation.

But for the other two, the man and woman standing off to the left, who waited like stone—obviously professionals—the myth meant nothing.

She had not known the woman before coming to this city, but the man was familiar. She had seen him in Halifax during another mission, one that had failed: An executive had contacted Treasury to report on a commodity fraud within his company. He was killed and the entire illicit operation was shut down.

The details scrolled through her mind, a comforting mantra. Vaccines meant for Africa left the country on a ship. In mid-ocean another ship met it, made an exchange, good vaccines for inferior product, point of manufacture unknown. The primary pharmaceuticals came back into the country by another route to be sold under another label at an inflated price. The company profited from the spread between the cost of the exchange and the new retail cost, doubling their initial profit. Detail upon detail, departure schedules, ports of entry, distribution points. Soothing, reassuring data. *I know things,* she told herself. *I am valuable, have been valuable.*

She had no hard evidence, but she knew that this man, now leaning quite peacefully against the wall of the warehouse, had been the one who had shut it all down and turned her investigation into a disaster. She had not expected to encounter him here. A mistake.

Well, she thought, *I always say if you're going to make a mistake, make a good one . . .*

Another vehicle approached. She strained to look behind her. Headlights blinded her and she momentarily closed her eyes.

"About time," the other woman said.

"I still think this is a mistake," the assassin said quietly. The woman glared at him; he shrugged.

Car doors opened, closed, more people joined the group. She could not hear what they said, only the sounds of their voices.

The group broke apart. She opened her eyes and looked around. Some returned to the van, a few stepped closer. The other woman squatted before her. Absently she fingered the lapel of her victim's shirt.

"I like your taste," she said. "Pity. We're going to take you home now."

Two men grasped under her arms and lifted her to her feet. Her torso rippled in pain and her breath came harsher.

She felt a heaviness in her right side and knew her lung was punctured.

They carried her to the car. She saw then that it was her car, a replica 1994 Cadillac Seville, its deep maroon the color of drying blood under the sodium vapors.

They took off the cuffs, opened the driver's door, and helped her behind the wheel. The van was backing toward her. She let her head fall against the headrest and closed her eyes.

"Time to stop hurting," the other woman said.

She opened her eyes and looked to the left. The woman stood by the open car door, smiling enigmatically.

The van stopped a few meters from the front of the Cadillac.

A pneumatic gun pressed to her neck; she felt a faint pressure when the trigger was pulled. The cold seeped quickly through her body, stealing the pain. Curiously, she hungered after it even as it left her. She sucked air raggedly for a few seconds.

"Leave it in front of her house," the woman said. "Clean up and get out. Disappear."

The men all nodded and set about their business.

"Don't you think—" her companion began.

She looked at him.

"No," he said, "I suppose you don't."

"I'll see you downtown," she said.

He nodded and wandered back to the van.

One of his men opened the hood of the Cadillac. He worked on the navigational computer for a few minutes, installed a new module, then sprayed a mild solvent over everything he had touched. He closed the hood and sprayed, then joined the others in the van.

The remaining two men departed on foot, heading in opposite directions.

The Cadillac started up. The van pulled away and the car followed.

The woman waited until the two vehicles were out of sight, then touched her sapphire brooch. A few minutes later, a limousine pulled into the alley.

As she stepped into the car, she glanced at the time: three-twenty A.M. The limousine moved off, into the night.

The alley was quiet.

ONE

G rant Voczek stepped out of the umbilical into Lambert National Airport and spotted his contact immediately: the man wore the waist-length jacket of the liaison office. He greeted Grant with a short bow.

"Special Agent Voczek, I'm Rycliff. I have a car waiting. Your CID please?"

Grant handed over his Civic IDentification card and followed Rycliff to the air marshal's desk. Rycliff spoke briefly to the attendant, inserted Grant's card into the scanner, then waved Grant through the velvet rope, behind the desk, and out into the concourse.

"Here you are, sir," Rycliff said, handing back the CID. "Welcome to St. Louis. How was your flight?"

"Fast," Voczek said, unable to keep the fatigue from his voice. "Personally, I prefer airships."

"Much more relaxing, I agree. The car is right through here."

A narrow corridor led off the main concourse. Rycliff pushed open the door and Grant found himself outside in a small alcove. A midnight-blue limousine waited. Rycliff slipped his own ID card into the lock and the door slid open.

Gratefully, Grant relaxed in the plush calfskin seat. He hated the stiff seats on passenger jets.

Rycliff tapped a button on the navigator. "We'll go directly to the federal building. Assistant Director Koldehn is expecting you. Have you ever been to St. Louis before?"

"No, this is my first time."

"Ah. Well, perhaps you'll have time to see the city."

The car moved off smoothly.

"Do you know anything about the incident?" Grant asked.

"Only the gross details. A Treasury agent found murdered, in her car in front of her house, apparently beaten to death."

Grant nodded. That was about all *he* knew. He had received word to fly to St. Louis at five in the morning Washington D.C. time; an hour later, he was on a jet. His stomach churned slightly—he had not yet had breakfast, but it was still early, not even eight local time.

The limousine accelerated onto a highway. Grant gazed out at the passing cityscape, absently noting the mix of light industry and residential districts.

Suddenly, the ordered architecture of private houses and manufactories ended, replaced by a chaotic sprawl of tents, tempdomes, makeshift hovels, and old trailers. Smoke drifted over the shantytown; sunlight glinted off solar collectors. A few houses rose out of the mass of shanties, blunt steel from a past age.

"Barter commune," Rycliff commented.

"I know what a barco looks like. How many people live in there?"

"We're not certain. Somewhere between two and four thousand. It's grown in the last few years."

"It's the only one in the city?"

"The only major one. There are a few small enclaves of gypsies, nothing serious."

Grant stared at the commune until the highway took them past it. A concrete wall separated the next neighborhood from the barco. Residences in neatly maintained streets with tall elms and maples made a startling contrast.

"There's the Hall Street district," Rycliff said, pointing out the opposite window.

New buildings, a few with contemporary neogothic trim, mingled with older metal boxes in the densely packed manufacturing and warehouse district. Steam wafted across the flat roofs. As they approached the Salisbury exit, Grant glimpsed the river locks.

"Impressive," he said, sitting back. "Convenient for the barco to be so close."

"The Mayor isn't pleased. There was an attempt made a few years ago to shut down all the barter communes in the city. That's the main reason there's only one now. They were everywhere, small communes, mostly in the north and northwest, but with a couple down south. Raids were conducted, arrests made. All it did was consolidate them into the O'Fallon Park district."

"Rats."

"I beg your pardon?"

"Rats, Mr. Rycliff. Very difficult to eliminate rats once they've established themselves."

"Personally, I think *they* killed our agent."

"The gypsies? Why would you think that?"

Rycliff frowned. "As you say, sir—rats."

* * *

The federal building complex squatted on four square blocks in the center of the downtown district, near the other civic offices—City Hall, civil courts, police headquarters, the post office. Typically, it resembled a fortress as much as an office building. The limousine parked itself in the underground garage. Rycliff took Grant to the fourteenth floor, all of which belonged to the Treasury Department.

Grant surrendered his CID again and let Rycliff walk him through the brief security protocols. Like other Treasury offices, this one seemed understaffed. The hallways stretched past closed doors, many of which probably opened on empty rooms. Stylized labels identified offices with special functions—COLLATIONS, DATA PROCESSING, INFORMATION MANAGEMENT, CIVIL PRIORITIES ROOM 40—while others bore only numbers.

Rycliff brought him to a door with a brass plaque:

PHILIP KOLDEHN
ASSISTANT DIRECTOR
TREASURY

He knocked twice, then entered.

"Special Agent Voczek," he announced. "Agent Voczek, this is Assistant Director Koldehn." He glanced to the right, past Grant, and frowned.

Grant registered the presence of another person just as Koldehn came up to him, hand extended. "Welcome to St. Louis, Agent Voczek. Honored to meet you, sir." Koldehn was a short man, wide-shouldered and bald, with a thin, greying mustache. The current fashion of knee-length jacket exaggerated his compactness. "How was your flight? I hate jets myself, much prefer the train."

"Tolerable, sir," Grant said, gripping Koldehn's hand. "Thank you."

Koldehn glanced at the liaison. "Uh, thank you, Rycliff, that will be all."

Rycliff nodded. "Sir."

The door closed.

Clearly, Koldehn liked dark wood and leather. The office seemed to absorb the light from the row of tall windows. Mounted displays of old, obsolete currency notes glinted on the wall above the bar.

"Agent Voczek," Koldehn raised a hand toward his other guest, "may I present Special Agent Reva Cassonare? FBI."

She was a full head taller than Koldehn. She stood with her back to the windows so Grant could not see her features clearly. She wore a short blue jacket over a white high-collared blouse, and baggy pants that gave the impression of a full-length skirt.

Grant nodded. "Madam."

"Agent Voczek." Her voice was a wooly contralto.

"Agent Cassonare came directly from Chicago," Koldehn said.

"Bullet train," she said. "Fast and boring."

"The FBI still have offices in Chicago?"

"For now," she said. "Gubernatorial elections this year, though. We might lose our welcome."

"Please," Koldehn said, gesturing for them to sit down. "You've both been on the road early, so I won't drag this out. We have . . . an incident. I'd like it cleared up as quickly and neatly as possible."

"A federal agent is dead," Agent Cassonare said. "Too late for neatness."

"I don't want it getting worse. The local police are

already more than slightly upset with us over this. They're more than half convinced our agent's death was justified and I can't entirely blame them."

"Excuse me?" Grant said.

Koldehn shifted uncomfortably. "You have to look at it from their perspective. The agent—Elizabeth McQuarry—was discovered yesterday morning. She was in her car, parked in front of her house. Apparently she'd been beaten to death. We estimate time of death approximately five hours before she was found." He seemed embarrassed. "A neighbor found her."

"Beth McQuarry." Grant sighed. He had heard that she was working in St. Louis. He had hoped someone else was the victim.

"You knew her?" Agent Cassonare asked.

"Yes, we were acquainted. She was a good agent. What was she investigating?"

"That's the question," Koldehn said. "She'd been called in at the Mayor's request to investigate a commodity leak in the barco. A simple enough assignment, you'd think, but after two weeks she went off on a tangent. There were complaints. I spoke with her, of course, but she wouldn't stop. Frankly, I was preparing to have her recalled when this happened."

"Complaints from who?" Grant asked.

"Local business owners," Koldehn said. "Of unimpeachable character."

"Case files?" Agent Cassonare asked.

"Not that we've found. I understand you worked with her once before, Agent Voczek?"

"Twice. Once in Boston, once in Buffalo."

"Then perhaps you know something about her routines . . . ?"

Grant nodded. "Perhaps."

Koldehn waited. When Grant said nothing more, he cleared his throat. "As this is now a murder, we're required to have the FBI on board." Again, he seemed embarrassed. "I want this solved. I want her original mission completed and her killer or killers found."

"Do you believe they're related?" Agent Cassonare asked.

"You don't murder someone for no reason."

Agent Cassonare's eyebrows rose slightly. She pursed her lips into a doubtful moue, but she said nothing.

"She wasn't working with a partner?" Grant asked.

"She was assigned Agent Kitcher, but I gathered she worked alone. Coming directly out of D.C. gave her a certain autonomy."

"A commodity leak in a barco is a rather low priority investigation for D.C. Why would the Mayor here bring us in?"

Koldehn shook his head. "The Mayor is bidding on a research firm to locate in St. Louis. The prime location for it would be O'Fallon Park. You may have seen it on your way in, Agent Voczek—it's covered by the barco. The Mayor, in my opinion, was trying to force a deportation to clear the area."

"She could order a local sweep—"

"But she can't get them out of Missouri. Frankly, she'd like to be governor. If a federal deportation is ordered, the gypsies end up in Yucatan. Not her fault, not her responsibility, her electability remains unaffected."

Agent Cassonare grunted. "And, of course, gypsies can't vote."

Koldehn frowned. "Well, of course they can't." He cleared his throat again. "In any case, we now have a capital crime involving a federal agent. Whether the Mayor wished us involved or not, we now have cause. So, I want the threads gathered up. I want to know who murdered Agent McQuarry and I want to know if it involved her investigation. You will both be provided offices here."

"What about the residency requirements?" Grant asked.

"Ah, well, Agent Cassonare's people have leased her an apartment for the duration. Treasury had already set Agent McQuarry up in a townhouse. I perfectly understand if you'd rather not—"

"Agent McQuarry's house will be fine," Grant said. "A townhouse . . . that sounds rather long-term."

"Yes, well . . . see Rycliff for that. He'll show you to your offices."

Grant stood.

"I wish," Koldehn continued, rising, "that I could welcome you here under better circumstances. St. Louis is a quiet city—I quite like it." He shook their hands. "Good luck. If you need anything . . ."

"Right now I need to check in with D.C."

"Of course." Koldehn leaned over his desk and pressed a button. When Rycliff entered he said, "Take them to Agent McQuarry's office. See they have our complete cooperation."

"Yes, sir."

Grant followed Rycliff out. He heard Agent Cassonare's footsteps a pace behind him. He made a show of rubbing his eyes with thumb and forefinger and stifling a yawn.

"Late evening?" she asked.

Grant nodded. "Then the call at five this morning."

"I know what you mean. I arrived an hour ago."

Rycliff led them to one of the oak veneer doors and opened it with a passchit. "This one was Agent McQuarry's. We can arrange for you to have a new office—"

"No, this will do." Grant stepped past him into the small room. The desk was angled to a corner. A sofa, two straight-backed chairs, a bookshelf; no pictures on the walls, no mementos or bric-a-brac. As he expected.

He turned to Rycliff. "Her terminal hasn't been wiped, has it? No one's been through it?"

"Except for standard retrieval procedures after an agent's death, it is as she left it."

"Can you arrange for me to have the adjoining office?" Agent Cassonare asked.

"Of course," Rycliff said.

Grant looked closely now at Reva Cassonare. She was nearly as tall as he. Angular face, strong jaw and a straight mouth and nose, dark, deepset brown eyes that looked up from beneath black eyebrows. Her hair was thick and black and her skin was a light brown. One of those rare people, Grant noted with a twinge of envy, who look both hard and gentle at the same time.

"Mr. Rycliff," she said, "please tell the forensics officer in charge of Agent McQuarry's case to see us as soon as possible."

"Yes, Madam—"

"And have a pot of coffee delivered, would you? I've been up since four."

"Yes, Madam."

"Rycliff," Grant said. "Arrange Agent Cassonare's office first."

"Uh—yes, sir."

"Then I want to talk to Agent Kitcher."

"I'm not sure he's in the building at the moment, but I'll see he contacts you."

"Thank you."

Rycliff went.

"In a hurry to be alone?" she asked.

"I didn't think you'd want to stand around in the hall while I made a confidential call to my superiors in D.C."

Agent Cassonare flashed a small smile. "Courtesy. Thank you, Agent Voczek." She started to leave, then looked back. "If you don't mind, my name is Reva. We'll be working together and formalities can be tiresome."

He nodded absently and sat down behind the desk. He steepled his fingers over his nose, closed him eyes. When he looked again, she was gone.

Grant raised his eyes to the walls and turned slowly until he once again faced the desk. He sighed heavily. The next breath caught, stuttered. The next came evenly.

"Beth . . . I'm so sorry," he whispered. "I'm going to miss you."

Grant switched on the terminal and sent a standard note to his Washington D.C. office stating time of arrival and that he had contacted the local director. He indicated that he intended to move into the house Beth McQuarry had used and would report at length from there.

Then he requested Beth's case file. After a few seconds, the screen flashed NOT FOUND. Grant opened his briefcase and took out a small disk, which he inserted into the scanner on the side of the keyboard. DIAGNOSTIC RUNNING, the screen said, and Grant leaned back to wait. Almost thirty seconds passed. Then:

TERMINAL COMPROMISED/NONCOMPATIBLE/SEARCH PROTOCOLS RUNNING/AUTO ERASE INITIATED/UNREADABLE FILES SIXTY-FIVE PERCENT/OPERATING SYSTEM INTACT/STANDARD NET-WORK PROTOCOLS INTACT

"Hell," Grant breathed. He bent over the keyboard and instructed the terminal to set up a bubble memory, access keyed to his diagnostic program only, then began the task of pulling information from elsewhere. The department files on the case dumped into the bubble and he started piecing together what had happened.

Beth arrived in St. Louis almost a month before, just as Koldehn said, in response to a request from Mayor Poena and Police Chief Moore to investigate the growing barter commune. According to estimates from the Comptroller's office, the barco population had doubled in the last three years.

Her initial reports—little more than replies to questions from City Hall—confirmed the estimates, even suggested that they were conservative. She had found evidence of a significant flow of unregistered goods through the barco. It looked like the barco was being used to disseminate sub-market goods in exchange for commodity scrip, a common enough way to avoid the purchase tax automatically deducted through the CID, but she had yet to find the points of flow—the input of goods and the outflow of scrip. The quantities of scrip implied would be difficult to redistribute inconspicuously.

A week ago, her reports had stopped.

He pulled the coroner's data.

Grant made himself study the images of Beth McQuarry. The bruising on her face made her look much older than thirty-one. Both eyes swollen, left cheek broken, right lower mandible broken, damage to both eardrums. Curiously, her nose was not broken. Four teeth missing, three cracked. Left ankle broken. Pelvis broken. Six ribs broken, two puncturing the right lung. Both kidneys ruptured as well as the spleen. She only vaguely resembled herself.

At last he closed down. The screen went clear. Grant leaned back in the chair.

It seemed senselessly brutal. If she had been murdered because of her investigation, then a gunshot, asphyxiation, a knife wound, half a dozen other methods would have served. They would already have known who she was, what she was doing, so torture for information would have been unnecessary. Or her murderer had nothing to do with her investigation. If that were the case, finding who became nearly impossible—at least for him, since that would remove the investigation from Treasury's jurisdiction.

Beth had been a friend. He would have to make sure it remained Treasury business. He would proceed on the assumption that she had been murdered as a consequence of her investigation.

Grant opened his pocket watch. Two-twenty. He stared at the wide, ivory face. That seemed wrong. He checked the time signature on the screen. One-twenty, local time. He reset his watch, snapped it closed, and dropped it back in his vest pocket.

He gave the desk a quick search, but, as he expected, he found nothing. Whoever had searched her terminal—clumsily, destroying all the data they probably wanted—would not have let locked drawers stop them.

In fact, he realized, the violated terminal fell under Treasury jurisdiction. That relieved him of one concern and gave him another: the only people with access would be Treasury personnel. He opened the terminal again, slipped another disk into the second scanner, and transferred the file he had just created. He returned this and his diagnostic disk to his briefcase, then stood and stretched. He was hungry. He checked himself quickly in the mirror that hung on the inside of the closet door—burgundy cravat, white silk shirt, dark grey and blue brocade vest, pale grey jacket and pants . . . and bleary eyes—and headed out.

He opened the office door. Reva Cassonare smiled, hand raised to knock.

"Are you hungry?" she asked. "I'm starving. And I have things to tell you."

TWO

In the lobby, a few late lunchers waited by elevators. Janitorial drays moved over debris scattered across the marbled floor. Posters, flyers, and pamphlets, Grant saw. REED REX, TYRANT AT LARGE, he read. COMMON FRANCHISE NOW!

On the sidewalk, local police loaded handcuffed people, many well-dressed, into transports. Several more people were on their knees against the wall, waiting, while bulls in padded armor walked back and forth before them.

"Senator Reed is paying St. Louis a visit this week," Cassonare said. "From what your director said, he and the Mayor should get along marvelously."

At the corner they crossed Market Street to the strip of parkland that stretched from the monolithic civil courts building east to an open-air amphitheater.

"You said you had things to tell me," Grant said.

"What do you think of Director Koldehn?"

Grant glanced at her. "How do you mean?"

"Before you arrived he talked about Treasury's

relationship with the city, the community. He didn't come out and say it, but I had the impression that he was more worried about your department's reputation."

"More than what?"

"My terminal is compromised." She looked at him. "I'm not surprised, but I had hoped for a little time before your people clippered me."

"Are you sure it's Treasury? With someone like Reed coming, Secret Service is probably already here."

"I thought of that, so I traced the clipper."

"And?"

"It's been routed through a number of very sophisticated dodges, but I'm certain it's sourced within the building. Without any other likely candidates, I'll assume it's Treasury."

Grant felt himself losing patience. "Would you like to use my terminal?"

"I might as well leave the clipper in place."

"Have you done anything else in the last two hours? Something, perhaps, that bears on the case?"

They walked to the amphitheater silently. It seemed warm for an autumn day. Food vendors served quick lunches on the sidewalk all around. On stage, a modalist troop performed intricate geometries with rings and staffs. The seats were nearly half-filled.

"I hope you like Mexican," Reva said, stopping at one of the vendors. Before Grant could say anything, she inserted her CID and ordered. She handed him a wrapper and a tall cup, then nodded to an open café area behind the amphitheater.

Grant looked inside the wrapper at an incoherent mass of peppers, beans, and some kind of meat, ladled into a soft shell. He followed her to a small table under an umbrella.

Reva folded back the wrapper and bit hugely into her food. She closed her eyes and chewed slowly, then shrugged. "Not bad for this far north. What do you think?"

Grant sipped at his drink—lemonade—and looked across the table. "I think," he said slowly, "that it is not the best way to start a working relationship by criticizing someone's department, questioning the motives of its agents, and presuming to feed me without first asking what I'd like."

"You don't like Mexican?"

"Are we being honest now?"

Her eyebrows twitched and she almost frowned.

"I frankly despise Mexican," Grant said. "And I haven't had many exemplary experiences with the FBI."

"I suppose we *are* being honest."

"That would be a pleasant surprise."

Now she frowned. "Agent Voczek, let's understand the situation clearly. *Because* the victim was a member of your department, you are allowed access to my investigation. *Because* the victim was a federal officer, the FBI has priority. *Because* I am officially in charge of this investigation, your participation is at my discretion. And *if* you have had less than fulfilling involvements with the FBI in the past, then you have my sympathies, but I expect cooperation. *Willing* cooperation would be preferable. I want to be taken at my word. I am not the rest of the Bureau. When you've had a bad experience with me, *then* you may criticize my professionalism."

"Seems unprofessional to complain about standard security practices," Grant observed.

"Unless it pertains to the case."

"Does it?"

She bit off another mouthful of her lunch and looked away, gazing at a very old building nearby. Its greenish

dome gave it the appearance of a miniature capitol. The
surrounding structures towered over it. She swallowed
lemonade and looked back at him. Her eyes narrowed.

"It strikes me curious that there were no records from
your friend for the week prior to her death. I've known section heads to bury data rather than share it with another
agency." Reva finished her food, then leaned back and
wiped her mouth. "So tell me, Agent Voczek—was Agent
McQuarry enough of a maverick to disregard all field protocols and keep no notes?"

"I wouldn't have thought so, no. But . . ."

"At least her car kept a record."

"Her car?" Grant asked.

She regarded him now with evident amusement.
"Besides finding out who clippered my system, I've been
down to the garage asking questions. She was found in her
car, I wanted to see the car."

Grant looked away, watching other lunchers while he
thought.

"It is odd no one reported a disturbance. Beating someone to death is hardly a quiet affair. The neighbor said she
found her in the morning, but heard nothing the night
before." He nodded. "I see . . . so, what do you mean it kept
a record?"

"She had a recorder installed. The clip for the night she
died showed that she'd stopped three places before the car
was left in front of her house."

"And how was she left?"

"A slave module had been attached to the navigator. She
was murdered elsewhere and her car was towed home. The
module had been removed, of course, but it left a trace on
the recorder."

"The addresses?"

"I'm having them processed now. By the time we get back they should be ready for us."

"My apologies, Agent Cassonare."

"Accepted . . . if you quit calling me 'Agent Cassonare.' When you work with me, it's 'Reva.'"

"You're sure you want to work with me?"

Reva shrugged. "I don't know. Anyone who despises Mexican . . . something unAmerican about that."

Grant finished his lemonade. "That's me. UnAmerican as they come." He tossed his uneaten food in a trash bin nearby and returned the cup to the vendor.

"Hey, I was joking."

"Of course." He gestured at the foodstand. "I owe you for that."

"No, I should have asked first."

Grant shook his head. "No, no. Surprise is good. I intend to return the experience." He walked a few steps, then looked back. She was looking at him, lips pursed. He smiled. "I'm joking."

"Of course. Let's see about those addresses."

A loud clattering cut through the soft sounds of conversation around them. The lid of the trash bin into which Grant had thrown away his lunch wobbled on the sidewalk. People moved away quickly. He took a few steps toward it, then saw an inch-thick rod extending up a few feet from the bin. It shone dully, like buffed metal.

Three thick streams of smoke shot from equally-spaced points along its length. Blue, yellow, and red, the trails seemed to thicken as they flowed across the plaza in the direction of the amphitheater. Thin tendrils escaped in the light breeze. The individual streams came together about four feet out from the rod, but, surprisingly, did not merge; instead, they formed a tricolor river of vapor that ran out above the stage. Suddenly, pinpoints of metallic silver, gold, red, green, and blue began sparkling throughout the mass.

A pair of civic monitors came running across Market Street. One pulled off his dark-blue jacket and tried to wrap it around the rod while the other peered into the trash bin. The smoke flowed thickly from the jacket sleeves and out the top and bottom, billowing the fabric. The sleeves waved eerily as blue and yellow smoke escaped. Red poured from the neck. The monitor gathered the lapels together and twisted, as if to choke its invisible wearer. The smoke filled the trash bin and poured over the edge to pool around the civic monitors. They both started coughing.

The cloud above the stage, no longer fed from its source, dissipated slowly. The metal scintilla grew brighter.

The civic monitors moved away from the trash bin. Liberated, the rod pumped out a few last streams, but most of the smoke now curled a foot deep around the bin and spread out. The bright sparks danced chaotically. Citizens laughed, coughed, moved back, a few ran. The civic monitor without a jacket spoke into his comm while his partner leaned over, hands on knees, and hacked painfully.

"Taggers," Grant said.

"I wondered if they were here," Reva said, smiling.

Grant shook his head. "Nuisances."

"Aesthetic guerrillas. Artistic terrorists. Creative hit and run."

The cloud was nearly gone, a faint lingering haze in the amphitheater. The smoke billowing around the cafe area started thinning. A city utility van pulled onto Market Street from Broadway, emergency lights strobing, and lurched to a halt by the scene. A team of white-suited, helmeted monitors jumped from the back. One stuck the end of a tube attached to a backpack into the trash bin and pulled a trigger. Foam lapped over the rim. Two others brought up a hand truck. They wrestled the container onto it and hauled it into the van.

"That was a waste," Grant said.

"You don't approve?"

"No."

Reva shrugged. "It was a fascinating display. How do you think they managed to keep the colors from blending?" When Grant said nothing, she added: "You probably triggered it."

"What?"

"Your taco. I'd bet it was the weight of a whole taco that set it off. A pressure plate. It might not have gone off till late afternoon without that." She laughed sharply. "I love Mexican."

The department car glided to a halt against the curb. Grant looked out the passenger window at a sprawling neowright mansion. West of Kingshighway, just as it came abreast of the largest park within city limits, Lindell Boulevard became a single long stretch of mansions. Many of them looked like original Gilded Age survivors of both the twentieth century and the New Madrid Quake of 2012.

"Is this correct?" he asked.

"Beth's first stop that night," Reva said. "Maybe not this house exactly—this is only where she parked."

"We'll run IDs on this one and four in either direction." He shook his head and looked at the map on the dash display. "Where next?"

Reva pressed the PROCEED button and the car pulled away into the thin traffic. Grant absently admired the cars along Lindell. Not a single modern style in any driveway, almost all of them twentieth century replicas. The newest model he saw was a pre-Reform Lincoln, perhaps an '08. The neighborhood was distinguished by Rolls Royces, Mercedeses, and Packards. Grant even saw a Cord.

Lindell ended at Skinker, across from the entrance to the Washington University campus. The car turned right. They passed along a row of gated private streets until they reached Delmar and turned right again. Small shops lined most of Delmar. They went by a hospital complex, crossed a major intersection, and entered a district of apartment buildings and townhouses.

At Grand Avenue, they entered a district of stable residential enclaves, solidly middle class, interspersed by neighborhood confectories, service stations, boutiques, and civic halls. Most of the construction was less than forty years old, by the look of the mingled styles. Grant had read that large parts of the city had burned in the Quake, others had simply collapsed. The city was absorbing it all back into itself and, like old scars, the traces were fading over time. For St. Louis, it had been the New Madrid Quake; for the rest of the country, it had been the Reform.

The car crossed Natural Bridge Road and passed along the edge of another park. Back from the street Grant saw the bright tent of a free kitchen. The long tables and benches seemed to be about a quarter full.

They left the park behind. Grand made a slight northeast jag crossing Florissant Avenue and became East Grand. Ahead, an ancient tower, like some improbable alpine keep, rose from a small circle of parkland. The shingled roof was scabrous green. East Grand looped around it and continued on, under Highway 70, across Broadway, and into the industrial area known as the Hall Street District.

Grant tapped the display. "We're not far from the barco."

"Mmm," Reva murmured, nodding.

The car's program brought it to Hall Street, then left. On either side industrial buildings stood, the alleys and streets between them close and deep like knife-cuts from above. No one walked the narrow sidewalks. The dull drone of machinery, punctuated by heavy impacts, throbbed constantly.

The car turned down an alleyway between two featureless metal shells. The navigator took them into the maze, turning right, left, left, right, and right again. Grant kept his eyes focused ahead.

Finally, the car stopped.

Grant stepped out and looked around. The sky formed a strip of brilliant blue between sheer walls. Once a pale green, the walls now flaked and peeled in the shadows between them. Streaks of rust ran down from the roofs. The air smelled of machine oil and hot metal. Debris formed an amorphous crust at the base of both buildings.

The alley let onto a wider street. A trailer rolled by. Grant stepped out into the street alongside it. As the trailer pulled away, he crossed to the other side and looked back at the pair of old warehouses. The one on the left still had no features. Grant strolled back. Midway down the length of the other building, a loading dock extruded over the shallow sidewalk, the metal doors wide open.

Within, bright ceiling lights cast the interior in brassy relief. A wide concourse extended back between high shelves loaded with various-sized packages. Drays hummed in and out of access aisles, moving materials. Grant saw no people. Probably the entire place was automated, with a couple of shift supervisors in an observation booth.

Above the loading bay, bright red letters proclaimed MCHI DISTRIBUTIONS #4.

Grant continued on to the end of the block. The corner

of the warehouse was a glass entryway. The tall door bore the engraved legend OFFICES in ornate script.

"May I help you?"

Grant turned. Three men stood a few feet away. All wore dark-green coveralls, smeared with ground-in dirt, and thick-soled boots.

The nearest one said, "You look lost."

"I am," Grant said. "I'm looking for the DuPont complex . . . ?"

The other two exchanged amused looks while the first man grunted. "Dandies. Swear to morning . . . this whole section is MCHI, all right? DuPont is that way." He pointed with his middle finger somewhere over Grant's right shoulder. "DuPont's all red and amber stripes. Got it, dandy?"

"Thank you—"

"This is private property. I see you 'round here again, I'm clipping you, clear?"

"Have you found it?" Reva called.

Grant looked over his shoulder and saw her leaning across the seat of the car.

"Yes. These gentlemen have straightened me out." He bowed his head politely to them. "Thank you again."

He got in the car and gestured for Reva to turn left. She drove away from the intersection leisurely.

"Sorry it took me so long," she said.

"You were watching?"

"From the alley. What now?"

"Go to the next stop."

She nodded and circled the warehouse back to the same spot in the alley. She rebooted the navigator and pressed PROCEED. The car moved on and turned right.

* * *

Grant kicked a stone with the toe of his boot and watched it skip down the pavement. Reva knelt in the middle of the alley, scraping at small dark spots with a knife and dropping the shavings into a plastic bag. She finished and stood, glancing around, eyes narrowed, lips compressed in concentration.

The corrugated walls of one warehouse reflected brilliantly, stark white, into the shadows of the opposite building, which seemed to soak up the light like dry sand absorbing water. Both buildings rose only two stories, but covered several square blocks. Grant thought how easily he could become lost in this industrial labyrinth. The corporate colors helped, but only if you knew the code. At night, even that might be worthless.

Reva approached him. He gestured at the sample bag.

"Blood?" he asked.

"Yes. I'll have the lab run it, but I'm certain this is where McQuarry died."

"Not much blood."

"No. But the autopsy revealed massive internal bleeding."

"Still. It seems like there should be more blood."

"Why?"

Grant shook his head absently. "She was strong. It would have taken a lot . . . "

Reva slipped the bag into her jacket. "What next?"

"I suppose we should at least ride the program out. See what path they took her home." He gave the place one last sweep and returned to the car. When Reva got in, he said, "Check the police reports, see if anyone reported anything out of the ordinary. We can come back later and canvass the employees."

"At night?"

"It might be worth a try. Most of these places are automated, but there's usually someone on the premises. Someone might have seen something. Heard something."

She punched PROCEED, and the car continued on.

The trail wound a tortuous path south through the industrial district. At times they came within sight of the river and the lock complex.

Finally, they reached Branch Street and from there they turned south on Broadway. The car joined a heavier flow of traffic into downtown, then took Olive Street west. At the sprawling St. Louis University campus on Grand Avenue, Olive became Lindell. Full circle.

Almost. The program turned down a block short of Kingshighway and the eastern edge of the park, then up Euclid, into a cloistered neighborhood of stately townhouses and lush sycamores, elms, oaks, and walnuts. Shops and restaurants clustered at the intersection of Euclid and Maryland. One more block, and the car turned right onto Pershing Place and stopped in the driveway of the last house at the first cross street, Walton Row.

Grant looked up at the house through the windshield. Pale blue with white trim, shutters framing tall windows, a covered driveway leading to an old brick garage in the backyard. It looked nothing like the apartment he remembered Beth occupying in D.C., or the cottage she had taken when they had worked together in Buffalo, New York. He took the key from his pocket and sighed.

"Would you like me to come in with you?" Reva asked.

"No." He looked at her, realizing how sharp he sounded. "I'm tired. And—"

"No need to explain. You knew her."

Grant nodded. "Thank you. I'll call in. We need to start running a list of the stops, see who belongs to what—"

"Already noted." Reva lifted a portable secretary. "I need

to check my new accommodations, too." She frowned thoughtfully. "Are you sure it's such a good idea to stay here?"

"No, but I don't want to waste time or credit arranging for new." He opened the door. "After we've both had a night's sleep perhaps we can start over in the morning. I have the feeling I didn't make a very good impression."

"You didn't." She smiled crookedly. "You're sure *we're* going to get a good night's sleep?"

"If not, I'll pretend *I* did. That should help."

Grant got out of the car and shut the door. He watched her back out of the driveway and head back up Pershing.

In the stillness of late afternoon, Grant heard leaves rustling. He breathed in the tree-flavored air. For a moment he considered talking to the neighbor who had discovered Beth. He had the name and address; it was just across the street. Mrs. Delcampo. But it could wait. He did not think she could tell him anything new, not now, not tired as he was. He might miss things.

He went to the front door.

The foyer was plainly paneled. A coat closet opened to the right, a built-in bench on the left. The thick cut-crystal glass in the front door diffused the light in a pleasant, vague pattern across the grey carpet. A staircase led upstairs, dividing the hallway that ran to the back of the first floor. It felt close, almost comfortable.

Sliding doors opened immediately off the hallway to the left. Grant pushed them aside and looked into a large study. Built-in bookcases held few books, a few curios and knick-knacks, but were largely empty. A mock Empire writing table stood near the windows—that, and a plain sofa Grant recognized as Beth's.

He drew the curtains by the desk and went to the bookshelves and scanned the titles. Most of them he did not recognize, a potpourri she had probably picked up in a local used bookstore just to have something on the shelves. Then he found her books. The same twenty-two she had had since he had known her. He still did not know if she had ever read them.

He pulled out the Tolstoy. *Anna Karenina*, an ornate leatherbound edition with gold leaf. He took it to the desk and let it fall open to the middle, set it up on end, and bounced it twice. From the space between the stitched pages and the leather spine fell a thin sheaf of papers. Grant sighed, relieved, and took the book back to the shelf.

As he replaced it, he thought about the book's opening lines: "Happy families are all alike; every unhappy family is unhappy in its own way." He had always wondered which part of that sentence applied to Beth.

Which part might apply to Reva Cassonare?

He tucked *Anna Karenina* back in its place and went to the desk to read Beth's personal case file.

THREE

In the morning, Grant made coffee. He carried a mug to the office on the second floor and tapped his code into the terminal. The screen on the desk turned milky.

"Please stand by," an androgenous voice told him. Grant glanced over the papers spread across the desk, then looked up when the milkiness on the screen faded into an image of the Treasury Seal.

Abruptly, the seal changed to another image: Director Cutter. She glowered at him, a wide-faced woman with narrow eyes and a perpetually skeptical pout. The time signature in the corner of the screen said: 8:35 A.M. D.C.

"Good morning, Grant."

"Good morning, Madam Director."

"I've been over your report from last night. Not very much. Three names?"

Grant pulled the sheaf of papers across the desk. "That's all I recovered. You already have Beth's reports up to a week ago?"

"Yes . . . Recovered? There's a problem?"

"Yes, Madam. I didn't want to send it in a report. Her office terminal has been violated. Whoever did it triggered Agent McQuarry's prophylactics. The files are irretrievable."

"I see. And her home?"

"My initial search doesn't show violation. I haven't gone through the terminal here yet."

"Are we secured, then?"

"My own prophylactics are in place."

She nodded curtly. "What didn't you send last night?"

"Only a couple of items. I have a question first. Was Agent McQuarry being disciplined?"

Director Cutter's pout deepened to a frown. "Why?"

"The Department doesn't usually stipend an agent for a townhouse unless it's to be a long-term assignment. Since Agent McQuarry was not officially assigned to Assistant Director Koldehn's division, I wondered if the nature of her mission—"

"The answer is yes."

"May I ask why?"

"That's confidential."

"With all due respect, it could bear on my mission."

Director Cutter seemed to consider, then nodded. "I'll think about it. Proceed."

Grant suppressed a scowl. "Without her case file, I'll have to rework her investigation. Her private log contained the three names I sent you—"

"Mitchel Abernathy—local businessman; Aaron Voley—private citizen; and Representative Michael Tochsin?"

"That's correct."

"And?"

"Notes about the quantity of merchandise leaking out of the barco. She estimated ten to twenty percent of all gypsy trade was contraband, leaked out by a local business. Her estimates of the gypsy population don't jibe with local Treasury estimates by several thousand. There may be over ten thousand in the barco."

"Any pattern?"

"A lot of entertainment gear, clothing, new terminal modules, toiletries—a significant range."

"A consortium of businesses?"

"Or one large company, highly diversified."

"There shouldn't be too many of those."

"I'm running a search-and-collate." Grant cleared his throat and took a drink of coffee. "There's one more thing, Madam Director. Beth's last page was labeled 'Director's Attention Only.' There's one name on it: Harold Lusk."

Cutter's eyes registered surprise. "My, my," she said. "That adds something."

"May I ask who is Harold Lusk?"

She shook her head. "Let me answer your queries from last night. As far as his record goes, Assistant Director Koldehn gives no indication of corruptible behavior. He's by-the-rule, regulation front to back, unimaginative, and politically circumspect. He's been the local director in St. Louis for fifteen years."

"He seems concerned that we not make a mess."

"He's comfortable there, doesn't want to risk a recall. Paul Kitcher, however, is another matter. He used to be attached to the Montreal Division. His record shows him to be competent, unambitious. But he was transferred out after an indiscretion over commodity scrip disbursements. The matter faded, so we didn't have to take further steps. But his ability to function in Montreal was severely curtailed. We transferred him to Boston, then St. Louis. That was six years ago and his record is clean since, but he's been known to hold unconventional political opinions. Again, nothing severe enough to warrant measures, but still . . ."

"What sort of opinions?"

"He tends toward New Libertarianism."

Grant grunted.

"We're still trying to acquire more information about Agent Cassonare, but by reputation she is an achiever. She was principal agent in the Tamaulipas incident in '48."

Grant started. "Really?"

"Her involvement in this suggests that the FBI are looking into a different matter entirely."

"What matter might you suggest?"

"Well, the third name on Agent McQuarry's list—Michael Tochsin. That's Representative Michael Tochsin of Missouri."

"So there may be a political element. What about the other two?"

"Mitchel Abernathy is a local entrepreneur, one of St. Louis's principal citizens," Cutter explained. "He owns Mitchel Consolidated Heavy Industries, Abernathy Distribution, Incorporated, and is head of the Clayton Banking Consortium. His personal net worth is estimated at half a billion. He's in his seventies, unmarried, and a civic benefactor of above-average generosity. He ran for mayor once, shortly after the Reform, but lost."

"And Aaron Voley?"

"A principle citizen of a different sort. Neighborhood organizer. He used to be a lawyer, served on the State bench for one term twenty-five years ago, and has since become a community activist. He is a registered opponent to the citizenship and deportation laws. He's not nearly as substantial as Abernathy, but he has enough to fund several local benefices. He publishes political material, is seen in public rarely, and is a vocal opponent of the society of principle citizens."

"It's sounding more and more political. What about the last name?" Grant asked.

"Since it has already come up . . . Harold Lusk worked for us, till recently. He was a security codes designer in the Fiscal Technologies Division."

"He left the Department?"

"He disappeared from the Department last year. We haven't determined what happened. Frankly, we didn't want the FBI involved. Something like this is embarrassing. This is Department business, Grant. Understand?"

Grant nodded. "Code security—how good is he?"

"One of the finest. He wrote the last variation on card dedication protects."

"How long after that did he disappear?"

"Ten months."

"Was Agent McQuarry involved in his search?"

Director Cutter drew a deep breath and let it out slowly. Grant carefully did not react. "Agent McQuarry expressed certain unorthodox opinions regarding his disappearance. She compromised her other work over this matter. She was used to walking her own path in the Department. My fault— I should have stopped it before she thought it was her right."

"I see," Grant said.

"I gather she did not inform A.D. Koldehn about any of this?"

"Beth—Agent McQuarry—tended to work close to the vest," Grant replied. "She was here four weeks. As she wasn't one to waste time I suspect that she didn't make any of these breakthroughs till quite recently. No, she didn't tell Director Koldehn—at least, if she did, he has chosen to say nothing about it. Given certain impressions I've had, I don't think she trusted the people here."

"That would be unfortunate, to find a problem among our own." Cutter looked thoughtful for a few seconds. "A ten to twenty percent volume trade in contraband in a barco of that size could take a substantial bite out the community tax base. Could easily affect their return share."

"Director Koldehn told me the Mayor is trying to bring a new company here, a research firm. She wants the land the barco is on."

Cutter nodded. "And she wants a federal deportation, I know. Normally, I would have denied the request, but . . . well, you may be there for a time. Would you like an increased stipend?"

"Why not transfer what's left of Agent McQuarry's into my account? If I need more I'll let you know."

"Very good. Take care, Grant."

The screen reverted to the Treasury seal, then faded to transparency. Normally, she would have denied the request, but . . . ? In his experience, Grant had never known Director Cutter to leave thoughts unfinished.

Return share . . . Grant could not quite accept the idea that Beth McQuarry was dead because the percentage of tax distribution for St. Louis—for Missouri—might go down as a result of unregistered barter trade. It made no sense to him that the gypsies would kill her—that could only bring trouble for them, the kind they had become careful to avoid since the days of the national deportations.

So the Mayor wanted a federal deportation. Politics. That, Grant thought, would be worse still. He accepted that people killed over politics, but he had never been able to understand it—intellectually, but not viscerally.

And Harold Lusk, whoever he was. Treasury code writer.

Grant wondered why he had never heard of this man's disappearance. If he were as good as Director Cutter suggested, the news should have been all over the Department, especially in Grant's own division, Resource Securities. Obviously, it had been suppressed internally.

And the FBI had sent the agent who broke a slave ring in Tamaulipas. He remembered some of the details. Part of it had involved bogus identities, adulterated CIDs. The local department had been used to validate that part of the FBI mission. A coincidence that Reva Cassonare had "been available" in Chicago?

His own presence he believed pure coincidence. Cutter would never have sent him had she known how close he and Beth had become. They had both been careful about that. They were good investigators who worked well together and had become friends, no more, no less than anyone else in the Department. Grant remembered that his insistence on discretion had annoyed Beth. "You're so by-the-rule, Grant," she had said. He saw no advantage for either of them in displaying their relationship for everyone. It could only cause problems. They would be separated.

He laughed at that now. They had been separated anyway, just from the flow of the job: Beth sent to Montreal, he to Frisco, then she to St. Petersburg, he to Denver. They managed to meet in D.C. from time to time, but it wore on them. Grant felt it, the fading. Trying to keep a fire lit without fuel; he had thought Beth had felt it, too. He had never asked.

He had checked Beth's home terminal the night before and found nothing, protected or otherwise, that looked like a case file. As he expected. He ran a more thorough diagnostic to ferret out clippers or any other indication of corruption. The system was clean. He tapped in the connection to the terminal in his—Beth's—federal building office and set up a mirror bubble in the home system. He then accessed her itinerary with an old code that she had never bothered to change. Nothing beyond department appointments the first week, but after that she began increasing her range. She had attended a Saturday evening performance of the symphony. Grant found reservations for the theater for the next three weekends. A lecture at the Fair Memorial Museum in Forest Park. Several memos regarding someone named Richard—he had called, she had called him—the last one on the day of the night she had been killed. Grant checked her phone file. Several calls to and from Richard up to that day. The day after, nothing. His number was protected, only his first name was recorded. Grant wished he had an open warrant with which to access this kind of data, but a judge—any judge—would want much more substantiation than this before issuing one.

He opened the data log and checked the number of faxes received and sent: only four in three weeks. The first had been the largest, a full report on Paul Kitcher requested from personnel in D.C. The second, a few days later, was a packet of information from the Tapachula border police. Was that in Tamaulipas? Grant searched for the file, but Beth had hardcopied it and erased the data. The third had been from Paul Kitcher, a profile on a stock and securities company. The last had been a transmission to D.C., a request for information on someone named A. Taraquel. No reply.

The report on Kitcher was missing as well. That left the stock company profile. Grant printed it out—nothing more than a standard prospectus, he discovered—on the securities company, a small firm called Weston and Burnard. Then he sent an inquiry to the Director's Office asking to identify A. Taraquel.

Weston and Burnard dealt in municipal bonds, investment credits, and interstate capital exchanges. The previous year's volume reached eight hundred million, which placed it solidly in the NASDEC Gold Elite. Three quarters of their business was within Missouri's credit district. The other quarter channeled through Wall Street and would be impossible to trace without a warrant. Grant had a contact in SEC division; something might be "unofficially" known. He tapped Stuart's number. He was out, so Grant left him a message to call when he could.

Without knowing who Beth had contacted in the border police, Grant hesitated following it up. His inquiry might be rebuffed, departmental privilege.

Grant closed the system down and stared at the clear screen for a few minutes.

He went back up to the bedroom on the third floor. The east-facing window glowed pink and gold from floor to ceiling with early morning sun. The bed occupied the center. Black sheets. Scandalous. He remembered standing at its edge the night before, bone-weary, reluctant to lie down. Beth's bed. He could not tell what disturbed him more, that he would sleep in a dead friend's bed or in a woman's bed uninvited. Finally, exhaustion won, but it had taken a long time for him to fall asleep. Across from it were mirrored closet doors. To their left, the bathroom; to their right, Beth's open portmanteau on a low, long table. A richly-woven carpet covered most of the hardwood floor. In the corner, next to the west-facing, wall-tall window, a small desk with data terminal.

Grant pushed open the mirrored closet doors. Several of Beth's suits hung loosely within. A set of low drawers took up the bottom of the closet. Shoes and boots stood neatly on top of the drawers. He went through all her pockets. In the fourth jacket he found a slip of paper with a scribbled note:

COZY, B.C. CID

He continued on. From a red brocade vest he took out three condoms. He pulled that suit out—amber-hued jacket, chocolate brown pants, red vest—and tucked it apart from the others.

Completing the right side of the closet, he closed the door and opened the left. Four dresses, her best. He remembered them. Full skirts, tight blouses with high necks, ruffled sleeves, brilliant sashes. One was blue and gold with faint dashes of green, cut in a Spanish style with a waist-length jacket and a thick belt. Beth's eyes had been brilliant green.

Grant looked up. To the left of the dresses hung three suits that did not belong to her. Grant looked over his shoulder at the bed. He tossed the condoms onto the black sheets and pulled out the first suit.

He spread it out on the bed and stepped back. Tailored, pale blue with black piping around lapels and cuffs, and a plain cobalt-blue vest. Copper buttons. He turned the sleeves back and checked the stitching. Fine pinholes gave the illusion of quilting in the silver satin lining. Grant used his fingertips to rub the satin, braced against the palm of his other hand. It slid liquidly over an interior lining. Poromat. The suit was thermally efficient, the inner lining "breathed" by shifting heat away from the body. The vest was similarly made. The pants tapered to the ankles; the fabric was very light to begin with, and unlined. Grant found the label—GROUSIANS, BOSTON, SIZE 46. He held the pants against his own leg. The wearer was probably an inch or two taller than Grant.

He went through all the pockets. Finding nothing, he returned it to the closet and examined the other two suits, both from the same tailor, both the same quality. In the pocket of the cream suit he found ticket stubs to the symphony.

Grant sat on the edge of the bed and scooped up the condoms.

Richard?

A deep-green 1946 Mercury pulled into the driveway. Reva leaned out the driver's window, honked the horn twice, and grinned at him.

"What do you think?" she asked. "I picked it up last night."

"Yours?" Grant asked.

"Of course, mine. Hop in."

He studied her as she craned over the seat to steer the car out of the driveway. She wore a vague smile. When she turned back around, she winked at him. The car bolted forward down the street.

"Is this all you did last night?"

"You mean other than sleep?" She smiled. "My secretary's on the back seat." She jabbed a thumb over her shoulder.

Grant stretched back and pulled the leatherbound portable off the seat. He set it between them and Reva, glancing at it once, opened access. The four-inch square screen glowed.

"File STL.R.ONE," she said.

Grant typed in the code and the file name appeared, followed by text.

"MCHI is owned by—" Reva began.

"Mitchel Abernathy. He also owns Abernathy Distribution and is chairman of the Clayton Banking Consortium."

Reva's eyebrows rose fractionally. She nodded. "Mitchel Consolidated Heavy Industry is also an umbrella for fifteen various manufacturing firms, plus two engineering consulting firms."

"Either one of them cybernetics?"

"Elgin Light and Grafics. The rest are listed on page two."

Grant scanned the list of firms. "A little of everything. Consumer electronics, industrial motors, power cells, special packaging . . . what about his suppliers?"

"Pages four through eight. Not an exhaustive list, this was done quickly."

"I'm most interested in the bank."

"I thought you would be. Page ten."

"Done quickly?" He paged down till he came to it, then read the profile carefully. "Assets forty-six billion . . . available credit: three point seven billion . . ."

"Fourth largest bank in the state. Most of St. Louis's principle citizens are depositors or shareholders."

"I'm interested in their investment arms."

"I only discovered a few of those, all blue chip, one of them Wall Street."

Grant studied the text. Weston and Burnard was absent. He set the secretary aside. "You were busy. Did you sleep?"

"Did *you*?"

Grant looked at her. He liked her profile, he decided, as much as her full face or her three-quarter. With a slight shock he realized that it had little to do with her appearance. She appealed to him and that troubled him. It would be easy to sit back and accept her at face value, accept her help, eventually come to rely on her.

"We have an appointment in the examiner's office this morning," Reva said.

"You make me feel sluggish."

"I can change that."

"Really?"

At the next stop she typed in another code. "Recognize this?"

Grant studied the screen. He frowned. "That's from my case file."

"Boston, '47. Intellectual property violations."

"Smugglers."

"Three members of the Harvard library board of curators were pirating research material on current projects and transferring copies overseas," Reva explained. "Treasury knew it was happening but not how."

"They used foreign studies students. They hid the data in the ID buffer of their travel visas. On arrival, the buffer dumped its data automatically at an additional command inserted in the scanner at Customs."

"You proved the students knew nothing about it."

"I worked with a team of good agents."

"But it was your breakthrough. You made the arrests."

Grant looked out at the passing street. "Beth McQuarry was one of the team."

"I know. I'm sorry."

Grant gestured at the secretary. "You got that from the same place as the material on Abernathy. This was already prepared."

Reva frowned suddenly. She switched off the secretary and drove on in silence.

Grant stared at the scenery without seeing it. Abruptly, he recognized the ancient City Hall building, a bizarre duplicate of an even older French building from the eighteenth century. Sections of it showed signs of recent attempts to clean it, but overall it looked encrusted, like the surface of an old ship. Grant straightened self-consciously and glanced at Reva. Her face was expressionless, as it had been most of yesterday.

She pulled into the garage and parked in a reserved space near the elevators.

"Agent Cassonare—" he began.

Reva's eyes narrowed. "We're back to that, then. Fine. If you want to work this thing the hard way, then we can part company now. I'll file the appropriate recommendations and have you removed. I'm not required to have someone out of D.C. from Treasury, I can use local representatives."

"I—"

"Let me finish. I would like to work this case with you, out of mutual respect, and try—if at all possible—to bypass the usual agency rivalries." She tapped the secretary. "I admire the work you did on this case. That's all. That's why I pulled this data. I would like that to be the basis of our relationship."

"Then you can start by being honest with me."

"I have been—"

"No. You've given me facts. I have no idea what's behind them."

"Lies of omission?"

"Call it what you like."

"So what would like to know?" Reva asked.

"Why are you here?"

"Because—"

"You specifically. You broke the Tamaulipas case. Aren't you just a little overclassed for this?"

Slowly, she smiled, nodding. "Let's say my being in Chicago was fortuitous."

"For whom?"

Still smiling, she got out of the car. Grant resisted an impulse to grab her and pull her back.

"Are you coming?" She slammed the door. "And my name is Reva."

The physician in charge of Beth's autopsy was short and heavy across the shoulders. The light-green smock made her look stouter. She brought Grant and Reva into her office and sat behind her desk. She tapped instructions into her terminal, and a wall screen cleared.

"You've seen the preliminary report?" she asked.

"Yes."

She nodded and read down the list anyway. "Multiple fractures . . . six ribs, left ankle, cheek bones, left side of face, lower right mandible, left shoulder dislocated . . . torn cartilage on wrists, elbows, left knee . . . various contusions consistent with stationary beating—she was restrained while beaten—ruptured spleen and kidneys, punctured right lung . . . if they had just left her in her car, she would have died without any other additional aid."

"What does that mean?" Grant asked.

The doctor keyed her terminal and a close-up of the side of Beth's face and neck appeared. Grant winced at the grey pallor, the bruises around her eyes, along the jaw line. The doctor painted the screen with a laser pointer. She outlined an area of the neck.

"Carotid artery," she said. "We nearly missed this."

"I don't see anything," Reva said.

"Exactly. The surface is clean. Except for a nearly invisible trace . . ." She changed the wavelength of light. A pale circle appeared against the now-blue skin. "Shows up under UV."

"What is it?" Grant asked.

"Pneumatic injector trace?" Reva offered.

"Correct. The subject was given an injection of something. Once we spotted this, we did blood tests to isolate the substance."

"And?"

The doctor shook her head. "I have no idea. Whatever it was, it broke down into some trace alkalis. Enough to indicate that she was given a lethal dose of something. But the toxin was evidently designed to break down quickly in the presence of certain antibodies."

"What antibodies?" Reva asked.

The doctor pursed her lips for a moment. "Could be anything. But there were excessive quantities of the antibody associated with *treponema pallidum.*"

Grant felt his ears warm. "So, after she was beaten nearly to death she was poisoned."

"Yes. By a very sophisticated toxin."

"What about her clothes?"

"Ah." She cleared the wall screen. Charts with DNA spectrums appeared. "Nothing sufficient to give us an identity, so we can't even really petition for a warrant to do a genome search. But we found traces of dermis on her lapels. Enough to state that at least one of her assailants was female."

"Just from traces on the lapels?" Reva said, incredulous.

"Well, not *just* . . . the same person slapped her at least once, left some skin on the upper incisors."

"No blood?" Reva asked. The doctor shook her head and Reva sighed. "Unfortunate."

"Anything else?" Grant asked. He began to notice the faint medicinal odor in the office.

"Nothing. Oh, judging from the various bruises, it seems likely three people beat her. One wore a ring—right hand, middle finger—but we couldn't tell what kind. And lividity set in after she was placed in her car. Death occurred at 3:20 A.M."

Grant swallowed dryly. "Any . . ." He drew a breath. "What about sexual contact?"

"Do you mean was she raped? No."

"Other?"

"Traces of topical spermicide, commonly used on most brands of prophylactic. Evidence indicates recreational use." After a few seconds, she added, "No ejaculate."

Grant nodded. Reva watched him curiously. He stood. "Thank you, Doctor. If you find anything else . . ."

"I'll call you at once, Agent." She stepped around her desk and shook hands. "I understand the victim was an acquaintance. My sympathies."

"Thank you." He paused, then asked, "When will she be buried?"

The doctor shrugged. "I can't say yet. Not everyone has signed off on the body."

Grant started. "Excuse me?"

"There are three open files on this case—Treasury, FBI, and local police. Until all three clear the body for burial, it stays here, frozen."

"Who hasn't signed off yet?"

"FBI and local."

Grant felt his anger rise. Jurisdictional limbo. He glared at the screen, at the image of Beth's dead profile. He told himself it did not really matter, as long as it cleared up eventually, but he could not help feeling that it did matter.

"Thank you," he made himself say again, and left.

Grant waited for Reva in the corridor. She emerged from the office a few seconds after him.

"We should talk," he said.

"I agree."

"My office?"

"After you . . ."

Rycliff was coming down the hall toward them. "Agent Voczek, I've been looking for you. Agent Kitcher reported in this morning. You requested a meeting with him."

"Thank you—"

"And the Mayor's office called. She would like to speak with both of you this afternoon."

"The Mayor?"

"Yes, sir."

Grant nodded. "All right. I'll confirm the appointment." He started to move past Rycliff.

"We've also received confirmation that your personal belongings are arriving on the 1:10 at the Municipal Station. Would you like to have me pick it up for you?"

Grant rounded on Rycliff. "That would be fine, Mr. Rycliff. Have my car brought here. Everything else can be placed in storage until I get to it."

Rycliff backed away a step. "Yes, sir. I'll let you know when it's here."

"Thank you."

Rycliff bowed, bowed to Reva, and hurried down the hall.

"You don't have to take it out on the help," Reva said.

Grant glared at her. "Is there something you can do about expediting her burial?"

"I'll see what I can do, certainly."

"Good."

"You know, you don't really impress me as the maverick."

"I don't?"

"No. Your entire career looks very by-the-rule, very circumspect. Efficient." She nodded. "Yes, that's the word. You're very efficient. Working this alone isn't."

"Perhaps I'm trying a new method."

"Is this the one you want to do that with? You might make a mistake and let them get away."

"I'll trust you that far. If you think I'm making a mistake you can let me know."

Reva stepped up to him. "Absolutely. If you make a mistake you could botch my case, too. I wouldn't like that."

"You wouldn't?"

"No, not in the least. It wouldn't be the best way for us to become friends, either."

"I'm not concerned."

"Pity."

Grant waited for more, but she only looked at him. He nodded sharply and started down the hallway.

"So," she called, "are you interested in seeing the rest of my notes?"

He stopped. He listened to her footsteps come up behind him.

"I have to see Agent Kitcher first," he said.

"Fine. Afterward, we can use my office," she said. "I've already screened it for security."

FOUR

C ozy stepped from the shoestore into the crowded street and flexed his toes. He looked down at the new runners—sapphire blue with white piping, crimson lettering stenciled along the sole that read "Avante"—and sighed, pleased. He glanced back inside the store. Another customer stood at the counter, handing over her CID card. The attendant indicated the slot in the side of his register. The customer, thumb on the scanner plate on the card, slid the CID in and waited for the blue light on the register.

Cozy blew out a pleased breath and started down Cherokee Street. The runners, lined with poromat, breathed like skin and his feet, for the first time in months, felt comfortable, pampered. He absently patted his jacket pocket—a new windbreaker, purchased half an hour earlier further west up Cherokee—and felt the rectangle of the citizen ID card.

Across the street, he saw Old Cletus standing outside the J.C. Penny outlet, playing an ancient accordion. The noon sun glinted off his thick, black sunglasses. At his feet a wide, handmade basket waited to receive contributions.

Among the scant number of shoppers on the street, a pair of women strolled by, hesitated, and stopped to listen to Cletus play. Both wore ankle-length embroidered skirts and brilliant white blouses with ruffles at wrists and neck. Cozy guessed them to be fairly well off, suburbans visiting the city for bargains and adventure. He faintly resented them, but it was an unfocussed emotion. As close as he ever got to the elegant covenanted estates out beyond the city limits were fashion 'casts on the HDs. It was difficult to resent what never interacted with you. He just thought of them as foreigners, in-country for a short stay and to gather enough input to impress the rest of the foreigners Out There.

A small knot of people gathered around Cletus now, like flotsam caught up against the pair of women who had stopped. Cletus seemed to sense the audience and worked his way into a spectacular medley of *fin-de-siecle* tunes. Cozy leaned against the corner of a building and listened, tapping his right foot. Cletus might have been good enough for HD 'casts if he had a little more discipline. He bounced from one melody to another, played with their structures, combined them in weird jams. People did not like that, usually. Not enough order, not enough attention to traditions. Still, he kept the beat the same through five separate songs, and the listeners stayed for the wind-up.

They applauded politely, then one of the first pair of women opened her bag and pulled out a sheaf of commodity scrip. Cozy could not tell the designation—whether the scrip was for food, basic housing, clothing, or utilities—only that it was a fair stack that she dropped into Cletus's basket. She touched his hand to indicate that she had left something. Cletus nodded and mouthed a thank you as the group of people drifted away.

As much as he wanted to, Cozy did not cross the street to make a donation. Old Cletus was, largely, on the straight-and-up and would wonder immediately how Cozy had come into any kind of currency that would allow him to surrender some of his own scrip.

Next to the J.C. Penny was an All-Sensory Music & Video. Cozy considered it, but he had nothing on which to play any purchase. Yet. He grinned, pleased with himself, and considered what he could buy tomorrow—buy and not pay for. As he understood it, what his cousin, Harry Lusk, had done allowed these CIDs to infect a purchase scanner with a short-lived virus that made the sale register on the system and then later erased it. There was supposed to be a one-hour window, which made the cards good only for spot purchases. He could not rent an apartment or stay in a hotel on it. But for small items, like his jacket and runners, it was perfect. The idea made him chuckle. He patted his pocket again and pushed away from the storefront. The next stop would be the hardware store to get some materials for his next display. It would be wonderful to buy them new, from a legitimate source. He wondered how hard it would be to work with them, whether their freshness made them different than the discards and recycled materials with which he was used to working. He decided not. Better materials, better work. He was already one of the best taggers in St. Louis. This could, he thought, be a quantum boost to his career.

A large hand closed on his left arm. Cozy wrenched away automatically, turning and almost colliding with another pedestrian. His right hand flexed, unconsciously going for the knife in his back pocket.

"Chee-s!" he hissed. "George, don't you know better? Don't clutch, no?"

George was a few centimeters shorter than Cozy, but

wider across the shoulders. He wore one-piece, military surplus utilities, charcoal grey.

"Walk," George said, jerking his thumb in the direction Cozy had been going.

Cozy straightened his windbreaker with exaggerated care, tugging with mock-dignity at the sleeve George had grabbed. Giving George a look of dignified pain, he fell into step alongside him.

"You wish to speak at me, sir?"

"Yeah," George said. His face was closed, eyes tense under thick eyebrows. He seemed to scan the street anxiously.

Cozy looked around, suddenly concerned. "Shadows?"

"Maybe. Shut up. Walk."

They continued on, past a hair salon, a sandwich shop, a battery outlet, a used bookstore, and the South City Surplus Resource Center. George walked with a purposeful stride that bordered on too fast. People moved out of their way.

Just past the resource center George turned down an alleyway. Behind the resource center the neighborhood was abandoned residential. Burned out shells and empty, boarded up multi-unit buildings rose out of overgrown back yards. A few broken concrete slabs showed where garages once stood. Insects buzzed in the air above the weeds and grass. Halfway down the brick alley, an old Street Department sawhorse stood astride a hole.

At the end of the alley, George cut across Potomac Street and headed west, to the next street, then south. Block by block the neighborhoods became more populated.

George's pace had quickened.

"George," Cozy complained, "where are we going?"

"Somewhere to talk."

"We can talk here."

"No."

Cozy knew George well enough not to push. He walked on, matching stride, annoyed that Cherokee Street was falling further and further behind.

Out of the corner of his eye, Cozy spotted a familiar face. Only for a moment, then he was gone. He looked around. Two people walked quickly away from a pair of canisters in the middle of the street. Cozy's heart jumped. He reached out for George, excited.

The canisters' lids launched into the air, followed closely by dozens of colored streamers. Red, green, orange, yellow, blue, purple, silver, gold, the thin ribbons rippled up like striking snakes. Cozy heard the whine of small motors. The streamers began twitching, then writhing, gradually finding orbits in and out of each other in layers. Cozy watched, impressed. The ribbons were all different weights, which determined their height as their motors whirled them around. The event horizon expanded to fill the street. Smoke began to pour from three or four abandoned cars parked along the curb. The vapor met the streamers and the mix churned into a multi-layered, contoured cloud.

"Yes!" Cozy shouted. "It's *art!*"

Suddenly, George pushed him left, toward an eroded-looking two-family. Several people sat on the steps in front of the first-floor door. They shuffled aside quickly and let George usher Cozy through.

Inside, the light filtered in from the windows. Cozy blinked, trying to adjust to the abrupt darkness. George stopped at the first door and leaned in. Cozy peered over his shoulder. An old woman sat in an ancient rocking chair, fabric falling from her lap while her twisted fingers worked to turn thread to lace. A small flatscreen stood on a low coffee table before her. Her eyes stayed on the HD, flicking down occasionally to check the work in her lap. A news announcer spoke softly about something outside the country—Cozy heard the words "Europe" and "Russian Commonwealth" but little else. She glanced briefly at George and Cozy.

"Pardon, Ma'am, if you don't mind, we need to cut through," George said.

She nodded. "You're a nice boy," she said, and returned her attention to the flat.

George tugged Cozy along the hallway, to the back door, out through the overgrown backyard. They jumped the fence and sprinted across the alley, into the opposite yard. This house was abandoned and George led the way down into the damp basement.

"That was cover," Cozy said disdainfully. "You had taggers do that just for cover?"

"Move," George said, nodding once.

Cozy carefully picked his way through the debris to the front of the building. George shoved an old mattress out of the way, uncovering a tunnel.

"George, you know I hate tight places—"

"Then why do you keep sticking yourself into them? Shut up and come on."

Cozy swallowed and entered the low-ceilinged tunnel; after about thirty meters it joined a cross tunnel. George took the right-hand one. Cozy scurried along after him, trying to ignore the wet walls, the smell of sewer, while at the same time keeping from brushing against anything.

The tunnel let them into another basement. This one was cleaner, clearly in use. George went to the back door and they came out into the bright sunlight again.

Cozy stepped onto the sidewalk and looked around.

Winnebago. Suddenly he knew where he was going. "Uh, George, I don't think I'm in a proper frame of mind to talk to—"

George turned left, toward Jefferson Avenue, and Cozy followed. Cozy knew better than to try to run. George was shorter, but stronger, and a faster runner. He had been in the military.

"Hey, George," he called, slowing, "I don't want to talk to Voley."

George spun around and jabbed a thick finger into Cozy's sternum. "I do not give a particular shit what you do or do not want to do. Voley wants to talk to you." He jabbed him again. "Give me the card you took."

Cozy backed away a step. "George, look, I—"

"Don't run from me. Give me the card."

Reluctantly, Cozy pulled the CID from his jacket and slapped it into George's outstretched palm. George looked at the card and shook his head.

"Hope you like your new *things,*" he said. The card disappeared into his pocket.

"I don't see what good the CIDs are if no one ever gets to use 'em."

"Exactly. You don't see. Come on."

Cozy jammed his hands into his pants pockets and followed George a step behind. "Didn't mean anything," he complained.

"Enough, Cozy. Save it for Voley."

At the intersection of Jefferson and Winnebago stood a tented free kitchen. The smoke and aromas of the food wafted around Cozy. He looked into the blue shadows beneath the half-acre awning. Still early, the tables were largely unoccupied. Several workers lounged behind the long counter. By noon the place would be jammed and no one would be idle.

Cozy ran his hand over his chin. "Hey, George, how about some calories first? I haven't eaten yet."

George glared at him over his shoulder. "Should have thought of that before I found you."

"I didn't know you were *looking,* George!"

George kept walking. Cozy considered breaking off and getting food anyway, but he let George drag him along in his wake. They crossed Jefferson and headed for one of the elegant old three-story townhouses that lined the east side of the street. The ancient houses stood out in sharp contrast with the rest of the neighborhood. Somehow they had survived all the cycles of erosion and renewal St. Louis had gone through for most of its history. The very fact that they stood, whole and much as they had been when originally built two hundred years before, even after the New Madrid, gave them an almost magical aura. This stretch of Jefferson was very nearly sacred ground by virtue of these houses. Cozy felt immediately intimidated.

George led the way down the narrow gangway to the rear. A high wooden gate hid the yard. George knocked softly, three times, and leaned back against the wall. A few moments later the gate opened and a tall, slender black woman with close-cropped hair and large green eyes looked at them. Cozy smiled at Voley's live-in housekeeper/secretary. Camilla had always been with Voley, as far as Cozy knew, and had always looked about the same.

"George," she said.

Cozy smiled and bowed. "Madam."

"He's waiting," Camilla said, and stepped aside.

Cozy followed George into a lush garden. A brick path wound its way through dense foliage to a comfortable screened gazebo in the rear of the yard. Two men and another woman waited within, glasses of lemonade sweating on the stone table.

"George," the man to Cozy's left said. "You found him."

"Yes, Mr. Voley."

Voley looked up at Cozy. He was old, with thin, yellow-white hair and pale blue eyes. His face was round and friendly, a bit red. He wore a loose navy blue robe.

Cozy did not recognize the man opposite Voley, but he did know the woman. Not her name, nor had they ever met, but he had seen her. Up north, in O'Fallon Park, cruising the barco.

Cozy noted the man's suit—name brand, very current cut, the jacket hem almost knee length, a rich maroon with a violet cravat—and the manicured, tinted fingernails. A touch of bronze shade darkened his eyelids around wide, almost luminous green eyes. A dandy, Cozy thought. The woman was just as expensively dressed in a comfortable executive suit, closed collar, her white cravat just a thin hint of material over the rim. She wore no makeup, and a secretary hung loosely in her hand. Her eyes were dark brown, almost black, which made her orange-red hair all the more striking.

Cozy smiled at Voley. "Sir, Madam," he said. "Mr. Voley."

"Cozy," Voley said, his normally laconic voice edged with unfamiliar tension. Voley looked up at George. "Take him in the house, George. I'll see him in a few minutes."

George nodded and tapped Cozy's shoulder. Cozy smiled again, nodded politely at Voley's two guests, and followed George up the back stairs into the kitchen.

"Sit," George said, indicating a chair by the old, plain oak table.

Cozy felt his heart race. Perhaps he could run. No,

George would simply find him again, and then he might pound him. Cozy laced his fingers together loosely and tapped his thumbs together nervously.

Finally, the kitchen screen door opened, and Voley stepped inside. He walked over to sit across from Cozy. Camilla brought him a tall glass of lemonade. Voley motioned and she brought another for Cozy. George dropped Cozy's stolen CID on the table. Voley sighed and picked it up. "Cozy, Cozy."

"I didn't mean—"

"I'm sure." Voley took a sip of his lemonade.

"Cozy, a portion of our enterprise has recently been compromised. Were you aware of that?"

"Uh, no, sir, I didn't know . . ."

"The gentleman I was meeting with has a certain interest," Voley said, nodding toward the backyard. "He is, of course, unaware of the particulars, and would probably not be very helpful if he did. He is that rarest of creatures, a politician with integrity. But as the situation concerns the barco and the barco concerns me, he has come to speak to me about it."

"I'm not following you, Mr. Voley."

"There was an investigation. I don't believe it went very far, but there has been a death. That potentially complicates everything else. Especially since one of the primary suspects is the gypsy community."

"A death?"

"You needn't understand more than that," Voley went on. "But you do need to understand that this has complicated matters for us all."

"I'm afraid I don't—"

"Be still, Cozy," Voley said. "You took a card without

authorization. Without permission." He looked at Cozy appraisingly. "Nice jacket. What else did you buy with it?"

"Shoes. Just . . . shoes . . . I didn't get a chance—"

"George?"

"No alert went out," George said. "As far as we can tell, the vendors didn't even notice."

Voley nodded. "That, at least, is in our favor." He tapped his fingers against his glass for a time. "Cozy, let me explain one thing. It is important—very important, I can't stress this enough—that no one suspect these CID cards. Not yet. We can't afford attention just yet. And, after the events of this past weekend, we must be particularly careful. There are other factors involved. It is important that new goods—like your jacket and shoes—be demonstrably sourced from the barco. That is why, for the time being, only a few individuals have been allowed to use the cards. They give us temporary access to the credit system, but they are not infallible. We can't have people indulging personal whims. Not yet."

"I really didn't mean anything, sir."

"No, I'm sure you didn't. You didn't think, you didn't plan, you just acted. You pocketed a CID from your cousin's apartment. You imprinted it and took it without asking. And you bought a jacket and a pair of shoes. What do you think would happen if these cards could be traced to members of the barter communes?"

Cozy shook his head and shrugged. He fidgeted and covered his unease with a drink of lemonade.

"It might trigger an investigation we can ill-afford at present," Voley said. He was beginning to speak with a gentle, rolling lilt, as if Cozy were five years old.

"I was being careful, Mr. Voley," Cozy said, resenting

Voley's tone. "Harry had a hundred of them. He didn't know I took it—"

"But he did explain to us that you were the only likely suspect. Harry is a gentleman, Cozy, and much too loyal to you for his own good. You really shouldn't take advantage of him the way you do. Harry is very vulnerable. He's taking a great risk to help us."

"We're family, Mr. Voley. I wouldn't do anything to hurt him."

"I'm certain you wouldn't. Not intentionally. I'm also certain you were very careful. But it would be a great relief to me if you would start being careful sooner—as in, keep your thieving fingers off things that don't belong to you."

"I'm no thief, Mr. Voley. You don't have cause to call me a thief. I mean, these CIDs aren't exactly legal."

"Ah. So you think it's a question of like oughtn't criticize like. Well, there's some merit to that, Cozy." Voley stood, leaned on the edge of the table toward Cozy. "I don't really care how you feel, Cozy," he said, politeness fading from his voice. "Your sense of injured justice is worthless if things go wrong. You self-centered idiot, what would have happened had a credit flag arisen from one of your purchases?"

"I would've gotten out of there, Mr. Voley! They wouldn't have caught me!"

"But they would have the card!"

The blood pounded in Cozy's ears.

"They would have the card and a description and they would know who was using it! Someone without proper ID, without credit, without any legal standing in this country, without any protection! And that would inevitably lead them to suspect the entire barco and everyone in it and what would happen then?"

"I—"

"What then, Cozy? What would happen then?"

"A raid, I guess—I don't know—!"

"You *don't* know! Exactly my point!" Voley sat back down, his face redder. He took a drink. "Exactly my point," he said, quietly. "You don't know. You have no business improvising with this, Cozy, because you don't know. Do you want to see another series of deportations?"

Cozy started. "No, sir!"

"Do you know why there haven't been any in the last five years? At least not locally?"

"I, uh—"

"Because the barcos have given no one any reason to be upset. The barcos aren't enough of a nuisance to anyone. But if this—" Voley held up the CID card "—if *this* attracts their attention and they make the connection, however unjustly, to the barcos, you know very well there will be new deportations. You could end up in Salvadore or Guatemala, Cozy, unable ever to get back here."

Cozy lowered his eyes, angry. Angry at himself and at Voley and George, angry at his cousin who had clippered him to Voley. Angry . . . and a little afraid.

Maybe, he thought, fending off the fear. *Maybe, Mr. Voley, maybe.* Cozy had heard other ideas about why no deportations had happened. The city could not get along without the gypsies, he had heard that, and it made sense. City Hall released special issue scrip for community service, cleaning up litter, tending the parks, stripping graffiti, neighborhood beautification. They had tried offering rewards for ghost artists and taggers, which had gone nowhere, but the other things . . . there were special projects that required a lot of bodies. Cozy had worked on the River Des Peres dredging four years before. Dirty work, cleaning the silt off the walls of the city's major flood control facility, which doubled as an open sewer. But the scrip had kept a lot of people in housing and food over the winter that followed. Citizens refused to do that kind of work. Oh, they would get out and work on sandbag details if the Mississippi threatened to spill the levees, that was hero duty, romantic in a backbreaking sort of way. Cleaning sewage did not count. No, the barco was necessary. Perhaps it was the same all over the country. No news ever came over the HD about barcos, unless they had some relevance to national economic indicators, but the underground carried word from coast to coast. Cities needed the disenfranchised. They would not permit another federal deportation.

"Where were you born, Cozy?" Voley asked.

"Sir?"

"Where were you born?"

"Here. St. Louis. Down at Alexius Hospital."

"You'd feel quite violated to be thrown out."

Cozy nodded.

"When was the last time you voted, Cozy?" Voley asked.

Cozy looked up, surprised. "Voted? I never voted."

"Would you like to?"

Cozy looked up at George and laughed. "Of course! Shit, who wouldn't—oh, I'm sorry—but, *yes—*"

Voley patted the air with one hand and smiled benignly. "Then follow the rules, Cozy. Keep your fingers out of things that aren't yours. You may yet get to vote." He drank again, then nodded at Cozy's glass. "Finish your lemonade, Cozy. We have other matters to discuss and you have to leave."

"Leave, sir?"

"George is going to take you somewhere to keep you safe. Now, don't argue, Cozy, this is for your own good."

"But—"

"Don't—argue."

"Yes, sir."

Cozy walked away from Voley's house. George walked alongside him, stony and silent. A spot between Cozy's shoulders itched, but he kept his eyes forward and his stride even. The smell of the kitchen across the street reminded him of his hunger. He walked against prevailing traffic, most of which flowed south, toward the free kitchen, but Cozy did not want to be this near to Voley. There was another free kitchen at the edge of Benton Park, five long blocks north.

The visitor with Voley had seemed very familiar. Important personage, certainly, but Cozy could not place him. The redhead, now that he had seen her in another setting, had the look of hired enforcement—very expensive enforcement, but Cozy had never had trouble recognizing them, no matter how well-dressed—and the secretary had been new tech, also very expensive, with a huge memory store. Cozy remembered the notices on the Net about them, new front encoding, holographic storage, microbubble configuration, everything necessary for a complete, on-the-road portable office connectable to any mainline datasource—as good as anything the Feds carried. Better, maybe. Beth had had one like it. Her personal unit, she had said, because she did not care for the government issued units.

He remembered the last time he had talked to Beth McQuarry. She had told him to disappear after he had turned over the other card. Now word had it she was dead. He wondered why Voley had said nothing about the second missing card. Or had Harry kept that from him? Who else was Harry connected with?

He told himself to forget it; that path led only to trouble.

He was already overextended on Voley's credit. He had heard nothing worth telling Voley in months, nothing to keep him in Voley's good graces, and now he had been caught lifting tools. Cozy was amazed Voley had let him go. He thought about George's warning: shadows. Who else might be looking for him? A lot of local vendors, both licit and illicit, but not in this league. The hired enforcement? He wondered if she had had anything to do with Beth's death. Voley knew more than he had let on. Why else have George take him to a safe hole?

They crossed back over Cherokee Street and he looked west, up the length of shops. He would have liked a new pair of pants to go with the jacket and shoes. If George had waited another ten minutes . . .

Cozy would have to pay a visit to Harry and talk to him about his loyalties. Family should count for more than—

Than what? Voley had been in this neighborhood, in that house, since Cozy could remember. Longer than that, he had been told. Voley was a fixture. He had done a lot for the neighborhood. He had been a community activist back when the title had been invented, so it was said. Cozy had never found out just how old Voley was. There were stories, of course, but Cozy knew better than to credit any that came with no proof. Which was none of them.

He sighed, and his belly growled. One thing at a time, the best way to survive. Food was a couple blocks off. Maybe he could afford a little better than free kitchen fare. He had some food scrip. But he had been saving that for his girlfriend, DeNeille, for the weekend; then for a week west, in the country, disappearing per Beth's instructions . . .

Maybe, he thought, it would be best to forget DeNeille. Maybe it would be best to stick with George and ride safe through the rest of this.

Maybe.

He had liked Beth. She had been straight-and-up with him, not like a Fed at all. Cozy had problems with people who killed his friends. Was Beth a friend?

He had to think about that. When he figured it out he would know what to do.

His stomach growled.

"Let's feed that," George said, "before you drive me crazy."

FIVE

A man waited in the hall outside Grant's office. He stood facing the door, hands in his pants pockets, chin tucked against his neck. As Grant neared, he looked up. Dark rings circled his eyes.

"Yes?" Grant said.

"Agent Voczek?"

"Yes."

"I'm Kitcher. Rycliff said you wanted to see me."

"That's right." Grant opened the office door and waved Kitcher in ahead. As Kitcher stepped in, he looked right and left, then turned to face Grant. Grant shut the door. "Sit down, Agent Kitcher."

Grant sat behind the desk. Kitcher remained standing.

"I understand you worked with Agent McQuarry."

Kitcher nodded. "First couple of weeks."

"What happened?"

Kitcher shrugged and his entire thin frame seemed to flex. "I don't know."

"Then you didn't complain?"

"Verbally."

"To?"

"Both of them—Director Koldehn and Agent McQuarry. I was told there was nothing to be done. Agent McQuarry didn't want to work with me anymore, she was D.C., that was final."

"That's what Koldehn said. What about Beth?"

"Beth . . . you knew her?"

"We were friends."

"Then maybe I don't have to explain. She went maverick, took off on a tangent. She told me to stay out of it."

"Was that before or after you complained to Koldehn?"

Kitcher frowned. "Did you read the case file?"

Grant nodded.

"Then you know."

"Not everything is in the file."

He shrugged. "Maybe not, but you know what I know."

"Go over it with me, Agent Kitcher. What kind of an investigation was she running?"

"I don't know. We were generating spreadsheets on barco traffic. Nothing remarkable. I'd already done it twice this past year."

"Oh? Why?"

"Mayor's request. She didn't like my reports, so she demanded D.C. send someone. I don't know, maybe Agent McQuarry found my attitude unacceptable. I'd already been over this ground twice, I was a little tired of it. After eighteen days I was withdrawn from the investigation. Just when it was getting interesting."

"Interesting in what way?"

"The Mayor insisted the barco was growing, that the volume of unregistered trade was increasing."

"Wasn't it?"

Kitcher shrugged. "A couple tenths of a percentage point maybe, but not the emergency the Mayor made it out to be." He frowned. "Until Agent McQuarry got here. It was as if someone had turned on a spigot."

"Do me the courtesy of sitting down and going over it from the beginning."

"You have my report in the case file, Agent Voczek. If you don't mind, I have work to do—"

"And right now *this* is your work," Grant interjected. "I want to hear it, Agent Kitcher. Directly. Now sit down."

"All right." Kitcher grabbed a chair and pulled it closer to the desk. He looked at Grant curiously as he sat. "Several months ago—"

"How many specifically?"

"Nine—months—ago . . . Chief of Police Moore filed a report with us that indicated a suspicion of increased traffic in unregistered goods in the barco. We contacted her and the Mayor's Office to follow up. Normally, we have a very cordial relationship with City Hall. The Mayor insisted that we look into the population of the barco. In her opinion, based on Chief Moore's report, its population was growing significantly; as a result, illicit trade was also increasing. She named a number—five, six percent, something like that, she was just snatching for one. We looked into it. We filed a report with both Chief Moore's office and the Mayor's Office stating that, indeed, the population of the barco seemed to be increasing due to statewide migrations. The increase in barter was a natural consequence, but it seemed within acceptable boundaries."

"The Mayor didn't like that?"

"No. She became quite upset and bellowed at Director Koldehn. He suggested that this was far more a matter of local jurisdiction than federal, that the police could more than handle any excesses, and that she could file a lost revenue claim with the Governor's Office and probably get compensated for estimated tax losses due to unregistered trade. After all, the volume didn't appear inordinate."

"You said a couple tenths of a percentage point."

"The first time it was less than point two three."

"So . . ."

Kitcher held up his hand. "She demanded a new investigation. We complied and again filed a report suggesting local solutions. Our revised estimate was point three-oh. That's when she called D.C."

"And by the time Agent McQuarry arrived, traffic had increased again."

Kitcher frowned. "Between the time we filed our second report and the time Agent McQuarry arrived, yes, it had. Enormously. I didn't see the final tally, but it was edging up toward twelve percent."

"How do you account for that?"

"That's what I'd hoped to find out. Then your friend cut me out of the loop."

"You said population had increased as the result of statewide migrations."

"Last winter was harsh. A lot of small communities shut down their charities. A few had actual purges, sent their disenfranchised packing. There are only four cities they can come to when the small towns shut them out: Kansas City, Springfield, Jefferson City, or St. Louis. They're not likely to go to Jeff City—that's the capital, and Governor Baden is fulfilling campaign promises by lending state police to civic centers to rid them of their gypsies."

"What about the other two?" Grant asked.

"Small increases, not a severe problem. Most of them came to St. Louis. They're all packed into O'Fallon Park."

"How many?"

"Total population? Officially, less than four thousand. Truthfully, though, there must be ten or eleven thousand people jammed in there."

"Director Koldehn indicated that the Mayor is looking for a way to get rid of the barco. That a federal solution is politically preferable to a local one."

Kitcher raised an eyebrow. "He said that? Well, it's true. I'm surprised Koldehn would say anything bad about Mayor Poena."

"He said something about a bid for a new research firm."

"I wouldn't know. It sounds legitimate. Mayor Poena has been good for St. Louis in that regard, she's an efficient booster. If there is something to that—and I suppose it's probably true if Director Koldehn says it is—then it might explain why she was so anxious for the investigation to prove her numbers." Kitcher frowned thoughtfully. "If that's true, then maybe your friend started poking around in that deal."

"Only a guess?"

"As I said, she cut me out."

"Would Mitchel Abernathy be part of that deal?"

"Mitchel Abernathy . . . ? No."

"You sound certain."

"Mitchel Abernathy has . . . prejudices. He's about seventy-two, been in business since the turn of the century. He'd no sooner participate in something with a federal connection than he would enter a monastery for a life of poverty."

"Even if he benefitted from the connection?"

"He wouldn't see any benefit from it. He's a bedrock Reformist."

Grant leaned back. "What made her shut you out?"

"I have no idea."

"She didn't like you."

Kitcher shrugged. "The feeling was mutual. That's no reason to behave unprofessionally."

"What's your opinion about her death?"

"Like I said, she probably nosed into things she shouldn't have."

"That almost sounds as if you think she deserved it."

"No. But do I think it was unexpected? Not entirely. I don't think they were trying to kill her, to be honest. I think they were trying to scare her off and got carried away. Why else would they have beaten her so badly? There are easier ways to kill someone. If she hadn't gone off on her own, I might have been there to stop it."

"So it's her own fault," Grant snapped. "You don't think perhaps she had really found something and that is the reason she was killed?"

"Of course she found something. Whether it had anything to do with the barco and the Mayor's agenda, who can say."

"You were transferred out of Montreal under scandal, Agent Kitcher."

Kitcher stiffened. "That's not at issue."

"No? One indiscretion doesn't necessarily mean you'll commit another? Perhaps not."

"If you think I really did something wrong, ask why I wasn't simply discharged."

Grant nodded. "I know. You're just misunderstood."

"It's not so difficult to misunderstand someone. Behavior and motive don't always make a perfect match. Your Agent McQuarry was a good example."

"Oh?"

"She lacked a certain critical judgement in her personal

associations. Though I think it's likely that she was murdered because of her investigation, it wouldn't surprise me to learn that she was victim of private miscalculation."

"You're not a very conservative sort at all, are you? You seem to enjoy pushing your limits."

Kitcher shrugged. "I understand she had syphilis. One needn't be very radical to draw certain conclusions from that."

Grant prided himself on control, his ability to mute reactions. He knew he failed at times, but usually only when he forgot that fact. He sat very still now, and waited.

The anger did not pass.

"When I'm through," he said, "we can talk about that at length. Privately."

"Will the rabid dog bite me?"

Grant frowned. "I haven't heard that term in years. What is it, Kitcher? Something personal about me? About Beth? We're all Treasury, what's the problem?"

"You both share a shortfall."

"And that is?"

"You're from D.C. Outsider."

"Still, we're both Treasury. The same."

Kitcher shook his head. "No. Not the same. World of difference. *I'm* local. Despite the signature on my credit log showing who pays my stipend, I live and work locally, in the real world, as the locals say. Everyone in this building does. We do our jobs locally, by-the-rule, and we do a good job. At the end of the day we go home and have neighbors and social lives and we have to live with the consequences of our daily actions. Agent McQuarry—*Special* Agent McQuarry—and you are the kind of nuisances we locals dread. You come in, you know nothing about the local situation, you have no idea what you're knocking over, and you go back to D.C. and leave behind your messes for the locals to clean up. And because we're Treasury—just like you—*we* get blamed. By our neighbors, by the local authorities, by the community."

"Our presence was requested."

"Not by us. What annoys me is that Cutter took the Mayor's word over ours. This is a political problem. Neither of you should have been sent here."

Grant came around the desk and stood over Kitcher. "Thank you for your cooperation, Agent Kitcher. If I need anything else—"

"Ask Koldehn for it."

Grant opened the door. "You've been helpful. As I said, if I need anything more I won't hesitate to ask."

After Kitcher left, Grant leaned against the door. He felt warm around the ears, down the back of his neck. The walls of the office seemed close.

He checked his pocket watch. Eleven-twenty. Still early.

He knocked on Reva's door and leaned in. "Lunch?"

She gave him a questioning look from behind her desk, then closed down her terminal. "I'd be delighted."

As they descended the elevator to the lobby, Grant began to feel better.

"Your treat," she said as the doors opened. "And there's nothing I don't like."

Grant felt himself smile.

"He didn't seem to know that Beth's terminal had been searched," Grant said, staring out the restaurant window.

"Did you expect him to?" Reva asked.

"Beth wouldn't just arbitrarily cut an agent out of an investigation, especially not one like this. Kitcher was right—if she hadn't done that, she might not be dead."

"Or she might still be and Kitcher would have even more explaining to do."

Grant shook his head. "It doesn't tally."

"Well, here's something else to think about for now. The addresses on Lindell." Reva pushed a single sheet of paper across the table.

Grant blinked and picked it up. One name isolated itself immediately: "Mitchel Abernathy."

"The neowright house. He built it himself on the site of one that collapsed during the New Madrid."

Grant scanned the page. "What about the others ... ? Parker Reed, that's familiar."

"I imagine so. Senator Reed."

"The one coming to town this week."

"That's him."

"I didn't know he was a Missouri senator."

"He isn't. Nebraska. But his daughter lives here, so he keeps a house."

"Coincidence?"

"That depends on Abernathy's politics."

"Are they associated in business?"

"Not according to Reed's disclosures. But there are a lot of protected members of Clayton Banking Consortium. Perhaps later you can see what your Treasury people can come up with. Certain things I just can't get to."

"What about these other names?"

"Principle citizens. Nothing overtly linking them to Abernathy except their addresses." Reva reached over and tapped one. "But that one—"

"Paul Dirkenfeld?"

"Senator Dirkenfeld. And he *is* a Missouri senator."

"So Reed keeps a house near a colleague." Grant set the

sheet down. "All right, two of her stops that might involve Mitchel Abernathy. What about the third?"

"CoMart National Shipping, Inc. and Nelikar and Balista Manufacturing—they make magnetic brake systems. No affiliations to Abernathy as far as I could find. My opinion is the location was picked at random."

"Were any of MCHI's members a pharmaceuticals company?"

"No. That would be too convenient."

"Why? The rest of this seems to be falling into place."

"Really? We have two locations associated with one name and no explanation of why McQuarry was at either one. It's a good chance that Abernathy was the subject of her investigation, but how does that relate to the barco she was called in to investigate?"

Grant shrugged. "I don't know. But there *is* a connection."

"You mean McQuarry wouldn't waste her time if there wasn't?"

"Exactly."

"What if she got sidetracked? What if while investigating the barco she discovered something to do with Abernathy that's completely unrelated?"

"If so, then she found it investigating the barco."

"Do you have the original request from the Mayor's Office for Treasury involvement?"

"Not yet. We can pick it up when we go over to City Hall this afternoon."

The waiter came then, guiding the small dray that carried the food. He set the bowls in the center of the table, asked if they needed anything else, then left with a bow. Reva lifted the lid from one dish. The aroma spiked the air.

She ran the tip of her tongue over her upper lip and began ladling food onto her plate.

"Soy sauce," Grant said, brandishing the bottle, "is the universal palliative. With this you can make almost anything edible."

"Only if you have no taste buds left," Reva said.

"How could you after all that hideously hot stuff you eat?" He gestured at her plate. On top of the Szechuan beef she was sprinkling hot ground red pepper.

"Keeps me from developing ulcers." She took a mouthful and closed her eyes. Soon, beads of sweat formed on her forehead.

"Is that how that's done? I thought one simply tolerated them until retirement, then kept them like pets."

Reva smiled. "Why, Agent Voczek, you sound cynical."

"Realistic. It goes with the career."

"I disagree. I love this job. I'd be crazy to do it if I didn't."

"You love being subjected to endless terminal time? Being stonewalled by PETITS?"

" 'PETITS'?"

"People Too Important To Touch. You love looking at corpses? Never eating in the same restaurant twice?"

"I have a list of favorites. I get back to them when I can."

"You love being lied to on a daily basis?"

"Sounds like ordinary life to me. What are the parts that separate us from normal citizens?"

Grant frowned. "Hmm."

"Seriously, though, no. I don't love any of that."

"Then what? The pay is certainly exceptional, but given that we're occasionally in harm's way that's only fair."

"The money's nice. Travel. Meeting interesting people."

"Any branch of civil service could provide that."

"But not the juice."

" 'Juice'?"

Reva grinned. "Adrenalin. Endorphins. Thrills."

"I don't remember the last time I was thrilled."

"No? I have the feeling you were quite thrilled with Agent Kitcher."

"Enraged."

"There. See? It's like spicy food."

"I didn't enjoy it, though."

"No? Doesn't it make you feel that you're . . ."

"What?"

She shrugged. "Swimming in the right stream. Riding a whirlwind."

Grant shook his head. "No, it just makes me angry."

"Then why do you do it?"

Grant made himself busy ladling more stir fry into his plate. "That's a personal question."

"Yes."

"I'm good at my job, Agent Cassonare—"

"Reva. Please."

"—I can't see what more reason a person needs to do what he does."

"You *can't?*"

Grant shrugged. "It doesn't matter. All other reasons fade. After a while it's a matter of competence and habit. Perhaps comfort. I've never considered doing anything else."

"You went through school planning to be a Treasury agent?"

"No. I wanted to be in law enforcement. I considered reading for the Bar, but—"

"But there's no juice in courtroom banter."

"I'll admit when I was younger there was a certain

romance about enforcement work. Some of it even turned out to be true. But frankly, it's too formulaic to sustain the illusion."

"By-the-rule?"

"By-the-rule."

Reva shook her head. "I don't believe it."

"Oh? Why would I lie to you?"

"Not lie. Hide."

"I'm hiding from you?"

"Among others."

"Is that a professional assessment?"

"That's *my* assessment," Reva replied. "I'm a complete package. I am my profession, my politics, my religion, my 'sthetics. When you get one, you get them all."

"Doesn't that get a little confusing?"

"No."

"How convenient for you," Grant said sarcastically.

"I suppose you try to keep everything separate? Different rooms for different guests?"

"It provides clarity."

"What about vision?"

Grant laughed.

"What's funny?"

"I feel like I'm in a race."

"Who's winning?"

"Does there have to be a winner?"

Reva shook her head. "You just have to cross the finish line."

Rycliff informed Grant his car had arrived, down in the garage. Grant made arrangements to have his belongings delivered to the house on Pershing.

"Come on," Grant said to Reva. "I want to show you this."

They found the Duesenberg in the shop, the mechanics giving it a thorough inspection. The lines and curves bent the bright lights into reddish neon brilliance. Reva whistled appreciatively.

"A 'thirty?" she asked.

"Thirty-two. Model SSJ."

The car seemed to glow, a deep maroon with a white convertible top. Grant stepped up to the supervisor. "How does she check out?"

"Fine, sir. We changed the oil for you, timed it, ran a diagnostic on the navigator and loaded in the local nav directory. Here's the profile." She handed him a slate and he scanned quickly down the list.

"This cost you a percentage," Reva said.

"One of the things that helps keep my ulcers away."

"All set, sir," the supervisor said. "Would you care to take it to your parking space?"

"Care for a ride?" he asked Reva.

"Only if you promise it won't be the only one."

Grant held the door for her, then hurried around. He slipped his card into the scanner below the ignition and pressed the button. The engine rumbled. The myriad gauges on the crowded dash twitched. Grant put it in gear and moved between the blue lights, out into the garage proper.

"This is not a by-the-rule sort of car," Reva said.

"A concession to the romantic I used to be."

"What kind of an engine does it have?"

"Straight eight thirty-two valve Lycoming, centrifugal supercharger. Three-hundred-twenty horse power."

Reva whistled again. "My Sportsman only generates a hundred horse. What are all these gauges?"

"Speedometer, altimeter, barometer, brake pressure gauge." He tapped each one as he named it. "Tachometer, oil pressure, chronometer—"

"Slow down, slow down. You don't need all those, do you? Who built it for you?"

"Chrysler's custom reproduction division. No, I don't need all that, but if you're going to spend the credit on a replica, you might as well do it right. I wanted it for its looks. I think the late Twenties and Thirties were the *belle epoque* of motor cars. Duesenbergs were special even then."

"I take it you and Beth McQuarry disagreed on that."

"Among other things. She liked the later twentieth century."

Grant pulled into the space alongside Reva's Mercury.

"Who built yours?" he asked.

"Samson Historical Motor Company."

"They're in Virginia, aren't they?"

"West Virginia." She nodded. "This is fine, Grant." She looked over at him. "You're not so by-the-rule as you say."

"You don't think so?"

"No. I think you sit on yourself. Too much." When Grant said nothing, she patted the dashboard. "Impressive. What next?"

"We have an appointment with the Mayor," he said, grateful for the change of topic. "Then I think we should start finding out who these people on the list are."

SIX

They walked the short distance, across Tucker Blvd., to City Hall. Mayor Poena's offices occupied one wing of the second floor, near the landing of the broad, curved marble stair. Polished woods, brass, and stone gave everything the impression of being under glass, untouchable.

Grant and Reva handed their CIDs to the receptionist. He handed them back. "Would you please have a seat? The Mayor is with someone at the moment."

They went to the long bench opposite the reception desk. As soon as they sat down, the receptionist seemed instantly to forget them. Grant looked at the tall, carved wood doors that led to the Mayor's chambers and wondered how she would react if he simply barged in, the way he had heard of federals doing in the last century. Stories, he knew, that were apocryphal. Still, he sometimes wondered what it might be like to have the authority.

Twenty minutes later, the big doors swung open. A stout man in a dark-grey suit emerged. His short legs carried him quickly across the room. Wispy hair clung to his wide head, white hair that made the redness in his cheeks all the more pronounced. He glanced at Grant and Reva, scowled briefly, and continued on without a word. He paused at the exit to retrieve a hat and cane, then left.

The receptionist looked up. "You may go in now."

Mayor Poena stood before her enormous desk, waiting for them, hands clasped behind her back. She wore her rich auburn hair in wings that swept back to a blunt point at the crown of her head. Her high-necked jacket gave her a serious appearance that her plump face failed on its own to achieve.

"Madam Mayor," Grant said, bowing formally. "I am Special Agent Grant Voczek—"

"And this is Special Agent Reva Cassonare. I know. I am Mayor Allison Poena. Now we are all introduced. Thank you for being prompt."

"How may we help you?" Grant asked.

"You have the last agent's reports?"

"Yes—"

"Then you know what you can do for me."

Grant cleared his throat. "I'm not sure I entirely understand."

Mayor Poena sighed. "Your last representative from D.C. caused me complications. This was a simple, straightforward matter, nothing that should have resulted in a death. I want you both clear on my needs. I don't want this complicated further."

"At this point," Reva said, "it's as complicated as it's likely to get. We have to investigate every aspect—"

"You're FBI, aren't you, Agent Cassonare?"

Reva frowned. "Yes . . ."

"Let me save you some difficulty, then. Homicide already determined that Agent McQuarry was beaten to death by gypsies. I believe your local agent, Mr. Kitcher, concurs. You'll do us all a service concentrating on that."

"With all due respect—"

"My requirements, Agent Cassonare, are that you help me serve my city."

"And how may we do that?" Grant asked.

"I asked for a federal investigation of the barter commune, not scrutiny of St. Louis's principle citizens. I didn't get what I requested. Instead I have a mess to straighten out with my constituency."

"Madam Mayor," Reva said, "a federal agent is dead—"

Poena waved a hand, cutting her off. "Of course I'm sorry about that. More sorry than you can know. That has only added to my problems. Now, if you wish to take up the investigation I asked for, fine. But I want it clearly understood that you're to leave my principle citizens alone."

"And what if one or more of your principle citizens is responsible for Agent McQuarry's death?" Reva asked.

"Do you have any evidence?"

"Not yet—"

"Until you do, I expect you to leave my constituency alone. Are we clear?"

Reva stiffened. She went back to the doors and pulled them shut.

"I'm afraid that's not possible," she said.

Poena's eyes narrowed. "Why not?"

"Because one of ours was murdered in your city, investigating one of yours. A coincidence perhaps, but I'm afraid it gives us jurisdiction to look into whatever we decide is necessary. Now, you can either give us some assistance or we'll proceed to upset all your principle citizens."

"You have thirty days, Agent Cassonare," Mayor Poena

said, "before you are required to have a Governor's Letter granting you permission to operate in Missouri. Your Federal Circumstances Exemption does not give you carte blanche."

"Madam Mayor," Grant said, "I don't understand your attitude. You requested a federal investigation—"

"And your agent exceeded her mandate. You're lucky your department isn't being sued."

"Do you honestly believe the increase in traffic that you complained about could happen without a sponsor?"

"They're gypsies, Mr. Voczek. They steal."

"And, of course, principle citizens never do." Grant sighed. "What do you want us to do?"

"You could make life easier for all of us by simply filing a report recommending deportation of the barco population."

"That's what you wanted in the first place."

She nodded. "I didn't quibble about it with your Agent McQuarry. I told her the same thing: I want them out. I want them out of the state. I don't have time to be politic about this. I don't see what the trouble is. Agent McQuarry was murdered by one or more of them. Deport them and you're sure to punish the criminals."

"Along with a lot of innocent people," Reva said.

Poena looked surprised. "Innocent? Gypsies? Forgive me, but last time I checked we work for the citizenry, not the disenfranchised." She shook her head. "I want this cleared up and settled. You're on my time."

"Madam Mayor, *you* aren't even on your time," Grant said. He felt his control slip. "You have a contract with a developer. I'm sure there's a reversion clause to worry about, something to do with time."

Her eyes narrowed. "Where did you hear that?"

"Are you going to try to tell me it isn't true?"

88

Poena raised an eyebrow appreciatively. "Impressive. And you've only been here a little over a day."

"Madam Mayor, whatever your opinion of the federal government may be, we are not here to provide you with a political scapegoat for unpopular policies. We'll investigate, we'll report. Based on the legitimacy of your complaint—"

"Those *people* are a problem, Agent Voczek. Crime is up. City resources have reported a rise in emergency use, not to mention the health hazards. In the last year and a half, public disturbances have increased."

"What kind of disturbances?" Reva asked.

"Defacement—"

"Ah. Ghost artists."

"Taggers are not artists, Agent Cassonare. They are public nuisances. None of this is good for my city."

"And you, of course, don't wish to burden other municipalities in the state with a deported migrant population."

"Why should I, when there are perfectly sound *federal* laws regarding citizenship? A deportation is long overdue. I don't care what kind of formalities you have to fulfill to get it done, that's what I want. Now are we clear?"

"Perfectly," Grant said.

"Good. I don't want to see you here again until you bring me a federal deportation order to countersign." Poena turned and stepped behind her desk. She began looking over papers. "Good day, agents."

"Can you confirm what you said about a contract?" Reva asked.

"I just did."

Reva laughed. "Do you ever get the feeling that you're unappreciated?"

Grant glanced at Reva. "No. Underestimated, yes."

She smiled briefly. "I suppose we should talk to Police Chief Moore next."

"I didn't see any report indicating a local investigation, did you? Since when is St. Louis Homicide involved?"

"I suppose since the Mayor said it was."

Grant shrugged. "Then Chief Moore it is."

"Should we make an appointment first?"

"It's more entertaining just showing up."

The main police station stood further down Tucker, across from the huge city garage. Blue, white, and gold police cruisers slid by. Grant felt the eyes on him, human and electronic. Nothing overt, nothing intrusive, just a constant sense of attention.

A uniformed officer stood at the main entrance. Grant handed over his CID and waited for the man to scan it.

"Your business, sir?"

"We'd like to speak with Chief Moore."

"Ask at the desk, sir, but I doubt she's available."

The main desk stood high, surrounded by a tall chamber of fluted columns and red granite. The duty sergeant asked for ID and Grant inserted his card in the slot at the rail surrounding the desk.

"Yours, too, Madam," the sergeant said.

Reva pushed her card into the next slot.

The sergeant read them on one of his screens, hidden from view from the floor. His eyebrows bobbed once.

"Your business?" he asked.

"We'd like to speak with Chief Moore," Grant repeated.

"Very well. I'll see if she is available." He pointed off to the right. "If you'd be good enough to wait in that room, I'll let you know."

"Thank you, Sergeant."

Grant opened the door for Reva and glanced back at the desk sergeant. The man concentrated on something before him, his lips pursed and his cheeks lightly dimpled.

As he shut the door behind him, Grant said, "If we're not called in fifteen minutes we're leaving. I'll have her summoned to the federal building."

"She might refuse to come. Local prerogative."

"Sometimes . . ."

"I know. This sort of thing makes me wish for pre-Reform federal authority."

"Too bad those stories are myths."

"I don't think they are."

"No?"

"There has to be a reason why things are as they are."

The small room contained a few straight-backed chairs and a pair of long tables upon which printouts and disks formed uneven piles. Reva walked up to the nearest table and gazed down at a stack of papers.

"After this," Grant said, "we should see about interviewing Mitchel Abernathy."

"A principle citizen? Are we that lucky?"

"We can get a warrant."

Reva lifted a thin booklet and opened it. "There's a local federal judge I think will be very accommodating."

"The question," Grant went on, "is whether the Mayor's attitude is simple local prejudice, or was Beth investigating her, too."

Reva replaced the booklet and picked up another. She smiled thinly.

"What is that?" Grant asked.

Reva dropped the booklet back on the table and sorted through the disks. "Pornography," she said.

Grant stepped up to the table. Cheap mass productions

with garish covers, a few better quality magazines, and scores of disks filled the space. He flipped one open with a finger and stared at a diptych of three women facing three men, all in exaggerated displays of arousal. He turned the page to close-ups of genitalia.

"Doesn't this stuff ever get any better?" Reva asked.

Grant looked up to see her shaking her head and grinning down at a foldout of lovers impossibly entangled, limbs twining in defiance of joint and muscle limitations.

"You find this amusing?" he asked.

"There's no other way *to* find it." She glanced back at the door. "The sergeant thinks he has a sense of humor."

Grant lifted a palm-full of disks, reading titles: *Celebrity More and Who, Chrysanthemum Poise, Variable Viscosity* . . . all holographic media. Expensive. He separated out a few, looked over at Reva. She stood at the next table, back to him. Grant slipped the disks into his coat pocket and went to a chair.

When Reva turned around, her eyebrows went up questioningly.

"You don't approve?" she asked.

"There's a reason it's illegal."

She shrugged. "There's a reason for everything."

"Do *you* approve?"

"I think 'approve' is the wrong word." She faced him and leaned back against the table. "I do think this is a joke in poor taste."

"We've been thrown out of the Mayor's office and now tucked in with the garbage. This city is trying to tell us something."

"Something like, we aren't going to get any cooperation?"

"That's my reading of it so far."

Reva nodded decisively and headed for the door. Grant followed.

The desk sergeant looked up, surprised. "I haven't heard back from Chief Moore—" he started.

Reva held up a hand. "Give Chief Moore a message, please. Tell her we have significant data regarding the murder of a federal agent linking it to a principle citizen, whose initials are M. A. If Chief Moore wishes to discuss the particulars with us before we receive a federal warrant for arrests, she can reach us at Treasury. Thank you, Sergeant."

Reva strode out of the building. She was halfway down the block before Grant, sprinting, caught up, drawing disapproving looks from other pedestrians.

"Are you all right?" he asked.

"Yes." After several more steps, she said, "So what do we know?"

They were passing before City Hall now. Limousines waited in the semi-circular driveway, the chauffeurs buffing headlamps and hood ornaments, or sharing conversation.

"We know Treasury was brought in to rubber stamp a local problem," Grant said. "Common enough, but irritating. We know the problem is real enough, although the exact dimensions have yet to be proved. We know that Beth—Agent McQuarry—stopped trusting her local partner and began investigating a principle citizen. We may assume that the barco problem and Mitchel Abernathy are somehow linked, at least sufficiently for Agent McQuarry to make the connection. We know she was murdered while clipping a piece of Abernathy's property. Whether Abernathy ordered it or even knew about it is a matter of conjecture. But the Mayor, at least, understands something about it. She verified the existence of a deal involving the land the barco's on."

"You don't think it's likely she's involved in McQuarry's death, do you?"

"No. But whomever she has this contract with may be. We need to find out who. It's been suggested to me that federal funding may be at stake. That should be easy enough to check."

"If the recipient turns out to be Abernathy, we may have enough to obtain a full disclosure warrant."

They crossed Tucker and entered the federal building.

"Agent Cassonare—Reva," Grant said.

She stopped. "First name now? Does this mean you're ready to trust me?"

"I don't know. Perhaps."

"I'm beginning to get the feeling that we may have no choice."

Grant nodded. "I'm going home now. If Chief Moore gets in touch with you, set it up for tomorrow afternoon. By then I'll know what I want to do."

"But—"

"Please. Tomorrow?"

Reva nodded. "Tomorrow."

The information Director Cutter had promised waited in the fax buffer, and Stuart from SEC had returned his call. Grant initiated a printout, then went upstairs to change clothes.

He took the disks from his pocket and dropped them on the bed. He stared at them, uneasy. Perhaps they were blank, already wiped in the police station, the contents scrambled beyond accessibility.

The doorbell chimed. He scooped the disks together and put them inside his briefcase, then descended to the front door. Two men in dark blue overalls waited, one holding a manifest. The truck from the railway station filled the driveway.

"Mr. Vok-zek?" the man with the manifest asked.

"Vo-chek," Grant corrected him.

"Sorry, sir. Sign here, please." Grant took the proffered stylus and scribbled in the signature space. "Card, sir." Grant slid his CID into the end of the manifest. The workman studied the screen, then nodded. "Thank you, sir. Is there anyplace in particular you wish us to put things, sir?"

Grant supervised for the next hour and a half as the two men, with drays, moved his belongings into the house. Bookcases, chairs, tables, couches, an exercise machine, carpets—he vowed again to rid himself of all the excess, that he would never move half this stuff again, all the while marveling at the efficiency of the Department in rolling up an entire house full of things and transporting them, a day later, to another city. Each time he acquired more, each time he promised to leave with less.

Most of the furniture was utilitarian: plain shelves, plain chairs, plain tables. But a few things were originals. Old names, mid-twentieth century couches, end tables, lamps. And his paintings . . . he could never leave behind or get rid of his paintings. Obscure artists, mostly, but he had acquired them with an eye for period—early twentieth century, before the Second World War and the changes that resulted. Prairie lands, farm scenes, young cities with new buildings and excited people. And a few, a very few, examples of late twentieth century fantasist illustration, images that had once graced the covers of novels about the future or about different pasts. He owned several of the books, tattered objects tucked in plastic. He never read them. He had acquired them for the covers. The images had appealed to him and the paintings themselves meant more than the sub-jects ever would.

He stood in the living room after the workmen had left, glass of sherry held loosely in one hand, and gazed at the paintings stacked against the fireplace. Late afternoon light dappled the tall windows, setting the thin white curtains aglow.

"How long will *this* stay be?" he asked the figures.

The house looked cluttered. Beth had brought little, but along with Grant's furnishings some of the rooms were now crowded. He wondered if he would have time to put it in order before he had to go to another city.

He looked at his pocket watch. Five-thirty. Too late to call Stuart back.

He undressed on his way up the stairs, pausing at the second floor landing to pull his boots off. He carried them to the bedroom and stripped, then took a shower. It was easier now, with his own things in the house. He no longer felt uninvited into Beth's space. He stepped into his loafabouts and went down to the office.

A pile of paper lay in the hopper, each sheet bearing the seal of the Treasury Department at the upper right-hand corner. Grant hefted the mass. On top was the report on Paul Kitcher, a bright-red CONFIDENTIAL: PERSONAL stamped above the title line.

Grant brought the decanter of sherry up to the office and settled onto the couch to begin.

He did not notice when the lights came on. When he looked up, eyes burning, the window was black and the diffuse yellow glow from the ceiling fixture cast soft-edged shad-ows around the room. The skin across his forehead felt tight. The time signature in the corner of the desk screen read 11:16 P.M.

His tongue was thick. The bottle of sherry was a third gone. He rubbed his eyes, which made them burn briefly even worse. Only fifteen sheets of paper remained in his lap unread—the report on Harold Lusk.

Grant set it aside and stood. The stack of reports lay on the sofa, delicate red pen marks checking off specific paragraphs, circling particular sentences, underlining names and dates. His head churned with information.

Paul Kitcher had made the mistake of getting involved with a political movement, the New Libertarians. Whether he had done so as part of an assignment—he had been working on tracing stolen commodity scrip at the time, which was one of the most popular ways of illicit funding for unpopular factions, since the scrip could eventually be turned back over to the federal government for recycling through state block grants—or as an honest expression of his personal feelings did not matter. He adopted the party as his own. He had "made intemperate observations" in hearing of other Treasury officials. Within six months there was a question raised about the disposition of certain confiscated allotments of commodity scrip. It was impossible to determine the legitimacy of any of it. Grant was suspicious because all Kitcher received was a reprimand and a transfer. Kitcher had been right about that—it *would* have been better all around if they had simply dismissed him or charged him. Now they had a disaffected agent. Perhaps, Grant thought wryly, they believed St. Louis too bucolic for Kitcher to get into any trouble. St. Louis had always had that reputation and, as far as Grant had been able to tell, it had always been a deceptive label. Or, more likely, Kitcher had a benefactor.

In any case, Kitcher was unreliable; after Beth had shut him out of her investigation, doubly so. Grant made a mental note to check whether or not Kitcher had been stationed in Montreal when Beth was there. Perhaps she had deeper reasons for her actions.

Congressman Michael Tochsin was a junior member, into his second term, and had recently been named to the Methods and Allocations Committee. He spent almost as much time in his district, here in St. Louis, as he did in D.C. Excellent voting record, strict currency views, moderate internationalist. He was not a principle citizen of St. Louis. He had come from modest middle class neighborhoods and worked his way into his position.

Albert Voley lived in South St. Louis, in one of the oldest neighborhoods to survive the New Madrid Quake. He came from old wealth and had devoted most of his life to civic work. An outspoken opponent of the deportations, he had a reputation as a militant civil libertarian, once even devoting his time as an attorney to the long-defunct American Civil Liberties Union. His activities placed him in direct confrontations with government at all levels but he had never faced deportation or any lengthy arrest. The last twenty years he had lived more or less quietly, providing a locus for community activities among the disenfranchised and poorer citizens. He had once argued a case before the Supreme Court regarding the transition to full credit economy. He had been a consulting attorney on the tax exemption rulings that had led to the creation of commodity scrip. He funded more free kitchens in St. Louis than the city government, and had loudly refused principle citizenship. Grant found himself admiring the man. He could not see how Voley related to the other two.

Especially Mitchel Abernathy. His major businesses all

functioned as holding companies for dozens of smaller firms. Abernathy was a throwback, an octopus. Through his shipping firm he controlled several out-of-state companies. Everything legal, everything licensed, everything by-the-rule, but it felt wrong. Aside from his one brief flirtation with public politics, he eschewed all but the most personal forms of civic expression. He was an advocate of free currency, a return to unregulated consumerism, and an end to all but the most basic forms of credit. Still, Clayton Banking Consortium was one of the four primary credit agencies in the state. Abernathy held contradictory views on numerous topics, but judging by the success of his management skills his paradoxes did not hinder him. He made a point of refusing federal grants but signed off as a principle citizen when other companies, the state, or the city applied for federal funds. He funded enfranchisement programs to bring gypsies back into the ranks of citizenship, but publicly denounced the required voting laws. He was a staunch Isolationist but bought foreign bonds and held stock in British, German, and Georgian firms, and provided venture capital for several start-up companies in Macedonia, Romania, and Ukraine. These were easily traced through the office of the American Union Trade Representative, but his domestic investments disappeared in a labyrinth of intermediate corporations.

Perhaps in the morning it would all make sense. Tochsin, Voley, and Abernathy looked like an impossible trinity. Grant poured another glass of sherry and wondered if Reva were reading the same reports.

No, there would be one report she would have that he did not. His own file. Just as he had hers.

SEVEN

R eva Idolina Cassonare had graduated Florida State
University *cum laude* and immediately entered military service. That surprised Grant. Six years, one on
detached duty to the United Nations, retiring finally as
master sergeant, combat specialist. Her foreign service file
was United Nations classified, but her jacket contained a
sheet of medals and commendations. After release she
entered the FBI training academy and had been with the
Bureau since. The Foreign Office had once offered her a
position, but she turned them down. After graduation from
Quantico, the Bureau had sent her all over the country.
Except for a three-month stint in Data Collation, in the last
five years she had been involved in several major investigations, almost as many as Grant had been in twelve years.
More commendations, citations, merits. She had been
offered a promotion, an assistant directorship, which she
had refused, stating that she preferred field work.

She had been briefly engaged, but a month before the
wedding it ended. Personal. No details available.

Cuban extraction.

Grant made coffee. He found his liquor cabinet and opened the lid. Paper stuffing popped out and he pulled it off the bottles within. He selected a bottle of Irish cream and returned to the kitchen. He poured an inch of the milky liquid into a large mug, then added coffee.

There was nothing in her jacket to indicate that he could trust her. Nothing to indicate what direction she might go if the investigation went sour and it became necessary to sacrifice truth in the cause of career. The reasonable choice, then, was to not trust her. She was FBI. Departmental traditions drew lines between them. Tradition dictated caution. Use her but give her nothing in return.

He liked her, though. Tradition offered no solution for that.

He drank his coffee and wandered the house.

Cuban extraction. That explained her rich color, her hair. Did it extend, he wondered, already knowing that it did not, to her love of spicy foods? He smiled to himself. He came from an Eastern European background and he despised the heavy Slavic foods. Still, knowing such assumptions to be false, like the air one drew them in and recycled them, as if the body of groundless cliché, despite all evidence to the contrary, provided answers, *or* causes that transcended reason and logic. How else to understand the world, but through the distortions it embraced? Much easier to believe people were born to be what they became than to try to sift the sands of culture for trails of cause. Easier to base choices on common prejudice than to see past the veils and learn the new. Perhaps not easier, but comforting in a superficial way, to trust that all things are as they should be.

When he thought about it at all, Grant did not believe

that. He avoided thinking about it. Then something happened, like the death of a close friend, and he sat alone with
a glass or a bottle and worked it through again. So Reva
Cassonare was of Cuban extraction. Did that explain anything? No more than his own genealogy did, and he
believed it explained nothing. He had once met a black man
with a rich French accent whose name was Baravoshkof. He
had claimed his family had come from Egypt, emigrated to
Europe before the blockade. Great-grandfather had been a
Russian construction advisor who had come to work on the
old Aswan Dam. The family had moved to Algieria, then to
Marseille. Grant had met him in Toronto. What did all that
make the man? Did his "extractions" explain anything other
than a curious family history?

And did any of this help Grant decide what to do next?

Grant laughed to himself. He had a simple choice. Trust
Reva Cassonare or work the investigation without any help.
In this case, that might be impossible. But to trust . . . that
meant multiplying the possibilities.

"Damn this century," he said.

The phone chirped. Grant returned to the office and sat
down at the terminal. He touched the ACCEPT cursor on the
screen. "This is Grant Voczek."

"Agent Voczek, good evening. I'm Chief of Police Karen
Moore. I hope I'm not disturbing you?"

Grant sat up straighter. "No, not at all, Madam. How
may I help you?"

"I was told you came to see me this afternoon."

"Yes. I was given to understand that you weren't
receiving."

"No need for undue politeness, Agent Voczek. My people behaved . . . unprofessionally. Still, it would not have
been useful to see you then."

"What do you suggest?"

"Could we meet now? In half an hour? I know it's late—"

"No, no. Half an hour would be fine. Where?"

"My house?"

"If that's acceptable to you . . ."

"Do you have transportation?"

"Yes."

"My address is 2122 Longfellow."

"Half an hour, Madam. I look forward to it."

The link closed. Grant rubbed his eyes and looked at the time signature. Eleven-fifty P.M. He took his cup back to the kitchen, dumped its contents in the sink, and poured a fresh cup. He took a mouthful and winced at the heat.

He dressed quickly: crimson turtleneck, midnight-blue jacket and pants, his most comfortable boots. He slipped a palm stunner into his pocket and his panama on his head. A distant throb pulsed behind his eyes as he stepped from the front door.

He hesitated, wondering whether he should call Reva. With a twinge of guilt he decided not to. He entered the address into the navigator and the Duesenberg came to life.

Chief Moore's house stood along a curving lane of majestic trees, one of a neighborhood of mansions. In the yellow glow of gas lamps, the old manors seemed sunk in amber, tall pillars extending up into second floor shadows, broad porches dappled in light filtered through leaves. For all their size they appeared warm and welcoming, comfortable homes from an age before class distinctions became inextricably one with common politics.

The Duesenberg stopped before the programmed address. Grant switched to manual and pulled into the long driveway behind a Rolls-Royce Phaeton.

He stepped into the alcove and touched the bell. The front door was an elaborately carved wooden frame and cut glass. A woman wearing a silver-grey smoking jacket opened it.

"Agent Voczek?"

"Yes. Madam . . . ?"

"I'm Karen Moore. Please, come in."

She took his hat and set it on a sidebar below a ceiling-tall mirror. A chandelier cast soft yellow light over the inlaid wood. Chief Moore herself was the color of polished mahogany. High cheekbones caught and smeared the light and accented her light brown eyes.

"We can talk in here," she said, gesturing him through a wide doorway. A fire snapped delicately in a green marble fireplace. Large sofas formed a semi-circle before the hearth.

Reva sat there, a brandy snifter in one hand. She smiled and waved. She still wore the same clothes. Guilt made the back of his neck tingle. A moment later, though, he remembered that she had not called him, either.

"I appreciate you both coming on this short notice," Chief Moore said. "Agent Voczek, may I offer you some refreshment?"

"Thank you, Madam. Do you have coffee?"

"Always." She smiled brightly and went to the bar. "How do you take it?"

"Unfiltered, thank you."

She brought him a tall glass mug; steam spilled off the top. He sat across from Reva. Chief Moore squatted by the fire and stabbed at the logs with a brass poker. One cracked open and fell apart in an eruption of sparks.

"First, let me express my regrets at the death of your Agent McQuarry. I respected her." She glanced apologetically at Grant, then Reva. "She did, however, exceed her assignment."

"What," Grant asked, "is it about Mitchel Abernathy that has you all so concerned?"

Chief Moore's lips drew briefly into a pout, the only sign Grant saw that he had surprised her. "Did you ask the Mayor?"

"She beat us to it," Reva said. "Told us to stay away from Mr. Abernathy—and any other prominent citizens we might be inclined to look at. All but stated outright that Agent McQuarry had earned her fate."

"Mitchel Abernathy is a city benefactor. He contributes enormously to civic progress, the various religious charities, and the urban societies. I can tell you quite unreservedly that Mitchel Abernathy buys more peace and quiet, good will, and security than my department can ever provide."

"He bribes the disenfranchised and borderline citizens," Reva said.

Chief Moore nodded, put the poker up, and sat on the sofa across from the fire, between the two federal agents. "Crude but accurate. He also donates the use of several of his properties for city functions."

"Is he the one your mayor has a contract with for the barco property?" Grant asked.

"No. That would be Coronin Industries."

Grant noticed Reva's eyes grow suddenly more intense. Grant knew the name; most people did. Coronin was one of the largest pharmaceuticals companies in the country. Possibly in the world.

Grant asked Chief Moore, "Do you know who murdered Agent McQuarry?"

"If I did, they would be in custody."

"Any guesses?" Reva asked.

"None more plausible than any other, all for the moment unprovable."

"Who—" Grant started, then closed his eyes briefly and cleared his throat. "Who was Agent McQuarry seeing socially?"

Chief Moore frowned. "Socially?"

"Who is Richard?"

"I—" She shook her head, then suddenly opened her mouth in a silent "Oh" and nodded. "Richard Dirkenfeld. I didn't think they were actually seeing each other. He escorted her to a number of events, but . . ."

"Dirkenfeld . . . Senator Dirkenfeld?"

"His son, actually."

"Is there something about him," Reva asked, "of which you disapprove?"

"He's rather an embarrassment. The family is prominent in St. Louis. Besides the Senator, they're strong in local business. Principle citizens."

"What sort of businesses?"

"They own CoMart National Shipping."

Reva's eyebrows went up. Grant felt his headache recede.

"And what does Richard do?" he asked.

"*He* doesn't do anything." Moore paused, frowning. "Well, that's not completely true. He dances with scandal. He's married and is never seen with his wife. If he and Agent McQuarry . . ." She let the thought trail off, unfinished.

"She reported a significant amount of unregistered trade in the barco. What do you know about that?"

"In the last two years we've registered a drop of almost three percent in retail traffic. Some of that is part of the usual cycle, but most of it is the result of unregistered trade. My own officers have been participating. Of course none of them will admit it, but rumors are impossible to stop. My own staff has looked into it, and I've compiled enough surveillance to bring charges against several members of my department. Anyway, in the last six months there's been an additional two percent drop. As I understand it, your colleague confirmed a similar increase in unregistered traffic. There's a lively exchange going on in the barco."

"Where are the goods coming from?" Reva asked.

"I don't know. None of the distributors show any discrepancies in stock."

"What about thefts?"

"Minimal increase."

"Mayor Poena made it sound like a crisis."

"She responds to constituent pressure—three or four angry phone calls, and it's a crisis. My numbers indicate minimal increases in theft. But the question of where the merchandise is coming from, that's important. The goods being traded in the barco now can't be accounted for by common theft. That's why I cosigned the Mayor's request for federal involvement. I initially opposed Treasury's presence."

"The local officers indicated that the increased trade you mentioned didn't occur until this past year."

"The local offic*er*, you mean. Paul Kitcher. He's wrong about that, but I can see why he might understate the problem. Mayor Poena has been militating for a federal deportation for a couple of years now and Paul Kitcher blocked her. My own people provided more accurate reports than he did, but I couldn't get past him. Not until Agent McQuarry arrived."

"He was assigned to work with Agent McQuarry," Reva said. "She severed the relationship."

"They didn't trust each other. That was obvious to anyone who saw them try to work together."

"Could Mitchel Abernathy be supplying the barco?" Grant asked.

"I don't see how," Moore replied. "His books are balanced. He would have to be getting the merchandise from somewhere, and that means a public record. There would be discrepancies."

"I understand he's an advocate of free currency."

"A very loud advocate, which is another reason I don't think he's the sponsor. Don't misunderstand me—I believe if he could find a way to do it, Mitchel Abernathy would indeed sponsor illicit trade. I just don't think he's the one."

"Evidently Agent McQuarry did," Reva said. "And she was killed on his property."

Chief Moore jerked as if struck. "Do you know that for a fact?"

"She was investigating something at the MCHI warehouses the night she was killed. So if he wasn't involved before, he is now. At least as far as *I'm* concerned."

"Understandable." Moore shook herself briefly. "There is a reception Thursday evening for Senator Reed. I'm going to see that both of you are invited. Mitchel Abernathy will be there, if for no other reason than to start an argument with the Senator."

"And Richard Dirkenfeld?" Grant asked.

"Yes, I'm sure he'll be there, too. The elite of St. Louis, principle citizens and benefactors."

"The incorruptibles, eh?" Reva said.

"There will be people there you'll need to know," Chief Moore went on. "If you'll be working in St. Louis any length of time, that is. Not all of them are strict separatists."

"That's very accommodating, Madam," Grant said.

"Accommodating." Moore frowned. "Agent Voczek, this is my home. I try to keep it orderly. It's been my experience that federals who don't know anything about a place tend to tip things over without intending to. I'm doing this to forestall a mess in my home."

"Are you a separatist?" Reva asked. "Strict or otherwise?"

"I'm a pragmatist, Agent Cassonare. And consistent with that, I intend to give you what aid I can."

"You have officers undercover in the barco?" Grant asked.

"Of course."

"If I wanted to make the best purchases in there, or try to track a gypsy down, who would I talk to?"

"That's easy. Find Comber Blue—he runs the best scavenger clearing house in the barco. I warn you, though, Comber Blue decides who to tell what to. He's not our man, but he's been helpful in the past. Would you like me to arrange a meeting?"

"No. Kindly refrain from telling your undercover people anything about us until I say otherwise."

Moore frowned, but nodded.

Grant finished his coffee. "Thank you for your hospitality, Madam. If you don't mind, it's late. I have an early day tomorrow and a great deal of data to collate." He rose to his feet.

"Agent Voczek—"

"Yes?"

"The man you may wish to look into—this is only a guess, mind you—is Aaron Voley."

"Do you think he may have something to do with Agent McQuarry's death?"

"I wouldn't want to say about that. But he's deeply involved with the barco—always has been. He's a sharp tongue for the disenfranchised."

"And where does he live?"

"South Jefferson, near Benton Park. Ask anyone down there, they can point to his house."

"Do you think," Reva asked, "this Mr. Voley is capable of murder?"

Moore shrugged. "He's a survivor. He's been around a long time and for most of it he's been at war for one cause or another. He's jousted with the tallest windmills and they never unhorsed him." She shrugged again. "A suggestion. He's difficult for my department to investigate. Very popular in the area. But he is a focal point for the margins."

"Thank you again, Chief Moore. I appreciate your seeing us."

Grant nodded. "I'll see you both Thursday evening?"

"Of course."

"Good evening, then."

Reva chuckled as she walked alongside Grant to her car, parked further up the street in the shadows between two lamps. "It will be interesting to see if he remembers me."

"Who?"

"Senator Reed."

"You've met him?"

"Oh, yes. And he has met me."

"That sounds serious."

Reva shrugged. "It was a long time ago. I just think it's amusing how things come around. How did you find out about this Richard Dirkenfeld?"

"Beth's phone log."

"The coincidence is striking. Do you think whoever killed her was trying to implicate him? Or his family?"

"Then why move the car? Why not leave Beth there where everyone would know about it?" Grant shook his head. "No, it seems likelier to be a message. It would be interesting to know if Abernathy and the Dirkenfelds are rivals."

"Would it?"

Grant looked at her. "What do you mean?"

"Are you interested because of the connection to Abernathy, or because of the relation to Beth?"

Grant felt himself retreat. His words sounded false even to him. "I don't understand."

Reva leaned back against her car, arms folded. "Yes, you do. Beth was a good friend. A very good friend. Probably a better friend than it's polite to admit."

"Therefore . . . ?"

"Therefore it seems reasonable that you might take this investigation personally. I don't mind, really I don't. Unless it affects your judgement."

"That's no concern of yours."

"Oh, yes, it is. Someone killed your friend. I don't think they'd mind killing again. Bad judgement on our part helps them."

"So if I'm taking this personally I could get you hurt."

"You could get *us* killed."

Grant tucked his hands in his pockets and studied the grass at her feet. "What do you propose?"

"Give some of it to me."

He looked up, startled. "What?"

"Talk to me. Don't carry it all around by yourself."

"You mean trust you."

"We could both do our jobs better if you did."

"Uh-huh. Did it occur to you to call me tonight when Chief Moore contacted you?"

Reva frowned. "Yes. Did it occur to you?"

"Why didn't you call me, then?"

"I decided to see if Chief Moore intended to call you. If

she hadn't, that would tell us something about her reliability." She cocked her head to one side. "Wouldn't it?"

Grant sighed. "May I be truthful?"

"Absolutely."

"I don't want to trust you. It would be easier for both of us, I agree. But I don't want to."

"Why the hell not?"

"Because . . . trust complicates."

Reva frowned. "That doesn't make any sense."

"Doesn't it? Well. Then perhaps you don't understand what it is you're asking."

"Then explain it to me."

"Not tonight." Grant turned away and walked back toward the Duesenberg.

"You want revenge, don't you?"

"Good night, Agent Cassonare. I'll see you in the morning."

He waited for her to say something else, but instead he heard a car door slam, an engine start, and tires chirp on the pavement.

Then stillness.

Grant looked at Chief Moore's house. All the lights were on. He thought about her, remembered her expressions, her movements, her measured words. The lights remained on and he began to understand something else.

Trust? he thought. How do you trust when no one around you does?

He reached his car and stopped. He looked across the street, wondering what had attracted his attention. Seeing nothing, he got in and started the engine. He backed out into the street and pulled away. The street curved gently around. As he lost sight of Moore's house in his mirror, he turned off his lights and pulled quickly into the next driveway.

A few seconds later a car drifted by, slowly. Under the street lamps it looked black, and he could not identify the model. When he was sure it had pulled far ahead, he backed out and followed.

He saw it at the next cross street. He slowed behind it and suddenly it bolted around the corner. Grant mashed the accelerator. The other car ran the next stop sign. Grant chased it through two more.

Then it turned into a slide that carried its back end around. Its driver straightened expertly and came at Grant. He jerked the wheel, steering between two parked cars and up onto the sidewalk.

By the time he got back onto the street, the other car was gone.

Heart racing, his hands shook slightly. Tired, alcohol still working his system, Grant tapped the navigator and let the Duesenberg take him home.

EIGHT

From the second floor window Cozy could see the smoke of the barco catching and smearing the morning sunlight. Even here, five blocks north, the aromas of its cooking reached him. Cozy sat up on the futon and scratched his belly lazily, smiling into the breeze. A pity to be alone on such a fine morning, and in a real bed, too. He thought about DeNeille then, and how upset she probably was that he had not shown up last night.

The door opened, and George leaned in. His frown relaxed when he saw Cozy, as if he had expected to find the room empty. Cozy grinned at him. He had considered climbing out the window and disappearing into the barco during the night, but he knew Harry would feed him.

"Morning, George."

"Good morning, Cozy. Sleep well?"

"Not terrible."

"Hungry?"

"When am I not?"

George grunted. "Five minutes."

Cozy nodded and George closed the door.

Cozy wondered if he could shower. Later, perhaps. Five minutes before breakfast. He pulled on his faded jeans, his thick socks, and his new runners.

The only other piece of furniture in the small room was a patched recliner. Cozy went to the closet behind it and looked inside. Musty boxes filled the narrow space. No clothes. He picked his torn t-shirt off the back of the recliner and pulled it on. Maybe he could borrow one of Harry's shirts. If George had left him alone another hour or two he might have managed an entire new ensemble.

The floor creaked under his tread. It was a very old house, a survivor of the New Madrid. Most of the houses in this district were, though Cozy felt that they had come through less sound than people wanted to believe.

He grabbed his jacket and stepped into the hallway. A young girl wearing an oversized bathrobe walked by him.

"Morning, Stelly," Cozy said, bowing. "Are you showering this morning?"

"Of course," she said over her shoulder.

"There gonna be enough water for me?"

"You could use it. I think so. Faith's bunch left last week, so there's been extra."

"Good, good. Thank you, Stelly."

She opened the door at the far end—second floor bathroom—and smiled back at him. Cozy bowed again and she closed the door. Cozy shook his head and went the opposite direction. Too young, that Stelly, too young by far, he thought, and her father would wreck him if he touched her.

The stairs groaned loudly all the way to the first floor. The front door stood open. Two men sat on the stoop, backs to Cozy, sharing a cigar. Cozy wrinkled his nose automatically and headed for the kitchen. The strong odor of sausage filled the hall.

He pushed through the swinging louvered door and stopped short of colliding with a woman in an azure-and-gold skirt and a heavy, green brocaded vest. A purple scarf hugged her scalp, knotted at the nape of her neck, the ends mingled with thickly-curled black hair that spilled all the way down to the base of her spine. She held a platter in her left hand while her right hung in the air at shoulder height to fend off anyone—like Cozy—who threatened to get in her way.

"Morning, Sereta," Cozy said.

"You're late," she said curtly.

At the sturdy table, George already hunched over a plate. Across from him sat Vera, Stelly's sister—a little older, her round face dotted with acne. She glanced up at Cozy, smiled shyly, and looked back down at her plate.

Harry sat at the far end. Tall and thin, with large eyes that seemed to gaze off at things no one else could see when no one was talking to him, he chewed on the end of a sausage.

"Morning, Harry."

Harry looked up. "Cozy."

Empty dishes waited at three other places, one still clean. Cozy sat down before it and surveyed the center of the table. He reached quickly for the bowl of patties and scooped half a dozen onto his plate.

"Where'd the meat come from?" he asked.

"Harry waited all night at the distribution center," Sereta said. "Sausage, potato, butter, flour, milk—all set out for disposal." She glared at Cozy from the sink. "He could have used help."

"I could go back there with you this morning, Harry," Cozy said, piling potatoes on top of the patties.

"It's probably all gone by now," Harry said. He stared at Cozy.

Cozy looked at him. "Something?"

"You took—Cozy, you stay out of my things. George told me about it."

"George has a mouth. What's the problem? You have hundreds of those things, Harry. I didn't think one would be missed."

"*Two*, Cozy. You took two."

Cozy hesitated while reaching for the biscuits.

Harry scowled. "So where's the second one?"

"Good question," George said. He shrugged. "We'll worry about that later." He gave Harry a look. "You shouldn't leave things lying around where someone like Cozy can reach."

"I didn't expect—" Harry began, then shrugged.

"You going to your shop today, Harry?" Cozy asked. "I'd like to go along, watch."

"Why? So you can steal something else?"

"Hey, look. What good are they if nobody gets to use them?"

"People will get to use them. But not for new shoes."

"Oh, like *you* got a place to tell people what's important to them?" Cozy snapped. "You know, Harry, you spent way too much time in D.C. They infected your brain."

"That's enough," George said. "You aren't going with Harry to his shop. Harry isn't going to his shop. Nobody's going near it until the Feds leave."

Cozy looked up. "Feds?"

George nodded. "One before, now there are two more. Do you know anything about that, Cozy?"

Cozy laughed. "What would I know about Feds?"

George shrugged. Harry looked uncomfortably from George to Cozy, then resumed chewing his sausage.

Sereta set a large ceramic coffee urn on the table.

"Harry, you eat that, now," she said. "You still look like death."

"Thank you," Harry said, and shoved half the patty into his mouth.

Cozy poured himself a cup of coffee. Feds. Beth dying was bad enough, but two more? What good would Harry's reactivated CIDs ever be if they could never be used? Voley did not want them used yet, the Feds were doubtless looking for them, so they had to stay hidden. Not fair. All that free credit. Even if they only got used once or twice, the goods that could be acquired would mean a lot to the barco. And Voley had suggested voting.

Would that establish the gypsies? He did not see how, really. Citizenship was far more complicated than one cast vote. Funny, in a way, Cozy thought. The law required citizens to vote, but without a CID, voting was impossible. Without credit, no CID; without that, no citizenship.

Crazy.

Maybe, he thought, *that just means the law doesn't apply to us.* A lot of gypsies acted that way, certainly, but Cozy, besides tagging, never tempted the authorities, avoided provoking them. No one really gave a damn about gypsy rights and that was really the way the law failed to apply.

"Hey, George, do you really think there could be another deportation?" he asked.

"What makes you say that?"

"Well, Mr. Voley said something about it."

"I suppose that depends on how careful we all are."

Harry looked pale.

Vera finished her plate and mumbled "Excuse me" as she stood. Cozy watched her hurry from the kitchen. He remembered Stelly, then, and hoped she saved him enough water.

"George," Sereta said, "Comber Blue said he'd have fresh tomatoes for me today. Would you fetch them for me? I don't know how many he'll have, but last time it was more than I could carry."

"Sure," George said. "I'll take Cozy."

"George, I planned to take a shower."

"Take one when you get back." George gestured at Cozy's plate. "Come on, eat up. Comber Blue never saves anything for long."

Harry pushed away from the table. "I'll be in my room."

Cozy raised a hand in acknowledgement, then attended his breakfast. He always ate quickly in the morning, shoveling the food in as fast as he swallowed it. He wondered if there was a biological reason for that, because he never ate so fast at any other meal.

"That was marvelous, Madam Sereta," he proclaimed when he finished.

"Good, now go with George and get my tomatoes."

A Civic Health van passed slowly up the street a block from the edge of the barco. Cozy wondered if someone was going to be "cured" this morning, his or her name turned in to Civic Health as a carrier of this or that transmittable disease. People crowded front porches, spilled onto the sidewalks. Doors and windows stood open and the sounds of laughter, crying, music, and morning arguments punctuated the babble of conversation. The old buildings, two- and four-family flats, seemed to lean toward each other, like close friends huddled together. The pavements—poured concrete instead of the newer synthetics—were cracked and disintegrating.

At the end of the street an archway, its cast iron gates long gone, opened into the barco. From here the high grey wall that ran along the far edge of the park seemed insubstantial through the haze of smoke and steam that constantly drifted over the hovels. On the other side of that wall, Cozy knew, the neighborhood resembled the one behind him in many ways. Except that the pavement had not cracked in thirty years, and cars lined the sidewalks and the houses stood straighter, the doors and windows all closed to hold in the conditioned air; people did not gather on the street, except for the walking parties, nor did they lounge on their porches or front stoops; Civic Health vans—"ice cream" trucks—did not prowl those streets, and the water was not in short supply.

For the most part Cozy felt no resentment. He never saw it enough to truly hate them, their worlds were separate. The barricade was only a symbol, he knew, and could not really keep anyone from this side out. But it hid the better neighborhoods from view, allowed gypsies and borderlines the conceit of ignoring the secure classes. Only when he went south to visit friends or pass information on to Voley, when he walked through those clean, newer neighborhoods and saw the well-dressed, mannerly people did he start to think about them and feel the stirrings of envy.

But usually he was among friends. What, after all, did the credit-soaked secured classes have to compare with the barco? None of them knew what was Real, that was what the gypsies said. The secured classes had made a world for themselves to keep out the real world; they never changed, not much, as if they had stopped time for themselves. He felt himself grin as he walked alongside George, through the old gateless arch, into the chaos of St. Louis's barter commune.

The grass had long since been beaten to death, though here and there shocks of it sprouted, unruly and desperate. Dirt pathways wound off what had once been a slab side-walk and now was a gravel walkway that curved into the recesses of the park to join with others like it. Plywood, two-by-fours, sheet plastic, and canvas tarps underlay clumps of tents, prefab domes, lean-tos, and shacks built of salvaged wood, cardboard, plastic, and metal slabs. Here and there a larger, stabler structure provided the locus of a constellation of shanties. Ancient truck shells, buses, and trailers competed with rusting mobile homes for grandeur. On this side, half a dozen flats still stood, left over from the New Madrid, all that remained of neighborhoods that had collapsed and never been rebuilt, now absorbed into the park and the commune. Between hovels people slept in sleeping bags or piles of fabric mingled with various other portable materials. Everywhere, in the tiny "courtyards" arranged among clusters of hovels, cookfires sent smoke and steam up to join the thin cloud hovering above the barco. Dozens of aromas—most appealing, some awful—mixed and roiled between the people and shacks. Sewage trucks came every third day to collect the waste in the open latrines and cart it off for reclamation. Usually they came before dawn, providing a grinding wake-up call for the inhabitants.

Already this morning the sounds of artisans cobbling together barterable goods filled the air: delicate noises, small taps and grindings, the rattle and scrape of tools on metal and plastic. Gypsy makers making.

Invisible from here, on the northern edge, just on the other side of Highway 70, the federal resource distribution warehouse covered five square blocks. The only thing the Feds were good for, in Cozy's opinion. Citizens could go there to exchange their monthly allotment of resource scrip for food, medicines, or utilities. Most citizens demurred, turning their scrip back to the government in exchange for added credit. They preferred to pay premium costs at retail vendors than make the trip here. Or they came into the barco for grey market goods, which they could get with their excess scrip or by trading in kind. Most citizens were poor barterers, so they often got cheated, but Cozy did not believe they came looking for bargains.

The distribution center never threw anything away if it could help it, a policy established around the time of the Reform, so whatever did not go directly to citizens in exchange for their allotted scrip went out the "back door" to the gypsies or anyone else who understood the schedules and did not mind mingling with the disenfranchised. A lot of businesses took advantage of it, though none ever admitted to it. No one asked. It was wrong to throw away food. People, citizens or otherwise, ate. The country had enough, more than enough. After a downturn early in the century, exports soared again. Cozy had heard that North America produced more than a third of the food for the planet. He could not imagine that, but did not doubt it, either. Free food was everywhere.

For the disenfranchised, though, it sometimes proved a challenge to get it. The back door policy of the distribution center notwithstanding, resources were, by law, intended for citizens. Myriad dodges filled gypsy bellies. Sometimes food could be gotten directly from the center. But when an audit was going on, the food had to be accounted for. The free kitchens all over the city received a lot of it—all of them arms of registered charities or the religious unions. Or pools collected scrip spent by citizens in the barco until there was enough for a general purchase and the take was spread throughout the barco by numerous outlets.

Like Comber Blue.

"Be simpler to just use Harry's cards," Cozy groused.

"Enough," George warned him. "Keep still about that."

Cozy gave him a mock salute.

Comber Blue's stall stood almost in the center of the barco, not far from the West Florissant overpass, down a trammelled pathway between two rows of filthy sheets draped over jagged frames. The pathway opened onto a kind of raised plaza that fronted Comber Blue's. Boards underlay a mosaic of sheeting—old advertisements, painted wood, plastic—and already a small crowd gathered at the bar just beneath the overhanging plywood roof. Comber Blue and his wife, Billy, talked to customers in low, confidential tones. Comber Blue spotted George and raised a finger, then continued bargaining with the citizen standing before him.

Cozy was surprised to see the man. Usually citizens stayed away until late afternoon, but here stood a tall, well-dressed one. Light brown skin, close-cut hair, broad shoulders, and easy stance. His suit was current fashion, east coast: knee-length cobalt blue jacket, onyx buttons at the small of the back, and comfortably loose pants over a fine pair of black boots. Cozy ran a quick estimate in his head and decided that the citizen must be from out of town.

Comber Blue ended the conversation. The citizen turned around and Cozy saw wide-set, narrow blue eyes in a face that seemed too young for them: small mouth, slightly curved nose, a faint scar along the left jawline. He wore a black velvet cravat tucked between the high collars of his saffron shirt. Cozy caught the golden glint of a watch chain across a dark blue vest.

The citizen sauntered off and disappeared up another path.

George watched him, too, a suspicious scowl tugging his mouth into a pout.

"George," Comber Blue called.

Cozy followed George behind the bar and into the shadows of Comber Blue's sprawling establishment.

"Who was the citizen?" George asked.

Comber Blue glanced back over his shoulder. "I don't know, but he's looking for Cozy."

Cozy felt his scalp tingle. "Me?"

"That is what he said. Did I know anyone named Cozy. I don't think he knows what you look like."

The stacks of boxes formed a maze beneath the variegated roof. On a low table near the back, Cozy saw ten shallow boxes with their federal ID codes slashed.

"Tomatoes for Sereta," Comber Blue said. "I told her I'd get her some. You tell her I expect those quilts. I already have a customer waiting on them."

"I'll tell her," George said. He handed five of the boxes to Cozy and lifted the rest.

"Back way," Comber Blue said. "I've told half a dozen people already this morning that I'm out of tomatoes."

He led them to a flap, nearly invisible against the draping fabric that comprised the rear wall, and held it open for them. Cozy wrinkled his nose. A latrine ran behind Comber Blue's. George jumped across and Cozy followed, quickly.

"So somebody else is looking for you now," George said. "He looked Fed to me."

"Did he? I wouldn't know."

George raised an eyebrow, frowning. "No?"

Cozy gave him what he hoped was an appropriately injured look. "George, what would I know about Feds?"

"A lot less than you should. Come on. Maybe we'll have to move you again."

Vera sat on the front porch, crying. Her chest heaved and her chin puckered. Her upper lip was moist and her eyes red, but she made no sound.

George stopped, leaned toward her. "What?"

"Harry. The . . . they . . ." She sucked a breath loudly, held it, and controlled herself. "The ice cream truck stopped."

"Harry?" Cozy blurted, grinning, instantly regretting it. Vera lowered her head.

George sprinted up the steps, into the house. Cozy adjusted the weight of the tomatoes and walked up one step at a time.

Sereta bellowed within. Other voices snapped back until she thundered orders and dominated them. Cozy carried the boxes to the kitchen. Stelly sat at the table, eyes wide. All the adolescent sexuality he had noticed earlier was gone, displaced by the look of a frightened child. Cozy set the boxes on the table.

"Didn't George come in here?" he asked. Stelly shook her head. "Well. Be a help, put these away. Sereta's tomatoes."

Stelly nodded and stood, clearly happy to have something to do. Cozy went down the hall, following the voices. Everyone was in the living room. George had set his boxes on the floor just inside the entryway. Cozy carried them into the kitchen where Stelly was fitting them carefully into the refrigerator.

Cozy went back to the living room.

"—bastards came barging in here!" Sereta said. "Didn't ask no permission, didn't check nothing with me! Just tackled poor Harry!"

Harry lay on an old sofa. His left arm was swollen just below his shoulder, and bruises were starting to appear on his wrists. He seemed to be shaking slightly.

"What did they say?" George asked. "Did they show any documents?"

"That's just it! They asked for Cozy! I told them there was no Cozy here, then Harry came down the steps. One of them pointed and said 'That's him' and no matter what I said they didn't listen. They read Harry the Declaration of Civic Health and told him he had been named as a carrier. They grabbed him, tested him, and then cured him! Had to bind him, Harry kept squirming. I tried to tell Harry to just let it happen, didn't make any sense to fight them, and if the test said positive, then I guess he needed it. They got all done and left and then Harry collapsed on the floor."

Cozy looked closer at Harry now. He looked feverish. George leaned over him and raised an eyelid.

"He might be going into shock," George said. "Be just like Civic Health to give him the wrong juice. We better get him to the mission."

"George," Cozy said, "the mission can't handle shock. Not this; they can't do reactions like this, you know that."

"Then what do you suggest?"

"Harry's got a CID, take him to regional."

George glared at Cozy.

"What would Mr. Voley say if you let Harry die?" Cozy asked.

George bared his teeth, clearly frustrated. "We try the mission first. Where's Carlos? Does his car still work?"

"Emil," Sereta said to one of the other two men. "Go get wheels. Now."

Emil sprinted out of the house.

"George," Cozy yelled, "you're wasting time on the mission!"

"Cozy is getting very popular," George said. "Did you give yourself a dose of something, Cozy?"

"No! I stay clean! Only woman I've been with is DeNeille, and I'm the only man she's been with."

"Lately," Sereta said caustically.

"You were supposed to see her last night," George said. "Would she turn you in for spite?"

"What, and get paid a visit herself? I don't think so."

"Then somebody else is looking for you."

"Harry looks a little like me, but—"

George nodded. "Better call Voley, let him know what happened."

Harry shivered violently.

"Go get one of his cards, Cozy," George said. "Just one."

Cozy ran up the stairs, all the way to the third floor. Harry's room looked almost too neat for any to live in. Bed, desk, rug, chest of drawers, everything clean and orderly. Cozy opened the bottom right-hand drawer of the desk. A stack of CID cards was stacked in the corner. Cozy grabbed them and shuffled through to the one with Harry's name on the edge. He dropped the others, then hesitated. He took another one, slipped it in his pocket, and slammed the drawer.

NINE

Grant's alarm woke him before sunrise. His head throbbed. He took an antox, then showered. By the time he descended to the second floor office, his head had cleared.

Reva had called three times since two A.M. Grant wondered if she ever slept. Stuart from SEC had called again shortly after he had left the night before. He would be in the office by nine, call then.

Representative Tochsin had called to request a meeting, earliest convenience. It was only seven now. He messaged Tochsin's office that his earliest convenience would be in the afternoon, around one.

With an hour before he could call Stuart, he went down to the kitchen, made himself breakfast, relieved to discover that the Department had restocked the larder for his arrival, then accessed the local newsnet.

Senator Reed's visit took pride of place as the biggest story. Clips of Reed's speeches were spliced into quotes from local principle citizens—including the Mayor—to underscore

his strong states' rights sympathies, his intractable isola-
tionism, and his anti-federalist leanings. Grant marvelled at
the mixture of sentiments. Oil and water. Reed explained
his position on immigration, how he believed the current
laws—tough as they were—failed to address the coming crisis. Even after decades of tighter and tighter control, the
borders remained permeable. The world seeped in through a
thousand cracks.

Immediately following this came a report on efforts by
the World Health Organization to isolate and control a new
outbreak of an unidentified hemorrhagic fever in Pakistan.
Vivid images of overcrowded facilities, blood, and frantic
medical personnel in isolation suits contrasted with the flat
voice of the reporter who offered statistics, projections, and
a brief history of twenty-first century world epidemiology.

Next was a report on another bill before the Senate to
institute subdermal CIDs. Grant winced. An old debate, it
never died, only faded from time to time, to reemerge even
louder and more strident. Ever since the Reforms someone
had been trying to pass this one, but, security-conscious as
people were, this still crossed a line most were unwilling to
erase.

He switched it off and rubbed his eyes.

Lusk's file lay on the couch where he had left it. He
sighed and picked it up. Leafing through it, he found a
photo of Harold Lusk. It showed an intense young man,
dark-skinned with short black hair and a thin mustache. He
did not look old enough to have the responsibilities Director
Cutter claimed, but Grant knew that meant little; code-
writers, the best of them, had always been young. The
report said Lusk was from St. Louis. That surprised Grant. If
Beth had found him here, then why would he come back? It
made more sense to run somewhere unexpected.

The phone chimed.

"Agent Voczek," Grant said.

"Grant."

"Stuart." He tapped the vid and a pleasant-faced man with thin, light-brown hair appeared on the screen. "I was about to call you."

"I got in early. Your message said you needed data. How can I help?"

"Weston and Burnard. Do you know anything about them?"

Stuart looked thoughtful. "The name is very familiar. We've been watching them."

"Why?"

"Is this part of an on-going investigation?"

"It is. Do you remember Beth McQuarry?"

Stuart nodded. "Certainly."

"She was murdered. I'm investigating it."

"Oh, god. I'm sorry, Grant. I know you and Beth . . ."

"Thank you. I appreciate that, Stuart. Can you give me anything?"

Stuart frowned, clearly uncomfortable. "Is this strictly Treasury? No one else involved?"

Grant nodded. "No one else."

"All right. Weston and Burnard broker sales of bankrupt companies or companies that have, for one reason or another, closed down. We suspect them of dumping."

"Illegal transfer of assets from one state to another."

"Exactly. If so, they aren't likely to be the only ones involved. We're trying to find out who else."

"What companies? What states? Anything involving Missouri?"

"Well, they're headquartered in Missouri, but they're licensed to operate in several states and on Wall Street.

Several companies, nothing with a pattern. Just firms with a lot of assets and no liquidity. Are you looking for anything specific? Maybe I can confirm or deny. This is ongoing, so I'm not at liberty to just—"

"I understand. The name Mitchel Abernathy has come up. And the Clayton Banking Consortium."

"I'll check, but neither one chimes at the moment. Anything else?"

"Y-yes . . . Coronin Industries."

"What would *they* have to do with this?"

"I don't know. But the center of Beth's mission involved property they were in the process of acquiring. Just see if any of those other names connects with them in any way."

"I'll see what I can do, but . . . Coronin? God! Why don't you pick a *big* target?" he asked sarcastically.

"This was Beth's call."

Stuart nodded. "Sorry. Didn't mean to criticize. How soon do you need this?"

"Can you just fax it to me as soon as you have it? I'm in and out, I don't know with any certainty when I'll be here."

"I can send it to the local offices—"

"No. Send it here."

Stuart gave him a quizzical look, but said nothing. "Soon as soon is, Grant."

"Thank you, Stuart."

Grant did not want to talk to Reva yet. He did not know what to do with her offer of trust. Habit, reflex, logic all supported his normal course. Do not trust. Take nothing on faith. But Reva did not seem to fit any profile. He felt guilty closing her out, treating her as he treated everyone else, though he could not define why. Perhaps because this involved Beth his instincts gave him no clear resolutions. Time alone, working, might help.

The note from Beth's jacket lay open beside his brief-case. COZY. CID, B.C. He put the note in his pocket along with his palm stunner and a handful of clippers. He pressed a receiver against the skin behind his right ear, called a cab, and went downstairs.

The big Checker took him north, up Broadway, and let him out a few blocks from the barter commune. The driver handed him a flasher. "When you need me, just squeeze it. I'll find you, sir."

The cab pulled away. The sun was well above the horizon now and the cloudless sky seemed to glow. Grant walked along the strip of offices and crossed the street at the next intersection. Carrie Street bridged Highway 70 and descended into the barco.

Standing at the crest of the bridge Grant could see almost all of it. The high wall that marked its southeast boundary ran along Linton Avenue. The park proper extended back to West Florissant, which rose up over the barco from Linton all the way to the north side of Highway 70. The neighborhoods around it had never been rebuilt after the New Madrid and the barco spread over the razed area, making it nearly a mile across. The curve of the high-way marked its last boundary.

Smoke muted the colors. Metal glinted amid rust and grime. Greasy odors mingled with fetid—the smells of open-air human habitation, earth, ammonia, sweat, burnt food, lye. Grant saw movement here and there—gypsies up early to start on a day of hand-to-mouth survival. Later in the day, he knew, when more citizens arrived—hunting for illicit bargains or indulging the thrills of dangerous associations, exploiting those they did not know, could not understand, and would not tolerate outside this area—the barco changed its flavor, became brighter with banners and hawking and barbecues and the color of poverty turning an expected face out for the benefit of the tourists. Grant had seen dozens of these places, though few so large. Each one was different, but they were all the same in their uniqueness.

The street was pockmarked and cracked. Where it touched ground in the park its disintegration accelerated, turning it into a gravel road that wound into the maze of hovels.

He had learned the hard way years before not to try to pass as a gypsy. No matter how well he learned the jargon, copied the mannerisms, or dressed the part, he never blended for long. At night, sometimes, he could manage for an hour or two, but during the day there was no point trying. So, like a tourist, he strode down into the commune.

"This time o' the day only Comber Blue is open," one old man told him. He looked Grant up and down with his single eye and snorted. "Bit early t' be goin' native, eh, sir?"

"Not if you want to catch fresh before the flood," Grant said.

The old man made a sound almost like a laugh and shook his head. "Whate'er yer wantin', Comber Blue get it or tell you where." He pointed. "That way, nearly half through."

"Thank you."

People watched him as he worked his way through the twisty paths. Grant saw a lot of military surplus uniforms, some fairly new. He heard thin music drift from somewhere to his left. He came out of one path alongside an open trench. Several people looked up from their morning ablutions and smiled at him, amused at the discomfort they imagined Grant must feel.

He asked more directions the deeper in he went until he

finally stepped onto the makeshift plaza fronting the ragtag mass of sheeting and tents of Comber Blue's stall.

It was larger than he had expected. The chaos of its construction gave it a deceptively hunched look, but Grant estimated the place to be a thousand square feet. A couple of gypsies leaned on the battered bar that formed the front of the stall, talking to a large woman with grey and brown hair hanging around her shoulders. They all looked at Grant for a few seconds, then the woman turned to shout into the interior of the stall.

"Comber! Citizen!"

A short man with thinning white hair emerged from the shadows. He grinned and leaned wide hands on the bar.

"Yes, sir?"

"Are you Comber Blue?"

"I have that distinction."

"I'm told you can get or find anything."

"Well, within reason. What, in particular?"

Grant leaned on the bar and lowered his voice. "I'd be interested in a projector."

"A projector, sir?"

"Full holo, ambient presence." He smiled, embarrassed. "The model I want is out of my range."

"If it's out of your range, what can you want from me, sir?"

"Something close. Maybe you know a source."

Comber Blue shrugged. "Sources, maybe. Would you might appreciate something—say, a Delphi-Vintron? Model, say, ninety-nine hundred series?"

"As a matter of fact I was looking at a ninety-nine-fifty."

"Well, say, possibilities abound. Now, I'll check. But sources, you know . . . ?"

Grant reached into his inside jacket pocket and pulled out a sheaf of notes. "I have four issues of commodity scrip here. Food, utilities, clothing, and medical."

"I might need six."

"Six? My good vendor, with six I could acquire one over the counter."

"Then why don't you?"

Grant tucked the notes away. "Damn robbery, that kind of price."

Comber Blue shrugged sympathetically. "Regulations. Makes everyone a slave to taxes, eh, sir?" He held out his hand. "Give me the four issues. A gift. I see what I can find for you."

Grant gave him a dubious look. "How long?"

"Give me a minute?"

Grant handed over the notes and Comber Blue disappeared back into the stall. Grant glanced over at the others. They looked away at once. Grant took one of the little clippers from his pocket and casually flicked it up into the recesses of the stall.

A few minutes later Comber Blue returned with a small, thin box. He set it on the counter and smiled at Grant.

"I must thank you for your generosity," he said. "We poor folk need all the largesse citizens might provide. Your gift is welcome."

"Oh, no trouble. What's this?" Grant pointed to the box.

"I don't know, sir. Something I found. Maybe you know what it is."

Grant opened the box. Within, nestled in its form-fit packaging, was a sleek blue component with delicate white lettering along the edge. Delphi-Vintron 9960. Grant lifted the machine from the box. It was slightly larger than his palm. He turned it over. Below where the source ID had been removed it read MADE IN NORTH AMERICAN UNION, PATENT PENDING.

"My," he said. "A projector. You're lucky you found this."

Comber Blue shrugged. "I have nothing to play in it, sir. It does me no good. Perhaps you should keep it?"

"Well, if you insist." Grant put it back in the box and slipped the whole thing into his jacket pocket.

"Now, generous citizen, will there be anything else?"

"As a matter of fact, yes. I'm looking for someone, perhaps you might point the way."

"I know a few people. I doubt any of them would know you."

"True enough. But I think this is the sort of person you're more likely to know than I."

"A name?"

"Cozy."

Comber Blue blinked, then slowly shook his head. "Cozy? Not much of a name." He looked past Grant's shoulder and gave a sign of recognition. "I can ask around, but I don't think anyone will admit to it without encouragement."

"That might be arranged."

"Would you care to leave a location just in case someone should turn up?"

"No. I'll come back tonight. You can tell me then if your acquaintances extend to Cozy."

"As you wish, sir."

Grant nodded and turned away. Two men stepped forward. One was a little shorter than him, broad shouldered, powerful-looking, dressed in dark-grey military utilities. The other, tall and slim, wore old jeans and a brand new windbreaker. Grant looked away, giving them a polite nod and strolled on.

The tall one looked like Harold Lusk. No mustache, less intensity, but . . .

Out of sight of Comber Blue's, he reached back and pressed the tab behind his ear.

"Who was the citizen?"

"I don't know, but he's looking for Cozy."

"Me?"

"That is what he said. Did I know anyone named Cozy. I don't think he knows what you look like."

Grant listened to the sounds of movement, boxes shuffled, a grunt. Then Comber Blue spoke again.

"Tomatoes for Sereta—I told her I'd get her some. You tell her I expect those quilts. I already have a customer waiting on them."

"I'll tell her."

"Back way. I've told half a dozen people already this morning that I'm out of tomatoes."

Grant looked for a path that doubled back. He hurried down a narrow squeeze between a huddle of dome tents. He stepped out alongside another open latrine, but no one was using it. He followed it toward Comber Blue's, then stopped. Fabric flapped, followed by footsteps. Grant moved to the side, between a pair of shanties, and peered out. He saw the two men who had approached Comber Blue when he was leaving step out, carrying crates. They headed west.

He followed along until he found an access to a main path. He took a chance on losing them, but the impossibility of discreetly following them here in the barco made it worthwhile. He hurried west, toward the area where the few remaining flats rose up out of the press of shanties, trying to keep roughly along the same trajectory.

The habitats thinned out on the other side of the West Florissant overpass. He waited in the shadows, leaning against a support pylon. Perhaps he had already lost them. They might have veered north or south, might have stopped somewhere along the way. No telling where Sereta lived.

Then he spotted them, about thirty yards north, winding their way west in roughly the same direction as before.

It became both easier and more difficult to trail them now. They were more visible in this part of the barco, especially the taller of the pair with that bright new jacket. But Grant was more visible, too. He followed at a distance, stopping at intervals to look like a tourist shopping for barter bargains.

They left by way of a stone-and-brick archway that led into a neighborhood of multifamily flats. Grant hurried up to the old arch and watched from its cover until the two men were out of sight.

Grant opened his watch. Nine-thirty. He could come back later and find out where Sereta lived. He at least had a face and a neighborhood.

He walked back across the barco.

The cab let him off in front of his house. Reva was waiting on his porch.

"Early day," she said, standing.

Grant slipped his card into the lock. "May I offer you breakfast?"

"Coffee. People might talk if I had breakfast in your house."

He looked back and saw her smiling. He opened the door for her.

"Were you waiting long?"

"Only half an hour. One of your neighbors—Mrs. Delcampo, just across the street—told me a cab took you away just after sunrise."

"Early day for her."

"She's about seventy and I got the impression nothing happens in this neighborhood that escapes her."

Reva looked into the living room, nodded appreciatively at the fireplace, then peered into the study.

"Your desk?"

"Beth's. I think. I don't remember her owning it."

Reva pointed down the hallway. "Kitchen?"

Grant nodded and followed her. "Is there something you wanted to talk to me about, Agent Cassonare?"

Reva quickly inspected cabinets until she found the mugs, then poured what remained of Grant's morning brew. She set it aside and began programming the maker.

"Reva, please."

"I'm not comfortable with that."

"Get comfortable. I'm not comfortable with 'Agent Cassonare.' Not from someone I'm supposed to be working with."

"Last night—"

"Last night you annoyed me. More than that, you really pissed me off." She picked up her mug and leaned back against the counter. "As a formal concession, call me Reva."

"All right . . ."

"And as a further concession, please tell me why you took off for the barco this morning without notifying me."

"Is this an official request?"

Reva scowled. "What is it with you? Your record doesn't read like such a by-the-rule Department boy."

"If you've read my jacket then you know that I'm exactly by-the-rule."

"No. Not breaking the law isn't the same as following it to the letter. I was impressed with the Boston incident. Then I read about New York. Stock transfers to South America channeled through an off-shore commodities smuggler. The Securities and Exchange Department couldn't break it, and you did."

"It was a subtle crime."

"Just the sort of subtle crime SED is supposed to deal with, but it never occurred to them to buy submarket commodities from the smugglers. *They* wouldn't violate the tax laws; *you* didn't mind."

"There are certain methods a Resource agent may use that other departments may not. I simply took advantage of my flexibility."

Reva shrugged. "Well, if you want to put it that way. What about Albany?"

"What about it?"

"Local director of the commodities distribution center was transferring scrip into the account of a nonexistent farm combine in which he held stock. He paid himself a dividend on goods never made, never delivered, never distributed. How did you break it?"

"He became greedy. I approached him as a legitimate commodity venture and offered a reduction in transfer costs with a stock kick-back."

"Very creative. Not what I expect from a by-the-rule sort."

"What's your point?"

"You're shutting me out. Why? Was I right? You want revenge?"

"You have your investigation to run, I have mine."

"It's *our* investigation."

Grant slammed his fist on the table. "How do I know that? How do I know you're not reporting directly to someone who might interfere?"

Reva set her cup down. "That's better. That's something I can live with. In fact, you don't know. You can't."

"Then I can't trust you."

Reva laughed. "This system we've got—it doesn't work, you know that? This separation of powers nonsense, I understand it had good reasons, but it's become pathological. Because I'm FBI and you're Treasury, we can't talk to each other. Why? Because we might combine our resources and energies and destroy the country? Is that reasonable? My god, Grant, we've got a murder to solve! We're supposed to be on the same side, at least morally."

"You make it sound silly, but you're right. There are sound reasons—"

"Good, solid Reformist crap. Do you believe that?"

"It has a kind of logical consistency."

Reva shook her head. "Pretzel logic. Closed loop reasoning. Look—why would anyone interfere with this?"

"You've heard it already. Beth was a maverick. She danced with scandal, played things close to the edge. Some of the methods she used were barely legal. I'm not sure—" He stopped, looked away.

"Not sure what?"

Grant felt foolish. The thought had not occurred to him till just then, but it must have been in the shadows all along, an unrecognized suspicion. Now it surfaced.

"Oh," Reva said softly. "You aren't sure that she wasn't removed by our people."

Grant felt himself nod. Odd, he thought, how he had kept the idea carefully out of reach. But it made its own paranoid sense. Tochsin's name on her personal report lent a kind of credibility to it. Beth had finally overstepped on an investigation, involved a congressman. The almost complete lack of local cooperation, including his own department's representatives . . .

Grant sat down at the table and closed his eyes. "I saw a suppression once. Or should I say I *didn't* see it. A colleague of mine investigated a governor for interstate smuggling. There was a rumor that the governor in question had internal support. My colleague was warned off, but he went to a federal judge and secured an open warrant. My colleague was found dead in another state—not one of the states involved—and six months later the judge lost his bench. The investigation was closed. The FBI looked into the death, worked the case for a month or so, and filed an unrelated death report. Gypsies, they said."

"You didn't believe the report."

"No. Deportations are forever."

Reva sat down across from him. "Grant—Agent Voczek— I swear to you I am not involved in a suppression. If one has gone down here I want to know. If it hasn't, then the only way to solve this is together."

Grant felt anxious. She did not look away. To move further along the path of cultivated mistrust would be easy, he knew, easier than the alternatives. Except that the result was self-destruction. He could not be effective this way. He could not do his job without the ability to rely on the systems he worked with.

"Tell me one thing," Reva said. "What suggested this to you? What have we seen so far that feels like a suppression?"

Grant thought about it. If he answered this question, he knew, the pattern would be established. Trust, distrust. Work together or accomplish nothing. Or maybe something, but certainly less than satisfaction.

He breathed deeply.

"The syphilis," he said, and joined himself to Reva.

TEN

Beth was too careful. She was compulsive about health. She had regular examinations and she was . . . cautious . . . about her pleasures."

"That doesn't mean contracting a social disease is impossible," Reva said.

"But unlikely in the extreme for Beth."

Reva frowned. "This isn't Secure Class prejudice, now, is it? 'People like us don't get things like that'—"

"No. Beth's dead—she was murdered. I don't normally indulge useless sentiment, but under these circumstances it would be criminal not to consider all possibilities."

"All right. Then the question is, where did it come from? Something to scandalize her? She was beaten badly enough that she probably would have died anyway, but she was poisoned. You're suggesting she was deliberately infected. Why? It's almost as if someone wanted to kill her over and over."

"Certainly the scandal would tend to discredit her. Maybe a way of deflecting a follow-up?"

"Get us to investigate the agent instead of her case?"

Grant shrugged. "Possibly. Probably."

"It did cause us delays."

"Minor. What's really bothering me is the silence. Not even Moore was completely forthcoming, although she acted the part of an honest citizen with dangerous knowledge."

"Is that how you see her?"

"Not you?"

Reva shook her head. "Whatever other motives Chief Moore had in talking to us, there's more than a little self-serving bum shielding there. The question is who to look at next."

"We have to look at it all." Grant took the projector out of his pocket and laid it on the table. "My morning purchase."

Reva opened the lid and whistled. She took the machine out and turned it over. "You got this in the barco?"

"Four issues of commodity scrip. That's not only way below market value, that's below designated distribution cost. The thing is, I went there looking for someone. I needed an excuse to ask, so I requested a purchase. I never expected to receive what I asked for. This is newer than the model I named. That machine is less than a year old. The source code has been excised, but I still think I can trace it. That validates Beth's investigation."

"I'd say so." Reva set it down. "All right, so there is a leak. New goods are spilling out of the legitimate avenues into the barco. The Mayor was right, your people here were wrong, and Beth McQuarry was killed for substantiating it."

"She was killed for finding the source."

"Abernathy?"

"He fits a kind of profile. Old radical commercialist, rabidly anti-federal, an advocate of free currency, wealthy enough to think he can get away with anything."

"Supplying the barco with contraband? Why?"

"A slap in the face to the government. A way to circumvent trade regulations. Any number of reasons, but one we always watch for is an attempt to destabilize credit. Someone like Abernathy ... by himself he couldn't do it, but along with others it's possible to upset the local economy by feeding a black market."

"To what end?"

"Anything. Tax evasion. Something as simple as creating a small panic on the exchanges and profiting from the margin to attempting a push for free currency." He grunted. "Seems strange that after more than forty years of running the economy this way some people still want to see it fail."

"He'd need a partner in D.C."

Grant nodded. "Tochsin?"

"He's on the Methods and Allocations Committee."

"It doesn't make sense."

Reva turned the projector around with her index finger. "We need to establish that the leak is from Abernathy."

"Beth hadn't requested any warrants yet. I don't want to either. That could get out and Abernathy could shut the whole thing down before we proved anything. I want to know before I move."

She nodded. "Agreed."

"A visit to the barco at night, perhaps ..." Grant suggested.

"Both of us."

"How good are you at passing as a gypsy?"

She smiled. "Are you kidding? Look at me."

"If you like."

She opened her mouth, then seemed to change her mind. She smiled instead and picked up the projector. "Do you have anything to play in this?"

Grant hesitated, thinking of the pornographic disks he had appropriated from the police station waiting room. *That* certainly had not been by-the-rule behavior. . .

The doorbell chimed.

"You have company," she said.

"No one I'm expecting . . ." Grant stood. "Excuse me."

He opened the front door. The woman waiting towered over him by nearly six inches. She smiled brightly and leaned forward slightly, brushing a strand of blondish hair from her thin face.

"Good morning," she said. "I'm Alicia Porter. I live a few doors down?"

"How do you do. I'm Grant Voczek."

"Voczek? Is that Russian?"

"Czech."

"Oh, how interesting! Are you a refugee?"

"No, Madam, I was born here. How may I help you?"

"I'm on the Walton Row Neighborhood Association committee. On behalf of the area, I'd like to welcome you."

Grant resisted the urge to shut the door and walk away. "Thank you."

Porter gestured at the house. "Madam McQuarry—well, we're terribly sorry about what happened, of course. We hadn't gotten to know her very well. She kept unusual hours. Did you know her?"

"She was a friend."

"I see. Well, we made her as welcome as possible, let me assure you. I hope—we all hope—that your time in the Walton Row area is more pleasant."

"Did you speak with Beth much?"

"The first week, almost every day. If not to me, then to several others I can introduce you to."

"After the first week?"

"Well, then she was preoccupied." Porter straightened slightly; her smile became briefly rigid.

"With a Mr. Dirkenfeld?"

Her smile faded. "It's not my place to—"

Grant held up a hand. "Madam, did you know that Beth McQuarry was a Treasury agent?"

"I—she made it clear that she was federal, yes."

"Ah. Then allow me to make it equally clear."

Porter started. "Oh."

"Your place or not, I would appreciate any information that might help me discover who murdered her."

"Murdered?" She frowned briefly. "Yes, I suppose she was, from what I heard."

"Who found her?"

"Mrs. Delcampo. She's the early bird in the area, up before the rest of us. At her age one needn't sleep."

"Is there a reason you questioned the fact that Beth was murdered?"

"Well, I understood she suffered a malaise."

"Who gave you to understand this?"

Porter blinked twice, smile gone. "Am I being interrogated?"

"No, Madam, we're merely having a conversation. I assure you, your name will not be connected to anything official."

That seemed to relax her. "The police told us."

"Told you what?"

"That she had been known to frequent certain Speaks. That she had gotten herself into difficulty at one of them."

"Did she attend these Speaks in anyone's company, or is this just a rumor?"

Porter frowned. "I don't ordinarily traffic in rumor—"

"Of course not," Grant said politely, "but she *did* keep irregular hours. And she *was* seeing a married man."

She nodded sharply, once. "We pride ourselves that we mind our own business, but Mr. Dirkenfeld was hardly an inconspicuous indiscretion."

"How long had she been seeing him?"

"Since just after her first week here."

"Did you know Beth was beaten to death?"

"Mrs. Delcampo said as much, but . . ."

"But you believed the police. Was it an official statement or from one officer in particular?"

"Nothing official, but—"

"What was the name of the officer?"

"I don't think—"

"Madam," Grant said sternly, "this officer lied to you. Hardly something worth defending."

She frowned. "True." She narrowed her eyes. "My name will be on nothing official?"

"Nothing. We're just conversing."

"Officer Van Belz."

"Thank you, Madam. That will help. How many local officers came before our people arrived?"

"Two cars. One unmarked, very official. But that one didn't stay long."

"Just two cars." Grant sighed. "You may correct the rumor. Beth McQuarry was murdered. Beaten to death."

"But—no one heard anything. Not even Mrs. Delcampo."

"Still, she was beaten to death."

"Awful." Porter shook her head. "Which brings to me to the point of my visit. As part of the neighborhood association, I'd like to invite you to attend our Walk this weekend."

"Walk?"

"Our Neighborhood Walk, from eleven till dawn. It's traditional, going all the way back to before the Reform. A vigilance. It was a nightly affair then, but now we only have one a month."

"Oh, I see." Grant considered it briefly, then nodded. "Yes, perhaps I shall. Where do you gather?"

Porter waved a hand in the air. "Oh, everywhere. We have a carnival of a time, Mr. Voczek. Will you come?"

"Certainly. Assuming I'm not otherwise occupied."

Porter smiled. "Of course. Well, thank you, sir. And welcome to the area. I do hope to see more of you."

Grant bowed and watched Alicia Porter move on up the street.

"A Neighborhood Walking Party."

Grant turned. Reva leaned against the wall nearby, arms folded.

"Sounds quaint," she said.

"It's not. When I was growing up we had them, every night, like she said. Most effective deterrent to crime. People don't risk much when the streets are full of people all night long."

"It doesn't sound like they need it anymore."

"Probably not in this neighborhood, but I'm sure there are areas where it still retains its original idea." He closed the door. "You didn't grow up with them?"

"Dade County has long been a bastion of peace and tranquility," Reva said, a hint of sarcasm in her voice. "There's enough wealth to buy the best security. Crime was something that happened in other places."

"How did you become interested in police work, then?"

"The best use of my abilities. After leaving the service, it seemed the only worthwhile career."

"You were in the service?"

She cocked an eyebrow. "Grant, let's at least not lie to each other so artlessly. You've read my jacket, I'm sure."

He nodded.

"And," she continued, "I could ask how *you* became interested in law enforcement with just as much expectation of a straight answer. Let me see, how did it go? 'Primary and secondary education demonstrated chronic indifference to set curricula, low self motivation, and wide disparity between potential and achievement.' You hated school. I imagine you hated authority. You ran away from home five times before your father finally had you placed in Newark Polytech."

"Touché."

"Well?"

"Well what?"

"Your father was a refugee?"

"No, he came over before the German absorption. *He* hated authority. A real libertarian, but too European to embrace the doctrinaire version over here. You?"

"My great-grandparents were. They came over from Castro's Cuba. Marielitos. They weren't very welcome. There was a Cuban community already established in Miami and they didn't want us. The whites didn't want us. When we started succeeding, there were others who didn't want us."

" 'Us'? I thought we were talking about great-grandparents."

"My family, yes." Reva frowned.

Grant shrugged. "I don't even know who my grandparents were."

"You could find out. There are immigrant associations—"

"Assuming I want to, yes. I could. So, what made you join the military?"

"I'm a patriot. I wanted to do something important for my country."

Grant felt himself smile.

"Do you have a problem with that?" she asked.

"No, it's just . . ."

"Just what?"

"I think I should talk to Mrs. Delcampo."

Reva grabbed his arm. "Have we come to terms?"

"I'm trusting you to back me up tonight."

"That's tonight."

"Did you overhear all of my conversation with Alicia Porter?"

"Most of it."

"There's a local officer who told her that Beth died at a Speak. Officer Van Belz."

"Would you like me to find him?"

"Yes."

"And the unmarked car?"

"If you can."

She let go of his arm. "We aren't finished with this conversation."

Grant nodded. "I have a meeting with Congressman Tochsin at one."

"It might not be wise to suggest to Tochsin that we're really working together."

"Fine." She stepped by him, and he caught her hand. It closed briefly, reflexively. Warm, dry. "Reva—we have terms."

"I won't turn on you," she insisted.

"Your word?"

"My word."

Mrs. Delcampo invited Grant into her house and insisted on serving lemonade. She brought a tray into the living room and poured him a tall glass.

She was small, her chalky hair tied back in a long ponytail. Her smile seemed permanently set, the folds trained over the decades to hold one dominant position.

"I had scoliosis once," she said. "But I took the cure in Pittsburgh. I feel forty-five all over again." She sat down on a short divan with her own glass. "I suppose you'd like to know about Beth."

Grant nodded. "You were on first names?"

"Tradition is boring. One week of 'Madam' and my jaw aches. I only call people I don't like by title."

"I understand you found her."

"You might say that. I saw her brought home."

Grant started. "Excuse me?"

"It was about three-forty, three-forty-five in the morning. She was towed. A van brought her car. I saw them pull up from my upstairs window. I thought something had happened to her motor. A man worked under the hood of her car for a few minutes, then the van left."

"The report said you found her body at seven-thirty."

"Yes, that's true. I mean, it wasn't my place to go down and snoop. How she conducted her life was entirely her business." She smiled. "I was impulsive when I was her age. That was before the Reform, of course, and all this stodgy nonsense you have to put up with today. I liked Beth because she didn't seem bound by it."

"I spoke earlier with Madam Porter—"

"*Mrs.* Porter."

"She said the police told all of you that Beth had died from misadventure in a Speak. She seemed unaware that Beth had been beaten to death."

"I found Beth's body and called the police. They came very quickly, and the body was taken away before anyone else saw it. I gave a statement to Officer Van Belz. I had the distinct impression that he didn't care what I had seen. He took almost no notes. Then I was sent home."

"Mrs. Porter said there were two cars that answered your call."

"One, first. Then about fifteen minutes later a second one showed up—the unmarked one. By that time I'd been sent home."

"Did you get a number off the second car?"

"I'm sorry, no. But it was a federal car. It left after a few minutes. Then the ambulance showed up. I went back out to make sure they understood what had happened, but Officer Van Belz stopped me and sent me home again."

Grant leaned forward. "Do you think Beth went to Speaks?"

"Oh, probably. She enjoyed."

"Enjoyed?"

"Enjoyed. Life, pleasure, everything. I don't believe she caused her own death, though, which was the implication of Officer Van Belz's comments. She was badly beaten. Beth struck me as being much too careful. And I never heard of Speaks towing a car home with a body in it. Usually, the river gets the corpses."

"You don't seem very shocked at the idea of her attending Speaks."

Mrs. Delcampo laughed softly. "Well, very little shocks me. Disturb, yes. Things disturb me. Like the way everyone now pretends to be shocked. Lying disturbs me. This whole period disturbs me. The one thing I want—I don't want much anymore, it's a habit I've lost—but one thing I do still want is to live through this time and see the world let its pretenses down again. I was in my twenties during the first decade of the century. It was an incredible time. Babylon.

Not in the sense of the prophets who kept telling us the world was about to end, but in the sense of . . . well, everything was present and at hand. The best and the worst. It seemed we had finally brought ourselves to the brink of honesty."

Grant raised an eyebrow. "Honesty? It seemed to me, reading about the period, that it was nothing but excess. Indulgence for its own sake."

The old woman nodded. "That, yes. But so much else. The gene therapies that have given us so much came to fruition then. Space stations were going up, it appeared we were going to go back to the moon. Agriculture underwent another productive revolution. The excess you hear about is the excess of pleasure, of indulgence, of our frantic pursuit of ecstasy. But everything came in excess. Hope and debauchery in equal measure. And we turned our back on it, retreated into—what do the gypsies call it?—Faketime."

She finished her glass and poured herself a fresh drink. "But once in a while I meet someone who reminds me that the possibilities aren't dead, just waiting."

"Beth?"

Mrs. Delcampo smiled thinly. "I'm very disappointed that we've killed her."

"Have we?"

"In one way or another, yes. Whatever she was doing it was because of this age. She ran into it. Rather than yield to her intrusions, we killed her." She looked at him directly. "Do you think I'm eccentric?"

"No more than anyone else."

She laughed again. "You're kind. The neighborhood values me because I'm up all the time. I don't sleep much. I only need a few hours a day, so I see what goes on. I don't tell them all I see, just enough that they think I'm valuable.

It gains me access to certain circles where there is at least intelligent conversation."

"Honest conversation?"

"No. But one can't have everything."

"Did you know who Beth was seeing?"

"Richard Dirkenfeld. I told Officer Van Belz that, too. He didn't even write it down. Certain names do not get written down in this city."

"Did she see him that night?"

"No. She left alone, quite late. She had been doing that more and more. That was the third night in a row that she went out alone."

"Who is Richard Dirkenfeld?"

Mrs. Delcampo lip curled. "A piece of social slime."

"Why do you think Beth would have anything to do with him?"

"An interesting way to put the question. She certainly wasn't seeing him for pleasure." She shrugged. "Maybe she was. But I think she used him to gain her access to people she could not normally get to without a warrant. His father is one of our senators. So is his father-in-law, for that matter. I don't think Richard would have liked that. They fought a few days before she was killed."

"The question then would be, why would Richard Dirkenfeld have anything to do with Beth?"

"You'd have to ask him that. But I suspect it was because Beth was better than him."

"I'm not sure I understand."

"Richard has never been particularly worthwhile. He has always sought women better than him. It's a pattern. He married far out of his league."

"Who did he marry?"

"Teresa Reed. Senator Reed's daughter. The Dirkenfelds

have been waiting for the divorce since, but she's never done it. I'm not at all sure why. I suppose they've come to an arrangement, like everybody else. No honest rage, just smooth it over and pretend it's all right, even while everyone knows it isn't. But I suppose it is all right if no one gets upset."

"You don't very much like these days, do you?"

"Life can be subdivided into genres: tragedy, high drama, opera, comedy. Each one has something worth watching or being a part of."

"And what is the present?"

Mrs. Delcampo laughed sharply. "Farce."

ELEVEN

Shortly after the Reform the federal building contained apartments for officials, dorms for lower echelon workers, a self-contained arcology. At twenty floors, covering five square blocks, it squatted in the middle of the downtown area. Whole sections were empty, sealed-up rooms and offices ready for the day when either federalism became more desirable, or another wave of reactions drove federal employees inside the walls. The space was available, to defend or administer.

Congressman Tochsin's offices occupied a corner on the opposite end of the structure from Treasury. Most of the fourth floor was empty. Thick sealant followed the seams of the doors.

Grant hurried down the silent halls. He had never cared for empty buildings, nor had he liked the community poly-tech to which his father had consigned him. Empty corridors disturbed him.

A male receptionist looked up when he entered.

"May I help you, sir?"

"I have an appointment with Congressman Tochsin. Special Agent Voczek, Resource Security Division, Treasury."

The receptionist touched his throat and announced Grant. He looked up. "Go right in, Agent Voczek. You're expected."

"Thank you."

Michael Tochsin looked up from behind his desk. A woman leaned over him, pointing to something on a portable secretary. She glanced up briefly.

Tochsin wore his hair short. He dressed in current fashion, a sky-blue jacket over maroon satin cravat and white shirt. There was something pliant about his face, as if it had not yet found its true shape. He wore make-up.

The woman had bright red hair that she let hang. Sharp features, and green eyes Grant suspected were contacts. She wore a black, loose jacket that hung to her upper thighs, and a tunic blouse of dark blue. A ruby clasp held her collar close to her throat.

"Special Agent Voczek," Tochsin said, standing. "Welcome. I'm glad you came. This is Tess, my personal assistant."

Grant bowed to her, nodded to Tochsin.

"Were we finished?" Tochsin asked her.

"Yes." She gathered up the secretary and crossed between Tochsin and Grant. She paused. "Pleased to meet you. Perhaps we'll see each other again."

"A pleasure, Madam."

She left the office by a side door.

Tochsin gestured to a chair in front of his desk. "Well, Agent Voczek, have a seat, please. Can I offer you anything?"

"No, thank you." Grant lowered himself into the chair. "How may I help you, Congressman?"

"I understand you're investigating the murder of your fellow agent, Elizabeth McQuarry. I wanted to extend the services of my office. I don't know what I might be able to do for you, but if there is anything, please don't hesitate to ask."

"That's kind of you."

"I would like to know, however, if your investigation involves anyone prominent."

"Prominent in what sense?"

"Principle citizens."

"You mean like Mitchel Abernathy?"

Tochsin frowned briefly. He reached into a polished wood box and withdrew a cigar. He offered it to Grant, who shook his head.

"Like him, yes," the congressman said slowly. "Others."

"'Others.' Say, the Dirkenfelds?"

Tochsin cut off the end of the cigar with small scissors. "Like them, too."

"Have you been approached, Congressman? Asked to intervene?"

"I wouldn't presume to intervene in a Treasury investigation, particularly with a barco problem the size St. Louis has. No, I'm offering to act as go-between, to smooth over any possible instances of possible misunderstanding between Treasury and St. Louis's citizens."

"Forgive me, Congressman, but I'm not following what you're suggesting."

"Agent McQuarry seemed to have been looking into areas outside her mission."

"It's fairly common knowledge that where there is an increase in unregistered trade in a barco there's a benefactor. The leak is from legitimate sources. It's fully within our mission to investigate those sources."

"I thought that was just hearsay."

"No, sir," Grant replied. "Barter communes generally trade only in what they themselves make from discards or from salvage. The merchandise available in such a barco is usually distinct. Rarely will you see new goods. When you do, it's coming from an otherwise legitimate dealer."

"Why? I mean, you make it sound like collusion. I think they just steal it."

"Sometimes, yes, but security systems are incredibly difficult to bypass. Most gypsies won't even try."

"So you mean to continue where Agent McQuarry left off."

"That is my mission."

Tochsin frowned again. "There are proprieties to observe in any relationship, Agent Voczek. I'll put it to you bluntly, sir, that I have a responsibility to see that innocent citizens aren't shamed by a sloppy investigation."

Grant folded his hands on his lap and waited.

Tochsin lit the cigar. Smoke drifted around his face. "Now, Agent McQuarry was called in here to investigate the barco, not principle citizens. If she had stuck to her mission, I doubt she would have been here long enough to be killed."

"That sounds like a threat, Congressman."

"No, no. Fact. Twenty-three days, Agent Voczek. That's much too long for an investigation that could be done in a couple of days."

"I didn't realize that you understood the procedures of Treasury investigations."

"My point is, I believe she was looking for something because her investigation had turned up nothing. She looked into the barco, found nothing, and instead of simply filing a report to that effect she started trying to build a case."

"The Mayor called us in on this—"

"Because of election politics. Now, I'm inclined to do her a favor in this, but I think her judgement was in error. She wants the barco deported. Fine. It seems evident that your fellow agent was murdered by gypsies. If you're so inclined, you can write a report that will take care of the problem."

"For that matter, Congressman, so could you. All you have to do is petition the House for a deportation order. Authorize it, and the army will be in there by the end of next week, load them all up, and ship them wherever you suggest. Or the committee. I'm not really certain how that part of the decision gets made. Brazil would probably appreciate the new labor."

Tochsin shook his head. "I can't do that unless it's based on a field report from someone like you."

"If the barco was indeed a threat to community, threat to commerce, threat to tax distribution, then Agent McQuarry would have found that out in a few days and acted."

"Exactly my point. She didn't. Instead, she went off on a tangent, making allegations against our finest. I'm suggesting to you that this need not be repeated."

"So I should just look at the barco and agree with you that it has exceeded acceptable limits and file a report so stating. Never mind the source of the increased trade."

Tochsin glared at him for a moment. "I'm not without some sympathy, Agent Voczek. But frankly, the gypsies have done it to themselves. They make themselves targets by living the way they do. If they then take revenge on the system by killing one its officers, I can no longer afford the luxury of coddling them."

"And their source?" Grant asked.

"Assuming one exists, once the barco is gone, the source will have nowhere to dump its illicit merchandise."

"But we still won't know who it is."

"Nor do we need to as long as the problem is solved." Tochsin pulled on his cigar, then relit it. "I understand there's an FBI agent working on this as well."

"Yes, sir."

"Is she giving you any trouble?"

"The usual."

"Has she learned anything?"

"I wouldn't know. She's FBI."

Tochsin grunted. "And you're Treasury. Well, then, that seems normal enough."

"Congressman, might I point out that you're dangerously close to intervening."

"This is my city, Agent Voczek. I represent these people. I keep D.C. as far out of their lives as possible. That way I keep going back to D.C. to represent them."

Grant made a show of pulling a handkerchief from his pocket and dabbing at his forehead. He slipped a clipper from his pocket in the same movement and dropped it on the floor. Its chameleon skin matched the carpet.

"I'd advise you strongly not to push this, Congressman."

"And I'd advise you strongly not to violate anybody's constitutional freedoms, Agent Voczek. You're a guest in this city. You should enjoy your stay, not antagonize your hosts."

Grant stood. "I may well be here long enough not to vote for you, Congressman. Is there anything else?"

"I'll be calling your superiors."

"Give them my regards. Good day, sir."

He left the offices and walked unhurriedly down the corridor. At the next intersection he ducked around the corner and pressed the patch behind his ear.

"—inept way to handle it, don't you think?" Tess's voice.

"He irritated me."

"He worked you."

"I *do* have the authority—"

"Which you tried on the other one, with even worse results. Michael, you should stop trying to be D.C."

"And you should stop trying to be my conscience. It's bad enough that you have such a crippled one yourself—if you damage mine, it will be a felony. What is it?"

"Nothing. What about the rest of your appointments? Shall I cancel them?"

"No. I have to go over to the MAC in half an hour. Late lunch with State Senator Robertson and Aurora Campbell of Coronin Industries. Move the rest to tomorrow morning."

"As you wish, sir."

Grant took his finger off the receiver. She knew, he thought. The change in their voices had been smooth, but . . . he told himself to look into her background.

He heard the office door open. He sprinted on the balls of his feet down the corridor to the next intersection and ducked around the corner. Pressed against the wall, he controlled his breath, listening. Nothing. He looked back down the hallway. Empty. He let go a relieved sigh.

This corridor ended at another door. Something about it was different than the other doors along the hall. Grant approached it silently. No sealant. He lowered himself to his knees and studied the carpeting, running his fingers lightly over the nap until he found a small, irregular lump. He teased it loose from the threads. It looked like molten plastic, translucent and hard. The edges of the door seemed clean. Near the knob, though, he found tiny gouges in the veneer. With a fingertip he felt along a line from the gouges both up and down and discovered a few others.

Grant pocketed the lump of plastic and took out his palm stunner. He turned the knob slowly and pushed the door open.

Desks and office chairs, boxes of old file disks, papers, spilled packing kernels. In the direction of Tochsin's office the wall was solid. Boxes blocked the door in the opposite wall.

Grant closed the door behind him. Plastic panels covered the windows, letting in milky light. The carpet was standard medium grey, institutional norm. He studied it closely but saw nothing irregular. As he stepped away from the door he could see that everything had been cleared away from the path to that blocked door.

He checked the top box—disks, and some very old paper manuals. Six boxes. He knelt and ran his hand over the carpet and found indentation marks. When he traced them he found that they conformed to the boxes against the door, as if the stack had been moved out and left sitting for long periods, then moved back.

Grant slid the stack out.

"Hey."

He turned, bringing up the stunner. His vision clouded and he smelled the sharp tang of citrus. He wiped at his eyes and squinted, his ears growing warm, the warmth spreading over his face, down his neck and across his scalp. He felt himself fall against the door. Beyond his groping fingers he saw two shapes looming over him, dark, featureless.

Then he saw nothing, consciousness encased in rippling brown and black. He heard footsteps, voices muffled as though coming through a wall.

"Damn it!"

He moved toward the exclamation, fell. He smelled the acid odor once again, then heard nothing.

He felt satin in his hands. He rolled and his stomach heaved. He caught himself, waited for the sourness at the bottom of his throat to pass.

"Hey . . ."

He opened his eyes and saw nothing. Darkness. His eyes felt gummy, uncooperative. He blinked and noticed light from the left. He thought about that carefully. He lay on his right side and he could smell his own harsh, humid breath. Satin brushed his face. He closed his hands and the satiny substance collapsed. Sheets, blankets, cloth. The light was reddish. He blinked again, then brought a hand—his left—to his face, wiped at his eyes. Sleepers peeled away.

"Ready to go again?"

He pushed. His head came out of the mound of sheets and started pounding behind his eyes, throughout his sinuses. His stomach worked threateningly. The voice came again, said something else he did not understand. Female. He moaned, then sneezed, hard, once, twice more. He sniffed back and smelled blood. Was that the acid tinge . . . ?

Other odors underlay this. Pungency, like sweat, and a fuller aroma, like fine seasoning . . .

"Maybe three's enough then? I don't mind. As far as I'm concerned, you can come back anytime for one on the house."

He slowly rolled onto his back and looked up. Someone sat on the other end of the bed. In the dim light he saw a thin face, hair tangled, stuck to her cheeks and jaw, her neck. Breasts . . .

"Where—?" he tried and his throat filled with acid. He choked, coughed, held his stomach.

"Just take it slow, darling, you'll be fine. Bit much tonight, perhaps. Sister Amy helps those who need it and those who want it, but I told you I didn't think you needed any help. You managed just fine without it. But the customer's the one who says what and when, so—"

Grant opened his eyes again. The laces of a corset traced paths across her belly. Bare legs . . .

He cleared his throat. "Where'm I?"

"I'm hurt, darling. You don't remember?"

He managed to sit up. "Clothes . . ."

"So soon? I thought you might stay till morning, darling. Better you than some of the others come in here."

Another light came on, a harsh white one. Grant looked up, squinted into it, and saw her scowl.

"Shit. Clothes it is, darling."

She bounced across the bed and onto her feet. Grant stared at her naked buttocks, jiggling as she hurried away. He reached. His arms felt weighted.

"Here, darling, let me help you. As bashed as you are you might make it out."

She dangled a pair of pants. Grant swung his legs in that direction and found the edge of the bed. He wanted to vomit, purge himself of all the sourness and bite that caused his stomach to spasm, but something about that white light that winked on and off told him he needed to wait with that.

She helped him stand, then helped him into his pants. He pulled them up and straightened and felt briefly dizzy. He closed his eyes until it passed. She held up his shirt.

"I must say," she said as his slipped his arms into the sleeves. "You *do* have a body, darling."

Grant buttoned the shirt. Someone banged on the door and he jumped.

"Hurry," she said. "They're almost here."

"Who?"

She deftly finished buttoning his shirt and tucking it into his pants. He wanted to push her away, but all he could manage was to look aside.

"I'm tucking your socks in your pockets."

He felt her hands push into his front pants pockets. Then she draped his cravat around his neck, worked it into his shirt. She helped him on with his jacket. Another bang on the door.

"Put your boots on outside."

"What—?"

She shoved him to the back of the room, into the bath-room. She turned on the overhead light and he winced. She opened the shower door and stepped in. A moment later another door appeared in the shower wall.

"Come on." She took his arm and guided him past her. "This'll take you about three blocks away, let you out in Calvary. You want to head away from the river, darling, and you'll find Florissant Road."

"Uh—yes. Thanks . . ."

"Anytime, darling. I hope you come by again."

He looked at her then, in the direct light. The thin face seemed gaunt, but that came from the smeared rouge that deepened her cheeks, and the heavy mascara and eye-liner that gave the impression of large eyes. Her front teeth over-lapped slightly.

"Go on," she said.

She handed him a pair of boots and shoved him through the door into a narrow stair. He stumbled on the first step, but grabbed the rails and eased his way down.

Above, the door closed.

It took a few minutes to adjust to the dark. Ahead, dim orange lights showed him a passageway. He drew a lungful of air, smelled moist earth, and stepped forward.

As he moved, his head seemed to clear a little. His feet were cold and he remembered his boots. He dropped them and fished his socks from his pants pockets. Leaning against the wall, he managed to pull them on. He slipped to the floor and rolled up his pants legs.

"This is not the best place to get dressed."

He looked up, startled, and saw a man bracing himself with both hands against the walls of the tunnel. His shirt was open and his jacket was dangling from one hand. His face seemed eyeless in the inadequate light, but he was smiling.

Grant finished pulling his socks up, then put on his boots. He rolled his pants back down and tried to get up.

"One feat of prowess a night is enough," the stranger said, and hooked him under the arm. He heaved, and Grant managed to stand.

"Thank you."

"Walk, please, before they figure out our escape route."

Grant nodded and continued down the tunnel.

"You must be the one who got Chloe. I'm perfectly jealous, you know. Chloe's a dear."

"Who?"

"Oh, my, I hope you remember more than that. I pity you if you've forgotten Chloe already."

Grant shook his head. The tunnel stretched on.

"But I got on all right with Sarah. Room next to Chloe's. I'm surprised we're the only ones in the tunnel. Must've been a slow night."

"This is the only tunnel?" Grant asked, not knowing exactly why.

"No, no, there are three others. Most Speaks only have one escape route, but Messalina's is one of the best in town. Oldest, too, from the days of the riots, you know." He laughed. "Back then they lopped parts off for this sort of thing instead of just the stocks. So I take it this is your first visit?"

Grant nodded. Acid burned his throat again.

"Ah. Well, lucky Jonathan. First time and tap Chloe. I had to work my way up."

"How far?"

"That's rather a personal question."

"How far up the tunnel!"

"Oh. Not much, now."

Suddenly, the tunnel ended at a steep stair. Grant rested and looked up into blackness. His companion tapped his shoulder and indicated that he should go on up. Hesitantly, Grant mounted the stairs.

He came up against stone. For an instant he began to panic. Then the stranger reached up and pressed a button. The stone lifted.

Greenish biolumens glowed in the corners of the chamber. Grant climbed over the lip of a rectangular shape and stood. As his eyes adjusted, he realized he was inside a crypt.

"Don't throw up in here," his companion said, emerging from below. "Bad luck, puking on the dead." He touched a spot on the lip and the lid of the sarcophagus lowered back in place. He pointed. "That way."

Grant staggered to the wall indicated and found the door. He managed the latch and fell out into the brisk night air. He smelled grass and loam. He took a few quick steps, fell, and heaved. There was little in his stomach, but he continued until, exhausted, his muscles gave up. He rolled onto his back.

The night sky was clear. For a while he searched and found constellations.

"We shouldn't stay," his companion said. He sat against the crypt, a brighter shadow against a darker.

"Right," Grant said and managed to stand.

Behind the crypt the horizon glowed blue and yellow. He heard the faint hiss of traffic. The cemetery spread out around them, stones delicately outlined by the spilled city light.

"West," he said.

"Correct." The stranger stood and tilted his head back. Grant heard liquid against glass, swallowing. "Care for some?"

"No, thank you."

"West, then." He pointed in the opposite direction from the horizon-glow.

They started through the tombstones. Grant stumbled once, but caught himself. He looked around and saw his companion, several feet to the right, a vague outline against the star-filled sky. They did not talk. Only the sounds of their boots sinking in soft dirt mingled with their breathing, the rustle of fabric.

Grant checked his pockets, then. His clippers were gone, as was his palm stunner. He still had his wallet. He fished in all its pockets, but his CID was missing. Anxiously, he rifled through all his pockets again, but the card was gone. He wondered for a moment if Chloe had taken it, but it did not really matter. If he got picked up without it he would spend a night in jail and have to answer a number of unpleasant questions. Whoever had engineered this might also have arranged for worse consequences. He returned his wallet and continued on, glancing uneasily at his nameless companion.

Abruptly, the man stopped. Grant halted automatically.

To the north he saw a patch of yellow brightness. As he listened, he made out voices. One voice, followed by a chorus. Chanting?

His companion chuckled softly. "What a night," he said. "Come on."

Crouching, Grant followed him toward the light. As they drew nearer they slowed, then began moving from tombstone to tombstone, staying under cover. Finally, Grant was crawling forward until the other man stopped. Grant came up beside him.

All the while the voices grew louder, clearer. The light changed from an indistinct glow to torches at the heads of staves, held by a circle of people in robes.

The stranger, grinning—Grant saw his features clearly now; mustache, pointed sideburns, arched eyebrows, and a straight nose—moved closer, behind a large stone. He beckoned Grant.

From the cover of the monument, Grant looked into the circle the group formed. One of them strode around a gallows in the center, shouting.

"—purge our cities of their presence, eradicate the bureaus and the vermin that infect them! This land is *ours,* this soil is *ours,* our ancestors *took* it, *worked* it, *built* on it, *made* it *America,* and we have labored in the service of Babylon since we gave up the vision of the frontier! I say *no* more, *no* longer, *no* deeper! Our fathers and grandfathers drove the unwelcome from these lands, called on those we paid to reclaim the birthright of those who truly belong here! They took the land back for us! They re-made the country! We set them to pass laws to protect our children from all that might take away what our forefathers fought for! But it wasn't enough! They let the beast live! They did not kill Baal and Beelzebub and Moloch and Magog! They stopped short of ridding the land of the disease that nearly destroyed us in the last century! *They did not finish the job!*"

"What—?" Grant began.

"Shh!" his companion snapped.

"Who do you say should manage your lives?" the group leader asked.

The circle responded: *"Us!"*

"Who should tell your children what kind of lives they'll lead?"

"Us!"

"Who must set policy for you and your neighbors?"

"Us!"

"What do you say to those who would deny you that power?"

"Burn!"

"Did you say 'burn'?"

"Burn!"

"With fire?"

"Burn!"

"Like witches and demons?"

"Burn!"

"How do we purge ourselves of scourge?"

"Burn!"

"Burn?"

"Burn!"

"Burn!"

"BURN!"

The man in the center waved, and two others came into the circle, carrying a body between them.

Grant started forward. His companion grabbed his arm.

"Wait. It's not real."

Grant watched as they mounted the gallows and tied a rope around the body. Then he saw the featureless face, the boneless way it hung.

They hoisted it. The dummy turned lazily. Across its back hung a sign—FEDERAL.

The three men joined the circle then. Suddenly, the torches arced through the air and landed on the gallows. Quickly, the wooden construction caught fire and went up.

"What a night," the stranger said. "Messalina's, a raid, and now this."

"This is illegal," Grant said.

"Hah! So is what we were doing back at Messalina's, my dear sir. Doesn't stop people from indulging their vices."

"You consider this just a vice?"

The man seemed to think about it for a moment, then nodded, grinning. "The vice of self-confident irrationality." He lifted his bottle and drank it empty. He dropped it on the ground and began crawling away from the stone and the circle and the burning effigy.

TWELVE

Cozy stared at the HD without recognizing the images. Some nonsense about the former Czech Republic. Nothing real, he decided, but the pictures held his attention. He scrunched down in the plastic chair of the waiting room, head propped on his fist, ankles crossed, and worked the morning through his mind again.

George made them go to the mission first. Cozy told him it was a waste of time, but George insisted. After the doctors at the mission said they could do nothing, they were not equipped to handle anaphylactic shock—the law, they said, apologetic, all cases of misadministered pharmaceuticals had to go to a fully certified clinic—Cozy had yelled at George.

Another drive, Harry shivering, dropping deeper into shock, all the way to Regional North. Cozy had told him to go there first, told him the mission would be unable to help, told him again and again until George nearly punched him.

George sat at the opposite end of the row of seats, staring

through the glass partition at the admissions desk, hands folded in his lap.

Now it was one-fifteen. Harry had been in there with the doctors for over an hour. Cozy tried to fix his attention on what the HD was saying, but his thoughts kept shifting to Harry.

And Comber Blue telling them that someone had asked for him. He glanced at George. George had suggested shadows, Voley told him to stay hidden. Who was looking for Cozy? Beth was dead—she was the only one outside family and the commune who knew.

He had used a reactivated CID. Maybe that alerted the shadows, whoever they were. He remembered the woman at Voley's with the pricey security.

George was worried. He had been reluctant to bring Harry here, had winced when Cozy had handed over Harry's CID. This was exactly the sort of situation in which they were likely to fail, where the debit monitors might have a chance to notice that it had a virus that kept trying to erase a particular account. Cozy wished he could have found Harry's legitimate CID, but Harry had discarded it, afraid of being traced.

He jumped when someone tapped his shoulder. George stood beside him.

"Problem," he said, and jerked his thumb toward the admissions desk.

A couple of people gathered around the terminal, all looking puzzled, frowning. One looked in Cozy's direction. Cozy felt a chill in his chest.

"What?"

"Reactivated CID. They figured it out. Told you we shouldn't have come here."

"So we had what choice? Let Harry die?"

"We need to leave," George said.

"Have to wait till we hear."

A third man had joined the group at the counter, staring at something with the others.

"You can wait if you want..." George started. Then: "Shit."

The third man was holding a CID, frowning. He glanced into the waiting room, said something to the other two, and went back into the office area behind the desk. One of the others picked up a handset.

George walked away, toward the door that led to the restroom. Cozy uncrossed his legs and sat forward. He wanted to wait for word about Harry. This was family, even though Harry had left years ago and only showed up now because he needed a place to hide. But where else could you hide, other than with your family?

He glimpsed the dark-grey uniforms of hospital security. Cozy followed George. Harry at least was a citizen, with legitimate ID. His name and profile were in the system, they would find that out soon enough. He would live or die by secure class rules. With a sharp pang, Cozy closed off his conscience and ran. Behind him he heard shouts, footsteps. He did not look back.

His long legs outdistanced the security guards. He saw no sign of George. Fine, George could look after George. No doubt he would head south, back to Voley. Cozy had other options.

He rounded a corner, almost collided with a gurney. He saw stunned faces whip by on his run down the corridor. Distantly, he heard more shouting. He took another corner and slowed down, looking into the rooms he passed. He found an empty one with a window and ducked in, closing the door behind him.

The window slid open sideways. He punched out the screen and crawled through. He let himself hang, then dropped the six or seven feet to the ground.

He ran for the parking lot. Never mind looking for the car, he decided, just go. He pumped his long legs, finding a rhythm halfway across the lot. At the other side, grass sloped down to the street. He jumped over the low wall lining the sidewalk.

He saw no police cars anywhere. He ran to the next street, crossed diagonally, and jogged into the residential area. He fished the other adulterated CIDs from his pocket and tossed them down a storm drain. Shifting to a mix of jogging and brisk walking, he worked his way west and south. After about two miles he began to relax.

The neighborhood did not look familiar. Century-old homes side by side with more recent ones, a lot of neowright, dating back to the time of the Reform. Walls surrounded small clusters of houses—enclaves against threats real and imagined. Cozy thought of the old joke, "just 'cause you're paranoid doesn't mean they aren't out to get you." Gypsies did not find it funny. He kept up a brisk pace and did not return any looks from the locals.

He came out on Jennings Station Road and suddenly knew where he was. He slowed a little, trying to behave normally, as if he belonged. A couple miles southwest and he reached West Florissant. He blew out a relieved breath and headed southeast, toward the barco. He could connect with George there, or maybe at Sereta's.

A bright flash of silver overhead caught his eye. He looked up and it was gone. The airport was nearby. Cozy had always wanted to fly. He remembered slipping into Lambert National Airport once, standing by the tall, arched windows, and watching for hours while the big Lockheeds, Hercules semi-ballistics, and MDB-898s took off and landed. He planned to stow away once on one of the orbital shuttles and run away to Island One or Oneil.

Somewhere outside North America, but not to the usual dumping grounds for deporteds.

He was approaching Goodfellow. Cars drifted by, a few plain models, current utility designs, most some reconstruct of a twentieth century car. A cherry red Cadillac—he did not know the year—rolled by, convertible top rolled back. Two women, smiling, hair pulled out by the breeze. He thought of Beth and looked away.

A police cruiser stopped in the intersection. Cozy turned and headed back. Another cruiser approached from the north. He sprinted into the nearest sidestreet.

The street was short and ended in a cul-de-sac. A cruiser blocked the entrance.

Cozy took off for the end house, thinking he could jump the fence, cut through the backyard. But the front door of the house swung open and a man with a rifle stepped out.

Cozy cut left.

As his new runners came down on the sidewalk pavement, his entire body spasmed. Every muscle seized, pulled in every direction. His legs locked and momentum slammed him down onto the concrete of a driveway. Black and white points danced across his vision. His head ached, but not as badly as the rest of his body.

Police came running up. One leaned over him, pulled an injector from his belt, and touched it to Cozy's neck. Cozy wanted to say "no, don't kill me," but the coolness spread through his body, relaxed his muscles, and he fell immediately asleep.

His eyes opened and closed involuntarily, sometimes one or the other, then both. He had been stunned once before, years ago, and remembered the humiliation. He wondered if he had soiled himself, as he had then.

A restraining jacket held his arms wrapped around his torso. He could not feel his feet, but knew they had bound his ankles, too. From the vibrations he also knew he was riding a hover. That meant downtown, main headquarters. That meant as well a small cell and hours of questions and more humiliation.

The injection wore off by the time they landed. Cozy's eyes worked, though he pretended sleep. The hover's whine grew louder and for a few seconds he felt rocked as if by waves in the ocean, then a loud thud and stillness. Police moved around, securing things, and the rear hatch opened with a sinuous pneumatic hiss.

"Come on," one said, shaking the ring attached to the front of the restrainer. "You're here. Welcome to your new home."

She pulled him to his feet. Cozy nearly pitched forward, but she directed the momentum and sent him staggering toward the open hatch. The ankle chain gave him less than two feet of travel so his stride was short and jerky and he almost fell on the ramp. Two police caught his arms and guided him.

Cozy looked around and up. A square of sky grew smaller. They had landed on a roof elevator, now descending . . . where? He looked at the pair of cops and recognized the black semi-military field uniforms. Federal. Their helmet faceplates covered their features. In their dark polarizing surfaces, all he saw was his own reflection, pulled out of true and curved.

"Shit . . ." he breathed.

One of them laughed shortly.

The elevator stopped at a wide entry. The heavy doors slid up and Cozy entered a processing center. More federals—nearly the whole field contingent, he guessed, five uniforms, plus the two escorting him, the one in the hover—and a man behind the desk asking name and CID.

"Cozy," he said. "No ID."

The man looked at him and Cozy saw him recategorize, mentally place Cozy in the slot for "his kind" and nod. He entered the information on his terminal.

"Charge?"

"Credit fraud," one of the escorting federals said. "Regional Hospital North, call four."

The attendant nodded again. His face showed nothing now, it was all routine.

"File transferred. Holding cell nine. Agent-in-charge will see him there."

His escorts took him down the wide corridor. Thirty feet in it branched right and left into narrower passageways. They took him left, along a row of doors with numbers. At the one stenciled "9" the escort on his right entered a code in the pad on the door. It opened and they brought him inside.

The cell was small but not as bad as city jail. The sheets on the cot were clean, as were the sink and toilet. Opposite the cot was a fold-down seat. The cell had its own light switch.

"Sit."

Cozy sat on the cot. One of them took out his stunner

and placed it on Cozy's temple while the other unlocked and removed the ankle restraint and the jacket.

Then he was alone. The door closed and he heard their footsteps retreating. Then only the hum of the ventilator.

At the head of the cot, built into the wall and protected by a transparent sheet Cozy knew was steel hard, was a recorder. For his convenience, if, at any time of the day or night, he wanted to confess. Along the bottom of the cover sheet was a touch-sensitive strip that operated the machine.

"For my last will and testament," he said. "I bequeath all my nothing to nobody, being of sound mind and body and without the least property."

He stretched out. Voley had asked him if he wanted to be deported. No, sir, he had said, but look at me now, Mr. Voley, I'm in the first stages.

He felt exhausted—being stunned released a huge surge of adrenalin and endorphins, which, unused, just kept him in a state of continual readiness even though he could not move, until they depleted themselves and left him depressed and tired—but he could not sleep. That and his concern for Harry and George, plus whatever sedative they had given him, pulled him in several directions at once.

Credit fraud. Those damn reactivated CIDs. If Beth had only stayed alive long enough to make her case, maybe instead of this he would be in a new city with real citizenship, his own legal CID, and a future. She had promised him that. Beth was dead, though, and he could not figure how. She had been operating alone, except for him—on Realtime, as the gypsies would say—and he had told no one. Not even Voley knew about his relation with Beth McQuarry. If he *had* known, Cozy would be dead now himself, he was certain.

The door opened. Cozy sat up.

He recognized the man.

"I'm Agent Kitcher. Have you been read your rights?"

"No, sir."

"Do you need them read?"

Cozy grunted. "I've got no rights."

"Oh, that's not true. You have rights. Whatever rights we choose to give you. Call them potential rights. Based on your willingness to cooperate."

Cozy looked at the wall.

Kitcher sat on the far end of the cot. "You used an illegal Citizen's IDentification card at Regional Hospital North. I'd like to know about that—Cozy?—yes, I'd like you to tell me about that."

Cozy shrugged. "Nothing to tell. It belonged to a friend."

"The one in the hospital? The one who just died?"

Cozy started, turned to face the agent. "What—?"

"Yes, he passed away about fifteen minutes ago. They did their best, but . . ."

"The hell they did!"

Agent Kitcher gave him a puzzled look. "Of course they did. Why would you say they didn't?"

"Invalid CID. They probably dumped him straight in the morgue once they knew."

"Quite the contrary, Cozy. He was infected with something they were unfamiliar with. By law, they had to do whatever was necessary to save his life and identify the pathogen."

Cozy snorted derisively. His hands shook, so he drew his legs up and locked his arms around them.

"You can be sceptical if you want, and you might be partly right. Identifying the pathogen *is* more important than saving a gypsy's life. But we can't have epidemics running loose, Cozy, and someone who's alive can tell us where he's been, who he's been with, so we establish vectors. That's the law. But I'm not so much interested in him as in the CID you used to admit him."

"Nothing to say."

"You got it somewhere. Give me a name, Cozy."

"Harry Lusk."

"Is there more?"

"I don't know, he never said."

"Where can we find Harry?"

Cozy sneered. "He just died."

Kitcher frowned. "Cozy, you're right about one thing: you have nothing. Let me tell you how this will go. There are a couple of scenarios. The first is the most pleasant, of course. It goes like this: You cooperate fully in this matter, give us the names of all the people you know who are involved in this, and we round them up, try them, convict them, and in compensation for your help we review your status as a citizen. There could be schooling, training in a field of your choice, and, assuming you manage to prove yourself competent, eventually citizenship. A real CID instead of a fake. Legal status instead of no status at all."

Cozy laughed nervously. "And the more likely one?"

"Well, presuming you say nothing—"

"Or know nothing."

Kitcher shrugged. "Same difference. In that case, we hold you here until we determine that you are of no use whatsoever. No family, no friends—that is, none with any legal standing—no possibility that you can help us in this case. We then transfer you to the Federal Transit Authority at Guantanamo. There you will be processed for deportation. Your ultimate destination is a matter of several factors:

genotype, skills, and accessibility of certain markets. You could go to Brazil or Ecuador or Antarctica. Or you could go to Africa."

Cozy shuddered. "Africa's quarantined."

Kitcher nodded. "Not totally. There are ways in through Mozambique, Cairo, Tangiers. Personally, I would prefer that to one of the Islamic Nationalist states. As an infidel there, you would have less value than you do here. And believe me, here you have almost no value. What little you have resides in your willingness to cooperate."

The agent stood. "Personally, I'd prefer that you didn't, but I have a job to do. Personally, I'd just as soon use you for the piece of shit you are and bury you in a field somewhere. At least you'd make good fertilizer. So if you really have nothing to say, that will be fine. We have the card, we know what to look for, we can just scour the barco and find the rest. Then I can have the pleasure of tossing your worthless shell out of the country." He smiled. "Think about it."

Kitcher went to the cell door, then paused. He raised a finger and stabbed it toward Cozy. "You know what really disturbs me is that you look familiar, Cozy. And that bothers me. When gypsies start looking familiar that means they aren't staying in their proper place."

He touched the door and it opened for him.

"Think about it," he said again, then walked away. The door closed.

Slowly, Cozy stretched out on the cot again.

No options. Maybe he could have some say at Guantanamo where he got sent. Maybe. In reality, he could think of no reason why they might give him more consideration there than he got here.

Africa. He had heard rumors—everybody did, they cost nothing, even when true—that deporteds went there. The

OAS complained in the U.N. about them all going south; Brazil had been censured for trafficking in deporteds like slaves. Russia refused to take any more, but rumor said a lot of them still went to the steppes. But Africa . . . rumor said that was a death sentence. Too many viruses, too much strain on world resources. Officially, the quarantine ended, a bad idea that accomplished nothing but added to the burden of guilt already permeating the developed world. But relations had never been normalized, trade went through only a few, tightly controlled ports, no one came out.

So rumor said. Cozy did not pretend to understand it all. He tended to dismiss the rumors—North America was a closed continent, how would anyone here know what the rest of the world did or thought or felt?—but he knew, intuitively, that some of them were based on fact. American troops and equipment and funding fed the United Nations Enforcement Arm. Those people went out and came back. Ex-soldiers saw, heard, felt, tasted the world. Rumors, even true ones, came through the borders. The difficulty was sorting them. What to believe, what to ignore. The world was a complicated place, the more ominous because no one really *knew* anymore.

No more complicated than here, Cozy thought, staring at the off-white ceiling. Might even be better someplace else.

Maybe, he thought, just maybe. But this is home.

THIRTEEN

Grant straightened himself up as best he could in a dingy service station restroom. He resisted the temptation to use the shower in the corner. He washed his face in the sink and brushed his hair with his fingers. His eyes stared back from the mirror, milky red around the pale blue irises.

His boots and pant cuffs were muddy, as were the knees, and his jacket was badly wrinkled, with dirt on the elbows and around the hem. He looked like he had spent the night in a Speak. Apparently he had, but he remembered none of it. He shuddered and splashed more water on his face. His stomach kept up a mild unease, just enough that he felt constantly out-of-sorts. He retucked his shirt—rouge smeared the left side, just over his chest—and tried to arrange his cravat so that it looked fresh, but the wrinkles made it look like a used handkerchief.

He opened his watch—two-twelve in the morning—and replaced it in his vest pocket. He was amazed no one had stolen it.

The harsh white light made him look even paler. He leaned on the sink and tried to piece together everything, but there was nothing to piece together. He had been sprayed with some kind of fast sedative and he woke up with . . . Chloe . . . then the raid.

He needed regular sleep. He left the restroom and came out into the shop area of the station. The place was automated, but without his CID he could not use it. His companion drew a cup of hot water from the dispenser, then took a candybar off the shelf. He dropped the wrapper into the steaming water. It dissolved and made coffee. Bitter, acidic coffee, but coffee. He handed them to Grant, who chewed the candybar and waited for the drink to cool.

The station was quite a distance south from where they had come out of the cemetery. The glow of the rally fire was invisible from here.

"Cab in five," his companion said.

In the brighter light of the station, the stranger looked in slightly better shape than Grant. His suit was darker and the dirt from crawling through the cemetery did not show as clearly. He smiled cheerfully as he made himself a cup of coffee, as if he found this a wonderful adventure.

"What a night," he said.

"Mmm."

"By the way, my name's Dick." He extended a hand.

Grant shook it briefly. "Grant."

Dick laughed. "U.S. Grant! Like Vicksburg, eh?"

"What?"

Dick waved a hand. "Never mind. Obscure humor. A pleasure to campaign with you, though, General." He blew across his coffee. "I wonder what caused that?"

"The rally?"

"No, no. The raid. Messalina's hasn't been raided in

months. Usually only happens when someone's spouse complains loudly enough, or City Hall is trying to find a Damocletion instrument on someone."

"You sound like a regular."

"Well, it *is* the best in town, but there are a couple others with certain ladies that I quite enjoy. In fact, when I found out Chloe was occupied for the evening I nearly left." He leaned forward and stared hard at Grant. "You know, you're quite pale. I never get bashed before I'm banged—the odds are good you won't remember the best night of your life."

Grant finished the candybar. His stomach began to settle. "I'll keep that in mind."

Dick grinned. "Learn from your mistakes. Otherwise, what good are they? You might as well live perfectly. Ah. Our ride."

A cab pulled up in the station drive, right in front of the door. Dick swallowed a couple of fast mouthfuls of coffee, wincing, then dropped the cup in the disposal. Grant drank all of his.

They stepped from the door and Dick punched the retrieve button on the teller. It extruded his CID. Grant followed Dick into the back of the cab. The driver was slumped against the door, sleeping. The navigator was on automatic.

Dick started to tap in his destination, then looked at Grant.

"You should go first."

Grant shook his head. "Go on. I don't mind a longer ride."

"You have no CID, sir."

"Oh. All right."

Grant punched in his destination. Dick smiled and

tapped in his. The cab tallied the fare and returned the card. The cab pulled away.

Grant managed to doze until the cab stopped. He looked out the window at his house.

"You live here?" Dick asked.

Grant nodded and reached for the door. "Thank you. I appreciate your help."

"Yes, well, keep my advice in mind. Next time—"

"I'll remember. Sobriety."

Dick laughed quietly. Grant stepped out and the door closed. The cab waited a few seconds, then pulled away. As far as Grant knew, the driver had never woken up.

Reva waited on the front steps.

"Good evening," she said. "You never came back from your meeting. I started wondering if maybe you'd skipped on me again."

"No . . . it's . . . could you let me in?"

"Too bashed to work your lock?"

"No . . . yes . . . I lost my CID."

Reva stared for a moment, then went to his door. She inserted her card and tapped in an override command. The door clicked open.

He stepped past her and leaned against the wall inside for several moments. He ached. His sinuses still felt hollow with the smell of blood. When he felt steady enough, he climbed the stairs to the bedroom.

The suit needed cleaning. Wallet, watch, cravat all went on the dresser. He took off his jacket and checked it over and found the lining of the left sleeve torn. He spread it out on the bed and felt carefully for any irregularities. Nothing. They had not clippered him.

He shrugged off his vest, then the shirt, which he tossed

aside. He sat on the edge of the bed and pulled off his boots, his hand coming away with drying mud. Standing, he pushed his pants down and examined them for clippers. Still nothing.

Grant went into the bathroom and flipped on the light. He turned on the shower, then stepped to the bowl to urinate. Dried matter like dead skin that flaked off at his touch clotted his pubic hair and the base of his penis. He closed his eyes and let the shame and rage wrestle for dominance. With immense relief and pleasure he showered, letting himself fall back against the wall where the water struck his stomach and flowed down.

Finally, he shut off the stream and grabbed a towel. As he returned to the bedroom he heard a soft knock. He considered ignoring it—he needed sleep, needed to dream away the night—but he made himself put on a robe and answer it.

He opened the door. Reva looked at him, eyes wide with surprise and relief.

"Grant—?"

He made himself smile and come out. He walked to the head of the stairs.

"May I offer you something? A drink? Coffee?" He headed for the kitchen. "Coffee sounds good. Double strong."

"Congressman Tochsin said you left his office at about one-fifteen."

"Did he? Good of him to remember."

"Are you all right?"

He reached the coffeemaker and punched in the program. He turned and leaned back against the counter by the sink. Reva stood in the doorway, watching him.

"You look intensely concerned," he said.

"I am. Where did you go?"

He shook his head. "I have no idea. Someplace called . . . Messalina's, I think . . . a Speak."

She looked startled. "I would never have thought you the sort. Not exactly by-the-rule."

"I'm not the sort. I don't." The coffeemaker gurgled. "I was . . ." He felt himself frown deeply, almost a reflex. He blinked and rubbed his face. "I was . . ."

Reva came toward him, slowly. "It wasn't your idea?"

He shook his head. He felt the frown again, again rubbed his face. His hands came away wet. He stared at them. They balled into fists and he looked up, closed his eyes against the light.

Then he was on the floor, Reva holding him from behind, arms squeezing. She whispered in his ear, "It's all right, all right, Grant, it's all right," even though by the sound of her voice, tight and controlled, she knew it was anything but all right.

In the morning he lay awake, staring at the window across the room until Reva came in with a tray. She set it on the nightstand and poured coffee from the porcelain pot.

"Take anything in it?" she asked.

He shook his head.

"Sit up. Drink, eat."

He let her tuck pillows behind him. She set a plate on his lap. Bagel, butter, honey. Mechanically, he bit into it.

"Can you remember anything more than what you told me last night?" she asked.

What had he said last night? He thought about it, recalled bits and pieces of broken conversation, very little of it coherent. He had told her about being gassed in the federal building and waking up in a Speak, the escape through Calvary Cemetery, the rally, the cab ride home—

"No. The meeting with Tochsin, maybe." He sipped coffee. There was a mixture of chicory and cinnamon in it.

"Congressman Tochsin said very little about your meeting," Reva told him. "Says he offered you the services of his office and that you then left. He says he has no idea what became of you afterward."

"Lie."

"Of course, a lie. But why? And why the gas? By the way, that sounds like CSC—Crowd Suppression Compound. It's a riot control substance the military uses."

Grant nodded. "Whoever did it was certainly good. I heard nothing, felt nothing. He came up behind me without a hint. Could be military."

"And that's another why. We need to get into that room and find out what's in it."

"Agreed."

"And why dump you in a Speak? They could have thrown you in the river."

"Two federal agents murdered in less than a week? I don't think D.C. would have a bit of trouble overriding any local resistance whatsoever. Marshals would be in here turning everything over. A Speak is a good way to discredit me."

"*If* you'd been caught in the raid," Reva noted.

"I woke up too soon, I think. I don't think the—my hostess—knew anything about that part." He looked up at her. "If I'd been found without my CID it would have automatically initiated an official inquiry into my conduct."

"You'd be believed."

"By Cutter, yes. Some of my colleagues. But locally?"

"Might have made it difficult to function."

"Hm. Impossible." He sighed. "Military applications. We should check into that. Find out if Congressman Tochsin is involved in any Defense Department arrangements. And I think it would be useful to find background on his aide. 'Tess,' he called her."

Reva nodded. "There's another problem."

"Surprise me."

She smiled at that. "I try. I went through your hard copies. You left them lying out. My jacket's woefully inadequate."

"That's a problem?"

"Nothing I can't fix. But no. The problem is Harold Lusk."

Grant closed his eyes. "What about it?"

"Why do you have it? I mean, what reason would this investigation present for you to request Lusk's jacket?"

"His name was on Beth's case file."

"I didn't think she had one."

"She did. Handwritten. What do you know about Harold Lusk?"

"He's an embarrassment."

"For who?"

"D.C. in general, Treasury in particular. He's a code writer."

"I know that."

She fidgeted, frowning. "This changes the whole thing."

"Why?"

"If Lusk is involved, then we have to consider that Abernathy isn't."

"I don't think I follow."

"*We* have an open file on Lusk." She shook her head, as if denying an accusation, a private dialogue. Grant wondered which side won. "What do you know about the Tamaulipas case?"

Grant shrugged. "Only what everyone does. A slave ring. Do you think this is related?"

"I don't know. I need to verify a few things. The point is,

though, that with Lusk's name attached to this, the reason your friend was killed becomes more complex."

"How?"

"His name turned up in connection with a group of neolibertarians in Tamaulipas. This group was involved in a political kidnapping, which brought us in. They were doing other things. Opportunistic sedition, grabbing any chance that came along to cause damage. When we raided them they managed to destroy most of their data, but we salvaged a few items."

"And Harold Lusk's name was one of them?"

"Just a name and a number in D.C. We traced it to an apartment Lusk used to live in. With nothing else to go on we couldn't very well get a warrant to investigate him. Departmental privilege. But we opened a file and kept an eye on him."

"Did you inform Director Cutter?"

"I assumed she was told. That wasn't my call."

"She didn't even want to tell me about him. I didn't know anything about him till I saw the name on Beth's case file."

"I'm sure she wants Lusk recovered. Is it possible Beth McQuarry was really sent here for that?"

"And the barco situation is just a happy coincidence? I don't know. I doubt it. More than likely she stumbled on it. And what about the others?"

"The other names on Beth's file?"

"Tochsin, Abernathy, and Voley."

Reva frowned thoughtfully. "Interesting group . . . what's the connection between them?"

Grant ate more bagel. He watched her stare off, concentration bringing her eyebrows together. Then he glanced down and realized that she wore only a robe. The seam parted just above her left knee, which crossed over her right. Her foot flexed idly, tightening and loosening the calf muscle.

She looked at him, then noticed his attention. "I hope you don't mind my borrowing Beth's robe. I suppose it's hers . . ."

"It is. No, I don't mind."

"It's a little small."

"She was shorter than you."

"Finish your breakfast. We have work to do."

He nodded. He looked away, then, suddenly self-conscious and uncomfortable.

"Grant. Last night—what happened was—"

"It's all right."

"No, it's not. It shouldn't have happened. But—look, it may never be all right, it's not something you can shrug off and forget about. If you need someone to listen—or just need someone who knows you aren't to blame—please, talk to me. I would feel privileged to be someone you trust."

He smiled slightly. "There's that word again."

"Can't get around it. It's a people sort of thing."

"Mmm."

"Just don't damage yourself being brave about it. It's not the kind of pain you can just tough through. It can become malignant and kill you."

"That matters to you?"

"Yes."

Grant did not look up. He wanted very much to deny it all, convince himself that it had not really happened. Foolish, he thought, and completely contrary to who he thought he was.

She touched his arm. He started to draw back, but his hand crossed hers and automatically closed around it. She squeezed back. He nodded.

"Thank you."

"You're welcome." Then she patted his hand and stood. "Another cup of coffee. We have things to do before tonight."

"What's tonight?"

"Tonight we go to the ball."

He showered again. He put on his loafabouts and went down to the office to reread the report on Harold Lusk. For the time being he seemed in control. Reva . . . helped. That surprised him. Finding out who, she said, that was important now. Was this part of what Beth had been investigating or something else?

No, he decided. Part and parcel of Beth's mission. Tochsin's name was on her file, so Grant could presume his involvement. Their conversation more or less confirmed it. Stay away from St. Louis's principle citizens, operate through Tochsin, stick to the barco problem. He was on the Methods and Allocations Committee, so he had some contact with Treasury as a matter of course. It was possible he knew Lusk. Was he protecting him?

According to Lusk's history, he had come from South St. Louis. Grant checked a city map and located the hospital, the house Lusk had lived in, then traced a line to Voley's house. Not too far apart. Lusk's family had been borderline—several members had apparently lost their citizenship during the Reforms and later got caught up in the string of mass deportations following the riots. Lusk might well have been one of those to whom Voley had paid special attention. A tenuous connection at best, but Voley's name was on the list. Was Voley hiding Lusk? It would be easy to lose him in the barco, especially if his family still lived there. Grant thought of Cozy and the striking similarity of appearance to the image of Lusk in the file. So the family was still here. The "barco problem" the Mayor wanted dealt with suddenly lost its simplicity.

Barcos provided people like Tochsin and Mayor Poena with easy targets for their politics. Grant pitied the gypsies— they were powerless and, in his experience, mostly harmless. After the massive deportations finally came to an end several years ago, most communities tolerated them, primarily out of a sense of guilt. Those deported would never return. And those last nationwide deportations had been minor compared to just after the Reforms. Grant rarely talked to those who had been adults at the time. No one was willing to discuss it. A great shame, yet they did it again, and the mechanism remained in place for more. Political rage dictated when and how many, political expedience kept the laws active, a bone to the dogs of social intolerance. Tochsin's career showed a careful nod in their direction, never quite committing himself to neolibertarianism or hardline Reformists. But Grant detected a willingness to use those tools if he thought he would benefit.

Grant had never met anyone completely lacking in conscience. But people compartmentalized, sorted their emotions and reason and prejudices into rigorously separate spaces that mingled only at certain points and never at others. In so doing they could often separate out conscience from certain compartments and never seem to suffer its inconveniences when pursuing the socially æsthetic line.

He poured himself a straight whiskey and sat down with the report on Harold Lusk. Reva had been right. With Lusk involved, a top-level codewriter from Treasury's deepest parts, a simple solution became the least likely.

Tamaulipas. Grant frowned. A request for data had gone to the border police down there. Regarding Lusk?

He went to the desk and tapped Reva's number. The phone rang four times before she answered.

"Cassonare."

"It's Grant."

"Oh." The screen winked on with her image. "My, we're now on personal phone call basis? What next? A date?"

Grant blinked, then felt himself smile. "When we're on our own time, who knows? I have a question."

"Make it a good one, I only have one answer left."

"Beth's fax log showed she'd requested data from the border police in Tapachula. I didn't have a name to go with it, so I've hesitated trying to follow up."

"Hmm. I know some people there. Let me make the inquiry."

"By the way, you were being modest. You were the principle agent in that affair."

She smiled. "I don't like to brag."

"If the FBI are keeping an open file, I'd like to know what's in it."

"I'm not sure I'm comfortable with that."

"You want me to trust you."

"Good point. Let me think about it. What time shall I pick you up tonight?"

"What time is the reception?"

"Eight. Your car is still in the garage."

"Then pick me up at seven-thirty. I'll be here."

"What about our trip to the barco?" she asked.

"Postponed, obviously. I'm glad you didn't go without me."

"Do you think perhaps if the reception is really dull . . . ?"

"Tonight?" Grant considered, then nodded. "Maybe.

Everyone will be there, especially Abernathy. No one would expect us to, certainly."

"Good. Shall I bring you a corsage?"

Grant laughed.

"That's good," Reva said. "I'm glad you can do that."

"I assure you it's only to cover up a deep and profoundly sad character."

"Seven-thirty, Agent Voczek."

"Seven-thirty."

The screen cleared.

The note from Beth's jacket lay on the desk. COZY, CID B.C. Cozy was the connection to Lusk, and Lusk wrote code—the kind of code CIDs required to function in a complex web of electronic currency. Abernathy held free currency views, but to tamper in the system at this level . . . CID adulteration carried a charge of treason.

The phone chimed.

"Agent Voczek."

"Grant, it's Stuart."

Grant tapped for vid. "Do you have something for me?"

"Something, certainly. I told you that Weston and Burnard were under investigation?"

"Yes."

"They've been under investigation, on and off, for the last eight years. I have a list of SED people who have worked on it, only to be transferred off the case."

"Someone's protecting them?"

"That would be my guess."

"Would you care to guess who?"

"No, I wouldn't. But I can tell you who their major shareholders are. Mitchel Abernathy is not one of them. He does business through them, his own personal accounts. No funds from any of his other interests go through them. He uses Weston and Burnard to play."

"But—"

"But we have nine senators and four congressmen on the rolls as very substantial investors. Including Senator Reed and Senator Dirkenfeld."

"What sort of investments?"

"Highly diversified, but . . ."

"But?"

"Well, our investigation into Weston and Burnard dealt with illegal commodity distributions. They buy marginal companies and liquidate them—"

"So you explained before."

"Yes, well, I did some comparisons. They've done this in only ten states. The coincidence is that all those congressional investors are from one or another of those ten states with the exception of Missouri."

"Coincidence?"

"Could be," Stuart replied. "Until I factored in the last query you made and found out that each of those states is also home to a major facility owned by Coronin Industries. Now, Coronin doesn't have any investments in Weston and Burnard. But in each instance that Weston and Burnard have bought out and liquidated a firm, Coronin ended up buying the land and building new facilities on the sites."

"Interesting . . . no connection with Abernathy?"

"One. Coronin has plans to build a plant in St. Louis. By law they have to fund construction with local capital. They've applied to the Clayton Banking Consortium for the loan."

Grant nodded. "Can you send me the list of those states and the legislators involved?"

"Sure. That's no problem. But I have to tell you, someone

is watching over this little company. If Coronin is behind it, then you have a real problem."

"Why is that?"

Stuart looked surprised. "Come on, Grant, don't you pay attention to the newscasts? Coronin is the darling of the pharmaceuticals industry. They've developed and marketed more vaccines and treatments in the last twenty years than any other company. Right now they look like world saviors. I don't think any investigation that turns up negative aspects has a chance of being sanctioned by Congress, the President, or the States."

"Maybe it's just a coincidence, Stuart."

"Maybe. Well, I'm faxing those lists now. If you need anything else . . ."

"Thanks, Stuart. I owe on this one."

The fax buffer switched on as the screen cleared. Grant watched the pages emerge, ideas spinning through his head.

He checked the time. Two-twenty. His report to Cutter was overdue.

He hesitated. Director Cutter had given him less than the whole story about Lusk. No lies, to be sure, yet . . . Grant tapped in the code. This age. He hated it.

FOURTEEN

Aaron Voley's name was absent from Stuart's lists.
So was Congressman Tochsin. And according to Stuart's numbers, Mitchel Abernathy was a marginal player. Of course, his bank stood to benefit from a loan to Coronin, but enough to kill a federal agent over? Grant could not see how. Nothing about this, except the allegation of asset fraud on the part of Weston and Burnard, looked illegal.

And Coronin could build anywhere. Why so much trouble over a barco? That had to be the Mayor's issue, not Coronin's or the investors'.

Grant tapped in Tochsin's name on the terminal. He had evidently been asked to intervene, to keep Grant away from St. Louis's principle citizens. That and whatever was in that room near his offices put him close to the center of Grant's suspicions. Grant made notes.

Reed, Dirkenfeld . . . the others. He added in their names, their states. It would be interesting to see who among them might be Coronin shareholders. He tapped a number in D.C. and requested that list. The system asked if he wanted all of it— the file was extensive. Grant confirmed and let it pour into the bubble memory. He then initiated a search-and-match between the two. A few seconds later he had a partial list. Most of the family names appeared among Coronin's shareholders, but only one senator held stock directly: Dirkenfeld. All the rest boasted relatives as shareholders. Still, family counted.

Theresa Reed, Senator Reed's daughter, owned a large share.

Grant stared at the screen. An interesting set of connections, but again nothing illegal. Not strictly, anyway. Grant studied Stuart's lists again. The last state where Weston and Burnard had bought out a failing company was Ohio. Sheflan Diversified, a large firm that did some light manufacturing, but mainly functioned as a wholesale distributor. Grant checked the public records again. Entertainment goods, mid-level electronics. The original owner, David C. Sheffield, had died several years ago and the company began losing ground. Weston and Burnard had bought them out a year and a half ago, and nine months ago Coronin had acquired the remaining assets and begun building a new facility.

The new owners of Sheflan held shares of Weston and Burnard. Part of the purchase price had included shares of Coronin. There was no inventory of what, exactly, had been purchased.

Grant drew a deep breath. He tapped in Voley's name. So far, the only connection to Voley was his civil rights work with gypsies and borderline citizens. He was a public advocate. Would he have killed Beth for fear that she would sign off on the deportation Mayor Poena wanted? He needed to see Voley before he could begin to judge.

Grant went upstairs and took out his pistol and shoulder rig and laid them on the bed. The weapon was a replica .9mm Browning automatic. He was as pleased with it as he was with his Duesenberg. Like most replicas, it was better than the original in many respects, and the original had been a fine pistol.

He put it away and found his other palm stunner. He was afraid. Yesterday had shocked him, damaged his self-confidence. Though he would feel safer with the Browning, he knew it was only a crutch. The only way to find out if he could get along without a crutch would be to act as if yesterday had not happened. He dropped the stunner in his jacket pocket and called a cab.

Briefly, as he climbed into the Checker, his conscience bothered him. He promised himself to tell Reva everything, then tapped an address on Jefferson Avenue into the navigator. The driver read it on his dash, nodded, and drove.

The cab let him out across the street from a row of stately houses. As Grant stepped from the Checker he looked around at the neighborhood. A free kitchen sprawled over vacant ground on this side of the street; a pair of houses, companions to the block full opposite them, stood sandwiched by broken-down flats with small businesses at street level; old, barely maintained cars mingled with a few newer, contemporary styles; the mix of people ran the spectrum from middle class to gypsy. The three-story houses seemed at once at odds with the neighborhood and so much a part of it that Grant could imagine them nowhere else.

The one he wanted stood at the south end.

At his second knock the door opened. A dark-skinned woman in jeans and a sweatshirt looked at him. "Yes?"

"I'd like to speak to Aaron Voley, please."

"Who may I say is calling on him?"

"Grant Voczek. Special Agent, Treasury, Resource Security Division."

"What business do you have with Mr. Voley?"

"His name has turned up in connection with an ongoing investigation. I would only like to ask him some questions."

"Let me see if he's receiving today."

The door closed. Grant sighed and looked over at the free kitchen. A few faces turned his way, passed comments. What, he wondered, might it be like to live in a place like this all your adult life?

The door opened again. The woman stood to one side.

"He'll see you in the parlor," she said.

"Thank you." Grant stepped into the darkened hallway. He smelled mint and lemon, old wax and cedar. The door closed out the world.

"This way." She gestured to the left.

Aaron Voley waited in a highbacked leather chair near the window. The soft light through the yellow curtains gave his face a gentle glow. Sparse white hair trailed over his scalp. A loose shirt covered his wide torso, leaving his wrinkled neck bare. A tall glass stood on the small table to his left, and a cigar waited in a large cast iron tray on his right.

"Mr. Voley?"

"Agent Voczek. Please, be welcome. Sit. I must say I'm rather surprised at this visit. How may I help you? Camilla, bring Agent Voczek something wet. What would you like, Mr. Voczek? Camilla makes excellent lemonade."

"Um, thank you . . ."

Grant studied the man. Small, bright eyes, tolerant smile, a faint scar just below his left eye, perhaps fifty pounds overweight. He did not look his seventy-eight years.

"You have a fine house, Mr. Voley."

"Thank you. I've lived here most of my life; of course, it has been modified. I rebuilt it twice, updated the security systems four times, the environmental systems five. Two wives, eight children, all dead now. Sometimes I wonder if I've lived too long, but I always find a reason for sticking around. Maybe it's the house. What would it do without me?"

Camilla returned and placed a glass of lemonade on the table beside Grant.

"Do you need me to listen, Aaron?" she asked.

"No, I don't think so. Thank you."

Grant watched Camilla leave.

"Camilla tells me that my name has come up in connection with some investigation," Voley said.

"That's correct, sir."

"Would it have anything to do with that young Treasury agent who was murdered?"

"Yes, it would."

"Hm. Interesting. I never met her. I almost never leave the house anymore."

"You aren't going to the reception for Senator Reed, then?"

Voley sneered. "That bigot? No, young man, I am not. Is he on your list, too?"

"No, sir."

"It's a pity your colleague died. I'm sorry."

"Thank you, sir."

"I had nothing to do with it."

"Do you know Harold Lusk, Mr. Voley?"

Grant noticed the slightest twitch of the man's eyes, a momentary downward flicker that Voley changed to a deliberate squint. He rubbed his eyes and reached for his drink.

"Who?"

"Harold Lusk."

"I'm afraid not."

"He was born here."

Voley raised his eyebrows. "Young man, many people are born here."

"I mean in this neighborhood. Just a few blocks over. He went to primary and secondary at the Soulard Polytech, then attended Washington University."

"One that got out, then. Good. Why should I know him?"

"You have a history as a community activist. You've been involved in this neighborhood since you were twenty-eight. You opened the first free kitchen after the riots, helped establish the mission clinics. It surprises me that one of the local success stories would escape your attention."

The squint hardened. "If you think this Harold Lusk was the only success to come out of this district you know less than you should. Soulard Polytech graduated some of the finest engineers in Missouri history for a time."

"Do you have any dealings with Mitchel Abernathy?"

Voley shrugged. "I know him. I've occasionally gotten funds out of him for neighborhood projects. Otherwise, we're quite opposite. There's not an altruistic bone in the man's body, nor a single generous instinct."

"What about Michael Tochsin?"

"Congressman Tochsin? He represents this district—of course I know him."

"Does he do a good job?" Grant asked.

"As good as any other. He's not the worst, by far. I did some campaign work for him when he first ran."

"And since?"

"If it involves my work here, we talk. Otherwise . . ."

Voley cocked his head to one side. "Interesting string of associations for a murder. Abernathy, Tochsin, me."

"And Lusk."

"And him. Does all this relate?"

"I'm trying to find out."

Voley shook his head. "I wish you luck."

"Mr. Voley, if anything you've said is false I can take certain actions you might find unpleasant."

"Seize my accounts? Freeze my credit? That's about all you could do."

"That doesn't concern you?"

"Of course it does. I'm not young, I have needs. Too great an inconvenience and I might not recover. Have you ever killed anyone, Mr. Voczek?"

"No, sir."

"Would you, if you thought you must?"

"I don't know."

Voley played with his glass, gazing down at it thoughtfully for a long time. When he looked at Grant again it was with an appraising intensity.

"Would you always have answered that way, Mr. Voczek?"

Grant did not look away. He waited for Voley. The question hung in his mind, unanswered, perhaps unanswerable. It would require a lot of thought and he did not want the distraction now. Finally, Voley's lips curved briefly into a smile, and he took a drink from his glass.

Grant let his breath out slowly. "Mr. Voley—"

"How long have you been in St. Louis?"

"Four days."

"Ever been here before?"

Grant shook his head.

"How do you find it?"

"Layered."

Voley grinned and nodded. "It is that. Old city. Almost three hundred years old, did you know that? I'd like to live to see its tricentennial. I don't think I will, but one never knows. Like all old cities, it has its own secrets, habits, vices. It served as a capital until Missouri became a state. I sometimes think it never recovered from the loss of status. It contrives to impress itself in compensation." He shifted in his chair and folded his hands over his stomach. "People come and scratch at the surface and see things that look like plots and motives, as if an entire community can actually have a single consciousness. They hear names, connect them to others, and assume they've discovered something important, like a conspiracy. They follow trails from north to south and believe they can make sense out of the city. All they've really found are the layers, one atop the other, extending back, like the rings in a tree. They don't mean anything other than as signs that the city has grown."

"Do you mean to suggest that there is *no* connection between any of the people I've named?" Grant asked.

"No, not at all. There are connections. Just not the ones you presume."

"You have connections with the barter commune."

Voley nodded. "I'm an advocate for them."

"You've devoted a lot of time and credit to them."

"That's an understatement. I've devoted most of my professional life to speaking out about the barcos."

"Why? You had a promising career in law, you're wealthy, you could do anything you want."

Voley shrugged. "A hobby that became a passion. Actually, there's more than a little self-interest involved."

"I don't see it."

"A good choice of words, Mr. Voczek. No, you don't.

Nobody in the secured classes does. If you did you probably wouldn't be able to live with it."

"Perhaps you could enlighten me."

Voley shook his head decisively. "You'd think me insane or a criminal. In any case, it wouldn't change a thing."

Grant looked past Voley at the bookcases covering the wall. The shelves held leatherbound editions as well as more recent plastic printouts and disks. He stood and looked closer.

"Jefferson, Voltaire, Rousseau, Keynes, Locke . . ."

Voley sniffed. "Hmm. Rousseau was the only disappointment."

"Oh?"

"His understanding of how society functions is marvelous, but his conclusions are contaminated by a misappreciation of human nature. He believed that if people were left alone they would become naturally good. Terribly naïve. Marx suffered the same flaw, differently expressed. Both believed civic systems to be the constructs of a few imposed on the many, and that freed from them, the many would become just. Catastrophic lie."

"You don't believe in democracy, Mr. Voley?"

"You mean like ours? Do you vote, Mr. Voczek?"

"Of course. It's the law."

"Exactly. What sort of a democracy is that? But, no, that's not it. I don't believe in justice. I've spent my whole life looking for it. If such a thing existed, I would have found it."

"Are you sure you'd know it if you found it?"

"Touché. But you tell me. You're a policeman, you've searched. Have you ever found it?"

"I don't look."

"Why not?"

"It's not my job."

Voley smiled thinly. "Of course not. And that's why you'll never understand someone like me."

Grant went back to the chair and finished his lemonade.

"One more question, Mr. Voley. Do you know someone named Cozy?"

"Did he say I knew him?"

Grant shook his head. "Would he?"

Voley shrugged. "No, I don't know any Cozy. But there are a lot of people in the area I've met once and they go away thinking I'll remember them. The price of a high profile."

"Of course." Grant rose to his feet. "Well, thank you for seeing me, sir."

"I rather enjoyed it, Mr. Voczek. If you finish your mission here and have the time I'd like to spend an afternoon just conversing with you."

"I'll keep that in mind. Thank you, sir."

"Camilla will see you out."

Grant looked around and saw the woman standing in the doorway. She smiled politely and gestured toward the front door. Grant bowed to Voley, who nodded in return, and let Camilla escort him.

Late afternoon sun sent long shadows eastward as the cab let Grant out in front of his house. He checked his watch. Less than two hours till Reva picked him up.

He went to the office and tapped Chief Moore's number. Her face flashed onto the screen. "Yes?"

"Agent Voczek, Madam."

She frowned. "What can I do for you?"

"Just one thing. Could you check and see if your people took a man named Cozy into custody recently?"

"How recently?"

"Within the last five weeks."

"How soon do you need to know?"

"Let me know when you see me tonight."

"Very well. Anything else?"

"Not at present. Thank you for your help."

"I'll see you this evening, Agent Voczek."

The connection broke and Grant leaned back in the chair. He felt relieved, somehow reaffirmed in his abilities. The relief was mingled with puzzlement at the Voley interview.

He accessed the public library and made a search for "Voley, Aaron, writings of," directed the terminal to find anything concerning barter communes in them, and store them for later viewing. Then he went upstairs to shower again.

Voley as much as told him that Grant could not understand, that he lacked the facility to comprehend certain things. Grant resented the implication of stupidity. It annoyed him that it still stung. He had been slow in school, even though every test he took showed "promise" and his performance had always been just good enough to track him into the tougher courses. After his father left him in the care of the state polytech, Grant discovered the best way to stay out of worse situations was to be exactly at the level of achievement he found most difficult. When he thought about it he knew his stubbornness and fear had taken him to and through university. By then it had become habit more than anything else. He knew he lacked a certain quality of insight those around him exhibited like precocious talents, but he taught himself to concentrate and so kept up with those who seemed predestined for academic achievement. At graduation he stood thirty-sixth in a class of two hundred ten. His life since had been a steady rise in ability and achievement and no one thought him slow or ignorant anymore.

So Voley's suggestion bit deep. He had talked of layers. Layers hid things, masked old details, things forgotten. But they remained and sometimes one surfaced or was laid bare.

What had Beth lain bare?

He returned to the office in his robe. The search program flashed COMPLETED on the screen. He called up the menu and read down the list of publications. Voley had been prolific once, and most of his work had been published in law journals. Grant selected a few that sounded pertinent and printed them out.

The doorbell broke his attention. He looked up at the terminal and saw the time signature: seven-twenty. He dropped the sheaf of papers and scrambled downstairs to open the door.

Reva grinned at him. She wore a scarlet bodice and black skirt that fell open like wings over scarlet pants. She carried a long, thin package in the crook of her left arm. Grant stared.

"Are you wearing that tonight?" she asked. "You'll attract attention."

"Excuse me," he said suddenly. "I was preoccupied. I'll be ready shortly."

"Don't hurry on my account."

He ran back up to the bedroom and dressed as quickly as he could.

"What preoccupied you?" she called up the stairs as he buttoned his shirt.

"In the office, on the sofa," he called down.

He managed his tie and folded the tips of his shirt collar

down. White satin vest, black jacket. He checked himself carefully, then took his Muller-cut down from the closet and hurried to the office.

Reva sat on the sofa, browsing the articles. She glanced up and nodded approvingly.

"That's less conspicuous," she said. She held up the papers. "Voley's?"

"Uh, yes. I went to see him this afternoon."

Reva frowned. "Oh?"

"Yes . . ."

"Is there a reason you went alone?"

Grant nodded. "I thought it was necessary. For myself."

She seemed to think about that for a time. She nodded. "And how do you feel now?"

"Much better than I did this morning." He made a smile. "You've seen me at my worst."

"It's all right. I hope to see you at your best." She set the papers aside. "So what about Mr. Voley?"

"Aging anarchist." Grant bent over her and retrieved the articles. He breathed in a scent he could not identify; just a trace, subdued. He drew another breath and it seemed to recede. He straightened and found her watching him. Distractedly, he shuffled through the printouts.

"Listen to this," he said. " 'In the pursuit of a system that functions in the service of all citizens we have asked ourselves, in the tradition of Plato, what constitutes the citizen. Rather than assume all members of a community to be necessarily citizens by virtue of their presence within it, we have taken the position that the community can only function in the presence of a certain type of member, that member becoming the model for the citizen. Birth has become meaningless. We have taken a giant step backward to a time when property alone determined community status. But rather than accept that property is a malleable form, easily transferred from one to another, we have decided that property is an attribute that can be assigned, a package to be delivered to the deserving, a set of credentials that not only define the citizen but can also be stripped away, thereby removing citizenship. Participation has ceased to be a matter of choice and has become an act of law. The penalty for abstention is disenfranchisement and, inevitably, deportation. We have created a class of faceless, propertyless, statusless exiles within our own borders, to be used according to the whims of current politics and prejudice, the scapegoats of our obsession with control and security. Instead of Plato's high minded polis we are building a prison of the soul.' That was written right after the Reforms were passed. He seems to have mellowed, but . . ."

"Impressive."

Grant dropped them on the sofa. "In a seditious sort of way, I suppose."

Her eyebrows came together briefly. "So what did he have to say about Beth's murder?"

"He said he was sorry, but had nothing to do with it. Also denied having any connection beyond the obvious with either Tochsin or Abernathy. He denied knowing Harold Lusk, but I think he was lying about that."

"We're going to be late to the ball." She stood and picked up the package from the desk. "Here. A present."

Grant found the tape at each end and broke it with his thumbnail. He slid off the top of the box. Within, nestled in tissue paper, lay a polished cherrywood cane with a gold knob and tip and thin gold band six inches from the knob. He lifted it from the box and hefted it.

"This is . . ."

Reva smiled. "Don't restrain yourself. Appreciation makes me accommodating."

"A little ostentatious."

"A little ostentation is good for some people. You don't know just how much, though. May I?"

Grant surrendered the cane and watched as she gave the knob a twist, gripped the staff just above the gold band, and drew it apart. She held up an eighteen-inch black composite blade. She returned it, secured the lock, and handed it back.

"Right here," she touched a spot an inch below the knob. "Push that up and both ends will deliver a fifty-thousand volt discharge. It resets automatically."

Grant raised his eyebrows. "Do you think I need this?"

Reva shook her head. "I just think a man with a cane is distinguished and elegant. Happy birthday."

Grant thought for a moment. "My birthday is next week."

"Imagine that." She grinned again.

Grant laughed. "Thank you. I don't know what to say."

"Yes, you do. Now, let's get ourselves to the festivities and see what hornets we can stir up. On the way you can tell me all about Aaron Voley." She turned and stopped him at the door. "And now that you've satisfied any questions regarding your ability to function, please don't do that again. At least not without telling me."

"I—"

"I don't want to be shown your body in a morgue without some idea how it got there. All right?"

"All right. Under one condition."

"Yes?"

"You tell me what *you* did while I was at Voley's."

She slipped an arm around his and smiled. "I had every intention to."

FIFTEEN

Cozy slept on and off. City jail cells offered an H.D. at least. He wished he could doze off and stay that way, but he kept alternating between sharp fear and deep weariness. The combination ate at him, leaving him exhausted but alert.

The quiet bothered him. In city jail, open bars let out the cacophony of inmate voices. Prisoners saw each other across and through the steel grillwork. Cozy knew about the eighth floor, the high security quarter of city jail, but only as hearsay. The cells must be like this, he thought. He had never been there. Eighth floor meant transfer to a state facility, which meant long term or deportation. Cozy had only done a few overnights and one month-long stay in city jail. He missed the voices, the presence of other prisoners. Somehow he knew he was alone here, the only one in the whole block.

Realtime, Faketime, and now federal time, he thought sourly.

He jerked upright and back into the corner of the cot when the door opened.

Kitcher stepped in, leaving the cell door open. Cozy could see marshals standing in the corridor. The federal dropped the chair seat and sat down. "Have you thought about what I said, Cozy?"

"I thought about it."

"Come to any decisions?"

Cozy shrugged. "If I knew anything I'd tell you. I don't know about the CID—that was Harry's."

"Do you know anything about Harry's friends? Was someone else involved with him dealing in adulterated CIDs? Were you involved?"

"I said—"

"Cozy, did you know adulterating a CID is treason?"

"What?"

"Treason. A peculiar species of it, but it's treason."

Cozy laughed. "You're kidding. It's just . . ."

"Just money? Credit? Exactly. Which is what we all use to live with, what we all need for security and happiness. It's what makes everything run, Cozy, so when someone violates it, the whole system is violated. But it goes beyond that, Cozy. A CID means citizenship. It means you're part of something large and complex and important and that you're connected to everyone else who has citizenship. It means responsibilities and benefits and identity. And when someone violates that it says that all this complex system doesn't mean anything. You violate the citizenship, the identity, the meaning of everything this country represents. We call that treason. That's a crime against the foundations of our community."

"That's crazy."

Kitcher shrugged. "You knew this. Don't tell me you didn't."

Cozy shook his head.

"Well. For the time being, it's out of my hands. I'm having you turned over to someone else for questioning. When they give you back to me, then we'll have another talk about the meaning of treason. We'll have another talk about Guantanamo and Africa and who Harry's friends are and where you got that card. I don't really care about you at all, Cozy. I want to know about that card. Nobody adulterates just one card, it's not worth it. People who do that are very skilled people who have a lot of specialized knowledge and expensive equipment and they do it for profit. I want those people, Cozy. They're the real criminals here. You're just a stupid gypsy who thought he could get things for nothing."

"Where am I going?"

"To another part of the building. Just for a little while."

Kitcher stood and signaled the two marshals. In their black uniforms and heavy belts and helmets they seemed twice as large as normal human beings. "Go with them, Cozy. They'd rather not carry you. If they have to, they'll hurt you."

Cozy stood. His legs shook. "I'm not a traitor."

Kitcher shrugged again.

"I'm not," Cozy insisted.

Kitcher glared at him. "I don't really care."

Cozy did not look at the faceplates of the marshals as he stepped out of the cell between them. He let them guide him, trying all along the way to control the shaking of his hands and legs, the anxious quivering in his chest and stomach. He did not pay attention to the journey's twists and turns—there was an elevator ride, though—but he noticed that he was no longer in the prison area. Here were long corridors, carpeted, lined with closed office doors. Then more turns, and finally through an office door.

They brought him into a large area. Where once walls

divided the space into smaller offices, now tables, desks, and racks of equipment marked off areas. Three men in grey coveralls looked up when he came in.

"Delivery from Agent Kitcher," one of the marshals said.

The oldest man—thinning brown hair, pale eyes, heavily lined face—came forward. He stared into Cozy's eyes for several seconds.

"Fine. Thank you."

The marshals left. Cozy watched them go, suddenly wanting them to stay.

"Cozy?" the old man asked.

Cozy stepped back and looked at the three men. The oldest one, close to him, held out a hand in a gesture of invitation, and smiled.

"Come on, Cozy, let's go over here. We can talk."

Cozy let the man take his elbow and bring him past a large table filled with tools, monitors, stacks of parts—chips, mostly, that Cozy could recognize, other things he could not—and into a space that looked like a lounge: tables and chairs, a couple of lamps that cast indirect light, and a large dispenser.

"Thirsty, Cozy? Coffee? Something harder?"

"Water."

The man nodded and went to the dispenser. A few moments later he handed Cozy a glass.

"Have a seat, Cozy. We want to talk."

"Who are you?"

"We're not federals, if that's what you mean."

"No, I mean, who *are* you?"

"Sit down, Cozy."

Reluctantly, Cozy went to a chair and sat down. He gulped the water, spilling a little down his chin. The three men pulled chairs around to face him in a semi-circle. The oldest took the center chair. The one on his left was heavy-set, bald, with wide, dark eyes. The other one looked very young, thick blond hair heavily moused and stylish.

"We have questions," the oldest one said. "You have answers. Maybe the ones we want."

"I told Kitcher, I don't know anything."

"Of course you did. You lied."

Cozy finished his water.

"More?" the man asked.

"No."

"Cozy, we aren't concerned with the same things Agent Kitcher is concerned with. We want answers for different reasons. Lying to us . . . well, it's stupid."

"I don't know anything."

"Harry Lusk was your cousin, wasn't he?"

Cozy started. "How—?"

The man held up his hand. "Harry worked for D.C. Did you know that?"

"No."

"He did. Till he came back here."

Cozy shrugged. "So?"

"Do you know Aaron Voley, Cozy?"

"Yes, sure, everybody in the barco knows Mr. Voley."

"Did you get your CID from him?"

"No—"

"Did Harry give it to you?"

"No."

"Harry was making them."

Cozy said nothing.

"Did Harry work for Voley?"

"I don't know."

"Yes, you do. We want to know if Voley was hiding Harry."

"Hiding him from who?"

"The federals."

Cozy shrugged. "Don't know."

The man sighed. "Yes, you do. Cozy, come now. This can take as long as you like. We've got all day, all night, all tomorrow."

"What do you want me to say?" Cozy snapped. "I don't know what you're asking!"

The man glared at him. "Don't shout at me, Cozy."

"Well—"

"We want to know what Voley intended to do with the CIDs Harry was making for him."

"Harry wasn't making—"

"Harry was adulterating CIDs. That's a fact, Cozy—"

"No! Harry—Harry's *dead!* Doesn't anybody care about that?"

"Cozy—"

"Harry was family! He's dead! I don't know shit about CIDs or Mr. Voley or D.C. or you! Who *are* you, anyway?"

"Cozy, you had better be still."

"I don't know anything!"

The man shook his head. He looked sad. He seemed about to say something when the sound of footsteps interrupted him. All four men turned around.

It was a woman, standing by one of the work tables, elegantly dressed—just as she had been when Cozy had seen her at Voley's. He had identified her as hired security then; now he was sure of it.

"We're leaving," she said. "How's your schedule?"

"We're just beginning," the man answered.

"I'll be back around one, maybe two," she said. "I want something then."

"We'll do our best."

"I'm sure you will. Good evening, gentlemen."

"Good evening, Madam," the interrogators said in unison.

She gave Cozy a half-smile, turned, and walked away. She had a nice walk.

The old man loudly cleared his throat. "Don't stare, Cozy, it's not polite."

"She—"

"Yes? Do you recognize her?"

"I—no. Yes. Who is she?"

"You don't know, then?"

"No . . ."

"Turn around, Cozy. Look at us. Forget her, Cozy."

Cozy made himself turn back around. The heavyset man stood right in front of him. The man's fist snapped around and Cozy's head bounced against the top of the chair back. His sinuses filled with the metal scent of blood, and his lips felt numb. His chin was wet. He reached up and his hand came away red.

The heavyset man returned to his chair.

"Pay attention, Cozy," the oldest man said. "We have questions. You have answers. We'd like them before the night is out."

"I don't know anything," Cozy said, his tongue thick. He bled freely from the nose and upper lip.

The younger man came forward and dropped a white cloth in his lap. Cozy pressed it to his face.

"Now. Once more. We have questions. You have answers. We want to know what Voley's intentions were concerning the CIDs Harry was making for him."

The heavyset man went to the dispenser and drew another glass of water. He brought it to Cozy and waited until Cozy took it from him, then sat back down.

"I don't know . . ." He drank. "I don't—"

"You're lying. Let's start with something easy. Harry was your cousin."

Cozy nodded.

"Good. True statement. Harry worked in D.C."

Cozy shrugged.

"Maybe true, maybe not. It's possible you didn't know that. Will you accept my word for it?"

"Sure."

"Good. Harry worked in D.C. He left. He came back here. Yes?"

"Y-yes."

The man smiled encouragingly. "Good, good. Three facts in a row. Don't let me down, Cozy. Now, Harry was doing work for Aaron Voley."

Cozy shrugged again.

The older man shook his head. "You were doing well till now, Cozy. You *know* Harry was working for Voley. Now, what's so difficult about saying it?"

"I don't—"

The younger man sprang up and kicked Cozy in the knee, hard. Cozy screamed and almost pitched out of the chair. The water flew up and splashed him.

"Harry was working for Voley," the old man repeated.

Cozy grasped his knee. It felt odd, out of joint. Pain grew, knife-like, in the middle of throbbing.

"Harry was working for Voley, Cozy."

"Yes," Cozy gasped.

"Very good. Perhaps this won't take all night after all. What was Harry doing for Voley?"

Cozy groped for the cloth and pressed it back against his nose. He hunched over his knee.

"Cozy?"

Cozy shook his head. Let them draw what conclusions they wished from that.

"We aren't going to beat you very much, Cozy. For one, it's tiring. For another, it loses its effectiveness after a short time. Beating only proves that we don't mind doing things to you. What else we might do . . . well, I'll let you think about that for a time."

Cozy looked up. He blinked, his vision blurred through tears. He was scared and embarrassed. He had never felt those two things before with such intensity, and never together.

"What do you want?"

"Answers. We have questions. You have answers."

"But I don't know anything," he whined.

The old man scowled. "Lie. It's possible you don't know how much you know. But we'll never get to that part if you keep lying about what you very definitely *do* know."

"What?"

"Harry worked for Voley."

"Yes."

"What did he do for Voley?"

"I don't—"

The man slapped his hands together, grinning. Cozy recoiled. "You see?" the man said. "You *do* know. Let me explain how I know you know. You took Harry to the hospital, correct?"

"He was sick . . ."

"You took him to the hospital, correct?" the man insisted.

"They wouldn't treat him at the mission."

"Of course not. That's against the law. Harry was suffering anaphylactic shock. He had to go to a registered, state-approved clinic. So you took him."

Cozy nodded.

"You used one of Harry's CIDs to admit him."

"Used Harry's card."

"One of them. Because when the hospital staff realized it was an adulterated card, what did you do?"

"Ran."

"Ran before they confronted you. Correct?"

"Y-yes."

"Why would you do that if you didn't know beforehand that it was an adulterated card?"

"I—"

"You ran before they even said anything to you. True?"

"Couldn't stay . . ."

"Because you knew the card was bad."

"Yes."

"So you knew what Harry was doing. *Didn't* you?"

Cozy nodded.

"Good. Now. What was Harry doing for Voley?"

"Harry wasn't working for Voley."

"Oh, hell, Cozy. All the way back to the beginning."

"He wasn't."

"Who do you think you're protecting? Harry's dead. Are you protecting Voley? Why? He's a Secured Class, arrogant, condescending citizen who thinks he's buying a clear conscience by helping the gypsies. He doesn't care about you. Not Cozy, not personally. All you are to him is a way to live with himself, to feel good about having citizenship when you don't. Are you protecting that?"

"I don't know."

"Another true answer: You don't know." The man smiled coldly. "Well, Cozy, we have hours before us to discover these things. We can learn them together. You'll feel better for it. You'll be more aware of who you really are . . . and where your loyalties lie. Wouldn't that be a good thing to know?"

"Mr. Voley's a good man."

The smiled broadened. "Of course he is. The question is: good for what? Did you think he was going to give you all CIDs and somehow magically transform you into citizens? You couldn't even get your cousin into a hospital without the card betraying you."

Cozy stared at the floor. "Leave me alone."

"We're just having a conversation, Cozy. We're just talking."

The pain in Cozy's knee seemed to be subsiding. He moved it and winced. Carefully, he explored it—not broken, as far as he could tell. He pushed himself up straighter in the chair. The bleeding from his nose and mouth had stopped.

"Some more water, Cozy?"

"No, thank you."

The man shrugged. "Maybe later. Now, where were we? Oh, yes. What was Harry doing for Aaron Voley?"

"I. Don't. Know."

The man sighed. "You're being unnecessarily stupid, Cozy."

"Man's either stupid or he isn't. Can't help it."

"Where did you get the card, Cozy?"

"It was Harry's."

"And where did he get it?"

"It was his."

"But it was adulterated. You knew it was."

"So? Maybe he picked it up somewhere."

"Maybe. But we don't think so." He looked at the younger man.

Cozy watched him go to another table. He sorted

through some items, then came back, left hand tucked partially behind his back, out of sight. Cozy lunged forward, but the heavyset man caught him in the chest and shoved him back into the chair with enough force to knock the wind from his lungs. An instant later, he felt the cold touch of a pneumatic injector against his neck.

"No!" Cozy whipped an arm around to knock it away, but the younger man had already stepped back. He felt his face contort. He thought of Harry dying from the poison the Civic Health people had given him. "No!" he cried.

"What's wrong, Cozy?" the older man asked.

"I don't want to die!"

"You won't. Not yet, not from that."

"What—?"

"All that will do is relax all your various sphincters."

Cozy shook his head. "I don't—"

"You'll notice. Don't worry. We're going to put you in a room by yourself for a while now. You can think it over, decide what's best for you. We'll come back in an hour. I think that's plenty of time for you to stew in your own juices, don't you think?"

The heavyset man laughed.

Cozy let them carry him to a small room far from the lounge area. As they closed the door, he felt inexplicably grateful. Alone felt good, felt acceptable. He could control himself. He could think of some way to fight them, perhaps, at least a way to withstand them.

He felt damp, suddenly. He looked down. A stain spread over the crotch of his pants. He tried to shut off the flow, but his bladder simply emptied of its own accord.

"Oh, *chees*, no!"

He leaned back against the wall, in the dark, and waited through the humiliation.

SIXTEEN

Your friend was tracking down board members of Coronin Industries," Reva said as the car pulled away from the house. "Her inquiry went to Inspector Juarez in Tapachula. He's INS, but used to be Treasury. You might want to contact him to see if there's more, but Coronin has a facility in the Yucatan."

"Specializing in?" Grant asked.

"Pharmaceuticals research. I couldn't find out if there are any foreign connections; you'll have to do that. But I made a couple of other inquiries while I was patched through. The Tamaulipas investigation was a kidnapping ring."

Grant nodded. "I remember."

"What you may not know, mainly because the Bureau didn't release this information to Treasury, was that it also involved CID adulteration."

Grant frowned. "I *didn't* know. That's—"

Reva shrugged. "It wasn't my call. The people kidnapped never disappeared from public accounts because their accounts remained active. The cards were passed on to new holders. After a certain amount of time, the card was reported missing and a new one ordered and Treasury sent one, very accommodating. No red flags went up because somebody had managed to break the system so the profiles could be changed."

"That's not possible."

"Normally, no."

"Not without someone inside."

Reva nodded. "No other way."

"Harold Lusk."

"We never confirmed that, but he was one of our primary suspects. He had the background, coming from borderline people, with certain radical connections."

"What sort of radical connections?"

"When he got out of school, he refused all government offers. And I mean *all*—federal, state, local. He did database work for a net affiliation of neolibertarians: free currency advocates—which is our Abernathy connection—and voting law reformists—which is our Voley connection."

"I'm sure we knew all this."

"Of course, you did. But Lusk apparently is very good and Treasury—just like every other agency I know—employs people like Lusk all the time, just because they're good."

"So how did we convince him?"

"Money. You're paying him twice what his colleagues are getting. I suppose even the most rabid idealists have their limit."

"But if he's still doing work for his former connections . . . why didn't you tell us?"

"No proof. The Bureau assumed it might start up elsewhere. We didn't want to do anything to drive him to ground, so Treasury wasn't informed. It would be too easy to lose him completely."

"Still, that information—"

"A little late to stand on formality."

"So you shut down the ring and settled back to wait for another occurrence of CID adulteration. What about the kidnapped victims? Where were they?"

Reva shrugged. "We never found them. We found the halfway houses, the transfer points. But the people guarding them didn't know. It was set up in cells. We did find parts, though."

"Parts?" Grant asked.

"Body parts. Washed up on the beaches on the west coast. A few genome scans identified them as some of the victims. Once we shut down the acquisition end, it didn't happen anymore. The local authorities passed it off as simple murders involving gypsies or some other borderline group. The governor refused to extend our letter, and we weren't able to obtain an override."

"They wanted it over and done with."

"So it seemed. What always bothered me was that in some of those parts the tissues exhibited traces of foreign compounds, broken down and unidentifiable. Nothing to give us a chemical fingerprint."

"Test subjects?"

"I'm thinking along those lines now. It never made enough sense to follow through."

"So what were your other inquiries about?"

"Property IDs. I had them go through all the records and find everything that had been confiscated in the entire operation. I wanted to know who owned what and if any of the names matched anything we're working on."

"And?"

"We confiscated eight vans. They'd been leased from a local firm, open contract, no termination time specified. A holding company paid the bill. The holding company evaporated as soon as we moved; we found no one. But the parent company that owned the property—which was also leased—is owned by Weston and Burnard."

"You didn't pursue it then?"

Reva scowled. "Not in our area. We would have had to turn it over to Treasury for that end of the investigation. What we thought more important at the time was finding the insider for the ID changes."

Grant shook his head. "This system . . ."

"All we need to do now is find out who actually has the strongest connection to Weston and Burnard."

"No one."

Reva glanced at him. "What do you mean?"

"Abernathy dabbles with his personal finances through them, but it's not enough to amount to anything. Certainly not enough to kill someone over."

"In your opinion."

"But neither Voley nor Tochsin have any dealings with Weston and Burnard."

Reva laughed sharply. "Wonderful. We're back to where we started."

"Not quite." Grant sketched out what he had discovered from Stuart and his own surveys.

"Coronin?" she mused. "So what would Lusk have to do with that?"

"Let's stick to one thread for the time being. We find the end of it, maybe we'll find the others."

The Daniels-Bennington Hotel ran north along the riverfront from the small parkland that fronted the Old Courthouse. Its crystalline facets stood on ground that had once been warehouses and factories, then hotels and luxury apartments, then rubble. A valet took Reva's Mercury, and she and Grant walked through the diamond-shaped entrance into the enormous lobby.

The reception was twenty floors up, in a banquet facility capped by glass that overlooked the river as it passed before the nearly century-old steel arch.

Grant surrendered his hat and cane at the door. They descended four broad steps to the gold-carpeted floor. He paused to scan the crowd. The wealth of St. Louis was gathered in small clusters across the hall, as if this were a garden and each group represented a plot of exotic flowers.

"Do you think they can tell by looking that we're below stairs?" Reva asked, smiling.

"Worse. We're the running dogs of federal monsters." He lightly brushed at her cheek. "You have ichor on your face."

"Oh, dear, I forgot to clean my teeth."

"I don't see anyone fleeing in panic, so our disguises must be sufficient."

"What disguise? This is the authentic I."

Grant looked at her and saw her bob an eyebrow. For a long moment he watched her face, reluctant to turn away, and her smile changed from the simply pleasant to pleased.

"Mr. Voczek. Madam Cassonare."

Grant looked around and saw Chief Moore. Her suit, midnight blue and pleated, had an official cut. Grant bowed. "Chief."

"I'm glad you could come. May I introduce you around?"

"Is Director Koldehn here?"

"Not yet. He's often late to social functions, though. Since he's been here I've never known him to be late for anything else."

"Before we begin, did you make the inquiry I requested?"

"Yes. And yes, a man by that name was arrested twice in

the last five weeks, the second time at about three this afternoon. He was transferred almost immediately to federal custody, though."

"What charge?"

"Credit fraud. I assume that your people have him."

"Both times? Credit fraud?"

"No, the first time was for public defacement. Tagging."

Grant nodded. "Thank you."

Chief Moore led them into the garden. Faces turned, names mentioned. Grant shook hands, bowed, listened for anything that fit categories he did not quite define to himself, but which, he felt, he would recognize. Drinks drifted by on trays held by human waiters—an affectation Grant identified with a peculiar obsessiveness with the past, a narrow view of tradition, which certain people of wealth suffered.

"Mr. Voczek, may I introduce Mitchel Abernathy?" Chief Moore said. "Mr. Abernathy, Grant Voczek."

Grant's nerves all seemed to come alive at once. A short, stout man with thin white hair over a wide skull and pale blue eyes looked up at him. Grant extended his hand, found it encased in a strong, brief grip. He recognized him from the Mayor's office.

"Mr. Voczek. Welcome. And what do you do?"

Grant blinked. The voice was familiar, but he could not remember why. "I work for the Treasury Department, sir."

"Oh. One of Philip's boys. You're new to St. Louis, then."

"Yes, sir. I've only been here a few days."

"How do you find us?"

"Unique."

Abernathy grinned. "We are." Then he frowned. "You aren't here to replace the young woman who was killed in the barco, are you?"

"She wasn't killed in the barco, sir."

Abernathy waved a hand. "By gypsies, then."

"I don't believe it was gypsies, either."

"Are you her replacement?"

"I'm here to find out what happened, yes."

"Then you probably know that I had problems with her."

"It's come to my attention."

The group around Abernathy watched, none of them moving. Abernathy's voice nagged at Grant.

"Stay out of my business, Mr. Voczek, and we'll get along fine."

"You're a businessman, Mr. Abernathy. You have a diversified company—more than one—and holdings in a bank. In a general way, you *are* my business."

Abernathy grunted and looked around at the others. "Federals. They still can't get over the Reforms." The group laughed politely. "It's my theory, Mr. Voczek, perhaps you'd like to comment, that bureaucrats are a species."

"A species, sir?"

"Yes, their own phylum in the family of *homo sapiens*, only they breed by example rather than sexually. The fact remains that they breed true. Change the circumstances in which they thrive and you stifle them for awhile, but they always find a way to come back."

"I thought Social Darwinism died with the twentieth century," Grant commented.

"No, no. Social Darwinism is a belief of bureaucrats. It never did really catch on in the real world." Abernathy looked thoughtful. "Voczek. What is that, Polish?"

"Czech."

"What generation?"

"My father was from Teplice, near the border with Germany."

"Oh, one of the first places overrun. He escaped, eh?"

"No, sir, he left several years before."

"Political?"

"I have no idea. As far as I know he just wanted to make more money."

"What did he do in the Czech Republic?"

"We never discussed it."

"Is he still alive?"

"No. He died ten years ago."

Abernathy raised an eyebrow. "And you never looked into his life? Never studied your own country?"

"*This* is my country."

"Well, perhaps."

"I was born here, sir."

"To an immigrant. That makes you what he was." Abernathy stabbed a finger at Grant. "You're Czech, Mr. Voczek, not American."

"An interesting argument. What would you say qualifies one to be an American?"

"I have a definition, but this is hardly the place to go into it. Suffice it to say that, just as a quick guide, no one whose family wasn't here in the twentieth century is an American."

Grant glanced around at the gathered audience. More than half seemed to approve of Abernathy's assertions. The rest waited with polite anticipation, probably to see if Grant would puncture the old man's exterior. Grant had seen the game many times, and played it more than a few.

"That's rather arbitrary, isn't it?" he asked. "I could say, with probably a little more justification, that anyone whose family wasn't here in the fourteenth century doesn't qualify."

"But they're all dead."

"As you say, this is probably not the place to go into it."

"Nor is there really a good time. The topic makes people uncomfortable, just like talking about the Riots and the Reform in anything but symbolic terms is socially taboo."

"Or discussing sex and public inebriation?" asked a familiar voice.

Grant looked around. A man had come up behind him. He grinned and held his glass up in mock toast. He paused at the same instant Grant recognized him.

"Well, well, small world," the man said. "How's your head today?"

"Much improved," Grant said. "Dick?"

Chief Moore frowned. "Have you two met?"

Dick laughed. "Not formally, no."

"Then, Mr. Voczek, may I present Richard Dirkenfeld? Mr. Dirkenfeld, this is Grant Voczek of the Treasury Department."

Richard Dirkenfeld's face froze. He held out a hand, waiting. Grant stared at him. Out of the corner of his eye he saw Chief Moore looking uncomfortable.

"I only come to these things for the liquor and to see my wife," Dirkenfeld said.

Grant took his hand and shook. "Sir."

Dirkenfeld nodded, then looked around. "Is Mitchel haranguing you with his fascist theories? If you've never heard them before they can be quite amusing, but they do wear thin after fifty or sixty repetitions."

"Good evening, Richard," Abernathy said stiffly.

"I heard the bit about families from the last century," Dirkenfeld replied. "That's new, isn't it? Did you tell Mr. Voczek your idea that there's a nationalistic gene?" He turned to Grant and winked. "You'll love it. It's a brand new twist on Lamarckian genetics."

"Some families can be here for centuries," Abernathy

said, "and still produce a throwback. I suppose it's a recessive."

"Thank you, Mitch, I'm flattered. Recessives are old buried genes that go way back, aren't they? That means I'd be more in touch with my ancestors than you are and therefore closer to the real thing?"

Abernathy pursed his lips and slowly shook his head. "You are an ass, Richard." He nodded toward Grant. "It was a pleasure meeting you, Mr. Voczek. I hope your stay in our city proves pleasant and uneventful."

Abernathy turned away, then, and his entire small group drifted off with him. Grant watched them go, feeling both troubled and amused.

"Great tailor," Dirkenfeld said. "Same shop does his suits and his sheets."

Grant opened his mouth in a silent "Oh" and looked at Dirkenfeld.

"Yes," Dirkenfeld said, nodding. "One of his hobbies. He was master of ceremonies the other night. Was that last night? Seems longer ago, but then I spent most of today sober."

"Mr. Voczek . . . ?" Chief Moore said.

Grant looked around and spotted Reva with another group.

"Would you be kind enough to continue on with Agent Cassonare?" he asked. "I have some things to discuss with Mr. Dirkenfeld."

"If you wish," she said, frowning. "Excuse me, please."

Grant watched Chief Moore move toward Reva. She gave him a backward glance with a worried, warning expression.

"I shan't divulge your secret, Grant," Dirkenfeld said. "Or would you rather I called you 'Mr. Voczek'?"

Grant turned to face him. "What secret? Oh, you mean last night. I could care less. I wasn't there willingly."

Dirkenfeld smiled slyly. "I know what you mean. The place has this magnetism, this hypnotic attraction. I lose all my will power, too—"

"You knew Beth McQuarry."

Dirkenfeld's expression lost all humor. He nodded sullenly, then looked alarmed. "I had nothing to do with her death."

"Perhaps not directly. You saw her the night before she was killed and then stopped all contact. No calls, nothing. Did you know something?"

"I . . . Mr. Voczek, this is not the place—"

Grant stepped closer. "She was a very good friend. I want an explanation. If I find that you had anything to do with this—"

Dirkenfeld glared at him. "Don't threaten me."

"Or what? You'll have your father speak to me? Or maybe your father-in-law?"

Dirkenfeld snorted.

"Or maybe you'll tell your wife where you met and discredit me that way."

Dirkenfeld paled.

"We have matters to discuss, Mr. Dirkenfeld—*Dick*—and we *will* discuss them. Tonight. Afterward."

"I—"

"Tonight."

Dirkenfeld nodded. "I liked her quite a lot, Mr. Voczek."

"So did I." He surveyed the ballroom. "You say you came to see your wife? Is she here yet?"

"You don't really wish to meet my wife," Dirkenfeld said. "And I don't really wish to see her. I—" He stopped abruptly. "Damn. Well, there she is, regardless. Would you like me to introduce you?"

Grant followed Dirkenfeld's annoyed gaze to a woman just entering the ball. She was elegantly dressed in a deep crimson gown with gold trim. As she drew nearer, he recognized her: Tochsin's aide, Tess.

"We've met," Grant said.

"Then I pity you," Dirkenfeld said. "And am grateful that I do not really have to introduce you. We'll talk later, Mr. Voczek. Good evening."

Dirkenfeld faded into the crowd.

Grant walked toward the buffet table that stretched along the back wall, filled to capacity with ornate deserts and hors-d'oeuvre. The center was dominated by an enormous, multi-tiered cake with different flavors of frosting on each level, swirled into delicate designs. Grant navigated through the clumps of guests to the edge of the table, found a plate, and began absently filling it with small edibles.

He watched the slow dance of social choreography. As he saw people to whom he had been introduced he recalled their names—most of them—and noted who they spent the most time with and where they went next. Abernathy had a new group of people gathered around him.

Mayor Poena arrived, then, with three others. She surveyed the gathering, seemed to put on an appropriate expression, and dived in. A few minutes later Grant saw her with Congressman Tochsin, the two of them alone and speaking intently.

"Good evening, Agent Voczek."

Grant turned to his left. Tess Dirkenfeld stood beside him. She smiled politely.

"Good evening, Mrs. Dirkenfeld."

She made a small moue. "Please. I go by my maiden name: Reed. Even when Richard and I still pretended to be a couple."

"Forgive me."

"Were you speaking with my husband when I came in?"

Grant nodded. "You don't miss very much."

"Working for a congressman, you do learn to look everywhere at once. I wanted a chance to talk to you. Michael can be a bit formal, especially when he's acting in his official capacity. Sometimes it gets in the way of reason and practicality."

"I'm a supporter of reason and practicality. What would you suggest?"

"He has to be above suspicion in his conduct. Anything that might look like a compromise to his constituency could cost him votes, even an election."

Grant studied her for a moment. He saw a hardness about her eyes and in the set of her jaw that did not look like the result of a pampered life as the daughter of a wealthy and successful senator. There was more there than privilege. She had earned that hardness. Grant wondered how.

"So he leaves certain messy details to you?" he ventured.

"Messes are unavoidable in public life. How public they become depends on the skills of those involved." She met his gaze. "Don't you agree?"

"Absolutely."

"Perhaps we can meet and discuss these things in more detail."

"At a time and a place where it won't compromise Congressman Tochsin's image?"

Tess nodded. "We understand each other well, I think."

"I still have a duty—"

"Please. Duty has limits and compromise is the way of the world. We were doing so well, let me make it clearer. I handle all Michael's unpleasant business. So far, no scandal has touched him." She raised an eyebrow. "Are we clear?"

"Perfectly."

"Good. I'll be in touch. Enjoy the ball, Agent Voczek."

He watched her drift off. She blended effortlessly, showing no hint of the aspect she had just allowed Grant to glimpse. He was impressed.

Reva appeared beside him. "Any revelations?" she asked.

"I met Richard Dirkenfeld. And his wife."

"Was that who that was? I wondered."

"I can see why they don't share lodgings anymore. I think I was just threatened."

"You aren't sure?"

Grant gave her a sardonic look. Reva raised her eyebrows and nodded. "I see. What did you think of Mitchel Abernathy?"

"Delightful old bigot."

"Isn't he, though?"

"Did you meet him?" he asked.

She nodded. She picked something off his plate and popped it into her mouth.

"Did he tell you his theory of nationalistic genes?" he asked.

Reva gave him a dubious look. When Grant sketched it out for her she searched the crowd for Abernathy.

"Ass," she said, and took another morsel from Grant's plate. "I'd qualify, though."

"Do you feel better?"

"Oh, absolutely. I can see why he's here. He probably thinks Reed is a god."

"You really dislike Senator Reed, don't you?"

"Don't you?"

"I don't know much about him."

"Don't you vote? The man is a demagogue."

Grant sighed. "I vote because it's the law. If he's anything like his daughter, though, I'd be inclined to agree with you. Why is he a demagogue?"

"He's sponsored twelve amendments to the immigration laws in his career, and was on the oversight committee that monitored the last national deportation," Reva explained. "He's a doctrinaire isolationist who has proposed sealing all borders permanently and controlling illicit migrations with the death penalty. Eight years ago, he sponsored legislation to require all naturalized citizens to undergo review every three years, no exceptions. Two years ago, he began debate on a proposal to declare any area with a gypsy population greater than one-tenth percent of its total population a disaster area automatically under martial law."

"Won't happen. The states will never allow that much federal intervention."

"Probably not, but he has a lot of support, and not just in this state. There's talk of him running for president."

Grant shook his head. "Why would Abernathy support him? He's a strict Reformist according to his jacket. He's staunchly anti-federal."

"It's been my experience that bigots are ideologically opportunistic. They'll sacrifice a lesser evil in the cause of a greater one."

"You're being simplistic. They don't think any of it's evil."

"When people die because they don't fit your program, it's evil. Nothing simplistic about it. Just ugly."

"We aren't here to worry over people's politics."

Reva was silent for a time. Then she said, "You and I need to sit down sometime, quietly, and have a long talk."

Grant took a stick of rolled meat from his plate and offered the rest to Reva. More people entered. He spotted Tess Reed and pointed her out to Reva.

"We need to find out more about her," Grant said.

"She looks familiar," Reva said, frowning. "I can't remember where, but . . . "

Then Assistant Director Koldehn arrived. Congressman Tochsin greeted him almost immediately and led him off by the arm.

"That was interesting," Reva said.

"Were you planning to be here the whole evening?" Grant asked.

"Only till I thought I'd learned everything I could."

"How far along are you?"

"I already know everything I need to know about Senator Reed." She held up her wine glass. "But the Merlot is very good."

Mayor Poena emerged from a curtain of guests and walked up to them. "Agents," she greeted them. "I wasn't aware that you came to things like this."

"From time to time it's good to expand one's social circle," Reva said.

"How is your investigation coming?"

"Slowly," Grant said.

"How unfortunate. When do you think you might be able to get me a decision from D.C.?"

"Hard to say until we find out what is actually going on," Grant said. "Since there seems to be a paucity of coop-eration from the various offices, that may take some time."

"I intend to speak to the Governor tomorrow. I'd like to

be able to tell him something more positive than that. If I had some reason to expect a useful response I might request an extension on your stay."

"Extension?" Reva said. "I have a month. Agent Voczek needs no gubernatorial validation."

"You do not have a month if a local solution is found."

"Have you found one?"

"Perhaps."

Reva set down her glass. "With all due respect, Madam Mayor, I'm getting a little tired of this. Do you want this matter settled or not?"

"I explained what I want: I want the barco gone. If you can't facilitate that, then I'll deal with it another way." She smiled then and bowed her head. "Agent Voczek, Agent Cassonare. Please enjoy your evening."

"Madam Mayor," Grant said, "I understand Agent McQuarry's burial is being held up because your people won't sign off on the coroner's report. May I ask why?"

"No, you may not," Poena said sharply. "Good evening."

She walked away. Grant caught sight of her a few moments later back in Tochsin's company, which now included A.D. Koldehn.

"I think I'd rather be elsewhere," Grant said.

"Agreed," Reva said.

"Why don't you leave first and I'll meet you at the federal building."

"Any particular reason?"

"Something we need to check."

He walked with her a short way toward the exit.

A loud rush, like air escaping a pressurized container, filled the room. Grant looked back toward the banquet table. The centerpiece sprayed matter from its crown, bits of cake that struck the nearest people. The crowd backed quickly away. The sides of the cake split and the entire complex pastry construction opened. Plates and settings spilled from the table.

From the center a column rose to about three feet above the top of the cake, then began to inflate. As Grant watched, it took on the contours and proportions of a penis. From the open sides of the cake, a banner unfurled across the food. The left side proclaimed SENATOR REED IS COMING! The right read, NOW WE ARE ALL FUCKED.

Reva laughed, then covered her mouth. Grant felt himself smiling.

Reva squeezed his arm. "I don't think anyone will notice if we leave together, do you?"

SEVENTEEN

Reva parked next to Grant's Duesenberg. A single night watchman was reading a book at his post outside the elevator. Grant and Reva inserted their CIDs into the automatic scanner. The guard glanced at his screen briefly and nodded, then returned his attention to his reading. They retrieved their cards and went up.

The Treasury level felt empty, the hallways lit by dim service lamps. Grant tried the doors along the main corridor and found them all locked.

"What are we looking for?" Reva asked.

"I'm not sure." He came to his office and turned the knob. Locked. "Try yours."

Reva, frowning, went the short distance to her office. "Locked."

Grant continued down the hallway and rounded the corner, heading for Koldehn's office. He inserted his CID into the reader and tapped in his override code on the keypad beneath the knob. A moment later, the lock clicked open.

The light from the desk lamp, set low, turned the assistant director's office into a maze of indistinct shapes. Grant picked his way carefully to the desk and sat down. He slid his card into the lock slot beside the center drawer and fed his code into the terminal keyboard. A small green light winked on, indicating an open link to D.C. Grant waited patiently for verification from Washington to come back to Koldehn's desk. Less than a minute passed, and the desk unlocked itself and opened access to the terminal.

"I gather we've stopped being polite?" Reva asked.

"I may apologize in the morning. For now . . ."

He pulled open the central drawer: Pencils, pens, paperclips, a spare watch, a bottle of cologne, a pair of personal phones, and a secretary, all intermingled with scraps of papers and a number of disks.

Reva opened the large file drawer to his left. She took out several stacks of disks, all with neat labels in department code.

"You don't intend for us to go through all this, do you?" she asked.

"No. Those are probably handouts like we received—standard performance reports, declassified closed cases. Busy work."

The top righthand drawer held a palm stunner and a replica Walther automatic, several spare magazines of ammunition, and a field communicator. Grant opened the next drawer: extra cravats, gloves, stick pins, and handkerchiefs. The bottom drawer held paper boxes.

"What are we looking for, anyway?" Reva asked.

"Anything that might tell us whether Director Koldehn is part of the cover-up."

"Oh, so we're looking for a confession?"

"Beth stopped reporting to Koldehn. I want to know if she had a specific reason or if she'd just stopped trusting everyone here."

Grant pulled the top paper box out and opened it. The title sheet read VOLEY, AARON, B. 1976. Grant leafed through the hardcopy file. He grinned at Reva.

"Voley's history," he said. "Old newspaper clips, field reports from pre-Reform investigations . . ."

"Why hard copy?"

Grant shrugged. He set it aside and took out the second box. When he opened it, he hissed. "Beth's data from Tapachula."

It was a thin folder, with about sixty pages. Grant took it out and closed the lid. The last box contained Koldehn's personal notes, memoranda, trivia. Grant handed the Tapachula folder to Reva and went through the Voley file.

"Nothing here that looks new," he said. Almost at the bottom of the pile of papers he found a sheet with a string of code. He tapped on the terminal. The screen rose out of its slot at the head of the desk and the ready cursor flashed blue in the upper-left corner. Grant entered the code. The screen clouded, then a Treasury seal appeared. A moment after that, the title page of the hard copy file scrolled up. "He has it scanned in." Grant accessed his house terminal and sent it a copy.

"As long as you're in there," Reva said, "see what else you can find."

"No sooner said . . ."

Most of the file names in Koldehn's menu meant nothing to Grant. He found one labeled McQUARRY and another with his name. He opened Beth's.

"Koldehn lodged a complaint with D.C.—personal fitness

report, dated four days before her death. 'Regrettably, Special Agent McQuarry persists in unorthodox procedures. She has exceeded the limit of her mission, and several prominent locals have registered complaints against her investigation.' According to this, she made regular reports for ten days, then never again. Koldehn is on record as reprimanding her for deviating from guidelines."

Reva clucked her tongue. "Poor man. I *thought* he might have trouble dealing with deviants."

"Mitchel Abernathy complained to him directly, then the next day went to Congressman Tochsin. Tochsin came to see Koldehn. Koldehn called D.C. Abernathy came back to talk to both of them."

"No minutes?"

Grant shook his head.

"Who else complained?"

"Abernathy's attorney, a Roger Simson, and a Lynn Hightower." Grant requested IDs. "Simson is an attorney for CoMart National Shipping—"

"The Dirkenfelds."

"—and Lynn Hightower is . . ." His voice trailed off.

"What?"

"Curious. She's a comptroller for Agla Interstate."

"Who?"

"That's a new one. The complaint was over a breaking-and-entering. Says Beth gained unauthorized entry to Agla's lease property."

"Odd and odder. Anyone else?"

"Her Honor the Mayor, of course." Grant sent a copy of this file to his home terminal, then opened his own jacket. He laughed.

"What is it?"

"One comment: 'Seems of the same cut as McQuarry.

Less difficult to accept, though just as troublesome.'" He looked up at Reva. "What is this? No one wants this investigation solved?"

"So far they've all been very clear what they want."

Grant nodded. "A federal deportation order for the barco—nothing more, nothing less." He stabbed a finger at the screen. "The only one who seems to be out of this particular loop is Voley."

"Maybe we should have another talk with him."

Grant leaned over the keyboard. "One more thing. I have to find." He tapped for the daily logs. "Odd. Cozy isn't listed."

"Who is Cozy?" Reva asked.

"Someone Beth contacted in the barco. He was arrested today and turned over to us. Credit fraud. But there's no record of his being processed here."

"Anything about the fraud?"

"Yes . . . Regional Hospital North . . . adulterated CID . . . patient admitted suffering anaphylactic shock, registered with fraudulent ID . . ." Grant shook his head. "Nothing about the arrest." He read on, then whistled. "The patient died, cause to be determined pending autopsy. Patient's name was Harold Lusk."

"Lusk . . . dead?"

"No further details. Pertinent data of fraud case taken under seal by Treasury, see agent in charge. Nothing about Cozy. I wonder if they made a mistake."

"What do you mean?"

"I've seen Cozy. The resemblance to Lusk is remarkable—they could be brothers."

"So you're saying Cozy is dead?"

Grant shook his head. "Couldn't be . . . who was arrested, then?"

"Are you sure the locals turned him over?"

"Chief Moore said they had."

"Who's the agent in charge of the fraud case?"

"Paul Kitcher."

"Hm. So, is there anyone around here who can be trusted?"

"Besides you, no." Grant leaned on his fist, staring at the screen. Then he tapped for a different menu. "Typical."

"What is?"

"Koldehn has his personal accounts data here. I've seen it a lot—account vandalism is one of the most common crimes we investigate. Someone breaks into your personal file and trashes everything, moves things around, takes some of it out, jumbles the codes so badly you can't access your own records. A lot of federal employees store their personal records on protected systems at work, thinking they can't be gotten to through our data security."

"No one thinks someone might break into the building and access it directly?"

"Well, that would be unlikely. How many people do you know with access to federal offices?"

"Oh, I don't know—"

"And override codes?"

Reva pointed at him. "You have me there."

Grant sent a copy to his home system.

"You're piling up a lot of reading for yourself," Reva said.

"I expect to have help."

"Oh?"

"You're not busy tonight, are you?"

"Besides pilfering files, sneaking around secured areas, and tracking down killers, no. Is that an invitation?"

"If you wish."

"People might talk."

Grant indicated the screen. "They are, anyway."

"Different kind of talk."

"You're not shy."

"Don't you know by now?"

"That wasn't a question."

Grant closed the menu, then accessed a building directory. "Let's visit the holding cells." He closed down the terminal. The screen disappeared into the desk. He pulled out his CID and the desk locked itself.

"Do we keep this?" Reva asked, holding up the Tapachula file.

"I don't think he'll miss it." He stood. "At least, not before it doesn't matter."

Marshal Lang drummed his fingers on the console, his mouth set in a straight, unhappy line. "I came in early, that's why I remember the prisoner. Marshal Kenner logged him in."

"Was Paul Kitcher the agent in charge?" Grant asked.

Lang nodded. "I saw the prisoner processed. The log should show that, but . . ."

"Do you remember his cell?"

"Number nine."

"Let's see if he's there."

Lang tapped instructions into the console, then waved for them to follow him into the cell block. At number nine he inserted his own CID into the scanner and entered a code. The door opened on an empty cell.

Reva stared in at it for several seconds, then nodded. "Look at the sheets on the cot. Someone was in here recently, unless you have no custodial service."

"The cells are cleaned and prepped every morning," Lang said.

Reva stepped into the chamber, surveying each object.

"No record at all?" Grant asked.

Lang's mouth rippled briefly, and he avoided Grant's eyes. "No, sir. I don't understand that. Tampering with that system requires high-level clearance."

"Kitcher?"

Lang shrugged. "I have to file a report, start an inquiry."

Reva came out of the cell. "How many marshals are on duty tonight?"

"Just me, Madam. The other three who should be here are at Senator Reed's reception."

"Don't start your report yet," Grant said. "Can you access the security schematics for the building?"

Lang frowned. "Yes, sir, but—"

"I'll get you authorization, Marshal, but I need to get into a secured area."

"I don't understand. The only secured areas are in this section and the labs in your section."

"I think there's another." Grant gestured for him to return to his station. "Let's get those schematics and I'll show you."

Marshal Lang accessed the building plans. The original structure had been built just before the turn-of-the-century. Partly collapsed in the New Madrid Quake, it had been rebuilt and added to. During and after the Reforms, more sections were built, growing around the central structure almost like the chambers of some vast sea creature.

Sections had been rebuilt, refurbished, and redesigned during subsequent decades, and from the look of it, the schematics had been poorly updated. Whole floors were listed as UNOCCUPIED or DECOMMISSIONED.

Grant found the floor he wanted and traced his path to Tochsin's office, then back down the corridor where he had found the storeroom in which he had been mugged. The entire section, including Tochsin's office, lay within an area labeled UNASSIGNED. The only thing visible were the corridors. The rooms were listed by number, but no inventory identified their use.

Grant thought back to the room. Which side had the door been on? He tapped the screen with his finger. The opposite side from where this room butted against Tochsin's office.

He had heard no one enter the room behind him . . .

"What kind of security do you have in this section?" Grant asked.

"Standard," Marshal Lang said. "Motion, infrared, and sound."

"Can you shut it off from here?"

Lang looked uncomfortable. "That's Congressman Tochsin's offices—"

"And by this schematic," Grant interrupted, "they aren't anybody's. So my request can be treated as though for an unoccupied area."

The marshal nodded slowly. "I see. This is still your responsibility if you get caught, Agent."

"Of course."

"I'll see what I can do."

"Thank you, Marshal," Grant said, straightening. He gestured to Reva.

"Why Tochsin's office?" Reva asked as they walked away.

"I'm betting there's a direct access to . . ."

Reva looked at him. "To?"

"Let's find out."

The nighteyes Grant had borrowed from the tactical equipment locker threw Tochsin's office into sharp black-and-white relief. Lang had assured him that the security monitors all routed through his station and that he had shut them off. Still, Grant moved carefully.

Reva closed the door behind her.

Grant went through Tochsin's desk, unsure what he expected to find. No weapons. No loose disks. No files. A personal calendar. Grant opened it on the desktop. The pages contained dates, names, places, cryptic remarks. Grant tapped a finger on one name for Reva, then counted backward to see how many times it appeared. Congressman Tochsin had met with Aurora Campbell of Coronin Industries five times in the last two months. Reva nodded and indicated another name. He had met with Aaron Voley on twelve occasions in the same period. Abernathy appeared only once.

The rest of the desk was empty.

Reva led the way into the adjoining office for Tochsin's aide, Tess Reed. The desk faced the windows. A few framed citations hung on the opposite wall. A pair of comfortable chairs, a sofa, and an HD completed the furnishings.

Grant tried the desk drawers and found them all locked. He slipped his CID into the scanner and tapped in his override code. A moment later the desk spit his card out and remained locked. He tried again, but the system refused to accept his CID or his authorization.

Reva touched his shoulder and motioned him up. She inserted her CID and entered her own code. Nearly a minute went by. Then the screen slid up from the desk and a line appeared beside the cursor:

DOPPLER AJAX ENTER BETA REFERENCE.

"Shit . . ." Reva whispered. She hesitated, then tapped a string into the keyboard, sat back, and waited.

LEVEL THREE ACCESS ACKNOWLEDGED.

The screen cleared briefly, then a menu scrolled up.

Grant indicated her phone log and Reva opened the file. The screen filled with code references and dates. No names.

Grant reached over her and opened a link to his home system, then copied the file into his bubble memory. Reva sighed, closed the file, and studied the menu again. She shook her head finally.

"There's nothing here," she said quietly.

Grant started going through drawers.

The large file drawer contained weapons. Reva pulled one out and laid it on the desk. It was a heavy-looking plastic frame with a thin barrel about fifteen inches long, with a thick rectangle protruding at right angles from both sides just forward of the grip and trigger. A compact sighting mechanism rode along the top of the barrel, and the grip contained a battery pack. There were extra magazines. Reva thumbed out a round.

"Needle gun," she said. "High velocity, hollow shaft, fifty rounds per magazine, two magazines."

A standard-issue .10mm lay in the bottom of the drawer in a shoulder-holster, along with three palm stunners and a pair of nighteyes.

"Why—?" Grant began, then stopped at Reva's short headshake.

She returned the needle gun and closed the drawer, then closed down the terminal. She pointed to the certificates. Grant stepped closer.

Two of them were certificates of merit from Congress, one from the Foreign Relations Committee for exceptional service, the other from the Military Oversight Committee. The third was a graduation certificate from the Quantico anti-terrorist school.

Grant shook his head.

"Good question," she whispered. "This is all military. The security code on her terminal, that needle gun, the diploma."

"You said earlier that she looked familiar."

Reva nodded. "I still don't know from where. I think we need to get into that room you almost found."

"She could still just be a bodyguard," Grant mused.

"A senator's daughter?" She shrugged. "Maybe."

Reva went to the wall adjacent to the windows. She felt along the base. After a time, she stood, and gestured for him to follow.

Out in the corridor, they took off their nighteyes. "There's an entrance in that wall, but it seems to be secure-coded. We could alert whoever's on the other side if we force it."

"Then . . ."

"We go in the way you found."

Grant led the way. They walked silently down the corridor toward the door through which Grant had gone the day before. Halfway there, the door opened. Grant stepped to his left and stopped, back pressed against the wall. Reva had mirrored his move to the right.

A heavyset man exited the room, carrying something beneath his left arm. He closed the door behind him and walked off down the far corridor without glancing in their direction.

Grant hurried to the corner and peered around the edge. At the far end, a firedoor stood propped open. He glanced back at Reva, who indicated that he should follow the man and she would check the room. He nodded and moved toward the firedoor.

He stepped out onto a wide service stairwell. Only red

exit signs lit the cavernous chimney. He heard footsteps echoing from below and leaned over the railing. Three levels down, he saw the bald man with wide shoulders descending the stairs. Grant slipped off his boots and followed.

Grant slowed as he neared the bottom. He dropped to one knee and looked through the space between the upper flight and the railing and saw the bald man open the door into the garage. A board leaned against the wall. He propped the door open with it as he went out.

Grant eased open the door to see out. The bald man had already covered thirty or forty feet. Grant pulled his boots on, stepped through the door, and sprinted on the balls of his feet to the nearest of the wide support columns. The bald man did not look back. Grant started moving from column to column, then between cars, keeping thirty or so feet back.

The bald man stopped at Reva's car. He looked around quickly, then opened the door and popped the hood. As Grant watched, he set the object he carried on the fender, took something from within his jacket and leaned over the engine. Grant crept silently up to the side of the Mercury. The bald man seemed completely absorbed.

Bracing himself, Grant placed both hands on the hood, then slammed it down. The bald man yelped and jerked. The hood came back up and Grant slammed it down again. The bald man staggered from beneath it, his wide face stretched in pain, blood flowing from his nose. Grant hefted his cane, stepped forward, and brought it down on the bald man's neck. He stumbled back against a column. Grant followed and hit him again, dropping him to the floor.

Breathing hard, he rolled the heavy man over and cuffed his wrists behind his back. He noticed that a heavy faceted ring adorned the bald man's right middle finger, then turned to look at what he had been carrying. The object he found on Reva's fender was a small explosive device.

Grant hurried back up to the stairwell.

Reva waited outside the door to the storeroom.

"You'll have to check your car over later," he said.

Reva raised her eyebrows, then gestured for him to follow.

The boxes had been moved from the inside door. Reva pulled it open quietly and they stepped through. They saw no one immediately in view, only heard someone, only heard movement, the small shufflings of paper, and the background hum of electronic equipment.

Tables and shelves held components of various sizes, terminals, tools—a complete workshop occupied space to the right. A wall blocked half the view of the other end of the long room. There were more tables, stools, chairs.

Grant moved toward the wall. As he drew nearer, he saw that it was only one wall of a small chamber.

"Greg should be back by now, shouldn't he?" someone asked.

"Mmm. Want to check on him?"

"He hates that."

"Then don't."

Grant pressed against the wall. Reva stood by one of the workbenches, examining its contents.

"I'll check."

Grant heard footsteps approach. Reva looked up.

A tall man, with thick, stylish hair walked by Grant. He took about four steps before he noticed Reva.

Grant rushed around the corner, into the other part of the room.

"Hey—" he heard behind him. The back of his neck tingled as he recognized the voice. Then came the heavy, plo-sive sound of a palm stunner, and the loud crash of a body falling against one of the tables.

The other man looked around, then. He was older, short, with greying hair, and a lined, intent face that barely regis-tered a reaction to Grant. He moved, instead—fluidly and fast. His hand reached, stretching out toward something on one of the tables.

Grant hurried up behind him, thumbed the contact on his cane. As the man reached his target, grabbed, and began to turn, Grant touched the knob of his cane to his kidney. The charge released with a loud crack and the man stiff-ened. He fell to the floor, a pistol in his hand.

Grant switched the cane off and looked back. Reva came around the corner, nodded her approval, and smiled. "Do you like it?" she asked.

Grant hefted the cane. "Very much. I never thought I was the cane type, but this is good."

She looked around the room. "What do you think?"

"Looks like a very complete covert field operation."

"They're still working on it. *I* would have had sensors at all the exits." Reva picked up a device from one of the tables. "Aerosol. Looks like . . . yes, I'd say this is what you were gassed with." She went over to the man Grant had stunned and turned him over with a toe. "Well, well, it's a small world."

"You know him?"

She nodded. "From Tamaulipas."

Grant grunted. "Why am I not surprised? Do you know his name?"

"It was Peter Fishman down there."

"Do you see anything that looks like a database?"

Reva scanned the room. Grant looked around. They both spotted the portable secretary at the same time. Grant reached it first. "I've seen one like this recently. It's new, very current."

"Only the best," Reva commented. "Anyone we know?"

"Tess Reed." He studied it, frowning. "How hard would this be to crack?"

"Judging from what I saw of her desk system, it probably would wipe everything before we could secure it."

Grant nodded. "So, the question is, what are they doing here?"

Reva went back to the older man, knelt beside him, and began searching him.

Grant switched on the secretary anyway. The small screen immediately requested a password and authorized ID. He turned it off and put it down, then noticed a high-grade code scanner nearby.

"These are controlled," he said, picking it up. "Treasury registers them and monitors their distribution."

"Why?"

"They can open the secured codes in CIDs."

He opened the platen and found a CID. He picked it up and turned it edge-on to read the name imprinted.

"My, my. 'Harold Lusk.'"

Reva sighed. "Really. Why am I not terribly surprised?"

"You *sound* surprised."

"No, I don't."

"*I'm* surprised to find it here." He rapped the corner of the code scanner with his cane. "Why in this? How did they end up with it?"

"Kitcher?"

Grant pocketed the card and gestured toward the old man. "Did you find anything on him?"

"Nothing."

"What was he doing in Tamaulipas?"

"He ran security for the van rental agency. When we started making arrests, he vanished."

"What about the other two?"

Reva shrugged. "Don't know them."

Grant gestured to the small chamber. "Are you ready to find out what's in there?"

"Breathless with anticipation."

It was locked with a drop latch. Grant lifted it and pulled the door open. He stepped back from the thick odor that emerged. Reva curled her lips and waved her hand in mock disgust.

Within, a tall, young man in heavily soiled white utilities lay on the floor in a puddle of excrement and urine. His eyes shifted, uncontrollably, and drool ran down his chin. His fingers curled and opened, and his legs jerked ineffectually.

Reva looked at Grant. "Cozy?"

"One can only guess," he replied.

EIGHTEEN

Gradually, Cozy felt control return to his muscles. The twitching increased for a short while, then calmed, and he lay against the wall, practicing closing his hands and stretching his arms and looking where he chose to look. He vaguely recalled someone giving him another series of injections. Then he became more and more self-conscious of his mess.

The door opened, and a new man stepped into the small cell. He was dressed for the evening, incongruously elegant, carrying a cane and a mass of clothes.

"There's a shower," he said, gesturing with the cane toward somewhere outside the cell. He dropped the wad of clothes. "These ought to fit fairly well. When you're able, take them and clean yourself up."

Cozy avoided his eyes, more embarrassed than he remembered ever being. Once when he was a child and newly arrived at the state polytech, he did not know all the rules and no one would tell him if it was permissible to go back inside during recess to use the bathroom. A simple oversight, a passed-over explanation, no one was really at fault, and, in time, after his classmates tired of teasing him about it, the embarrassment faded. Now and then, though, Cozy remembered that day—just why, he never understood, nor could he pin down what triggered the memory—and a peculiarly intense sense of foolishness came over him and a desire to go back and undo the event. This was worse, though. Someone was at fault, the humiliation had been with intent, and, unlike children, adults never seemed to grow out of their embarrassments. He would have to live with this.

The man left and Cozy relaxed. He flexed his arms, his legs, worked them till he felt confident, then got to his feet. His legs quivered and he leaned against the wall. Bending over to pick up the clean clothes dropped him to his knees, dizzy. He closed his eyes and left his brain whirl inside his skull, concentrating on the threatening nausea. Slowly, his perceptions stilled and he opened his eyes. The floor did not shift, the walls stayed in place.

"—very well-equipped arsenal here," he heard someone say. He strained to hear more. The voice had been feminine.

"Anything here that looks like it might have been used on Beth?" the man asked.

"Pneumatic injectors. And look at this. You can build your own molecules with this, create custom pharmaceuticals. Raw materials here..." Her voice drifted off as she moved away.

"Who *are* these people?" the man muttered.

Finally, Cozy managed to leave the cell. He spotted the woman: she wore a scarlet-and-black evening gown, and was standing by one of the workbenches. She gave him a concerned look, then pointed past him. Cozy followed her finger and saw a shower stall in the far corner. He nodded and stumped toward it. He kept his eyes straight ahead, unwilling to risk the disorientation that might result from looking right or left. He reached the stall, his limbs weak with the effort.

Gratefully, he closed its door and hung the new clothes over the top. He peeled out of his sodden coveralls. The smell was pungent and nauseating, but he did not get sick. He dropped them in a corner and turned on the water. The spray needled his body pleasantly, the warmth working into him. He pressed for soap and turned his back to the flow and let it rinse the effluent from his legs and buttocks.

His memory was jumbled. He remembered the first injection, the first humiliating reaction, and he knew there had been others, till he lay in his own filth, unable to move at all. Questions about Voley, about Harry, about the barco—he could not recall most of them or when they had been asked—and another visit from Kitcher, the federal who had brought him here. None of his interrogators had beaten him after they put him in the cell. The federal had been angry about that. The older man calmed him down, told him Cozy would be cleaned up before they returned him, don't worry. The absolute sincerity in the man's voice had terrified Cozy. He had been certain they intended to beat him again. It would have been useless. Underlying his physical embarrassment, Cozy felt ashamed to know that he would have told them anything they wanted. He knew so little, though, and, convinced he had nothing to give them, he had remained silent. Sure, there were things he had heard Voley say, things George had said, and he knew where Harry's workshop was and what he had been doing, but they knew that, too. At least, they had known where Harry was; Cozy believed that. Though he had not seen them, he quickly convinced himself that these were the men who had killed Harry. So given that they knew just about everything Cozy might tell them, what point was there in giving them an early excuse to dispose of him? It was easy to resist when there was no other option. The trouble now was he could not remember what he had told them.

Cozy closed his eyes and leaned into the stream. He stood there, content for the moment to feel nothing but water running down his body.

Someone rapped on the door.

Cozy pushed himself out of the spray. He pressed for dry, and the water cut off. Warm air swirled up from the fans in the bottom of the stall. He wiped at himself, scraping water. A towel had been thrown over the top, next to the clean clothes. He pulled it down and rubbed his hair, his face, his chest and belly.

"Come on, Cozy," the man called. "We don't have all night."

Cozy pulled on the clean coveralls and stepped from the shower. The man waited there, holding a cup of coffee for him; hesitantly, he accepted it. Perhaps it was only coffee, in which case he would be glad. If it was something else, what choice did he have?

"I'm Special Agent Voczek," the man said. He pointed to the woman. "This is Special Agent Cassonare. You *are* Cozy?"

Cozy nodded and sipped at the coffee. He winced at the heat, then smiled. It felt good.

Agent Voczek pointed, and Cozy looked at the wall by the door through which he had been brought in. His three captors lay there, handcuffed and unconscious, between a pair of marshals.

"Do you have any idea who they are?" Agent Voczek asked.

"No, sir. Sons-a-bitches." He looked at the woman, Agent Cassonare. "Sorry."

She shook her head. "Don't be. I agree with you. What were they doing?"

"Asking me things."

"They beat you?" Agent Voczek asked.

"Not much."

Agent Voczek sighed. "Go on and have a seat, Cozy. Relax. Get some more of that coffee in you."

"They don't work for you?"

"Is there a reason you think they do?"

Cozy shrugged. "Another agent brought me here. Treasury man."

"Agent Kitcher?"

Cozy nodded.

"These men don't work for us," Agent Voczek said. "Sit down, Cozy."

Cozy looked around for a chair, but every part of the room made him uneasy. Finally, he took a stool by one of the tables across from the two agents.

Everywhere he looked he saw equipment he did not recognize. Parts of things he knew, like the scanner, and various tools and guns, but others . . . still, it all had the look of barco product, a polyglot of recycled components assembled into new things. With one difference: none of this had the unfinished, rough look that came out of gypsy shops. This was all polished and refined. These people had had no trouble getting just the right parts, and none of it second-hand.

The two agents seemed to be trying to figure it all out. Cozy cradled his cup and looked at his former interrogators. Who did they work for if not the federals? Watching them, Cozy recognized the look of indecision in both of them. Maybe they were just as illegitimate as those three. The idea frightened Cozy—from one set of rogues to another.

But, then, marshals were present. A few more arrived and the three unconscious men were lifted onto gurneys and strapped down.

"Marshal Lang," Agent Voczek said. "I want this room secured. I also want Congressman Tochsin and his aide found and brought in."

"Sir?"

"My authority."

The marshal looked uncomfortable, but nodded and started speaking into his comm again.

"You're sure about this?" Agent Cassonare asked him.

"I really think this qualifies. And I want access to that terminal."

Agent Cassonare shook her head. "If she's who I think she is, you won't get it."

"Then I want her in a cell."

Cozy listened, watched the marshals take away the rogues, and sipped his coffee. The coveralls itched. He missed his jacket and his new runners.

"So what are you going to do with me?" he asked.

They looked at him. Agent Cassonare whispered something to Agent Voczek, who nodded, and they both came over to him.

"Do you know what they gave you?" Agent Cassonare asked.

Cozy shook his head. "Some kind of muscle relaxant."

"Some kind, yes. I'm not sure how much they gave you, so I had to be careful administering the antigen."

Cozy nodded, though he did not entirely understand. "Bad stuff, huh?"

"Very. Military grade, actually. I'd be very interested in their source."

"Not the barco. We don't traffic in that kind of trash."

"No question. If there'd been even the hint that you might have this kind material, you'd all be in military quarantine on your way to Guantanamo."

"We absolutely don't deal in that kind of thing!" Cozy insisted.

"I believe you," she said.

Cozy swallowed coffee to cover his nervousness. "So. What are you going to do with me?"

"We're not leaving you here. We'd like to ask you questions."

"I don't know anything."

She jerked a thumb in the direction the marshals had taken his captors. "They thought you did. I'd be satisfied just knowing what it was they thought you knew."

"They kept asking me about my cousin."

"Cousin?"

"Harry. They wanted to know about him."

"Harry Lusk?" Agent Voczek asked.

Cozy looked up at him. "You know him?" He laughed derisively. "Of course you know him. You're federal. You know everybody."

"I don't know you, Cozy."

"Everybody with ID. I got no ID."

"Harry did, but instead of using it he used a fake." The agent held up a CID card. "Why would your cousin do that when he had legitimate citizenship?"

Cozy shrugged, suddenly feeling hopeless. They had Harry's card. Did they know where his shop was?

"Cozy, listen to me," Agent Voczek said. "A friend of

mine was killed not long ago. I think you knew her. Beth McQuarry."

That surprised him. "I knew her."

"You were working with her. I have a note from her with your name. I think she trusted you."

Cozy shrugged. He did not know if she trusted him, but she had been concerned about him. She had kept him out of the worst part of her mission, the part that killed her.

"She was a very good friend of mine," Voczek said. "I want the people who killed her. For me it's that simple. I'll do what I have to. I'd like to think you want the same thing, that you'll help us."

"Look," Cozy said, his heart hammering. "Beth was good, she knew a few things. I have nothing except what's in my head. No gypsy has anything but that, 'cause that's all that keeps us whole. When you got only a little you don't spend it all. I know things—maybe—and they're worth something— to you, to them. I give it all away and there's nothing left. What do I do then? What have I got to barter with?"

"We think these men work for the same people who murdered Beth."

Cozy thought about that. He nodded. "Maybe. It's not a bad guess. You need cause, though."

"That's right."

"Maybe something to do with my cousin?"

"Do you know why?"

Cozy drew a deep breath. "Maybe . . . Harry wrote code. Maybe it has something to do with that."

"Who was he writing code for? Mitchel Abernathy?"

Cozy laughed. "Why would he do that?"

"Aaron Voley, then?" Cassonare said.

Cozy looked away, feeling more caught now than

before. Finally, he decided that his choices had run out. "Yes. He was doing work for Mr. Voley."

"Why?"

Cozy shrugged.

"Do you know what has happened to Harry?"

"Dead. That's what Agent Kitcher said, anyway. He was in bad shape, so I think maybe that's true." Cozy finished his coffee. He had not known Harry well, barely knew that he was family. They shared a close similarity of appearance and an aunt, nothing more, and Harry had known Sereta. Acquaintances of acquaintances, a tenuous connection. Still, Cozy felt the loss, a sudden, profound absence in a place a week ago he would not even had known existed. He believed Harry had died in his place, that these men had been looking for him and found Harry instead. He tried to imagine them killing Beth and Harry. "Beth was good. I liked her."

"Will you help us?" Agent Cassonare asked.

Cozy looked up at her and thought, for the first time since he had seen her, that she was an attractive woman. Not like Beth, who was light-skinned and delicate-cute, nor like DeNeille, who was lush and florid and welcoming. Agent Cassonare looked solid, like someone who had seen a lot and could give pain or comfort in equal measure, depending on the situation. Deep eyes, a lot behind them.

Voczek reminded him more of Beth, though on him the delicacy was all facade, a mask over stone. Small, intense eyes, a feminine mouth, signifying nothing. He was a big man, wide shoulders, long legs, powerful. George would even have a problem with him one-on-one.

Suddenly, he recognized him. "You were at Comber Blue's the other day. You were asking about me."

"That's right."

"You were looking for me before they got me. Why? Beth's note?"

Voczek nodded.

"What are my options?" Cozy asked. "What do I get for my value?"

It was Voczek who smiled, when Cozy expected Agent Cassonare to be the one to understand. Cozy held onto his surprise, let it fade below the surface. He revised his estimation of Voczek and told himself never to take this one for granted. Voczek understood Cozy.

"What did Kitcher promise you?" he asked. "Citizenship?"

Cozy nodded.

"That wasn't in his power to promise."

"Is it in yours?"

Voczek nodded. "Is that what you want, though?"

Another surprise. Secure Class people assumed the only thing a gypsy ever wanted was citizenship. A legal CID, job options, secure class rights and privileges. It never occurred to them—most of them—that there were other things that might transcend membership in the club. Voczek did not make that assumption.

"I don't know," Cozy said.

"Your options diminish with time, Cozy."

Cozy tried to figure this agent, the way he had with Beth. She had been straight-and-up with him, told him exactly what to expect, what she wanted, what the consequences might be. She had not considered her own death, though, which had frightened Cozy. He had not considered that he would be pursued beyond her death.

"All I know," he said finally, "is that Mr. Voley thinks something bad is going to happen to the barco."

NINETEEN

Wat does Voley think is going to happen?" Reva asked.

"I don't know, but he's upset," Cozy said, clearly uneasy talking to them.

"Does it have to do with the leak?" Grant asked.

Cozy shrugged. "Maybe. I know he didn't want us to use it. But it seemed a shame not to take advantage of all that stuff."

"The quantities really increased this past year, didn't they?"

"Did they! I never saw so much leak out! Truth is, I can't help thinking maybe Mr. Voley's right, that it's just a trap. Bait, he called it, but he never explained why. Not to me, anyway."

"Who's leaking it?"

"I don't know. Beth—she was trying to find out, but I don't know if she ever did. Maybe. Maybe that's why she's dead."

"Could it be Mitchel Abernathy?"

Cozy shook his head. "It doesn't fit. It's not like him. He's never done anything like it before. I mean, sure, he's dumped some of his excess into the barco rather than pay penalties on overstock, just like everybody else, but he's never been generous."

"We need to have a talk with Voley," Reva said.

"Mr. Voley's a good man," Cozy insisted.

"At least, he's on your side," Grant said. "What was Harry doing for Voley? And why?"

"When Harry came back to the city, Mr. Voley fixed him up with a place to stay. Harry probably did something to pay him back. Harry came from the barco. That's the way we do."

"No, he didn't, Cozy. His family was borderline, close to losing credit, but Harry never was a gypsy—he was a citizen. Why'd he come back?"

"He said he saw things he didn't like. He said he needed time to sort out what to do."

"Do you know who Harry used to work for?"

Cozy shook his head, but Grant did not believe him.

"He worked for Treasury, Cozy. My people." He felt Reva look at him, hard. "He wrote code for us."

"Did he, now? Well, maybe he didn't care for it anymore." Cozy waved his hand to indicate the room. "Is that why they killed him? Do they work for you?"

"I swear to you, Cozy, I have never seen those men before."

"So? Doesn't mean they can't be working for the Department."

Grant shook his head and walked away. Unfortunately, Cozy had a good point. Grant did not know. He did not believe Treasury employed men like this, but the FBI did. In Cozy's eyes, there would be no difference.

"They're not ours," Reva said. "If that's what you're thinking."

"How do you know? The fact is, it could be anybody." He waved at the equipment. "Who set this up? This doesn't look like an outside operation—these people had access."

"You're right. But I don't know anything about it."

"No? You recognized one of them from Tamaulipas. You were down there, Beth was getting information from INS in Tapachula. You must have an idea what this is about."

She sighed heavily. "Theories, not much else."

"I don't even have that."

"From what you told me about the Weston and Burnard connections, it's obvious Coronin Industries is involved. They seem to have benefitted most from Weston and Burnard's acquisitions program."

"Agreed. But how? So far the only thing we can prove is that they want the land the barco is on and that they're taking out the development loan from Abernathy's bank. We can't really tie them to Weston and Burnard directly, and there's no connection between Weston and Burnard and *this*."

"Oh, there is. There *has* to be," Reva said.

"You're guessing."

She shook her head, but her expression was puzzled. "We haven't got it all yet. There's got to be something that ties all this together, but it's not just guessing. Look, Weston and Burnard has bought up failed companies in ten states. In each instance, Coronin Industries has moved into that property. The two names common to everything we've seen so far are Weston and Burnard and Coronin. Now, it could be a coincidence, but I don't think so."

"And Harold Lusk? And Voley? And this place?"

Reva scowled, frustrated. "The same two names still keep popping up. And now that we have Peter Fishman, or whatever his name is, we have a direct connection to Tamaulipas."

"And nothing tying any of it to Abernathy . . ."

Reva narrowed her eyes at him. "Other than the fact that Beth seems to have been investigating him, is there any other reason you want him to be guilty?"

"Look," Grant said, shaking his head, "we need to know more. Get Cozy out of here."

"Are we trusting anyone else?"

"Not at the moment. Take him to your place. I'll meet you there later."

"What are you going to do?"

"I don't know. I have plenty of choices, don't I? I should wait here until they bring in Congressman Tochsin."

"If you're not at my place in two hours—"

"A curfew, officer?"

She failed to suppress a smile. "Call me and let me know where you're going."

"Of course. Anything else, Madam?"

"Not at the moment. Maybe later."

Before he could think of a reply, Reva leaned toward him and kissed his cheek. She walked toward the exit. "Come on, Cozy, we're going for a ride."

"Check over your car," Grant called.

She waved over her shoulder. Cozy looked uncertainly at Grant, then the remaining marshal, then hurried after Reva.

"Marshal Lang," Grant said, "I want this place secured completely. I also want Congressman Tochsin's offices secured, no admittance unless I authorize it." *And while it's secured,* he thought, *I'm going to go through it again . . .*

Grant pushed open Kitcher's office door with the tip of his cane. The lights came up and he stepped in. One wall contained two neat rows of framed citations and commendations. Grant read the list of cities—Denver, New York, Toronto, Cincinnati, Montreal, Newport. Kitcher had been cited for valor, for meritorious service, for civic achievement. There were three from St. Louis, all for exceptional community service.

Grant sat down behind the agent's desk and slipped his CID into the scanner. He tapped his override code into the terminal and the desk unlocked. There were aspects of his job he loathed, and this was one of them: spying on his own, going through fellow agents' private places. He would go home later and shower, but the feeling would linger. He hated it especially when he found nothing—then the violation had been substanceless, and he had made himself feel dirty to no benefit. Finding something did not purge the disgust, but at least he did not feel worse.

The top drawer contained a revolver and three boxes of cartridges. The drawer below held bundles of correspondence. Grant read a few letterheads, but saw nothing that looked relevant. The third drawer was full of disks, all numbered.

Grant slammed it shut. It would take hours to go through all this. Added to what he had just retrieved and sent to his home system from Congressman Tochsin's office, the research alone could take days. He opened the file drawer on the other side.

Empty.

He tapped a command into the terminal. The screen

cleared and requested a password. Grant entered his override code. A few seconds later, a menu scrolled up.

Case files, numbered with names that meant nothing to Grant, climbed up the screen. He spotted one that looked familiar and backed up.

MCQUARRY, D.C.

He tried to open it. Instead, the screen requested another password. He tapped in his code again, but the menu vanished.

FILE DELETED.

"Damnit!"

When he accessed the menu again, McQuarry's file was absent. He connected with his terminal then and continued on. Finally, he came to two files: Dirkenfeld and Agla. He brought his bubble memory on-line and isolated the two files, then transferred them to his terminal. He ordered his prophylactics program to defuse the traps set on them, then closed down the connection.

He stared into the empty file drawer. Paper dust collected in the corners, a little of it scattered over the bottom. Something had been in there recently, judging from the looseness of the paper powder.

Grant reached into the empty space and felt along the underside of the drawer above it. His hand brushed against something rectangular taped against the plastic. He worked it loose with his thumbnail and peeled it away.

A CID. His.

He slipped the card into his pocket and relocked the desk.

There were too many things to do. He checked the time: eleven-twenty. Reva should be at her apartment by now, he decided.

Now what?

He wanted to talk to Richard Dirkenfeld. He wanted to go see Voley. He wanted to confront Kitcher. And Tochsin.

The door opened. Rycliff stood there, mouth open. "Oh. Agent Voczek."

"Good evening, Rycliff. Working late?"

"Liaison work, you know. Uh—forgive me, I'd come in for some information Director Koldehn requested and I noticed—"

"Come in, Rycliff. Sit down. You have some time, don't you?"

"Well . . ."

"I insist."

Rycliff stepped in and closed the door. He sat down and looked at Grant with an attentive expression.

"Do you know much about Representative Tochsin?" Grant asked.

"Not much, sir."

"Does he use his offices here a great deal?"

"He's here almost half the year."

"Why does he keep them all the way on the other side of the building?"

"For his constituents, sir. He has his own entrance, over on Clark Street, so they don't have to go through all the other federal offices on their way to him. Local prejudice."

"Would you say he's a good congressman?"

Rycliff shrugged. "I'm not fond of some of his internationalist opinions. I'm not a strict isolationist, but I see no point in opening the barriers any further than they are now."

"Can't do without any contact at all."

"No, sir. We have to be able to export, after all. But the rest?" Rycliff gave a definitive shake of his head. "When it comes to his service to Missouri, I suppose he's been better than most."

"How are his relationships with St. Louis's principle citizens?"

"Did you have anyone in particular in mind?"

"Mitchel Abernathy?"

Rycliff smiled. "Sir, Mitchel Abernathy has as little to do with D.C. as possible, *including* Representative Tochsin."

"I've heard *him* called a strict isolationist."

"Could be true, but I doubt it. He's a strict capitalist. No, the only times he ever involves himself with anything federal is when he feels violated by us or wants a federal contract."

"What about Aaron Voley?"

"Oh, well, that's different. They use each other, he and Tochsin. They've made numerous public appearances together. Voley is constantly calling on Representative Tochsin to help with some civic benefit. I think they find each other indispensable in many ways."

"How do you know all this, Rycliff?"

"I'm liaison. It's my job to know the community, the agencies, the personalities—their public aspects, at least."

"You seem to do it well."

"Thank you, sir. Is there anything else?"

"What do you know about Richard Dirkenfeld?"

"Again, not much. His family is prominent. He's Senator Dirkenfeld's son. He, however, seems little more than an embarrassment to them."

"Any relationship between him and Tochsin?"

"Yes, sir, quite a peculiar one."

Grant raised an eyebrow. "Oh?"

"Mr. Dirkenfeld's wife works for Representative Tochsin as his personal aide."

Grant nodded. "So I noticed. Senator Reed and Congressman Tochsin—they aren't of the same Party, are they?"

"No, sir. Not even of the same state."

"So how does Tess *Reed* reconcile her job?"

Rycliff cocked an eyebrow. "You would have to ask her, sir."

"I may. What did she do before becoming Tochsin's aide?"

"My understanding, sir, is that she was in the military. Foreign duty."

Grant waited for more, but Rycliff seemed to be finished.

"Will there be anything more, sir?" Rycliff asked.

"One last question. Does Agent Kitcher have an association with Congressman Tochsin?"

Rycliff pursed his lips. "Nothing beyond what his job requires. But . . ."

"But?"

"He *does* seem to have an association with Madam Reed."

"Business?"

"Personal."

Congressman Tochsin had not yet been found. Grant told Marshal Lang to let him know as soon as the congressman was brought in. He also revoked Kitcher's access. He went down to the garage.

He reached across the wheel and tapped the self-diagnostic and waited while his car examined itself. When the blue light on the dash winked the all-clear, Grant started up the Duesenberg and drove out into the quiet downtown streets.

Outside the Daniels-Bennington Hotel, civil monitors wrestled with a mob of protestors. Grant heard the sirens of police vans. A fight blocked the entrance to the hotel lobby. Nightsticks flashed among picket signs, the sound of stunners punctuated angry shouts and screams.

Grant drove on past. The reception above continued, he knew, oblivious to all this on the street. The tagger display had probably long since been cleaned up, new food brought out, and the night set back on track with nothing more than added conversational spice. He had missed Senator Reed's address, which, he was certain, had been modified to include the display. Nothing new. More of Reed's programmatic rhetoric. Grant ignored politics except when it became part of an investigation, but he knew Reed was a power in D.C. His stand on the barter trade and gypsies and the immigration laws had kept him in the Senate for three terms now, and would probably keep him there till the next Reform.

Grant tapped in Reva's address and let the navigator take him there.

It was nearby, four enormous structures along the riverfront. The Duesenberg pulled up before the second tower and a valet hurried up to him.

Reva's apartment was on the fourth floor. She opened the door and Grant hesitated. She wore black loafabouts. She followed his gaze down at herself, then smiled and stood aside.

"I was beginning to wonder," she said as she waved him in.

"Where's Cozy?"

"Asleep. Let him. He's having reactions."

"Should we take him to a clinic?"

"Probably, but he needs sleep now. What he was administered isn't something a public clinic is going to have any experience with."

He stopped at the threshold of her living room. A long sofa stretched against the wall to his left, facing a wall containing mounted photographs. Between sofa and display stood an old, scarred coffee table.

"Sorry," Reva said. "I haven't had time to straighten up."

Grant laughed. He walked down the wall of photographs. Names of artists identified several—Weston, Callahan, Bullock, White, Lange, Cunningham—but most were unattributed: images of streets along ancient brick and stucco walls; a group of laughing children gathered before a fountain; thick-grassed countryside canopied by lush clouds.

"Those are mine," Reva said.

"They're good."

"Thank you. Cuba. In and around Havana, mostly, but that one—" she came forward and indicated an image of old wharfs lapped by dark water "—is from Mariel."

Grant suddenly felt awkward. "You take this seriously, don't you?"

She looked up quizzically.

"Your history. Family."

"Of course. Doesn't everybody?"

Grant shook his head. "I don't know anyone else who does."

Reva laughed. "Really. Maybe you just never asked. Would you like something? A drink?"

"I usually have a sherry by now."

"No sherry, but I've got a good cognac."

"Fine, thank you."

She returned shortly with two snifters, and handed one

to Grant. She sat on the sofa, legs drawn up under her, and looked past him to the photographs.

"My family was thrown out of Cuba. There was a purge, a deportation. Thieves, murderers, rapists—at the time, America took anyone from Cuba automatically. It was policy, no questions asked."

"What category of crime did your family fit?"

He had tried to make it sound like a joke, but Reva's expression turned serious. "Politicals. They questioned the current regime too much. There were others like them, thrown in with the trash, and put to sea in leaky boats. They had a difficult time when they arrived in Florida. When the government realized just what it was Cuba had sent over, they tried to contain the problem. Camps, jails, ghettoes."

"How did they manage?"

"Fortunately, there was already a well-established Cuban community in Miami; over time, the Marielitos were absorbed. My family started their own business."

Grant gestured to the photographs. "If Cuba didn't want you, why the fascination with it?"

"Aren't you fascinated by your homeland?"

"I was born here."

"And that's the end of it? You were born here, therefore there's nothing else?"

Grant shrugged. "Like what?"

"Well, like where your family is originally from. Aren't you interested in Czech?"

Grant shook his head.

Reva looked at him curiously. "Who were your grandparents?"

"I have no idea."

"Do you care?"

"Not really."

"What happened to you?"

Grant swirled his glass, watching the gemlike fracture of light in the brassy liquid. "Why is it whenever someone expresses an opinion at odds with current fashion, the immediate assumption is that something is wrong with him?"

"I didn't—"

"My father was a publisher. He ran a small house that specialized in fiction, but he occasionally took on other books. He did one that criticized the E.C. monetary structure, specifically the credit system. It was a theoretical work that used a lot of euphemisms, like 'freedom of choice,' 'sanctity of privacy,' things like that. It got my father investigated by the state censor. While they were at it, they looked into his fiction publications and decided that he was a general subversive. They closed him down. The book that got him in trouble was published by another house without any further complications, but my father was unable to acquire a license to start up a new house. He migrated here, thinking it would be better. He was allowed in under some old political refugee law, but his history followed him. As soon as it was disclosed that he had been shut down for subversive publications, he was unable to get a license here. They let him be a citizen, but he was barred from doing the one thing he loved."

"There's no federal law that bars someone—" Reva began.

"I know that. He didn't. He didn't speak the language well, he was new in the country, he got bad advice. There was a state law. All he would have had to do was move to another state. No one told him. By the time he found out the truth, he didn't care anymore."

"Your mother?"

"I never knew her. She left when I was two. I never

found out why. Then Germany absorbed the Czech Republic. That was the final blow for my father. He gave up completely. I never understood that—they took away his dream, threw him out, but he still . . . Anyway, a year after the Absorption, he assigned me to a state polytech and I never saw him again." Grant finished the cognac. "History destroyed him. I have no use for it."

"Is it better to be isolated?"

"I'm not isolated."

Reva looked doubtful. "Why do you do what you do?"

"I told you, I'm good at it."

"But—it was the state that destroyed your father."

"And the state that gave me a life. The polytech did more for me than he ever did. Why do you do it? A state threw your family into the ocean."

"Good point."

Grant shook his head. "There isn't an answer to that, is there? Why anything? I became interested. The more work I did, the more I wanted to do it. Where's the mystery?"

She stood and reached for his glass. "Another?"

"Yes, thank you."

"Come on. I want to show you something."

Grant followed her into the kitchen, where she poured more cognac. Then she took him into a bedroom.

Grant felt immediately uncomfortable. The bed was unmade, sheets rumpled. He saw clothes scattered across a bureau, spilling onto the floor. Portmanteaus stood against the wall near the closet.

"Here," Reva said, pointing to the wall alongside the door.

Grant stepped in and turned. Mounted on the wall was a diorama depicting a hillside with a grotto gouged into it. High up the wall of the grotto a statue stood within a carved alcove. The white stone statue showed a woman in gowns from head to foot, her palms turned out from her sides, her face lowered as if she looked down on a crowd gathered at the base of the wall. Off to the right, miniature crosses hung from the tree limbs, the bushes, leaned against the wall of the grotto. Candles in various stages of melting away lined the base of the diorama.

"What . . . ?"

"It's a replica of the grotto outside Lourdes."

Grant shook his head.

"You don't know the story? In the mid-nineteenth century a young girl named Bernadette Soubrious is said to have met a woman here named Aquero. Later, Aquero turned into the Virgin Mary, or turned out to be, whichever way you want to see it."

"That's a Catholic saint, isn't it?"

Reva nodded. "It's not talked about much anymore. After the American Catholic Church adopted the rationalist æsthetic during the Reforms, the saints were relegated to the same category with miracles—that is, quaint unsubstantiated stories."

"Are you Catholic?"

"No. I'm an atheist, which to some is just as bad."

"Then—?"

Reva gestured at the diorama with her glass. "This place—which is in France, by the way, in the Pyrenees—became a focal point of miracles. People with incurable diseases went there seeking cures from the Mother of God. That's who Mary was supposed to be."

"Did they find them?"

"Depends how you look at it. People came away cured, there's no question of that. Many others didn't. I checked. The numbers are hard to find for decades before World War II, but afterward it's not so difficult. So-called miracle cures happen all the time, always did. The fact is, the percentage of cures at Lourdes was about the same as spontaneous cures at any major hospital of the time. Some diseases simply turn off, or the body learns how to beat them before death. Medical science has never been able to fully explain it, only note that it happens."

"So these people would have had the same chance if they'd stayed home."

"That's what the statistics suggest."

"You don't believe it?" Grant asked.

"It's not that. I want to know—I want to understand—what motivates people to do what they do. People went to Lourdes because they believed in something, which pushed them. It formed their ideas, determined what path they took to achieve their ends. That belief—what is that? Why did they believe?"

"An interesting question. What does that have to do with us?"

"Everything. When you look at it, the thing that makes us successful is how well we understand our enemy. What makes them do what they do? Why would they do it? You, for instance—you investigate people who break trade laws. People go to barcos and trade their commodity scrip for goods they could just as easily get legitimately."

"Not all of them—"

"But most, true?"

"Yes . . ."

"So why would they go to the trouble of risking criminal charges?"

"Tax avoidance—"

"They never notice. Taxes come out automatically when they make a purchase on a CID."

"But the commodity scrip is not taxed."

"Of course it is—it's subsidized by CID purchases. So why would they go to the trouble of doing something that in no way makes rational sense?"

Grant pointed at the display.

Reva nodded. "Belief in another way, belief in something, or the desire to experience something different—to embrace the irrational because the rational is just too damn boring. I don't know. Sometimes I find reasons, mundane answers for bizarre crimes. But there are always other ways open. I don't know. So I look at this every night when I go to bed and I ask the questions over and over again. What makes people act on things? What makes them do things the way they do them? Why do they make the choices they make?"

"Does it matter?"

"I think it does."

"Even without understanding, you still find them, catch them. You can still do your job."

"True."

Grant shook his head. "So where's the point?"

Reva sighed. She gestured for him to leave. As he returned to the living room—looking again at the wall of photographs—Grant sensed that he had failed a test. He resented the sensation, but he said nothing, just gazed at the images. When Reva came back in and sat down, he turned.

"So what makes you do what you do?" he asked.

Reva regarded him for a long time. Grant thought she would not answer and started to look away. Then she said, "Because I don't trust anyone else to do it for me."

TWENTY

Grant drove slowly through the throng filling the streets as he returned home. The houses along both sides were brightly lit, and tables stood along the sidewalks, where people could stop for drinks or snacks. He remembered then that a Walking Party had been scheduled for tonight and the next night. He had not intended getting to his house and back out to take this long. They had agreed to go visit Voley together, but he wanted to look at the data he had transferred to his bubble memory first. He phoned Reva and told her he would be late picking her up and why.

"I'll meet you down at Voley's, then," she said, laughing. "Don't worry, I won't move without you."

She broke the link, and Grant worried his way to his house.

Richard Dirkenfeld waited on his front steps.

"So much for an inconspicuous meeting," Dirkenfeld said, grinning. "You changed Beth's lock code."

Grant walked past him to the front door and slid his CID

into the lock. He turned the key and waved Dirkenfeld in. As the man went by, Grant smelled scotch.

Dirkenfeld peered into the living room. "You've filled it up nicely. Beth didn't have much furniture."

Grant shut the door. "You had a key for here?"

"Don't tell me you're jealous. Were you a . . . ?"

"The question is unwelcome."

"Ah. So, then, do we fight about it?"

Dirkenfeld stood in the hallway, a few feet from the stairs, arms akimbo. His expression wavered between fear and defiance. He was unsteady; it would, Grant decided, be easy to knock him down. But what then? Kick him?

"Beth made her own choices," Grant said.

Slowly, Dirkenfeld nodded. "I feel lucky to've been one of them."

"Why did she die, Mr. Dirkenfeld?"

Grant could not read the changes in his face. "Could we sit down, Mr. Voczek? I'm . . . do you have anything to drink?"

"I'll make coffee."

"I meant—"

"I know what you meant. Coffee."

Dirkenfeld shrugged. "Coffee."

Grant went into the kitchen and started the coffeemaker. Dirkenfeld came in and sat down in the breakfast nook. He left hand rested on the table; his fingers drummed, listlessly, arrhythmical, while he stared into nothing.

"She liked Hanson," he said finally. He looked up at Grant. "Music?"

"I know Hanson. Was that what you heard at the symphony?"

He nodded. "It surprised me. We pretend to be a romantic

age, but . . . Hanson was the best romantic composer of the twentieth century and Beth genuinely liked him."

"She liked Sibelius, too."

"A real Nordic lover. You?"

"I'm afraid my taste runs more toward the electric. Hendrix, Fast, Beck."

"Hm! Another surprise. I would have said you were more baroque."

"Why would you have said that?"

Dirkenfeld waved at him. "Well . . ."

"Appearances, Mr. Dirkenfeld?"

"Ah. Well. And Beth preferred late-century cars and you drive that gorgeous—"

"Why did she die, Mr. Dirkenfeld?" Grant repeated, more loudly.

"I'm not certain. I wish I were. I wish I could *do* something, but . . . she used me to mingle with St. Louis's principle citizens. I understood that. It didn't bother me. I use other people for various things. It's all façade."

"You called her the day she died."

"I wanted to see her. She said she had other plans for the evening, but asked me to come over in the afternoon."

"What for?"

"She gave me something for safe keeping." Dirkenfeld smiled ruefully. "I asked her why she thought I would be a safe keeper and she told me the truth. She told me no one would believe that I would be the one she'd trust with anything important." He reached into his jacket and took out a disk. "She was right—no one *would* think that. She gave me a list of names and said if anything should happen to her, give it to one of them."

"My name?"

"One of four. You must rank highly in Beth's estimate."

The coffeemaker chimed. Grant poured two cups and brought one over to Dirkenfeld. He set the mug down and picked the disk up. "This is all?"

"She told me not to call her anymore until she contacted me. Fine, I said, I understand. Then she turned up dead and I stayed away from all of it."

"Were you going to give this to me?"

"Frankly, I gave serious thought to destroying it. Death isn't something I'm willing to risk casually. Whatever is on that, Beth died for it. I've felt under sentence since she gave it to me."

"Do you have any idea who killed her?"

"I have an idea, but it's preposterous, even for . . . well, it's preposterous, so I won't tell you."

"Mr. Dirkenfeld—"

"No. I don't have to, even if you arrest me. You can figure it out for yourself." He looked at his mug. "This probably isn't a bad idea." He lifted it to his mouth. His hand trembled.

"Do you think Mitchel Abernathy had her killed?"

Dirkenfeld laughed nervously. "No, I don't. He's a son of a bitch, true, but he wouldn't do that."

"But she was killed investigating his warehouses."

Dirkenfeld looked up, startled. "That's interesting. But hardly conclusive. Abernathy owns enough space that he sub-lets to smaller firms, out-of-state firms." He shook his head. "In all truth, if I knew anything, I would tell you. Personally, I think you should be looking at Congressman Tochsin and the Mayor."

"What about Aaron Voley?"

"What? He's not—no, I don't see how. Not his forté."

"Beth—she screened for syphilis, Mr. Dirkenfeld."

Dirkenfeld looked shocked. "Not from me, sir. She insisted on french letters."

"Attending Speaks doesn't reassure me."

He shook his head emphatically. "Not from me. As I said, she was insistent." He smiled thinly. "So, you see, in a way, I can honestly claim I never really touched her."

Grant did not remember moving, just suddenly *being* there, on top of Dirkenfeld in the narrow space of the breakfast nook, hands on his neck, thumbs pressed up beneath the man's ear. Dirkenfeld's mouth stretched wide, and his hands shoved uselessly on Grant's arms, his shoulders. His legs kicked weakly.

Then Grant dragged him out onto the floor. Dirkenfeld hung in his grip, unable to find his balance. Grant let go, and the man dropped heavily.

Dirkenfeld coughed, his breath ragged. "You know, I might suggest ... your presence at a Speak ... doesn't exactly let you off ... I mean ... unless *you* never touched her at all ..."

Grant felt the muscles of his leg and hip begin the motion to kick, but he stopped it. He stepped back and leaned against the edge of the sink.

"Thank you for bringing the disk, Mr. Dirkenfeld," he said stiffly.

Dirkenfeld got to his feet. He made a throwaway gesture, then stumbled to the breakfast nook. Coffee had spilled onto the table, but he drank what remained in the cup.

"You know, Mr. Voczek, you remind me of my wife. I never know what's going to set her off." He laughed. "And she can work me over just as well as you."

"I doubt that."

"No, no. She was in the military. Nasty bitch. Great

punch." He wiped at the spills on his jacket, then shrugged. "It was good wrestling with you, Mr. Voczek. If you don't mind, I'll be taking my leave."

"I'll see you out."

"Don't concern yourself. I remember the way. Good luck, Mr. Voczek."

Grant frowned. "Mr. Dirkenfeld . . . when did you and your wife separate?"

"Well . . . we were never really *together,* if you understand my meaning." He looked thoughtful. "It was her father's idea, to marry me. My father thought it was a capital arrangement—in every meaning of the term. Tess . . . she'd been out of the military and working in St. Louis over a year before I found out."

"Had you been lovers before?"

"Briefly." He smiled ruefully. "She told me once that my cock was the only part of me with any integrity—at least it stood up for itself. Good night, Mr. Voczek."

Grant watched him from the kitchen doorway. He considered making him wait so Dirkenfeld could take his clothes from Beth's closet, but Grant could not bring himself to say anything more. He felt the anxious vibration in his limbs from unfulfilled rage and knew he must stand still and let Richard Dirkenfeld walk out the door, untouched.

Dirkenfeld opened the door, turned, and gave him a little wave, almost like a salute. Then he was gone.

Why do people do what they do? Reva's question. Grant did not believe it answerable. He went back to the breakfast nook and stared down at the disk. No answers, he thought, only more information. Always only more information. Conclusions, perhaps, but no answers.

He picked up the disk and his coffee and went upstairs.

* * *

Grant stared at the screen, stunned. Beth had entrusted her complete case file to Richard Dirkenfeld. In a way, it made perfect sense. The man's reputation marked him as irresponsible. He probably did not even know what she had given him.

And his name was on the first scroll.

Not Richard himself, but his father, Paul. Senator Dirkenfeld.

Beth had targeted very large prey.

The Dirkenfelds owned twenty percent of Weston and Burnard. There were others, all the names Stuart had turned up for him, but Beth had managed to compile breakdowns of shares. She had also traced a lot of Weston and Burnard's acquisitions. By law, when a company was purchased, the assets had to remain within their home state. A number of legal dodges enabled firms to by-pass this restriction, but it all required careful monitoring. Assets transferred from state to state did not "disappear" unless the transfer was illegal.

Beth's numbers showed discrepancies in final sales totals. She had done an enormous amount of work. Grant skimmed over the columns of numbers. It was hard to pin down, but assets seemed to be disappearing *within* the states of origin. The acquired companies were all resold inside their state, but the mark-up was minimal, hardly enough to cover the expenses Weston and Burnard created. The buyers seemed interested only in the physical plants, not the stock. Where did the stock go?

Where did Abernathy fit into this? He used Weston and Burnard, too, but he did not own a share of it outright. The volume he transacted was substantial, but not nearly on a level with, say, the Dirkenfelds, and Grant saw no connection between the Dirkenfeld side of the ledger and Abernathy's.

Beth had started digging into Abernathy, then, and the Mayor had received a complaint. Abernathy knew about Beth's investigation. How? This was all data collation to this point.

Grant backed up. Beth had generated a list of all Abernathy's holdings. The only concern he did not own outright was the banking consortium, but he was a major shareholder. Not a controlling interest, no, but close. Another ten shares . . .

One of the other shareholders was Senator Reed's daughter, Teresa—Tess. Also not a controlling interest, but enough to combine with Abernathy's to give him a controlling vote.

But also, combined with her husband's shares, to accomplish the same thing. Grant thought about that. He doubted Richard Dirkenfeld knew the first thing about his own stock portfolio. And Beth had trusted him—to a degree, at least. It would be logical to assume Tess voted their shares together as a block. That would have suited Senator Reed's ideas of a "capital" marriage.

Everyone kept insisting that Mitchel Abernathy was not the sort to murder Beth. Then why was she investigating him? Aside from the shareholder lists, Grant did not see Tess Reed-Dirkenfeld's name anywhere else in Beth's reports.

Tess worked for Tochsin. What was his connection? Grant did not find his name in any of the lists of shareholders. But Teresa held shares of Weston and Burnard.

Tochsin's name was on none of it. The only connection he had seemed to be Teresa Dirkenfeld neé-Reed. How had she put it to him? She took care of the messy parts . . .

Tochsin *did* sit on the Methods and Allocations Committee.

But if this was, indeed, connected to Tamaulipas, how was

Tochsin involved? Reva's investigation had been four years ago and Tochsin had only been in Congress for three years, appointed to Methods and Allocations only this last year.

The next section was about Coronin Industries.

Beth had listed the states with Coronin plants and research facilities. Manitoba, Nova Scotia, New York, Ohio, New Orleans, Florida, Chiapas, Quintana Roo, Oklahoma, and Nebraska. Nebraska. Reed's state.

Chiapas—Tapachula was there. Right next to Tamaulipas.

The report she had requested followed. Missing persons, deportations, more lists. What was she looking for?

Reva suggested Coronin Industries had been involved in the Tamaulipas slave ring. One of their largest plants was in Puerto Morelas, south of Cancun.

Now they wanted a plant in St. Louis. Why?

Grant returned to the lists of shareholders. There was a partial list of Coronin owners, but none of the names matched anyone, not directly anyway—family members held stock. That did not necessarily mean anything, aliases were common enough these days. The privacy laws made it easy to hide investments behind a public façade.

Beth had detailed the Weston and Burnard purchases, the subsequent sales to Coronin. Also, the financing in each state had been arranged through a local bank that had connections, via Wall Street, to Weston and Burnard.

And in each state, in the time between acquisition and sale, almost as a coincidence, there had been a large deportation of disenfranchised following local complaints about expanded barter trade.

Grant sat back. It was an impossible trail. He marvelled at what Beth had done, but he still did not know what it meant. Conclusions. No answers.

He tapped into his bubble memory and transferred the file.

Everything seemed to revolve around Coronin Industries, and yet no one involved to this point had any visible connection to them—except the Dirkenfelds, but even that was inconclusive. Just business. The question remained, what happened to the merchandise from all those acquisitions? Transferred out through barter communes? And then the barcos themselves deported? Someone in D.C. would have to authorize that.

Grant dialed D.C. and tapped the Treasury database. After a few minutes' search he found what he wanted. Hundreds of complaints of barter commune transactions came in every year. Most proved frivolous—insufficient traffic to warrant federal action. State tax shares were not affected by unregistered trade until it exceeded one and a half percent of total volume. Barcos simply did not generate those numbers; they were too small, too widely scattered. Only when a concentration occurred, such as what had happened in St. Louis, did a problem arise. But there did seem to be a lot of such concentrations over the past few years in the states in question. Resource Securities agents had gone in and signed off on deportation warrants.

Federal deportation meant out of the country.

The points of egress were New York, Guantanamo, and Tapachula. Destinations . . . there were treaties with Brazil and Argentina, but after that it could be anywhere. The Third World had never recovered from the epidemics early in the century and suffered chronic labor shortages. Everyone knew what became of deported gypsies. The epidemics that had ravaged most of the world had sealed off the industrialized nations into nearly impenetrable enclaves, hopelessly paranoid about immigrants, the sanctity of their borders, the stability of their economies. With that came a cauterizing of conscience. As long as Americans did not send them into slavery directly no one mentioned it. Let the Brazilians and Argentineans do it.

Grant wondered how this fit with Reva's coup in Tamaulipas. Kidnappings, gypsies assuming citizen's IDs. Not many, he remembered that, the numbers were less than a hundred. That many citizens lost their franchise every year, through personal bankruptcy, or violation of the voting laws, or simple insolvency. Reva had said there were parts, though. Limbs.

Did the gypsies follow the merchandise? Or were they the price?

Or the couriers . . .

The last file on the disk contained a list of trade treaties negotiated within the last eight years with Third World nations. It was an incomplete list, with no explanation.

Grant dialed Reva's number.

The free kitchen across from Voley's house was empty this late at night. A security drone moved slowly among the tables, its small red light winking on and off. Grant walked the length of the block, looking for Reva's car. He checked his watch—after one in the morning—and crossed the street.

Reva stepped around the corner then, Cozy alongside her.

"I was wondering if you were ever going to come over here," she said.

Cozy looked nervous, eyes wide. He kept glancing up at Voley's house, then away.

"What's wrong, Cozy?" Grant asked.

"Nothing." He looked at Voley's house again. "What are we doing here?"

"We're going to have a talk with Mr. Voley."

"I don't think that's a good idea."

"Why not, Cozy?"

"Mr. Voley's a private person. He doesn't like surprises."

"That makes two of us. Come on."

"Why do I have to be here?"

"Because you knew Beth McQuarry. I wonder if Voley knows that."

"I'm a private person, too. He doesn't need to know everything about me or my friends."

"But I suspect he does. Come on."

The front door opened before he could knock. Aaron Voley stood, backlit, in his foyer, wearing a smoking jacket and pajama pants.

"I wondered how long it would take you to work up your courage," he said. Then he looked past Grant. "Cozy . . . I am surprised. I had heard you'd been arrested."

"I was, Mr. Voley."

"And now you're in the company of the two new federal agents. You have a penchant for people from D.C." He sighed, coughed mildly, and stepped aside. "Please come in. It is not a proper hour for decent people to be out."

Voley led them into his study. The air smelled musty. A tray of cups was on the sidebar. Voley sat down in his high-backed chair. "Cozy, Cozy, Cozy, I am disappointed in you. You might have trusted me more."

Grant looked at Cozy, who scowled.

"You didn't trust me, Mr. Voley."

"I trusted your good will toward your cousin."

"It's not my fault Harry's dead."

"Maybe not. I'm not sure you didn't precipitate matters. No, Cozy, you didn't kill him, but those who did acted only after you made some ill-advised choices."

Cozy looked down at his feet and said nothing.

Voley turned to Grant. "You've come back, Mr. Voczek. And this is . . . ?"

"Special Agent Cassonare," Reva said. "FBI."

Voley nodded. "The FBI. We've attracted the rabid dogs."

"Are you pleased with yourself for that?" Reva asked.

"In a peculiar way. It's about time something other than a Treasury agent showed up. Our problems are larger than that."

"I gather," Grant said, "that you're willing to tell us something now?"

"No, but I have few options. Please, sit down. You, too, Cozy. I don't intend to blame you for anything. Refreshments?"

"No, thank you," Grant said. Reva shook her head. "What's going to happen to the barco, Mr. Voley?"

Voley smiled sadly and shook his head. "I've spent a good portion of my life trying to undo the mess the Reform created. You're both young, you weren't even born at the time. It's hard to make people of your generation understand. It's hard for me to understand and I watched it happen. And I'm about to fail."

"What does the Reform have to do with any of this?" Grant asked.

Both Voley and Reva said simultaneously, "Everything." They looked at each other with open surprise and Voley chuckled. "Are you a student of history, Agent Cassonare?" he asked.

She nodded.

"Your associate is not."

"No," Reva said. "I don't think he sees its importance."

"Then," Grant said tightly, "enlighten me."

Voley grinned. "With pleasure."

*   *   *

"Things . . . were simply a mess," Voley said. "In the most technical sense of the word. Just when we thought the solutions to most of the world's problems were within our grasp, the world snatched itself away from us and ate itself up. Africa is still blockaded—unofficially, of course, but very thoroughly. The epidemics that swept across the Third World after the turn of the century were all blamed on Africa, even though they were far more victim than villain. Panic on a global scale. The expense was crippling for the developed nations and they finally just gave up. That's how the world began to look the way it does now. Borders were closed, trade ground to a halt, migrations were turned back, often by force. For all intents and purposes, it was a world war. Us against Them. Literally. Us being those with property in the western tradition of the term, and Them being everyone else. The depression that struck made the one a century earlier look like a minor slowdown. That only worsened the problem because the resources that had been flowing back and forth and keeping it all afloat ceased flowing, and everything sank. There's no way to estimate the death toll since the turn of the century. I remember reading an article shortly after the Reforms, a piece defending the continuation of America's space program. Through satellite tomography the population of the globe had been estimated. The tally indicated a decrease of nearly thirty-five percent. Personally, I think that's conservative, but enough is enough. It has resulted now in a global shortage of labor.

"Add to that the New Madrid Earthquake of 2012, which devastated the mid-west and diverted all remaining resources to the internal clean-up and rescue and you set the stage for the Reforms. In fact, the Reforms did a lot of good things. We have survived. For the most part, we have survived quite well. You would never know the world had been at the brink forty-odd years ago. You, Mr. Voczek and Agent Cassonare, have grown up in a society that has solved most of the problems that plagued it in the last century. Of course, there are new ones, but nothing is perfect.

"To whit: I give you Cozy and all those like him. Gypsies, you call them. People without citizenship because they have nothing. No property, in any case. Nothing that matters in the scale of things. Every society has had its margins, its groups that never fit properly. But we managed finally to codify it. We know who they are because we know who we are. We. The citizens. We who vote, we who work, we who spend. Everyone gets a CID. Everyone but those who don't get one. Those who get one must vote. It does so much. The state—or states—get the mandate, the census gets its statistics, the taxes get distributed by population, so much otherwise impossible bookkeeping gets done just by using that little card. And those who don't have one don't count. They have no say.

"Which has been convenient for municipalities. A ready source of cheap labor—just feed them. And the food is free, anyway. Shelter them—citizens are guaranteed shelter after all, and most of them don't use their housing quotient, give it to the gypsies. Clothe them, inoculate them, take care of them. And we do. Until it's time to scapegoat them for something. Until, perhaps, their own economic activities become embarrassing or the numbers grow to a point where the credit balances are affected. And then we just deport them. After all, there's a labor shortage out in the Third World, isn't there? We don't call it slavery because we don't actually sell them. Do we? But it's become part of business now, the kind you don't talk about *inside* the boundaries of the country because it only goes on *outside*. You and I can't own one—pardon me, hire one. Not legal. But . . .

"And they are defenseless. They have no voice. Except for the occasional political neanderthal like me. I jeopardize my own citizenship every time I open my mouth on their behalf. You see, it's become a convenient threat as well. All kinds of problems can be dealt with through creative use of the gypsy population. It's all just numbers somewhere in D.C. Or the state capital, but I think they're less perpetrators than middlemen.

"All this from the Reforms that supplanted pre-Reform constitutional law and civil liberties. The riots you've heard about—attributed to the hard times in the aftermath of the depression and the New Madrid. Partly true—nothing that large is ever from one cause—but they occurred *after* the Reformist platform was adopted and the first wave of changes instituted."

"What does all this have to do with what's happening now?" Grant asked.

"I'm coming to that. All this is necessary to let you see how we have allowed ourselves to become what we are. We have to have a certain mindset, a certain direction in order to act in certain ways. Without these things—gifts of history—we wouldn't tolerate this crap for a second."

Voley walked over to the sidebar and poured himself a drink. "I have a large database, Mr. Voczek. Spans the country."

"The gypsies?"

Voley nodded. "And what I have learned in the last several years scares the pants off me. You see, the epidemics—they've continued. Not the same ones, no, but once you break down a system of support and let the locusts loose, they perpetuate themselves. A dozen new diseases in as many months sometimes. It goes on and on. We're isolated, for the most part, but you simply cannot isolate a whole continent forever. We still have to find cures. Or vaccines."

"We have been."

"True enough. For some. But nature is magnificent in its mutagenic capacity—and its indifference. The work is never ending. Results are demanded constantly, faster and faster. The irony is there's no choice. It must go on."

"Coronin Industries?" Reva asked.

"Among others, but they're the largest. How do you develop, test, and market a brand new drug in less than a year? Less than six months?"

"The hard part is the testing," Reva said.

"Exactly. The only valid test, is a human test."

Grant looked at Cozy. "Gypsies."

Voley nodded. "And the survivors can be sold overseas. No matter what their condition."

TWENTY-ONE

That's what Beth said." Cozy stared at Voley, feeling suddenly displaced.

Voley gazed back at him, sadness softening his eyes, gentling the tightness in his mouth. Cozy looked at the two federals and felt his pulse quicken. "She told me she was trying to find out about the disappears, that she thought all the new stuff coming through the barco was connected."

"How?" Agent Cassonare asked.

Cozy caught the narrowing of Voczek's eyes. He knew. The federal nodded slowly.

"Coronin wants that area for their new facility," Voczek said. "It's close to the locks on the river. Except for the barco it's vacant. They can build what they want. Probably any local codes have been waived by the Mayor."

"So . . ." Cassonare mused. For a moment longer, she seemed puzzled. Then her eyes focused. "So someone starts dumping goods through the barco, enough to draw a Treasury investigation."

"We rubber stamp a deportation order to close it down," Voczek said.

"And what becomes of the gypsies?"

"Well, if Mr. Voley is correct, they end up belonging to Coronin. Part of the deal. Coronin gets a new site, close to major river transportation with ready access to the Gulf, and over ten thousand new test subjects and potential off-shore product."

"Beth found out?"

"Beth knew," Cozy said. "She told me she knew. From before she came here."

Voczek nodded. "The question is, who? Abernathy? Tochsin? Dirkenfeld? Reed?"

"Or all of them," Cassonare said. She looked at Voley. "Your last talk with Agent Voczek wasn't so forthcoming. Why are you talking to us now?"

"I have little choice," Voley said. "Harry's death has forced me to this. If you hadn't shown up tonight I would have come to you tomorrow."

"Harry . . ." Cozy said. "What does he have to do with all this?"

"Harry was going to get you all out of this, Cozy," Voley said. "Why do you think I became so angry with you?"

"The CIDs?" Voczek ventured.

"Harry was the best," Voley said. "And he was a decent man. It would be worth a lot to me to find his killers."

"He died of an allergic reaction," Cozy said. "An ice cream truck gave him the wrong cure . . ."

"They don't do that, Cozy," Voley said. "They don't get it wrong. Your cousin was murdered."

Cozy watched. The two federals said nothing, standing like statues, while Voley seemed to shift and alter, growing smaller, narrower, but remaining physically as he had always been. From his separate place—temporary, he knew, a point reached only by shock or indifference—Cozy tried to make it all form a pattern, like a tagger display. Voley was the centerpiece, the real locus from which the work unfolded. He knew what was going on. He always had known. The federals knew parts, some of which were larger than what Voley knew, but they needed Voley to make sense of them. They were learning. Power—the locus—was shifting to them. They did not have it all yet. Beth had known more than they, but even she had not managed to put the patterns together before the end.

So Harry had been murdered. Like Beth. In both cases the killer remained unknown. Cozy felt certain at least one of the three men who had interrogated him was involved, but they were employees. Who? Coronin Industries? Then how was Agent Kitcher involved? He was federal, apart from all this.

Cozy knew less than anyone, but he sensed the pattern.

Beth had gone after Mitchel Abernathy, but Cozy doubted that connection. Abernathy had benefitted the gypsies in the past, dumping surplus merchandise. It was a common enough practice when a company overproduced, overbought, and undershipped. Get rid of it. Keep the ledgers balanced. Excess stock tilted the projections, made the economy falter. All numbers, Cozy knew, like everyone knew, but he had never believed in them the way Secured Class citizens believed. To him it was always only a pattern.

Abernathy's participation in this did not fit the pattern.

Cozy looked toward the windows at the faint sound of car doors closing.

Cassonare went to the window. "Are you expecting any other visitors, Mr. Voley?"

"No . . ."

A loud shattering sound came from the back of the house. Voley pushed himself to his feet, eyes wide, mouth slack—fear, which Cozy had never seen in his face before.

Voczek took his arm, mouthed "Down!" and urged the old man behind his chair.

Cassonare turned off the lights.

Cozy pressed himself back against the wall. In the sudden darkness he felt caught, unable to move. His eyes adjusted slowly and he strained to hear. The house became a space of isolated noises, creaks and taps, rustlings Cozy could not make match to anything sensible. No pattern. He saw vague forms move about the room briefly, then nothing.

The streetlights showed the windows clearly. Where was George? Camilla? It had never occurred to him before to wonder about Voley's security, but now it seemed odd that the old man was alone at this hour. He considered sneaking to the back of the house and checking the sunporch, but he did not know where the two federals had gone. He did not want to be mistaken for an intruder by them. He had tried to run from Cassonare when they had arrived at her apartment complex and somehow he had ended up face-down on the pavement, a breath-stealing pain in the middle of his back. She had lifted him easily to his feet and moved him like a doll into the building. Beth had surprised him that way.

From the back of the house came a sharp crack, then a thud. A few seconds later, a gun went off. Cozy dropped to the floor, shaking. He crawled in the direction of Voley's chair.

"*Mr. Voley,*" he hissed. His hand found an ornate chair foot. "*Mr. Voley, it's Cozy.*" He pulled himself around and reached into the space behind the chair. He touched fabric, which jerked back from him.

"Cozy . . . ?"

"Yes, sir. It's me."

"Cozy . . ."

"We got to leave, Mr. Voley."

He heard Voley move. "We can't, Cozy."

"We *got* to! They killed Harry, now they're trying to kill you!"

"Check the window, Cozy."

Cozy nodded and began to crawl away. He stopped halfway across the room to listen. The house was still. He realized then that Voley would not have been able to see his nod and considered going back to tell him he was on his way to the window. Stupid, Cozy, he thought, and continued.

He edged up against the wall and peered over the sill. A limousine waited across the street. Further north another car was parked. He saw no one, which frightened him. He crept back to Voley and told him what he had seen.

"The back way," Voley said. "Only way, now."

"What about Camilla?"

"Out this evening . . ."

"We got to leave *now,* sir!"

A sharp pop made Cozy jump.

"The back way, Cozy. Go on."

"I'm not leaving you."

"I understand, Cozy. I'm right behind you."

Cozy moved in the direction of the entryway. Its outline was visible now, a large square of black in the dim grey wall. The hallway beyond was lightless. As Cozy reached the door he looked up. A window at the top of the stairs to the second floor let weak light glow in, outlining the banisters. It was enough for him to find his way.

The view down the length of the hall, through the kitchen entry, was unobstructed. The windows in the kitchen shone blue by the alley lights. Cozy crawled toward them, quietly.

As he reached the threshold of the kitchen, he heard a sound behind him. He glanced back, expecting to see, dimly, Voley crawling in his wake. He saw nothing, though. He stopped and stared. Then he looked up slightly. Two small ovals hung in the air, reflecting light from the kitchen. For a moment, Cozy did not understand. Then, about a foot below them, he caught the glint of light along a metal shaft, like a finger pointing toward him.

His insides churned instantly and his muscles seized.

Suddenly, the finger and the glassy eyes jerked to the right. A heavy impact sounded against the wall and Cozy heard a swift rustle, followed by a solid blow and a deep groan.

His paralysis ended. He scrambled forward, into the kitchen, across the tile floor to the sunporch, and out onto the wooden deck. A high, keening wail pierced his inner ear and he knew it was his own scream, held back tightly so that only a thin leak of air made a sound only he could hear. He fell down the back stairs, smacking his chin on a step, scraping his right arm from wrist to elbow. He kicked his legs and rolled down the last two steps, to the stone path, onto his feet. He bolted for the gazebo, yanked the door open, and fell inside.

He climbed beneath the stone table and sat there until his breathing slowed. The alley lights cast black shadows in the monochromatic jumble of the yard.

Cozy looked to the right and saw legs stretched out from a chair. He stared, disbelieving, until he also saw a hand hanging limply. He eased out the other side of the table and stood cautiously.

Someone lay in the chair, eyes open and fixed on the ceiling of the gazebo. Cozy touched him and he did not move. He felt his neck for a pulse and found nothing.

Then he saw another shape, propped against the low wall. He crawled on hands and knees around the table to this body. His hand slid in fluid, warm and slick on the bricks. He stared at the face.

The entire front of his clothes were wet. Cozy touched the fabric, felt a rip in the cloth. "George . . . ?"

Startled at the sound of his voice, Cozy dropped to a crouch behind the table. When he had heard nothing for long enough, he left the gazebo, keeping low, and went to the high fence between this yard and the next. He jumped and caught the edge. His feet swung against the wood. Cozy, terrified, pulled himself up and over and dropped into the next yard. He bolted to the next fence, which was lower, and into the next yard, and so on down the length of old, venerable houses.

When he reached the end, he vaulted the fence and came down, hard, in a vacant lot. Without a backward glance, he sprinted across the empty street and into the gangway between two businesses. He did not stop running until he reached Benton Park.

Cozy sat on the slope of grass above Highway 55; on the opposite side sprawled the old Busch complex. Once only beer came out of those buildings, but Busch Consolidated was a widely diversified company now.

George dead . . . Cozy could not get his mind around it. At least, he thought, George killed the guy that killed him, for all the difference that made.

Of course, it made a difference, he realized. That one had been on his way to the back door of Voley's house. Cozy would not have gotten out if George had failed.

It seemed a cheap trade, though.

He rubbed his face and tried to sort through everything. Lies, half-truths, this fact, that one—none of it added up right, all of it confused him. No one could be believed. The two federals knew too little, Beth had known too much, Cozy knew nothing at all. Harry might have cleared a lot of this up, but he was dead, and now George was gone, and Cozy had no idea if Mr. Voley was still alive.

Mr. Voley was the only one, Cozy felt, whose word was reliable. If the man did not intend to tell the truth he kept silent. It was hard to dislike a man who helped people. Cozy had never known his cousin Harry well, but he knew Voley had saved him from becoming one more disenfranchised body in the barco and helped him into Secure Class society. Cozy had taken pride in the fact that a member of his family—someone he actually knew—had a legitimate identity and a CID. And Mr. Voley seemed to be siding with the two federals. It was thin, but Cozy had nothing else to lean on.

Cozy stared across the highway, a new feeling working its way into him. The fear had passed with distance. He still jumped at odd sounds, but the tension faded quickly and he could think.

Word had circulated from one barco to the next for years about growing numbers of vanished gypsies. Word was that it was like the old deportations, only worse. A lot of them were secret and those that made the HD no one really cared about. There were reasons, causes, Secured Class anxieties to assuage. The world was a dangerous place, had always been, but Cozy had begun to think things were getting better. The stories he had heard about the world when he was little— about the epidemics and the border conflicts and the break-downs and the days of the riots—were about things that no longer happened, a dim, nontime kind of place.

The old stories no longer mattered. No one cared, he knew that, had always known that. They were just stories, told because they drew attention, made people feel hopeful that maybe things might be different, but nobody really took them seriously. If they did the world would be different, or become different. The stories had power to impress the naïve. Cozy had clung to them because it felt better than not having them.

But Harry—who had gotten out and made good—was dead.

George was dead, too. Somehow that was more disturbing. Cozy had always looked on George as being almost indestructible. He had been in the military, had served overseas with the U.N. George was *good*. So anyone who could kill him was better.

Beth had died first, though. And there were all those who had disappeared from the barco over the last several years. They had stories, too. The police, the federals—ghouls of one sort or another. Of course there were also slavers, but no one ever admitted that those stories were true. But none of those who disappeared ever came back to dispute them, vanished into nontime.

There was life, lived hard and close to the edge—that was Realtime, what the gypsies claimed to have. Whatever Secured Class did it never seemed real—they had Faketime. Death, the disappears, kidnappings, the vanished—Nontime. Waiting for death or oblivion, Cozy now thought of as Federaltime. No matter, he decided, everybody is on their *own* time . . .

Cozy could not work it all out. There was a pattern, sure, but he did not understand it. Clearly it all connected, became one thing, but he failed to make it resolve.

The Mayor, Mitchel Abernathy, Congressman Tochsin,

Senator Dirkenfeld—they all lined up on one side, under the heading of a company called Coronin Industries. On the other was Mr. Voley, Agent Voczek, and Agent Cassonare, all of whom might be dead now. Like Beth. So the federals were probably all right, which Cozy found an odd thought. Everything he had been raised to believe, everything he had been told the country had become since the Reforms, was based on the tacit belief that federals were not all right. But so far in this the only people who had seemed to want to help at all were federals.

Then, again, there was Agent Kitcher.

So nothing is a monolith, Cozy thought. Mr. Voley used to say that when he gave lessons in the park on politics and law and community action. Cozy had taken it for granted, but had always acted as if certain things, like governments, were monoliths. For the differences to matter one needed power. Gypsies had no power.

As it stood now, the only people who might have been trustworthy were dead.

So if he did anything it had to be based on that.

Who did the killing, though? He had names: Abernathy, Tochsin, Dirkenfeld, and Reed.

Perhaps he would start there . . .

The door opened after Cozy's fifth round of knocking. A dark face scowled out at him until she recognized him. The door swung wider.

"Cozy! Good Jesus, where the fuck you been?"

"DeNeille, hi. Sorry."

DeNeille, housecoat falling open, grabbed him by the collar and pulled him into the apartment. The door slammed and Cozy was enveloped by strong arms. His hands went automatically beneath the housecoat, finding warm, bare skin. She kissed him from the right ear, to his cheek, to his mouth.

"DeNeille—wait—"

She tucked at his zipper. With an effort, he grabbed her hands and stopped them.

"Wait," he said.

She gave him a puzzled look. "What's wrong? I haven't seen you for a week and—"

"Wait. Please."

She stepped away from him. Demurely, she pulled her housecoat closed. "All right."

"There's trouble. I need your phone. I need to call Sereta."

"At this hour?"

"At this hour."

"This *must* be serious. You don't want me, you want my phone so you can wake Sereta up."

"I don't think Sereta's sleeping."

DeNeille shrugged and waved him to follow. He walked across the small kitchen behind her, down a short hallway, into the oversized living room. Her bed was stretched across the floor from its hideaway in the wall. A reading lamp on the stand beside it shined down on an open book. Cigarette smoke curled up from the ashtray next to a half-empty glass.

"Help yourself," she said, gesturing to the replica turn-of-the-century vidphone on the opposite nightstand. She spoke with an exaggerated indifference Cozy found infuriating; she used it when she was completely baffled and did not want to admit it.

Cozy sat down on the edge of the bed and tapped Sereta's number. It rang twice.

"Yes?"

"Sereta?" The screen was blank; Sereta did not have a

vidphone. He glanced at DeNeille, who suddenly looked more interested.

"Cozy, is that you? Where are you? What's happening?"

"Sereta, Harry's dead."

"I know, I heard early this evening—"

"So is George."

"Oh."

Now DeNeille was frowning intently. She sat down beside Cozy and took his hand gently.

"Sereta, there's trouble. I need to talk to Comber Blue and the others."

"Where are you, Cozy?"

"I'm with DeNeille—she can bring me up. I need to talk to them as soon as possible, Sereta. It's important."

"All right, Cozy. I'll see what I can arrange. When will you be here?"

"Soon as I can. Is it safe? Nobody's watching you?"

"No, not that anyone's seen."

"Get somebody to watch. There's serious trouble."

"Be careful, Cozy."

"Nothing but."

The connection broke.

"Good Jesus, Cozy," DeNeille said quietly. "What the hell have you got into?"

Cozy closed his eyes and leaned forward. He felt DeNeille's fingers begin to work on his taut neck muscles.

"More than I ever thought there was," he muttered.

TWENTY-TWO

Grant put on his nighteyes the moment Reva turned out the lights. He adjusted the optical amplifiers, and the house snapped into stark black-and-white. Reva, wearing her own set, nodded once and disappeared up the stairs. Cozy and Voley lay on the floor. Grant stepped out into the corridor and heard the faint *snick* of the front door lock opening. He retreated into the hallway between the front hall and the kitchen and pressed himself back against the wall, hoping the frame of the entryway was deep enough to hide him.

The front door opened. Grant heard whispering, then a soft padding sound. He looked down and saw Cozy crawl past him, down the hallway toward the kitchen.

Cozy stopped just inside the kitchen and looked back. A man walked by, a long-barreled pistol in his hand, gaze fixed on Cozy. Grant chanced a look around the frame. The foyer was empty.

He stepped quickly up behind the assassin, brought his cane around, and jerked back against the man's throat. The assassin struggled briefly and Grant jerked the cane again, then heaved the man against the wall. He jammed the crown of the cane into the assassin's sternum, then again into his throat. The man slid limply to the floor.

Cozy was crawling quickly toward the back porch. Grant considered following, then heard movement on the second floor. He glanced back into the hallway, but saw no one. He heard something in the living room, though.

Grant crouched in the pantry and looked into the kitchen. Where was Reva? He had lost track of her in the first minute.

Tile creaked. Grant hefted his cane, thumbed the switch, and waited near the pantry door. Another assassin, wearing black head to foot and a pair of nighteyes, walked by the pantry. He held a short automatic rifle at waist level. He stopped and began to raise it.

Grant stretched out the tip of the cane and touched him below the armpit. The cane discharged with a loud crack and threw the man across the kitchen. The rifle clattered away. Grant stepped forward and picked up the rifle. It was a purely functional instrument, no grace to it at all—a military weapon. Grant aimed ahead of him and went back down the hallway.

Voley sat in the entryway to his study. As Grant came around, into the entrance, he saw someone kneeling beside Voley, reaching toward his neck with a pneumatic injector. Grant kicked out and caught the wrist. The assassin did not lose the injector, but stumbled backward, off-balance.

Grant moved forward, swinging his cane down, and missing. The assassin scurried back, out of reach. Grant raised the rifle.

"Don't," he ordered.

The assassin hesitated a moment, then lunged for him.

Grant turned the rifle to fend off a blow, but the assassin collided with him. He sprawled across the floor, losing his cane. He tried to hold the assassin and roll over to get leverage. The attacker seemed small, but moved fast. Grant caught a kick with his upper thigh, hard fingers pressed against his face, searching for his eyes. He felt a hand work on the strap of the nighteyes and he twisted his head, but lost his grip and the assassin jumped away. A toe impacted his left shoulder. His leg ached and his breath came hard, but he managed to get to his feet. As he straightened, he saw the assassin running out the front door.

"Grant?" Reva called.

"I'm all right!"

Grant pushed himself up. His head swam for a few seconds as he staggered to the front door. The lenses adjusted for the brilliance of the street lights in a moment. The assassin sprinted across the street and into the back of a limousine parked across from the house. The car was beginning to move. Grant fumbled with the adjustment on the left side of the nighteyes and suddenly the scene enlarged, the car jolting forward to fill his vision with nauseating abruptness. In that instant he saw nothing to distinguish the vehicle, no labels, no odd marks, but he was certain it was the same car that had followed him from Chief Moore's house.

"Grant?"

He went back to the study. Reva knelt beside Voley.

"I'll stay with him," she said. "Check the rest of the house."

His leg throbbed and lungs ached, but he went upstairs. Two bedrooms, another study with more books, a bathroom, walk-in closets. Grant found another body on the rear balcony. He looked down into the yard, but saw little through the dense foliage. He limped back downstairs and checked the dining room and the parlor. Empty. He went out into the backyard.

Cozy was nowhere to be seen, but Grant found two dead men in the gazebo. One looked familiar, but Grant could not place him. His stomach had been ripped open by a knife that lay nearby. The other's neck had been broken.

Grant went out the back gate, into the alley. Nothing.

Reva switched on the lights after he returned. Grant peeled off the nighteyes, grateful for color once more.

Voley still sat propped against the edge of the entryway. He did not appear injured, but his face was disturbingly vacant. Reva gave him a quick, efficient examination.

"No wounds," she said. "Help me get him to his chair."

Grant, ribs and leg protesting, took an arm and lifted. They walked Voley back to his highbacked easychair and set him in it gently.

"Mr. Voley?" Grant said. "It's all right now. They're gone. It's over."

Voley shook his head listlessly. "My home. They . . . my home."

"Grant." Reva stood over the one she had taken down in the hallway. As Grant came up to her she gestured. "Look who we have here."

Grant looked down at Kitcher's dead face. "Shit."

"Gesundheit."

Grant glanced at her, chagrined, and she smiled. "What about the rest of them?"

Two of them had been in custody earlier. The others Grant did not recognize, nor did Reva.

"Agents . . . ?" Voley leaned forward, elbows on knees, hands dangling, crossed over each other. He looked better than he had a few moments earlier, but his skin was pale and damp.

"Sir?" Grant prompted.

"It's come further than I thought," Voley said.

"What has, sir?"

Voley shook his head. "You must take me to the barco."

"Mr. Voley," Reva said, "you don't appear to be hurt, but you should be examined—"

"No one touched me, Agent Cassonare. I'm just . . . frightened. But I must go to the barco. Tonight."

"Why?" Grant asked.

"I have responsibilities—"

"So have we."

Voley's attention seemed to sharpen as they watched. He gave a decisive nod. "It's the barco that is being used by these people. If you want answers, that's where you'll have to go to get them. They won't talk to you unless someone vouches for you. That will have to be me. Otherwise, you'll likely never find out what's going on. It's your choice. I'm going to dress. You think about it."

He stood with an effort and left the study. Grant heard him ascending the stairs.

Grant saw something at the foot of the stairs. He picked it up. "Well, well." He held the injector out for Reva. "The one that got away was about to use this on Voley."

Reva took it. "Like the ones in Tochsin's lab. It's still loaded. Good." She slipped it into her pocket and waved up the stairs. "He's direct," she said. "What about it?"

"What about what?"

"Do we take him?"

"We have a mess to clean up here—"

"They're dead, Grant. They won't go anywhere."

"He wants us to help him break the law."

"Is that a problem for you?"

"It's not for you?"

Reva shrugged. "How else are we going to get at this thing? Kitcher is lying in the hall. He was here to kill Voley. Someone—probably Kitcher—let those other two out. That happened too fast for my comfort. Kitcher was working for the same people. I want to know who they are before they succeed in killing me. Or you."

"I'd left instructions to bar Kitcher access." Grant looked around the living room until he found the phone. He tapped the federal building code and waited, then entered the department number. "Marshal Lang, please."

"Marshal Lang isn't here, sir."

"Where is he? He was on duty earlier."

"He was called away, out of the building, sir. May I give you to Marshal Kenner?"

"Yes."

A few moments later, a new voice came on the line. "This Marshal Kenner, how may I help you?"

"This is Special Agent Grant Voczek. Where is Marshal Lang? I left him on duty with a special assignment."

"I don't know, sir. He was called away at the request of Assistant Director Koldehn. I believe he went to assist with a disturbance at Senator Reed's party."

"I left three prisoners with him, restricted access. Where are they?"

"Just a moment, sir . . . my log doesn't show anything."

"Nothing?"

"No, sir."

"Did A.D. Koldehn come by there earlier this evening?"

"I wouldn't know, sir. I was called in to replace Marshal Lang after he had already left. Let me ask." Grant heard a muffled exchange. "No, sir, no one here remembers the manner in which Marshal Lang received the call."

"Have either Congressman Tochsin or his aide been brought in?"

"Sir?"

Grant sighed. "Never mind, Marshal. If Marshal Lang returns this evening, please have him contact either me or Special Agent Cassonare."

"Yes, sir."

Grant hung up the phone and looked at Reva.

"I think we should take Voley where he wants to go," she said. "At this point I don't think we can rely on anyone."

Grant wanted to reject her analysis, but he could not. Even as he tested it for flaws his intuition embraced it, told him she was correct. His reluctance, then, baffled him. "Do what is necessary" had always been his personal prescription. If he did that, now, Reva became the only dependable ally. The enemy. He discovered himself both attracted and repelled by the idea. FBI and Treasury did not mix, the same with every other agency. Cooperation was discouraged, distrust promoted; that was the way it had been since the Reforms. Probably before that, even. To trust her meant letting go of by-the-rule. But by-the-rule gave him no options. As far as he could tell, no one could be trusted.

Was that the only thing?

No. He had wanted to settle this alone, for Beth. Accepting Reva's assessment—and all its consequences—meant abandoning that particular quest.

"What's more important to you?" Reva asked.

Grant shook his head. "I don't know."

"Then maybe you'll find out."

"Are you always reckless?"

"No . . . in some things I'm very careful."

"What things?"

"Associations . . . friends . . ."

Voley came thumping down the stairs. "Well?"

Grant looked up. "Where exactly in the barco, Mr. Voley?"

Reva raised her eyebrows, startled. Then she grinned.

The thing that never made sense to Grant about barter communes was how quiet they were at night. The jumble and chaos of them seemed at odds with such peacefulness. During the day the babble of people, the crash and stutter of hammering and drilling, the general cacophony of a hundred pieces of music and conversations and children playing all fit the landscape. At night the smoke from cookfires and small smelters glowed above the mass of bizarre architecture, lit by every possible source—fire, gaslight, carbon, LEDs, fluorescents, halogens—spreading in all directions. Deep within it, sense of place faded, the improbability of it worked against acceptance and peace of mind. And the stillness made it dreamlike, a phantom landscape stepped into from the real—an encampment on the edge of Acheron.

Grant followed a few steps behind Voley and Reva, who helped the old man as he led the way through the labyrinth of tents and shacks and hovels. Occasionally, Grant saw a face looking out from under a flap, gazing up from its position amid a jumble of other artifacts, or someone walking the same path. Each time he saw recognition as Voley passed by, replaced then with suspicion when they saw Grant. As they moved closer to the center, Grant felt as if the attention of the barco turned on him, like the gaze of some enormous predator.

Voley stopped. "Wait here, both of you. I have to talk to them alone first."

Before Grant could speak, Voley stepped beneath the flap of a sprawling tent. In the dark, Grant could not tell how large an area it covered, but it was possibly the largest single mobile structure in the barco.

"Don't worry," Reva said with mock seriousness, "I'm here."

"Thank you, officer, I'd be so afraid without you," he returned dryly.

"May I ask you a personal question?"

"Always."

"But will you answer it?"

"Maybe."

"What made you the way you are?"

Grant laughed, surprised. "I thought you'd ask if Beth and I had been lovers once, or something difficult like that."

"Well?"

"I thought we already had this conversation."

"We started it. You never finished."

"Why do you want to know?"

"Do I need a reason?"

"Probably not. But maybe I need a reason to tell you."

"True . . . I guess I thought you already had one. Was I wrong?"

"Mmm. I don't know. I suppose that depends on what way you think I am."

"You're very by-the-rule."

"Ah."

"Formal."

"Forgive me, but I'm not very comfortable talking about myself."

"I know."

"Well . . . the polytech my father put me in had more than an average allotment of immigrants."

"I thought you were born here."

"I was, but try to convince people of that when your parents weren't. At least, my father wasn't. My mother . . ."

"You said she died?"

"She left. Anyway, I ended up classed with the real immigrants. By the time I graduated I learned two things. The first, be formal. People can't get a real handle on that, it's difficult to attack. Insults . . . well, it's no fun teasing someone who simply doesn't react."

"And the second?"

"All you really have is what you carry in your head. Everything else is just decoration."

"That includes family?"

"What family?"

Reva nodded, though Grant saw doubt in her expression.

"May I ask you something now?"

"Fair is fair," she replied.

"Why didn't you take the promotion?"

"I told you I prefer—"

"That nonsense about 'juice'? A promotion doesn't mean you retire from field work. Besides, that just doesn't feel right."

Reva paused. Then: "All right. It was a bribe. The promotion was to a section where I wouldn't be able to pursue the Tamaulipas case anymore. It was offered to stop me."

"Does this have anything to do with Senator Reed?"

"No, we'd crossed paths before that."

"Your three-month tour on a desk?"

"That was the result of an investigation into an alleged cover-up. Two Interpol agents had been investigating a black market weapons corridor. Hardware was being sold across the Balkans into Ukraine. They came here with information that one of the primary shippers was American with former military connections. Both of them were found dead in their hotel. The murders were classified almost instantly. Senator Reed is on the Foreign Relations Committee. His office contacted Interpol outside of normal channels. Shortly after that, Interpol retrieved the bodies and asked that all further investigations be discontinued. That's when I got into it."

"Sounds like a cover-up to me," Grant said.

"But why? Obviously, someone connected to the Committee—or Reed himself—was involved in the arms trade."

"You never found out who?"

"No. Only that before I got very far I was relieved of field responsibilities and put behind a desk. I learned later that the order had come from Reed's office, but I never found out why. I asked him."

Grant's eyebrows went up. "Personally?"

Reva nodded. "I believe in going to the source."

"What did he say?"

" 'Young lady, you must be mistaken. You should be careful about that. Mistakes can be fatal.' "

"Subtle."

"My military sources verified that it was someone who knew the military, probably someone who still had access. Reed had never served, though, so I thought it might have been a colleague."

"But you never found out."

"No. Shortly after that I was down in Tamaulipas."

"And then you were bribed. Any connection?"

"Do vinegar and sugar taste the same? I don't see it. No, it was a different source this time: Senator Dirkenfeld."

"And now the two of them seem to be involved in this."

"Could be coincidence."

"Is that what you think?"

Reva shook her head. "That wasn't the sort of personal question I expected," she said. "Don't you ever think about anything but the mission?"

"Of course I do. Just not during a mission."

"Sounds terribly by-the-rule."

"I have the feeling you would really rather not bother with rules. You'd be just as happy with anarchy."

"Maybe as a vacation, but no more. I just don't think you should let rules define you. They're tools, you use them."

"I agree."

"Then . . ."

"Then what? You want something from me. What?"

"I like you. I want to know you."

"So—"

"So comparing career profiles doesn't quite satisfy."

Grant shook his head. "I don't know what you're asking for."

"What did Beth ask for?"

"She didn't."

"Really? You were lovers, weren't you? Lovers give things to each other."

Grant felt his ears warm, a tingle spread over his scalp. "Is that what you want?"

"I don't know. You haven't shown me enough yet for me to decide."

"But enough for you to consider it."

"Enough to interest me."

"I don't think you want to know more."

"Oh? You have *secrets?* Things that bother you when you take them out and look at them?"

"Something like that."

"Do you think that makes you unique?"

"No."

"Then what?"

"How I manage them does."

Reva frowned. "I'm willing to share mine."

"And in return I'd be obliged to do the same. Friendship as barter. You'd make a good gypsy."

"Do you see everything in terms of economies?"

"No, not at first. But everything seems to become that."

Reva looked off across the barco, her face momentarily lost in shadow. "Every Treasury agent I know collects old money. Like Koldehn, with his mounted bills, like its some sort of symbol for what you do. I haven't seen yours."

"I don't have one."

"Why?"

"I think it's silly. An affectation. I'm not interested in things that don't do anything anymore."

She nodded thoughtfully. "So what do your secrets do? What makes them worth collecting?"

The tent flap opened. Voley looked out at them. "Would you both be so kind as to come in now?"

The man called Comber Blue sat on a camp chair at the center of a semi-circle of older gypsies. Grant counted eighteen. Gypsies did not have leaders in any organized sense, in Grant's experience, but they had a group that held the community's respect—older gypsies usually, ones who had survived and prospered, whose visible assets demonstrated their intelligence. Not so very different, he had always thought, from any other part of society. But there was no formal title, no election, no process whereby the community designated a spokesman or a leader. As far as Grant had been able to tell, a group like this just spontaneously formed whenever a barco grew large enough.

"Aaron says you helped him," Comber Blue began. "He's been a good friend to us. We thank you."

Grant nodded his appreciation.

"I know you," Comber Blue said. "You came here the other day looking for people."

"Yes."

"Now what do you want?"

"A friend of mine was murdered investigating a commodity leak into this barter commune," Grant said. "I want who did it."

Comber Blue grunted. "That would also stop the leak, wouldn't it?"

"Presumably. Depends on whether or not the people who killed my friend are the same ones causing the leak."

"They are."

Grant started. "You know them?"

"Them. Not who they work for. The question here is do we want to stop the leak. It's been good. Lots of product. Lots of component."

"Has Aaron explained to you what we believe is going to happen?"

"Yes. But it's your theory."

"No, it's his."

Comber Blue shifted his gaze to Voley. "Aaron?"

Voley nodded. "That's why I had Harry making cards."

Comber Blue scowled. "Never fails. We find a good place, business is good, problems are few, and always—*always*—there's a fucking catch." He drew a deep breath. "Question is, do we accept this? And if we do, what next?"

"Why wouldn't you accept it?" Voley asked.

"Aaron, friend, you're Secured Class. Doesn't matter what you've done for us. In the end, you and the federal here are on the same side."

Voley looked crushed. "I have never—how . . . ?"

Comber Blue shrugged and looked at Grant again. "Some gaps can't be bridged. You are what you are, you can't change that. At least, not with a little piece of plastic with some coding. Give anyone here one of those and at the end of the day all you got is a gypsy with access, not a Secured Class citizen."

"People change," Grant said.

"Sure," Comber Blue agreed. "But only a little and not easy. Look at Aaron—he's been a friend to us, helped us. Has he done it for us or for himself? He's the only one can answer that. But one thing's obvious—he thinks helping us means making us one of you. He accepts the standard."

"Realtime versus Faketime?" Grant asked.

Comber Blue grinned. "You know about that?"

"I don't," Reva said.

"A question of what's real," Comber Blue said. "Secured Class, they try everything to keep reality out. You don't want to know about dying, you don't want to know about sickness or worry, you don't want to know about struggle. Everything you do, you do to shut all that out. You make a nice, polite world to live in that's everything reality ain't. Faketime."

"The gypsies, on the other hand," Grant said, "because they think what they have is closer to the bone, claim to live in Realtime."

"Every day's important," Comber Blue said. "No time to waste, it's real, it's currency, it's what you have."

"So what's yours is yours and we can't have it."

Comber Blue shrugged. "You don't get it."

Reva grunted. "So what makes you any different than us, then?"

Comber Blue stared at her for a long, uncomfortable

moment before shifting his gaze back to Grant. "You want to stop a leak. That's your job, I respect that. It's your law, I don't respect that. But . . ."

Grant felt a smile begin and stopped it. "But?"

"Aaron might be right and maybe we ought to be thinking about that. It might be even Secured Class can tell the truth. So . . ." Comber Blue's eyes seemed to brighten. "Maybe we can trade."

TWENTY-THREE

Sereta told him not to do anything, just get himself to her place as quickly as possible.

"I got work to go to in the morning, Cozy," DeNeille said as she dressed. She managed to look deeply worried and angry at the same time.

"Things are falling apart," Cozy said. "Don't worry about your job."

"Easy for you to say. When was the last time you had a steady job?"

Cozy glared at her, but she was not paying attention. He did not bother to answer. She was only venting, anyway. If she were really angry, he thought, she wouldn't be taking me to Sereta's.

He looked around at the apartment. It was tiny, barely large enough for DeNeille and a couple of friends to sit around and talk. The fold-down bed took up most of the living floor, so she had to move furniture out of the way every night. The kitchen had room enough for one person to cook in, two people to sit at the small table and eat. One closet and a shower. For this DeNeille worked four days a week, ten hours a day, bussing tables at a restaurant she could not afford to eat in. The only reason she had the job, Cozy thought grimly, is because the law required it. Drays did work like that better than people, and, in fact, *did* do the work, but someone—like DeNeille—had to supervise.

The doorbell rang.

DeNeille looked at Cozy, frowning.

"Are you expecting anybody?" Cozy asked.

"At this hour? Good Jesus, no!"

She started toward the front door, but Cozy jumped up and grabbed her arm. She opened her mouth, but he shook his head insistently and held a finger to his lips.

Cozy went to the front windows and looked down at the street.

"Ice cream truck," he said.

"Not for me!"

Cozy frowned. "No . . . I wouldn't think so . . ."

"Cozy, I am *not* doing anybody else!"

"Keep it down." He moved away from the window. "You still got that old stunner?"

"Y-yes, but it hasn't been charged in I don't remember how long."

"Get it."

"Cozy, it's just Civic Health—"

"No, it's not. An ice cream truck killed Harry."

"What?"

"Just get the stunner."

DeNeille squatted before her dresser and dug around in the bottom drawer. The bell rang again, followed this time by a heavy knock. DeNeille waved the stunner in the air and Cozy held out his hand. She closed the drawer and brought it to him.

He switched on the charge. The small meter on the grip indicated that it was charging, but it was slow.

"Get your card and your coat," he whispered to her. "Get ready to move. Back stairs."

"Cozy, it's just—"

"It's *not!* Just—listen. Please."

She nodded and fetched her things, then went to the kitchen door. Cozy could see her from the living room.

Cozy went to the front door. The stunner finally indicated a charge, but it was weak and he only had one. He swallowed hard and held it chest-high and waited. Another knock came.

He yanked the door open. A man in white coveralls stood there, hand still raised to knock. Another man stood behind him, to the right. Cozy recognized the first man instantly—the older man, the one who had directed his interrogation. Cozy shoved the stunner forward, against his chest, and squeezed the contact.

The weapon discharged. The man stiffened, seemed to jerk in mid-air, eyes wide, teeth bared. Cozy shoved him with both hands into the other man, who tried to dodge. Cozy charged out the door, head down, and caught him with his shoulder. He rammed him back against the wall, heard a sharp gasp. He fell with the man, who raised his arms to grab Cozy. Cozy pushed the arms away, stood, and kicked straight down onto the man's face.

Then he was back in the apartment, door closed, locked, and running after DeNeille, who was already halfway down the back stairs. Cozy plunged down the steps, waiting for the shot from behind, amazed when he reached the ground. DeNeille started her car and reached across to open the passenger door. Cozy looked up at the back porch and saw no one. He climbed in and DeNeille, grim-faced, hands clamped around the wheel, mashed the accelerator and shot down the alley.

Cozy's breath came hard and fast. They reached the end of the alley.

"Turn left!" he shouted.

"What for?"

"*Do* it!"

She obeyed, the little car slewing sideways almost onto the opposite sidewalk.

"Go around front," he said.

"Cozy, we—"

"*DeNeille!*"

She slowed and turned down the street in front of her apartment building. The ice cream truck was still parked.

"Pull across the street," he said.

"What are you going to do?"

"You go to Sereta's and stay there," he said, getting out. "Don't go to work tomorrow. They know where you live, then they know where you work."

"Who?"

"Those are the sons-of-bitches that killed Harry. *Please*, DeNeille, don't make me explain it now."

"But what do you think you're going to do?"

"I'm taking the truck."

Her eyes widened. "Good Jesus, Cozy—"

He slammed her door and waved for her to go on, then bolted across the street.

The doors were unlocked. He climbed in and crouched low. The back was unoccupied. Relieved, he studied the dash and realized that the vehicle was still running. He checked the ignition scanner and found a CID in place. He laughed sharply. The arrogant shits, he thought. They left the damn thing on.

Cozy glanced back at the building. No one had come out yet.

"Shit," he breathed, and laughed again. He put it in drive and pulled away.

He took a winding path down side streets until he had to use a major avenue, then drove downtown. He had stopped long enough to check the contents of the van. He found another pair of white coveralls and put them on. The rest . . . dispensers, analyzers, a couple of rifles—since when had they been standard issue in a Civic Health van?—and a lot of equipment he simply did not recognize. It did not look legal, though he could not have explained why.

He did not want to take it up to the barco, fearful that it could be traced. But he did not want to simply return it to the owners, either. He drove to the federal building and parked in the garage. Somehow it did not surprise him that the automatic security had passed the van without question. He left it in the longterm section of the garage, where older, decommissioned vehicles waited. It was the best he could think to do. Walking away from the ice cream truck, he looked up and down the length of vehicles with a twinge of nostalgia. As a child he had played in here—what was the fun in playing where playing was allowed? The riskier the venue, the better. He and his friends had dodged the security drones, pretended to be cops or federals, ran from hiding place to hiding place. Sometimes they were caught, but usually they managed to spend most of a day in here, and in other places around the city where they should not have been. What amazed him now was how familiar it looked. Perhaps some of these cars were the same ones . . .

He left by an old service conduit. The hinges on the exterior door ground slightly, long unused, but no alarm went off, and he sprinted east, toward a shuttle station.

A foot patrol lounged outside the entrance, nightsticks hanging from their belts. One other person preceded Cozy through the doors. Cozy forced himself to act normally. He smiled at the officers and they nodded back to him. He almost laughed out loud when he stepped through the entrance.

A new stunner was in one pocket, a second CID in the other. He used the CID from the van ignition in the autoteller and was passed through. It felt strange and exhilarating to actually ride the metro like a citizen. The interior of the car was all dark wood paneling and velvet. People gave him odd looks because of his Civic Health coveralls, but, as he expected, no one said anything. He took a seat near the doors and pretended to nap.

He had no idea what he intended to do. Talk to Comber Blue maybe, tell him what had happened. They should pick up camp and leave. That much Cozy understood. Even if most of what the two federals had said proved false, St. Louis was not a safe place for gypsies anymore. And after that? Go elsewhere. Cozy did not want to think about that. He did not know anyplace else. All other cities were just names, and the rest of the world meant Guantanamo, Brazil, Africa—Europe was impossible and nobody said anything anymore about the Russian Federation. China? Cozy did not even know where that was. No matter. The only way he could leave the country was through deportation, and that automatically limited his choice of destination.

Or so he had always been told. What if that was a lie, too? George had been overseas. He had almost never talked about it. When asked, he had told Cozy, "No place you ever want to be." George could have stayed in the military, too, but he chose to be a gypsy instead.

The sexless voice from the metro's loudspeaker announced the arrival at the Hall District station. Cozy got out and ascended the stairs to the exit. He pushed through the doors, out into the night air, and found himself at Broadway and Branch St., just at the southern edge of the maze of warehouses and factories, easily two miles south of the barco.

"Aw, chee-s!" He looked back inside at the metro schedule. The next car was scheduled half an hour later. Shaking his head, he started trudging up Broadway.

Highway 70 ran under the Adelaide overpass. Cozy looked down onto a convoy of trucks rolling down the exit, turning toward the industrial area. He stopped to watch them, impressed as always by their size and power. Seventy-odd feet from cab nose to trailer apron, the massive machines seemed to slide along as though they weighed less than a car, the hum of their turbines generating a deep vibration in his chest. He wanted to drive one someday, though he knew there was little chance.

The last one moved away from him and he sighed. He noticed that the poo-tag on the rear bumper listed point-of-origin as Ohio. He turned and headed across the overpass and into the barco.

He kept his head low and his hands in his pockets as he hurried toward Comber Blue's. Dressed as a Civic Health monitor made him stand out in the barco. Not many people were still awake at this hour, few were out on the paths, but he caught looks from open shanties, felt resentful gazes follow him. He only hoped to get through before someone decided to challenge him.

As he drew near Comber Blue's, he looked behind him. Several people followed. Cozy's pulse quickened. Another ten yards to the sprawling tent and he might be safe. He took the chance and broke into a run. Someone shouted behind him and he heard them start running, too.

He made the tent and flung wide the flap.

"What the fuck do you want?"

Cozy looked up at a large man with dark, deep-set eyes and an aluminum baseball bat in his left hand.

"Straight-and-up!" Cozy said loudly. "It's Cozy! Harry's cousin! Cozy!"

Hands closed on his arms and pulled. Cozy felt himself slip away from the light within the tent.

"Hold! Let him go!"

Cozy fell backward amid a tangle of legs that closed around him. He threw his arms up to cover his head, but the blows never came. Suddenly, he was lifted to his feet and dragged within the tent.

"Hell of a disguise, Cozy!" someone called out.

Cozy looked around, laughing nervously. The faces around him grinned, a few laughed. Then he saw Voley, sitting alongside Comber Blue, and he raised a hand.

Next to Voley sat the two federals.

"Good Jesus, Cozy!"

He spun around. DeNeille pushed through the first row of gypsies seated on the ground. Sereta followed.

Cozy opened his arms and she came into his embrace, quickly, heavily. Then she pushed away from him and punched him solidly in the chest.

"What—?"

"You have got me in *trouble,* Cozy!"

"DeNeille—"

"My *job,* Cozy! I have a job! It's four in the morning! How am I supposed to do my job without any sleep?"

Cozy felt his relief transform to anger. "You'll get another one! You ain't the one about to be sold down the river!"

"Cozy."

He looked around. Voley shook his head. Comber Blue stared at him, mouth cocked in a half-smile that did not look in the least amused.

"Cozy."

It was Voczek, the federal. Cozy felt a flare of rage at him, but it faded quickly. "What?"

"No one's selling anyone," Voczek said. "I'm going to prevent it."

"You think you can?" Cozy snapped.

The other federal, Cassonare, said, "By himself, no. But with me? What do you think?"

Comber Blue got to his feet and waved Cozy to follow him. They went back into Comber Blue's stock, through the narrow aisles between crates, and stopped near the back. Comber Blue turned to him.

"Cozy, we all know you worked for the federal that died. That doesn't matter now. I want you to tell us what you know."

Cozy felt anxious. He wanted to leave as badly as he had wanted to come here. "I—"

Comber Blue held up a hand. "Don't confuse loyalties now. It's not the time. Mr. Voley, those two federals, everything we've been seeing the last year—something's wrong, Cozy."

"Listen to him, Cozy," Voley said. The old man stood at the end of the aisle, leaning on a box, looking very tired in the dim, scattered light.

"Mr. Voley, you never told me what the cards were for," Cozy said. "You weren't straight-and-up with me."

Comber Blue jabbed him with a pair of stiff fingers. "You weren't straight-and-up with any of us, either. You did work for a federal. For some, that's as good as treason."

Cozy wanted to argue. His actions with Beth had seemed perfectly reasonable at the time, but now he could find no way to explain. "What do you want me to do?"

"Come back in there and tell us what she had you doing. Answer the federals' questions. Now's the time to be straight-and-up. We got a problem."

"None of us are free of guilt," Voley said. "We all thought we were doing the right thing. It's turning on us."

Cozy looked at Voley. "Why do you have a problem? You're Secured Class, a citizen. So you do charity for gypsies, so what? That's no crime."

"No," Voley agreed, "but credit fraud is. Come on, Cozy. We're all involved now. It's time for complete honesty."

"Look, who's to say those two won't do the same thing to us that the mayor's trying to do? We tell them everything we know and they go out and be heroes and what happens to us?"

Comber Blue nodded. "Good questions, Cozy. Fact is, we don't know. But they tried to kill Mr. Voley tonight, which means our problem is their problem. It's possible . . ."

Cozy waited. When Comber Blue and Voley added no more, he grunted. "You don't know what to do any better than I do, and I don't know shit. All right, I want something for this."

Comber Blue's eyes widened briefly, then he nodded. "What's the trade?"

"I'll go in there and be straight-and-up, but I want out before the cage closes. I want a couple of Harry's CIDs and passage out. I'm not staying around to get sent south or have my heart stopped."

"Fair enough," Comber Blue said.

"And for DeNeille," Cozy added.

"It can be arranged," Voley said. He looked sad, almost frail. "Shall we?"

When they came back into the main area, the quiet babble of conversations ceased and everyone looked at Cozy. He stepped into the center of the group, swallowed hard, and cleared his throat.

"I did work for Beth—Agent McQuarry. She paid me. The deal was mutual, a fair trade. I didn't think she'd end up dead."

As he talked he fell into a kind of trance. He did not see the gathering around him. He saw Beth. She smiled and laughed more than his experiences with any other law had led him to expect. He remembered little of their talks together, which bothered him because he could not trace the route by which she had convinced him to snoop for her.

He remembered the first time he saw her, though. He had been arrested for tagging. Not the first time by far, no doubt not the last time. Waiting in the common cell in city jail for arraignment and process, after which he expected to be assigned civic duty—cleaning parks, painting, removing tags, street monitor—for which he would receive a certain amount of pay-in-kind, like clothing, food, surplus commodities, he remembered looking up and seeing her staring at him through the bars. At the time he had tried to ignore her, but the expression on her face had been one of recognition, and that bothered him more than he wanted to admit. A few hours later, he had been pulled out of population and brought to an interrogation room where she waited.

"What's your name?" "Cozy." "Want to earn some extras?" "Sure." "It's federal work." "Hell." "Does that bother you?" "Only if you want somebody dead." "Good. My name's Beth McQuarry."

And it started. So simple. His civic duty became federal work. All he had to do was go find out what she asked him to, all work around the edges of the barco. At first, it had been fun. She had him slipping into places in the Hall District where gypsies were not allowed. Go in, check out an address, find out what the traffic is like, tell her. Count things. It had been random. Cozy had seen no pattern then, but gradually one began to emerge. She started seeing that dandy, Dirkenfeld, and he had told her he had a reputation. Why did it matter to him? He liked Beth McQuarry, she treated him better than any other Secured Class citizen. It was narcotic, that treatment, something Cozy felt he could get used to. He had even found himself contemplating his future life as a citizen.

So he did not break it off when she started asking him more direct questions about certain traffic. He gave her answers, tried to tailor them to hide people he knew, but she had been sharp. What he held back she had figured out, and the next talk had better questions, more details. He knew he should have disappeared when she asked him directly about Harry and Voley.

What was worse, he had stolen for her. One of Harry's new CIDs. Yes, she had one. Cozy did not know where it had gone, and it bothered him when Voley asked him for only the one he had kept for himself.

He had liked Beth McQuarry. When he had learned of her death, his first reaction had been rage, anger that he had been betrayed, that his friend was gone. Then resentment that his passage into citizenship had been taken away.

Then fear.

He had found the source of the leak for her. He had told her. Pointed it out. And she was dead. He should have left St. Louis then.

But this was home.

Why should he have to leave his home?

TWENTY-FOUR

Grant listened and remembered. Beth had been one of the most persuasive people he had ever known. Like Cozy, he had never been able to pin down how she did it. He had felt oddly relieved when he realized that she did it as a matter of course. It was as much a professional skill for her as a personal trait. But that only made sense. She had been very much what she did and that clear mingling of surface and center had drawn him to her.

Cozy finally wound down. He stood in the center of the gathering, hands in pockets and head low, looking like a caught child.

"So where is the leak, Cozy?" he asked.

Cozy looked up. "I tell you that and you'll stop it."

Grant nodded. "You knew that when you told Beth."

Comber Blue cleared his throat. "It's a little late to assert gypsy loyalty, Cozy. Tell the man."

"Why don't *you* tell him, then?" Cozy said.

Comber Blue waited silently. Grant thought he understood. Cozy had broken the faith, stepped outside the gypsy line. Comber Blue knew what Cozy knew, but he would not say. *He* had not betrayed gypsy trust.

"All right," Cozy said. "The MCHI warehouses. It's all been flowing out of there. But that's not the whole thing. It's what's been flowing *into* those warehouses that Beth needed to know. Those warehouses are just the end-point of the leak. The leak's being supplied from all over the country."

"How do you know that?" Grant asked.

"One of the things she had me do was follow poo-tags. A lot of truck convoys carry stuff in there that never comes out in the legal market."

"Poo-tags from, say, Nebraska and Oklahoma?"

"And Ohio. Matter of fact, there was one tonight."

"Shit," Reva hissed.

"Beth was killed at those warehouses," Grant said.

Cozy nodded and looked away.

"So it *is* Abernathy," Reva said.

"I don't think so," Grant said.

"He's got to know, at least—"

Grant shrugged. "Cozy, who killed Beth?"

"I don't know, but I'd take odds that those men you got me away from were part of it. The older one showed up at DeNeille's place tonight."

"DeNeille told us. She said you drove off in the van. Where did you take it?"

Cozy grinned. "Parked it where they won't figure to look."

"That van is evidence, Cozy," Reva said. "It better still be there or you and I will have a private talk."

Grant got to his feet. "I want to see it, Cozy. Take us."

"It's all the way downtown—"

"Not the van. The delivery. I want to see MCHI."

Cozy looked worried. "Now?"

"If it's there now, yes. A little late to have reservations, don't you think?"

"I'm not dying for you, federal. You know where it is; you go alone."

Grant stepped up to him. "Your information helped get my friend killed. If I find out you were part of that—"

"No!"

Grant grabbed Cozy's collar. "You're coming with us. To be sure."

No one else said anything. Grant watched Cozy look around frantically for support, but found none. Grant sympathized a little. Cozy was alone now, over the line. They might let him back in, take care of him if he survived, but they would never trust him again. He had to choose.

He nodded.

Grant walked down the service alley between the pair of warehouses, Cozy a few steps ahead, to the right. The textures of decay along the walls showed as fine etching and black holes in the harsh night lights. The sounds of trucks vibrated the early morning air.

Cozy edged up to the corner and looked quickly around, then leaned toward Grant.

"They're still queued," he said.

Grant moved by him and saw two trucks waiting for access into the eastern warehouse. He glanced west, toward the corner where he had encountered the workers his first day. No one.

"There's another way in here," he said.

"There is?"

He glared at the gypsy. "Cozy . . ."

Cozy scowled and started back down the alleyway. Grant brushed his lapel, felt the small head of the clipper. Not far from here Reva listened to them, kept track of them. Grant felt vulnerable without more back-up, but he agreed with Reva that no one else locally could be trusted. Not till they dumped the whole thing over and saw where everyone fell.

He had left his cane in her care. He had a stunner in his pocket and his Browning in its shoulder-rig under his jacket.

Cozy stopped at the opposite corner and peered around. Then he waved Grant to follow and slipped out of sight. Grant hurried to the edge. For an instant, he panicked— Cozy was nowhere in the street. Then he heard a small tick and looked up. Cozy was halfway to the top of the building, climbing a thin, metal ladder.

Grant clambered after him and caught up at the top. Cozy pointed in the direction of the forest of vents and housings that erupted from the roof. Grant motioned him to continue, and Cozy led him straight to a manhole cover.

"This is one way we use," Cozy said. "There's a couple others, but this is the safest."

"It's not alarmed?" Grant asked.

Cozy shrugged. "Maybe, maybe not. Nobody ever got caught."

"Beth did."

"I don't know about that. She came down here alone that night."

Grant surveyed the other objects for options. None looked any more promising than this one, so he undogged it and flipped it open.

Cozy climbed down first.

Grant pulled a cowl from his pocket and tugged it over his head, then slipped the nighteyes on over it. The roof leapt into stark black-and-white relief. The tunnel down which Cozy descended looked like a white tube with etched black rungs. Cozy looked back up and his face was a complex of lines around dark eyes. Grant donned a pair of gloves and zipped his jacket all the way up, which activated the electromagnetic layer of his clothes. He was invisible now to almost all scanners and alarm monitors.

He followed Cozy down into the warehouse.

The tube opened above a catwalk that ran alongside a bank of ducts and coils, part of the elaborate environmental system that allowed different parts of the warehouse to maintain different temperatures, humidities, and ion levels for special products with delicate requirements. A few of them rumbled with the passage of gasses.

At the end of the catwalk a short ladder took them down to a service nodule. Grant examined the equipment quickly—all of it related to the environmental systems—and motioned Cozy through the opposite hatch.

He came out on a walkway high over the warehouse proper. The nighteyes adjusted themselves constantly to compensate between the pitch black on the catwalk and the bright lights below.

The tops of the trucks were visible in the wide passageway between the storage areas. Cranes carried crates and nacelles along the webwork suspended above the stockpiles. Drays moved smaller containers down various aisles. The clank and hum of efficient machinery reverberated throughout the enormous space and Grant heard no voices, saw no people.

Far down the walkway, nearly at the front of the warehouse, Grant spotted another ladder that descended into an enclosed area. On the roof of the boxlike structure, Grant recognized junctions fed by power lines and communications cables. He tapped Cozy on the shoulder and pointed. Crouching low and taking the lead, Grant jogged the distance to the ladder.

The nighteyes registered everything within as sharp lines. The shed contained all the primary automation for the building. From here the cranes and drays received commands, and in return fed back location and task into the monitors. Grant moved along the banks of displays until he found the inventory monitor. He watched the display for a few minutes, then spoke into his clipper.

"Reva, contact our judge. This building has a disconnected inventory monitor. That's our warrant. We can search the whole damn thing now."

He traced the connections carefully until he found the one that tied the database at hand to any external, manual monitoring systems. Patiently, slowly, he disconnected the shed so that no command from outside could erase anything. He then opened one of the panels and found the small switch that allowed such connections to be made and removed it.

He went back up to the walkway, where Cozy waited, anxiously watching the floor of the warehouse.

"Can we leave now?" Cozy asked.

Grant shook his head. He sat back in the corner and took off the nighteyes. The brilliant saffron light of the warehouse floods startled his eyes. He squinted, blinked, and then watched.

This was probably where Beth had intended to be that night. But she had known something might go wrong. Kitcher, he suspected. She must have sensed that he was wrong. She had left a disk of her case files with Richard Dirkenfeld—surely, Grant thought, one of the most unlikely hiding places—and come here to finish the hard part of the mission.

And died.

Grant checked his watch. Twenty minutes passed since his message to Reva. He pocketed the timepiece and stood.

The stairs down to the floor hugged the rear wall. The offices were a dozen feet from them. As he reached the bottom landing, he pulled the hood off and pocketed it, then reached into his jacket for the Browning.

He opened the office door and stepped in. Three people looked up from where they sat around a terminal, all smiling until they recognized that Grant was not someone they expected. All three began to stand and then stopped when Grant raised the pistol.

"Special Agent Grant Voczek, RSDT."

The one closest to the terminal stabbed a button. The one nearest Grant grinned humorlessly.

"I suppose you have a warrant," he said.

"On its way. If any of you move again, I'll kill you."

The three men frowned uncertainly, but none did anything. Grant glanced around the office. A stack of disks sat on the edge of the console near the man who had pushed the button. Grant picked one up. A bright-red logo proclaimed it to be the property of Agla Interstate.

A few minutes later, Grant heard the sirens, then the shouts of police giving orders. Grant opened the door and called out for back-up. In seconds, the room was full of local police, cuffing the three men and asking Grant questions. Grant sighed heavily and holstered his weapon.

He felt suddenly very, very tired.

The trucks were loaded with components from a company in Ohio. Grant tapped D.C. from the warehouse offices and checked the registry, and discovered that it had been a recently defunct company purchased first by Weston and

Burnard, then by Coronin. He made another inquiry, and found Agla listed as a subsidiary of Coronin, their shipping division.

A room in the rear of the warehouse contained equipment for excising the product source code. Stacks of goods on metal shelves lined one wall. Grant found himself hurrying from point to point, overseeing the police impound operation. Reva finally made him stop, rest. He propped himself against the edge of the main door, watching the activity of uniformed police in the brilliant lights of their vehicles.

A limousine pulled up. Mitchel Abernathy got out of the back, followed by a pair of assistants. He looked around at the jumble of trucks, police cruisers, and law enforcement until he saw Grant.

"Here it comes," Reva said from where she sat on the apron of one of the Ohio transports.

"Special Agent Voczek," Abernathy bellowed. "Of the Resource Securities Division, Treasury."

"Yes, sir. How may I help you?"

"You better have a damn good explanation for all this!" He took the whole scene in with a sweep of his arm.

"Yes, sir, I do. I trust you also have a good explanation?"

"For what? This is my property, Agent Voczek. I don't have to explain what happens on my property to a federal."

"Unless what happens violates federal law."

Abernathy frowned. "What the hell are you talking about?"

"By law, under the Credit and Resource Trade Act, every warehouse receiving interstate shipments is required to have, on-line, an automatic receiving monitor to log in all product going in or leaving the premises."

"Yes. So?"

"Yours, sir, has been disconnected. Or is malfunctioning, which amounts to the same thing. It gave us grounds for a complete search and we have, as a consequence, discovered several counts of product fraud."

Abernathy turned to his assistants. "What is he talking about?"

Both of them shrugged and looked at Grant wide-eyed.

"You have a warrant?" Abernathy demanded.

"Yes, sir."

"Issued by who?"

"Federal Judge Thoc Le Ngao—"

"That goddamn immigrant!"

Grant pushed away from the doorway and stepped toward Abernathy. "We're also pursuing a charge of murder, Mr. Abernathy. A federal agent was killed while investigating these premises. We realize that the facility has been subleased, but that doesn't let you off completely. As owner-operator, you are liable for certain charges. If we prove that the action was taken with your knowledge or under your instructions, you will be prosecuted to the full extent of the law." He stopped inches from Abernathy, towering over him. "Now, do you have any other witty comments? If so, use them now, while I still have a sense of humor."

Abernathy sneered. "Don't threaten me."

"No threats. I would advise you to consider how best to help yourself in this, though. Even if you aren't directly involved, passive collusion carries a penalty of property loss and fine."

"You piece of federal shit . . ."

"If we can demonstrate that you knew about the murder

of Special Agent McQuarry, *that* carries a charge of accessory and worse penalties, up to and including the death penalty."

"You're fucking with the wrong man."

Grant raised an eyebrow. "I'm terrified. Will you visit me in your sheet in the middle of the night and frighten me with your pointy hood?"

Abernathy's face froze, mouth slightly open. For several seconds, he remained fixed in place. One of his aides came up and lightly touched his arm. Abernathy violently shrugged the hand off. He glared hatefully at Grant.

"We didn't go far enough in the Reforms," he said. "You better have your case put together flawlessly, or so help me I'll have your shield. You'll end up cardless and living in a barco somewhere."

"I suggest you consult with your counsel, Mr. Abernathy."

Abernathy backed away, then, and stumbled back to his limousine. Grant followed him and caught the door before Abernathy closed it. He leaned in.

"I would also consider the possibility," Grant said, quietly, just loud enough for Abernathy to hear, "that your peers have been using you and expect you to take most of the responsibility for this. Stop being so quick to blame the federal government and consider that your friends have relied on your prejudice to look the other way."

Abernathy's mouth opened, but he hesitated. For a moment, his eyes narrowed. Then he pushed Grant away and slammed the door. The car moved away.

Grant stared after it until Reva touched him.

"How do you feel?" she asked.

He shook his head. "It's not finished."

Reva sighed. "You mean, we still don't know who killed Beth?"

"*He* didn't."

"I know. But it *was* on his property."

He looked into the warehouse. "But he wasn't here."

"Neither was she."

Grant blinked at her. "She?"

"Remember, we determined from skin samples that one of Beth's assailants was female?"

"Tochsin's aide? Tess Reed?"

Reva nodded. "She's at the top of my short list."

Grant shook his head wearily. "On whose behalf? Tochsin's?"

"Or her father's."

Grant blew out a breath. "There's too much to do."

"We don't have to do it all personally. You haven't stopped since we got here. All the documentation has been filed, you've signed off on all the necessary procedures, it's being taken care of. You can go off government time now."

"Then what?"

"Sleep."

"That sounds wonderful."

"Would you mind having company?"

Grant shot her a surprised look.

Reva smiled. "With our killer still on the loose, it might be a bad idea for either of us to be alone."

"Oh."

"Oh." She looked very amused. "Yours or mine?"

"I need to report . . ."

"Yours. Come on, I'll walk you to your car."

He gestured at the operation going on. "But—"

"They're good people. They won't violate a federal

warrant, no matter how much they dislike us, and Chief Moore is already on her way. We don't need to be here now. You talked to Rycliff?"

Grant nodded. "He said he'll inform Director Koldehn when he gets it."

"And he'll handle the rest, too. Come on. You're almost useless."

"Oh, thank you." He frowned. "Where's Cozy?"

Reva looked around. "I imagine halfway to somewhere else by now. Worry about it later."

Grant let her pull him away. He stopped by the officer-in-charge cruiser and told her where he could be reached and what protocol to follow. The officer nodded, asked a couple of procedural questions, then bade him good-night. All without a hint of sympathy, compassion, or tolerance. It was a job she clearly did not care for, doing federal work, and he felt it in her attitude, heard it in her voice. Yet, he knew, Reva was correct. They would do the job. They were professionals, and sometimes that counted for more than any merely human connection.

Tired as he was, Grant found this infinitely sad.

He slept while the Duesenberg took them home. Reva shook him awake in the driveway. The sky was lightening as he thumped robotically to the door and let them in.

He went to the second floor office and tapped Director Cutter's code, then filed a brief report, details to follow in the morning. He almost fell asleep in the chair. Reva roused him.

It was easy to let her help him—so easy it surprised him. She gave him mock support up the stairs, to the bedroom, sat him on the edge of the bed and pulled off his boots, worked him out of his jacket, his shoulder holster, his shirt, his pants, stood him up and drew back the top sheet and tucked him in. His head pressed into the pillow and sleep came instantly.

Thick, fuzzy sleep, dreamless and thorough. He woke up once, sunlight shining into his face from the window. When he rolled over, he found Reva lying on top of the covers. She had kicked off her boots, her jacket, her weapons, and unbuttoned her shirt. She slept with one arm thrown above her head, hand pressed against the wall at an odd angle. Her mouth was open and a trickle of moisture trailed from the corner, down her jaw. Her eyes shifted beneath their lids.

Grant drifted to sleep watching her. He dreamed briefly of Beth and woke up to discover his arm around Reva, her back pressed against him, one hand holding his against her breast. He almost pulled away, but hesitated. She was warm and seemed, to his sleep-distorted consciousness, comfortable. He could see no way to disentangle himself without waking her, so he relaxed and soon fell asleep again.

The next time he opened his eyes, he forced them to remain open and sat up. Reva was gone. Grant pushed himself back against the wall and tried to recall his dreams. As usual, he failed.

He sat there until the pressure in his bladder forced him out of bed and to the bathroom.

Reva was toweling herself off.

Grant stared, stunned and embarrassed, frozen as in a dream where one must flee but cannot move.

"Don't hurt yourself," she said, smiling. She reached behind the door and took down a robe and slipped it on. She draped the towel over the stall and stepped by him. "Excuse me."

Then Grant looked down, felt himself redden, and mumbled an apology. He entered the bathroom and closed the door.

The room smelled of soap and hot water and clean skin. He stood before the bowl, waiting for his erection to diminish so he could urinate.

When he finally finished, he was reluctant to leave the bathroom. He stripped the rest of his clothes off and took a shower. The steaming water cleared his mind and he laughed, at himself and the situation. Another robe hung in the small linen closet. He gathered up his clothes and came out into the bedroom.

Reva was not there, but her robe lay on the bed. Grant put on his loafabouts and went downstairs.

He found her in the kitchen, wearing another set of his loafabouts, making coffee. The time on the oven read 3:22 P.M.

"Short day," he said.

She glanced at him. "Sorry. I thought I'd be finished before you woke up."

"Don't apologize. I enjoyed it."

She gave him a speculative look. "Truthfully?"

"On my honor."

"Hmm. Most men think I'm too muscular."

"No."

She smiled. "My military service. I was always athletic, but that gave me an edge I've never cared to lose."

"I like it."

"Thank you."

For a moment, Grant wanted to walk away. It was a curious experience, to see something as a branching of choices and knowing that he had the power to select and thereby determine the course of the next hour, day, year. To say nothing, leave the room, and wait for Reva to join him meant one path. A safe path, leaving them where they had begun, separated by traditions and customs and an unspoken agreements. The other . . .

"I have to finish reporting," he said, and retreated back up to the office.

Director Cutter had left three messages on his system. He tapped her number and waited.

"Grant," she said. "I was beginning to wonder if anything was wrong."

"Nothing a few more weeks of sleep won't put right."

"After this, you deserve it. Your report from last night was intriguing, but—"

Grant nodded. "Incomplete. I wanted to make this one directly." He told her about the raid, his conclusions, the events of the last few days. She listened intently, asking only a few questions, until he finished.

"We are on thin ground," she said. "Your raid—barely legal."

"Under the circumstances, I think there was little choice. I had no time for subtlety. I have a witness—"

"A gypsy."

"Given the surrounding aspects of the situation, his word ought to do. Judge Thoc Le thought so."

Cutter nodded. "We'll make it work. What about the murderers?"

"Unfortunately, still at large. But I don't see that they have much time left. I have warrants issued to pick up Teresa Reed-Dirkenfeld. I still don't have a positive ID on the man, but I think he may be—"

"Alvin Taraquel. You requested an ID on the name four days ago."

Grant blinked, momentarily puzzled. "Ah. Yes, the name Beth had inquired about."

"Taraquel is classified—that's why she never received a response."

"Classified . . . by whom?"

"Military. Covert operations. Officially, he retired five years ago, but he has no known whereabouts."

"He works for Coronin."

"You sound certain."

"He was involved in the Tamaulipas affair, running a small security operation for Weston and Burnard."

Cutter stared at him for several seconds. Then: "Grant, I recommend you allow me to take care of this. Your mission is complete."

Grant started. "Excuse me? With all due respect—"

"Your mission is *complete,* Agent Voczek."

Grant wanted to argue, but he said nothing. Cutter waited until he nodded.

"Very good, Grant. Send me the balance of your records on this." She narrowed her eyes briefly. "We are not burying this. Please believe me."

"Yes, Madam. I'm sending you everything I have."

"You've handled this very well, Grant. You deserve time off. I'll be in touch."

"May I—"

"Yes?"

"May I be present at final arrests?"

"Of course. I'll let you know."

"Thank you."

The screen cleared. Grant set up the transmission of his data and sent it, then shut down the terminal.

Reva stood in the doorway with two cups of coffee.

"How much did you hear?" he asked.

"Most of it. Do you believe her?"

"I don't have much choice." He accepted a cup. "Would you care to use my terminal to make your report?"

She shook her head. "I'm not sure I'm finished."

"Oh?"

"I'm supposed to find the murderers, remember? You've found the leak and stopped it—"

"But the barco isn't going anywhere. The Mayor won't be happy."

"The hell with the Mayor. You've done your job."

"So why aren't you out there tracking them down?"

Reva shrugged. "Because I'm not completely sure who they are yet. Taraquel and Dirkenfeld, certainly. Maybe even Kitcher, but he's dead now. Still, there are gaps."

"No investigation is seamless."

"True, but there are some gaps that you can live with."

"You haven't answered my question," Grant said.

"Yes, I have. At least, the one you asked."

"There's a question I haven't asked?"

"Always." Smiling, lower lip caught by upper teeth, Reva tilted her head in the direction of the stairs. "Bring your coffee."

He thought that perhaps afterward he might regret it, might question himself about why he did it. As they undressed each other, he wondered if this were the right thing to do, if their situations really allowed them the privilege. But once he touched her, felt the texture of her skin, kissed her flavor, smelled the richness of her, nothing else concerned him. Joined, it felt completely right, overwhelmingly natural. There was no other choice, no other course that made any sense compared to this.

She was very strong. She moved him where she wanted

him with as much ease as he moved her. Later, he wondered at all the rest—time passed differently, his exhaustion left him while they coupled, she seemed to know what he wanted—a catalogue of mythic experiences he had never before encountered. There were mistakes, yes, periods of awkwardness, but these faded as quickly as they passed, and all Grant retained was a retrospective perfection.

He never questioned its rightness after, no more than during. When they had sated themselves, they slept, legs tangled, sweat drying, sprawled like survivors thrown from the catastrophe.

When Grant opened his eyes in the darkness, his first thought came complete, a shock: *My life will never be the same again.*

To learn what happened to Cozy, log on to the *Realtime* web page at www.ibooksinc.com/realtime to download the exclusive e-chapter.

TWENTY-FIVE

Voley's house looked worse in the full light of day. Cozy winced at the bloodstains in the gazebo, on the stone floor, out on the path. George must have put up a struggle. Cozy hoped he had.

The porch door had been burned open, he saw now. A torch right through the lock, probably a military laser or something similar. Chalk lines marked where the invaders had fallen. One in the kitchen, one in the hallway, one in the parlor, two upstairs. Cozy tried to imagine the two federals moving through the darkness, killing this efficiently. Now that he saw the battleground, he wondered at how quietly it had been fought.

He still shook a little. Agent Voczek had scared him, dragging him down into Abernathy's warehouse. He recalled the calm way the man had walked into those offices and arrested the people there. He had had no idea how many people were there; no notion of how many might have been on the premises, or if any of the drivers in the convoy would move on him. Cozy tried to imagine what

367

kind of confidence or bravery or stupidity a person needed
to act that way and failed. He shook his head. Federals.

For himself, just getting back to the barco had taken
nearly the last of his nerve.

Only to have Comber Blue and the others impose on him
to bring Aaron Voley back home.

Voley walked slowly from room to room, Camilla near at
hand. He looked older than Cozy had ever seen him. He was
not a frail man, but he was old. His home had been invaded.
Last night must have cost him.

Camilla had called the police when she came home.
Someone from the barco had let her know where Voley was.
She looked shaken, uncertain. Too much had come home
this time for both of them. Maybe back in the days of the
riots and the Reforms Voley had seen worse, suffered worse,
but Cozy had always known him to be comfortable, coddled
the way all Secured Class were. He wondered if Camilla had
ever been through anything like this.

Voley went into his study, then. Camilla stared after him
for a time, then came into the kitchen with Cozy.

"Thank you, Cozy," she said. "For bringing him home."

Cozy shrugged. "It was nothing."

She opened the refrigerator and studied the contents for
a time, then pulled out a bottle of ale. She offered him one.
He did not care for it, but he accepted it. Camilla went to
the table and sat down, gazing out into the backyard
through the open door.

"At least it's over," she said.

Cozy did not agree, but he kept his opinion to himself.

"You know," she continued, "Aaron used to tell me stories about the early days, when he was involved with the
pipeline, moving deportees north. There was supposedly an

exit out of Cape Churchill on Hudson Bay. Half a dozen countries, mostly in the Russian Federation, would take them. Some of the stories, though . . . you know that's where all the tunnels came from under the city?"

"I heard something about that."

"Well, Aaron told me a lot of them go back even further, to the last century and a time called Prohibition, whatever that was. But he was a little of everything then—lawyer, engineer, pirate, spy." She shook her head. "After this, I don't see how anyone could stand it."

Cozy nodded and drew on the ale. He did not think Camilla wanted to hear that Voley probably had a taste for it. He was worn out now, true—other things had become more important to him, and he was incapable of letting them go—but Cozy had seen flashes of it last night, as Voley sat with Comber Blue and the others. For a time he seemed almost powerful, thriving on the edginess around him. Cozy could easily imagine a younger Voley craving it, putting himself at risk because that was the place where he lived.

"I'm going to miss George," Camilla said.

"Me, too."

"What was this all about, Cozy? I still don't understand."

Cozy shook his head. "I don't know."

The silence continued until Cozy became self-conscious. He took another swallow of the bitter drink.

"Uh, Madam, if you don't need me . . . ?"

Camilla looked up. "Oh. Of course, Cozy, you don't have to stay around if you have other things to do."

"I need to check on DeNeille. She was awfully upset."

"Of course. Thank you again, Cozy. Please . . . come back later, would you? Bring—what's her name? DeNeille?"

"Yes, Madam."

"Bring her with you. I'll make dinner. I'm sure Aaron would find the company . . . well . . ."

"I understand. Of course. I'll be back."

He set the bottle on the sink and hurried to the front door. It felt odd coming and going that way, but he enjoyed it. He glanced into the study as he walked by, and saw Voley sitting in his highbacked chair, staring at nothing.

He stepped out the door into the bright late-morning sun. Across the street, the free kitchen was filling up. Steam drifted away from under the awnings, glowing in the light. He thought about sitting down to a free meal, but he was not hungry.

He headed north. He wondered if DeNeille would even let him in after last night. He tucked his hands in his pockets and walked, long strides carrying him quickly down the street.

She answered his knock at the back door immediately. She smiled quickly and waved him inside.

Suitcases lay open on the sofa.

"Going somewhere?" he asked.

"I thought it might be a good time to visit Chicago. I've never been there."

"Oh."

"I have a sister there."

Cozy nodded. He watched her continue to pack, and tried to ignore the hollow sensation growing inside. "I, uh, I've been thinking about leaving, too."

She looked at him, eyebrows raised, a silent question.

"Don't know where I'd go . . ."

DeNeille straightened. She seemed to be reading something, her eyes moving back and forth.

"Well, Cozy . . ." she said finally. "Would you consider coming with me? Or is that what you're asking?"

"What?"

"Something you didn't hear?"

"No, no . . . I just . . . you want me to come with you?"

She gave him a stern look. "Things would be different. They'd have to be."

Cozy stared at her, stunned. He had given no thought to leaving St. Louis, but now that DeNeille had brought it up, it immediately appealed to him, especially in her company. What things would be different? Oh, he realized, yes, they would. I'd need to go straight-and-up, get franchised, a legitimate ID. As long as he had a sponsor he could do it. Maybe. That, or DeNeille would have to take care of him. He wondered if he could live with that.

"Why?" he asked.

"Why am I offering you this?"

He nodded.

She shrugged. "Good Jesus, I'm damned if I know."

Cozy laughed nervously. "Not what you thought you wanted?"

"I never had a notion what I wanted. If I *had*, though, you probably wouldn't have been it. But—Cozy, we've been seeing each other for what? A year?"

"More or less."

"That should be enough time to know if you want more."

"Truth, DeNeille, I never thought about it. I always felt lucky to get what I did. Doesn't make sense for gypsies to have much in the way of aspirations."

DeNeille nodded, frowning. "I think that's it."

"What?"

"You've never lied to me, Cozy. If there's a reason, that's it."

Cozy thought back and laughed. "You know, I believe you're right."

"Of course I am. I think that's worth trying to keep."

"Maybe."

She returned to packing. "But I don't think I want to be in this city for a while. I need to go somewhere else. Chicago sounds good to me."

"It's starting to sound good to me, too."

"After you went off with that federal agent last night, we kept talking. There's a way we can get you a proper CID and everything. Mr. Voley said he'd be willing to help, so it wouldn't be like you'd still have to live in a barco or anything."

DeNeille snapped the case closed and came to him. She draped her arms on his shoulders and kissed him lightly.

"Oh," he said. "Camilla asked us to come to dinner at Mr. Voley's."

"Who's Camilla?"

"Mr. Voley's—" He stopped. Mr. Voley's what? Lover? Housekeeper? He had never quite understood her relationship. "She's Mr. Voley's companion."

"I'm leaving in the morning, Cozy. It'll have to be tonight."

"I can call her. May I use your phone?"

She kissed him again, nodded, and went to her bureau.

Cozy tapped Voley's number. The line connected and started ringing. He glanced back at DeNeille with a curiously warm appreciation. Travel with her, stay with her, settle with her. The more he turned it over in his mind the more it appealed. There was nothing, really, to keep him here anymore. His credit with Comber Blue and the barco was gone, spent last night. A new town, the possibility of a different life.

He shook his head at his sudden prolepsis.

The phone continued ringing. He broke the connection and tapped it again. At the fifteenth tone, he disconnected.

He climbed over the back fence. The door on the sunporch still stood open. Cozy moved as quietly as he could. He stood on the porch a long time, listening, trying to hear inside the house.

The kitchen was empty. He went down the hallway to the study, close to the right-hand wall. At the doorway, he leaned forward to look within.

Camilla and Voley sat in chairs, eyes open, lifeless.

Cozy swallowed hard, his heart pounding. He stared at them, struggling for control. Finally, he made himself explore the rest of the house. He touched nothing, not out of caution, but from fear. He went through the entire house, room by room, slowly and methodically, until he was certain no one else was in it. Then he returned to the study.

He stood between them and stared. *I shouldn't have left,* he thought. Then: *They'd only have killed me, too.*

Neither body looked damaged, though. That meant nothing. He remembered the injections he had received, and shuddered. There was no odor of voided bowels or urine here. They looked like statues, lifeless renditions. No pain, no peace.

Voley was dead. Cozy said it a few times, but it was a nonsense statement. Voley had been old when Cozy had been born. Voley was forever, so the gypsies believed. Here, at least, someone made them more than their status said they were. Dead.

Cozy did not know when he began to cry. He wiped his face a few times, then did not bother. He stood in the study and wept. He was still weeping when he left.

* * *

DeNeille had not sounded happy. Cozy broke the connection and leaned his head against the phone. The metal and plastic were cool. He felt slightly feverish.

A knock on the door brought him up. He looked through the glass of the booth at a woman who indicated that she needed to use the phone. He opened the door and stepped out with a muttered apology.

He sat down in the booth near the rear entrance of the tavern. Cozy had asked DeNeille to wait for him, but she said no, she would not. But she agreed to contact Agent Voczek and tell him what had happened. He hoped she understood.

The man he had met here slid back into the opposite bench, grinning.

"So, citizen," he said. "Your merchandise awaits."

Cozy nodded. "You have it?"

The man feigned dismay. "Of course! I'm not an alley-cat! I do an honest trade." He leaned on his elbows. "As long as I'm traded with honestly."

Cozy slid the CID across the wooden table toward the other man, who snatched it up and slipped it quickly into a scanner under the table. Cozy watched the play of light from the screen on his thin, aged face.

He grinned again. "Very excellent, citizen. We don't see many military quality dubs like this."

"Military . . ."

The man set a bag on the table and pushed it toward Cozy.

Cozy took it and set it on the seat beside him. He opened the bag and pulled out the heavy shape inside. Wrapped in cloth, the pistol gleamed darkly. Cozy picked up the magazine and thumbed out shells. At four he stopped and nodded.

"As advertised," the man across from him said. "That piece has no history. A perfect throw-down."

Cozy reloaded the shells into the magazine, rewrapped the weapon, and put it back in the bag.

"I'd better not be stripped when I leave here," Cozy said. "I'm an—"

"An honest trader, yes. You said."

The man nodded appreciatively. "The rear entrance is unlocked. For your convenience."

"Thank you."

Cozy tucked the bag inside his jacket, finished his soda, and stood. He walked out the front door, onto Euclid Avenue. Night was close. He zipped up and crossed the street. A block up, he entered another tavern, relieved to find it jammed with patrons. He worked his way to the back, ducked into the kitchen, and hurried to the rear entrance. Someone shouted at him, but he did not stop. He burst into the alley and ran.

Six blocks later, he felt confident no one had followed him. He started making his way west, to Kingshighway and the park.

Maybe he could catch up with DeNeille later. Maybe. After tonight, he doubted he would be able to go anywhere by choice. Only if he did not get caught.

They had killed Voley. "They." Since he was a child, "They" had colored his existence like a fairytale monster threatening to eat him if he took a wrong step. As he grew older, he came to believe that They did not exist, that They were only a target for frustrated talk among people caught powerless in circumstances, looking for a place and a person to blame. It's Them, it's Their fault, They did it. No one real, he had told himself, just things, history, coincidence, the times. But it was easy to slip back into that kind of thinking, easy to believe in a They. Cozy found himself sharing the talk, the frustration. He told himself, though, that They did not care about Cozy, that it was nothing personal. He could live with that.

Till now. Now They had killed something Cozy had believed in.

This time, though, Cozy had Their names:
Reed. Dirkenfeld. Abernathy. Tochsin.

TWENTY-SIX

Grant opened his eyes to a dark room. The street lights set the window aglow; he saw the blue time signature on the terminal in the corner.

Reva snored softly beside him. He reached over to touch her, found her shoulder. Her skin was especially warm to him. He traced the line of her arm, down to her wrist. Her hand twisted around and caught his, a tight squeeze. She snorted, moaned, and rolled toward him. When she opened her eyes, Grant saw the faint light from the window catch in her pupil.

"Good morning?" she said speculatively.

"Still evening. I think."

"Mmm."

"How are you?"

"You need to ask?"

Grant laughed quietly. "I meant—"

"I know." She sat up. "I need the bathroom."

"I can wait."

"A true gentleman."

Grant watched her shadow cross the room. She did not turn on the bathroom light and after a few seconds he heard her water.

The terminal chimed. Grant looked over at it and groaned to see the phone cursor. He went to it in the dark, unwilling to turn on the lights just yet, and tapped the accept.

"This is Agent Voczek."

"Transfer call from Treasury offices."

"Accept."

A moment later: "Agent Voczek?"

"Yes, this is Agent Voczek."

"They put me through this way, I tried your office. I don't know if you remember me from last night. I'm DeNeille—Cozy's friend?"

"Of course I remember you. How may I help you?"

"It's Cozy. He asked me to call you, but he wouldn't tell me where he is. I think—Cozy's going to do something stupid and I'm scared."

"What's he going to do?"

"I don't know, but he has this voice when he's really upset. Cold. Good Jesus, it's a scary thing to hear. He called me a little while ago."

"DeNeille, calm down. Why is Cozy upset?"

"Mr. Voley—he said Mr. Voley is dead."

Grant felt the hair on his neck thrill. "Dead. Where?"

"His home. Cozy told me to call you and tell you."

Reva leaned over Grant. "DeNeille, this is Agent Cassonare. You remember me? I was with Agent Voczek."

"Yes, I remember. You're both working together."

"That's right, DeNeille. Where are you?"

"My apartment. I—"

"Is there someplace you can go? Right now?"

"I was leaving tomorrow for Chicago. I have family there—"

"No, DeNeille, I mean right now. After we get off the phone."

"Well . . . yes, but—"

"Don't tell me where. Just go. Tomorrow, contact Chief Moore and request protection, tell her we told you to. We'll set it up from here. She'll take your call. You aren't safe where you are now."

"I—I don't *care* about that! It's Cozy I'm worried about!"

"What is it you think he's going to do?" Grant asked.

"I don't know. He told me to tell you 'They' did it. He said you'd know what he meant. He said it's not finished yet."

"They . . . All right, DeNeille, do what Agent Cassonare told you to do. Right now."

"All right."

"Thank you, DeNeille. We'll take care of it from here. We'll find Cozy."

"He worshiped Mr. Voley. Lots of people did."

"I know. We'll deal with it."

As he broke the connection, Reva hissed. "I guess it was too soon to celebrate," she said.

"We knew it wasn't over. I should have thought to have Voley put under security." Grant tapped Chief Moore's number and waited. No answer at her home, the terminal said, would he like a trace? He touched YES and waited. The time signature said six-twenty P.M.

The trace found her at police headquarters, her office. "This is Chief Moore."

"Agent Voczek. We have a problem."

"That's no exaggeration. Mayor Poena is ready to eat your liver."

"Aaron Voley is dead."

379

There was a long silence. "Oh, God . . . when?"

"I'm not sure. This afternoon some time. At his home. I need the premises secured."

"Right away. What else?"

"Find and secure Senator Dirkenfeld, Senator Reed, and Congressman Tochsin."

"What in God's name for?"

"Their lives may be in danger next. I'm going to go see them myself."

"That won't be difficult. They're having a small gathering at Reed's house on Lindell this evening. Private party."

"Very convenient. Thank you." He told her then about DeNeille and what he wanted.

"I'll take care of that."

"Now, will Mayor Poena be at this party?"

"As a matter of fact, yes. A few others."

"You?"

"No. Unless you want me there."

"I don't think it would be a bad idea."

"I'll put the rest of this in process and meet you there."

"That will be fine, Chief. Thank you."

He shut down the terminal. The lights came up, then, and he squinted. Reva leaned against the wall, arms folded under her breasts, one ankle crossed over the other. Her thick hair billowed in a wild, black halo.

"Are you up for crashing a party?" he asked.

She smiled. "I think that would be the perfect way to top off the evening."

Four limousines were lined up in the driveway of the Reed mansion. The entire house was lit up—all the windows, the grounds lights, the paper lanterns on the veranda that wrapped around three sides of the granite-facade tudor revival. Grant noticed that only one window seemed lit in Mitchel Abernathy's neowright, four lots away.

Grant and Reva got out of his car. He gazed into the dense shadows of Forest Park. The replica early-twentieth century street lamps lining the twisty paths of the park gave off a gauzy light, more nostalgic than useful.

The police had not arrived yet. Grant looked back at Abernathy's house.

"What is it?" Reva asked.

"I'm wondering if Cozy might not consider Mitchel Abernathy part of Voley's death."

"Do you want me to check on him?"

"No. I want you here when Chief Moore arrives. Go in with her—I don't want any jurisdictional problems with Madam Mayor or the congressmen. I'll bring Mr. Abernathy."

"Be cautious. Cozy might not respect us if we get in his way."

Grant nodded, took his cane, and walked down the street.

The neowright felt immense as he approached it. The lone window with light, in the upper left corner, lent no perspective. Grant felt his way up the front stairs. The doorbell mount glowed. He pressed the button and waited.

"Yes?"

An androgynous voice, a house system. Grant was surprised. He thought Abernathy would employ human servants, but this, in its way, was even more extravagant.

"Special Agent Grant Voczek to see Mr. Abernathy. It's important."

"Mr. Abernathy is receiving no guests this evening. Please call—"

"This is official business. Please inform Mr. Abernathy of my presence."

"Please wait." After a time: "Mr. Abernathy is receiving no guests this evening. Please call back another time."

Grant jammed his CID into the scanner below the door-bell.

"Checking override authorization," the system said.

"Judge Thoc Le Ngao."

Then: "Do you wish to exercise override?"

"Yes. Special Agent Grant Voczek, Resource Securities Division, Treasury Department."

"The lock is disengaged."

"Where is Mr. Abernathy?"

"Second floor, southeast corner office. Do you wish house lights?"

"Yes."

Grant took back his CID and entered the house. A chandelier above the main hall winked on. A wide staircase ascended to a landing, then split in two and continued up to the second floor. Grant hurried, barely glancing at the rich furnishings and artworks.

He knocked lightly on the designated door. Again. When no answer came, he went in.

The office was classic neowright, built-in furniture arund the walls, low-ceilinged, the lights encased in ornate boxes casting pleasant yellowish illumination. A few paintings decorated the walls. The one odd piece was an ancient rolltop desk, before which Mitchel Abernathy sat, facing the door, a pistol in his hand. He wore a velvet housecoat. His hair was neatly combed, but he stared at Grant with the metallic gleam of someone on the edge.

Another desk, opposite the roll top, contained stacks of disks and papers.

Grant raised his hands slowly. "Mr. Abernathy."

"Mr. Federal. *Special* Agent Voczek, fucking Treasury."

He had not raised the gun yet. It lay against his thigh, pointed at the floor.

"There's a problem, Mr. Abernathy."

Abernathy smiled. "I know. A big one. I've been sitting here since this afternoon trying to think of a solution. I considered killing you. Then I considered killing myself, but frankly I never thought much of suicide. Cheap way out. I'd only use it if I were dying of some painful disease. As much as I might claim it, I don't quite consider meddlers from D.C. that disease."

"But close?"

"Hm. I never like it when one of you has a sense of humor." Abernathy tossed the pistol noisily onto the desk. Grant relaxed.

"I didn't want to see anybody tonight," Abernathy said.

"I gathered as much from your house system."

"But you overrode it. You can still do that?"

"Under certain circumstances."

Abernathy shook his head. "No matter how much we change the rules, you people still find a way. Incidentally, I don't think your case will hold up in court."

"Perhaps not. It doesn't matter. The leak is stopped. And the case isn't against you anyway."

Abernathy's eyebrows cocked. "Do you think I won't have to answer for my share of the responsibility?"

"Did you authorize the disconnection of your scanner?"

"Of course not."

"Then I don't see a problem."

"Oh?"

"No. All you have to do is turn over to me the paperwork you have on the sublease."

Abernathy smiled. "That simple, eh? And if I refuse?"

"Why would you? You aren't responsible for the leak."

"Maybe," he said, waving a hand in a broad gesture, "I just want to make a statement about how little I respect federals."

Grant stepped forward. "Principle? Does that extend to murder?"

Abernathy scowled. "I didn't kill your agent."

"I know that. But the people who did just murdered Aaron Voley."

Abernathy's mouth fell open. It seemed to Grant that he went pale. "Aaron . . . ?" He glanced at the pistol on his desk, then shook his head. "He and I were friends . . . once . . ." He seemed confused for a moment, then fixed his gaze on Grant. "Do you know who?"

"I can't quite prove it yet, but yes. If you refuse to help me—"

Abernathy raised a hand. "Don't threaten me. No need."

Grant decided to change the direction of the conversation. "Were you aware that they'd increased the barter commune leak by two thousand percent in the last year and a half?"

Abernathy nodded. "Usually, I check more carefully, but I've got staff to do that. They didn't do a good job this time. I suspect some of them were bought. Two thousand percent did you say?"

"Mr. Abernathy, I would really like to discuss this with you, but as I said—"

"You have a problem, I heard you." He scowled at the gun on his desk, then scratched his chin thoughtfully. "The Mayor knew all about this, that bitch."

"Mr. Abernathy—"

Abernathy held up his hand for silence. "I said I've been sitting here trying to figure out a solution all afternoon. I'm being fucked, young man. I'm old, I'm tired, I'm more interested in showing off now than taking care of business, but I will never get to the point where I like being fucked. In this instance, it seems my only option is to decide who is going to get to stick it in further."

Grant held his breath and watched Abernathy think. Finally, the man looked up.

"Shit." He drew himself up and concentrated on Grant. "You came here to protect me?"

"Not just you, sir. We have reason to believe Senators Dirkenfeld and Reed and Congressman Tochsin are also targets. They're at Reed's house just down—"

"Yes, I know. They asked me to that little gathering, but they're just politicians."

"I'd like you to come with me so we can keep you all secured this evening. It shouldn't take very long to catch the man."

Abernathy's eyes narrowed. "It's not the same one who killed Aaron?"

"Or my colleague. No, sir, not that one. This man is coming after you all out of anger."

"Then it's revenge. Maybe you should let it happen."

"Don't tempt me," Grant said tersely.

Abernathy looked startled. "That doesn't sound much like a public servant."

"A very good friend of mine died investigating your warehouse. Revenge has crossed my mind a few times in the last week. Now get dressed."

"Don't bark at me, little dog. You might make me choose the wrong solution." Abernathy got to his feet and went to his other desk. He cleared away some papers and tapped his terminal. "Give me a minute to check something." After a few minutes, he asked, "What was your friend's name?"

"Elizabeth McQuarry."

"Oh. Her. Persistent. I wanted her to back off, not die. My condolences." He returned his attention to the screen.

Grant went to the window and looked up the street. Police cruisers had joined his Duesenberg. He spotted officers on the street by the park.

"That's what I thought," Abernathy said. Grant looked around. The old man stood. "I'm having this downloaded for you. Come here and look for yourself. I think I'd like to be a nuisance tonight."

"I hope you won't be too disappointed," Abernathy said as they walked toward Reed's mansion.

Grant did not answer. Police waited at the foot of the walkway. Grant presented his CID and they waved him through. More police strolled the veranda.

In the foyer, Chief Moore talked with Reva. They looked up when Grant and Abernathy entered. Chief Moore frowned.

"Good evening, Karen," Abernathy said, extending a hand. "Good to see you."

"Mitchel . . ." She took his hand hesitantly.

"Is everyone here?" he asked, looking right, toward a wide archway.

"They are now," she said.

"Good, good. Excuse me while I go say hello."

He strode through the archway. Grant heard his voice, loudly calling names. Laughter.

"Nothing yet," Reva said. "Congressman Tochsin is here,

though. I didn't say anything about last night. Cozy hasn't shown up. Is it possible he changed his mind?"

"I don't know. I don't know him that well. Thank you for responding, Chief Moore."

"The last thing I need are dead congressmen in my city, Agent Voczek."

"Mr. Voczek," Abernathy called, "Madam Cassonare. Have you met everyone? Please, come in."

The ceiling arched overhead in a confusion of heavy wooden beams. An immense hearth covered the far wall, a thick fire blazing within. Drays stood against the wall near the service entrance, hors d'oeuvres platters ready. Several people lounged in the heavy sofas around a broad central table.

Senator Reed stood out from the others. He seemed taller, his greying hair thick and mythic. He wore an expression of reserved amusement, like someone listening to a joke he may not enjoy. He anchored the people around him—Congressman Tochsin, Mayor Poena, and Assistant Director Koldehn. Another man completed the immediate group, one sharing the same demeanor as Reed, and Grant assumed him to be Senator Dirkenfeld.

Richard Dirkenfeld sat in one of the sofas nearby, nursing a drink. He lifted his glass in greeting to Grant and smiled sadly.

Three other people Grant did not recognize occupied a circle of chairs near the hearth. They watched Abernathy warily.

Reva touched his elbow and he waited. She leaned to whisper.

"That's Dirkenfeld . . . those three are connected to Coronin, a contracts team. The woman is Aurora Campbell."

"Everyone's here," Abernathy said expansively. "That's good. I am still invited, Senator?"

"Of course, Mitchel," Reed said. "You're always welcome. You never come, though, so I'm curious. What's the occasion?"

"I thought it was time to straighten out our misunderstandings."

"Do we have misunderstandings?"

"Indeed we do. And it's getting worse instead of better. I've learned this evening that a friend of mine from way back has died today. We didn't talk much lately, but I still counted him a friend. This has distressed me. That and I have learned that my trust has been abused by people who ought to know better."

He went to the bar. Everyone watched him while he poured himself a straight bourbon.

"I've invited Agents Cassonare and Voczek to hear about my discontent. I doubt they'll be able to do anything about it, but they've been trying to discover the truths of certain events lately and I think they deserve at least that much." He raised his glass toward Grant and Reva. "I didn't have all the pieces. Since they are the legally deputized agents of destruction, I'll let them have the floor."

"Very generous of you, Mitch," Senator Dirkenfeld said. "You usually don't give us federals the time of day."

"There are federals and then there are federals, Senator. With all due respect, I wouldn't cross the road to piss down your throat if your stomach was on fire."

"Mitchel—" Mayor Poena began.

Abernathy raised a hand. "Patience, patience." He cleared his throat, mock drama, and Grant began to like him. He glanced at Reva and saw her holding her hand up to cover her own smile.

"A couple weeks ago," Abernathy said, "it came to my attention that I was being investigated. A federal agent—Treasury, to be precise—was snooping around my property, digging into my public records, asking people about me. I found out about it from the manager of the property, a woman named Hightower. The property in question was leased two years ago to Agla Interstate and she works for them. I thought it was odd that she'd tell me and not her superiors, but when I found out that the questions being asked involved me, too, I thanked her and thought no more about it. I didn't like the idea of being investigated. I still don't, but it was her job. I asked her what it was she thought she was looking for and she refused to tell me. Since it was Treasury, I assumed she was trying to find some trade irregularity. My relations with the gypsies are hardly out of line, certainly not sufficient to bring a special agent from D.C. in, so I started making inquiries. I found out that she was poking around at the request of our esteemed Mayor. I paid Madam Mayor a visit and we had a frank exchange of view. Allison seemed reluctant to do anything, so I put it to her bluntly—get the federal out of my business or I will open the affair up in court. She relented. Now, since I had achieved my purpose, I went away and thought no more about it. My mistake. The agent in question turned up dead. There are two more—" he pointed at Grant and Reva "—to find out what happened, and I find I cannot blame D.C. If someone killed one of my employees I'd damn well want to find out what happened. Since Agent McQuarry's death followed closely my request to the Mayor, perhaps she'd care to tell us what she did with it."

Mayor Poena glared at Abernathy, then at Grant and Reva, but her resentment seemed built over a substrate of embarrassment. She looked at Tochsin, then Senator Dirkenfeld.

"Daddy, dear," Richard said, "what did you do?"

Dirkenfeld frowned at his son but said nothing.

"I spoke with Michael," Mayor Poena said. "Congressman Tochsin."

Grant stepped forward. He was still trying to sort everything into place, but looking at all these people now, faces with names, the bits gathered, the pattern assembled. "Why would you speak to Congressman Tochsin? He has no direct say in what Treasury does."

"He's our congressman," Poena said.

"But A.D. Koldehn is the one who could have helped you," Grant said. "Or had you already spoken to him?"

Poena said nothing. Grant turned to Congressman Tochsin. "What action did you take in response to Madam Mayor's request?"

Tochsin also looked at Senator Dirkenfeld. "As you said, I have very little say in what Treasury does. I asked Senator Dirkenfeld for advice. We discussed it and he offered to look into it himself."

"So you passed it on." Grant looked at Senator Dirkenfeld. "And what was your advice, Senator?"

"I told him to take it up with the local Treasury representative."

"At which point," Grant said, "A.D. Koldehn tried to suppress Agent McQuarry's investigation. Unsuccessfully. She'd been working with a partner when she first came here—Agent Kitcher. Did you speak to him, Congressman?"

Tochsin frowned. "No. I said—"

"You spoke to Senator Dirkenfeld, yes. Did *you* speak to Agent Kitcher, Senator?"

"Is there a point to all this?" Senator Reed asked.

"Oh, yes. A big one. Let me see, where do I begin?"

Grant rubbed his chin in mock thought. "Agent McQuarry started snooping into Mr. Abernathy's business because she learned that the barco leaks were originating from his warehouses. Once Mr. Abernathy learned this, he protested to the Mayor, who took it to Congressman Tochsin, who passed it on to Senator Dirkenfeld. He spoke to A.D. Koldehn, who was already filing bad fitness reports on her. But there wasn't enough yet to get her off the case. The warehouses she was investigating, though, turned out not to be operated directly by Mr. Abernathy, but sublet to Agla Shipping. Agla has an interesting collection of shareholders. They all use the same brokerage, too."

"Weston and Burnard," Abernathy said.

"The same. You do a great deal of business with them personally, Mr. Abernathy, although you aren't a shareholder. Now, I looked into the terms of the agreement Mr. Abernathy had with Agla and it turns out that he leased his property to them at no cost. A gift—because somewhere along the way he'd entered into a conditional partnership. Is everyone following me so far? Technically, it could be said that he had leased his own warehouse to himself. To what end and for whose benefit? I suppose you could untangle all the various legalities to find out who is actually using his property, but I don't think it's necessary to go through all that here. We all know who that would be."

"Really, Agent?" Senator Dirkenfeld drawled. "And who would that be?"

"Coronin Industries," Grant said. "The same company that is currently applying for a loan from Mr. Abernathy's bank. It's a development loan, with a contingency. But that's beside the point. The fact is, were he to grant it, he would be open to charges that he had loaned funds to a company in which he had direct connections, which, not having declared that, would be illegal. His property would then be subject to seizure. I can imagine who would then acquire it at auction."

"Which is why I've decided to decline the loan," Abernathy said.

Dirkenfeld's mouth opened slightly. Reed lost his smile. Congressman Tochsin looked confused.

"Don't you understand, Congressman?" Grant asked. "I would have thought you'd grasp the beauty of the arrangement, given your own involvement in credit fraud."

Tochsin glared at him. "What the hell do you mean?"

"Oh, please, don't disappoint me," Grant said. "Don't tell me you didn't know. I might be inclined to believe you. You've been recycling commodity scrip through the barco. You and Aaron Voley. He's been using you to secure benefits for the gypsies. I've seen it before, but I must admit I'd never seen it being done partly for altruistic reasons."

"You have no proof—"

"I do, Congressman. But we're getting off the subject. I don't really care about your petty larceny. This complex arrangement with Coronin, though . . . You see, the loan application would be guaranteed by federal money. Perfectly legal. I'm certain Coronin can pay it back, that's not an issue. But it's that contingency that's a problem. They specified location, which is the contingency. They want the barter commune. There are other areas where they can build, but none of them are as suitable. A few have potential resident-protest problems. None of them have such a combination of government support as this one. The only problem is there's a nice big barter commune on it. But that's not a real problem if you can get it moved. How do you get it moved? You make it a threat to the community. It could be argued that your Mayor already had sufficient cause to deport them. But she didn't want to risk her chances in next year's gubernatorial race. So she demanded Treasury do something about it. And Director Koldehn obliged. That's when Agent McQuarry was sent in. Soon enough, Mr. Abernathy knew he was being investigated and he predictably complained. That's when other measures came into play."

"I did my duty," Koldehn protested.

Grant nodded. "In a sense. You could have told the Mayor to go to hell. You had reports from your field people telling you that the illicit barco trade had gone up less than half a point. Those reports were false, of course. Still, Beth McQuarry was called in, she did her usual thorough job, and set the stage for the next step. Her murder prompted a second investigation which showed that the barco trade was far worse than reported, and all the evidence was aimed directly at Mitchel Abernathy. Had we been less imaginative, Mr. Abernathy would be in custody right now and all his holdings would be up for auction within a year. The barter commune would be closed down and Coronin would have its loan, and construction of the new facility would begin."

"Very imaginative indeed," Senator Reed said. "But I'd like to know what gives you the authority to interrogate us?"

Abernathy shot him a look. "You work for me, you piece of federal shit, just like these two agents do. I'm the people. You answer to me."

Senator Reed smiled. "No. I don't."

"You—"

"Mitchel, there's enough evidence now to convict you of unregistered trade and credit fraud. I wouldn't push it if I were you."

Abernathy stared at Reed.

"Excuse me," Grant said, stepping forward. "Mr. Abernathy doesn't have the authority, true." He faced Reed directly. "But I do."

"Agent Voczek—" Koldehn began.

"No, sir. Please keep out of this. As far as I know, you had very little direct involvement. It was Agent Kitcher."

"Kitcher?"

Grant nodded. "The one thing I couldn't figure out was the discrepancy in the two reports on the size of the leak in the barco. It never made sense that the quantity of illicit goods would jump that much in so short a time. Once I knew that Kitcher was your man, Senator, then it made sense."

Reed raised his eyebrows. "I wasn't aware that I had 'a man' in your department, Agent."

"Of course you were. That's why you're here. It puzzled me why a Nebraska senator would make a public appearance in St. Louis off-season. But your daughter lives here and you keep a house. Nebraska is also the headquarter state for Coronin Industries. Coronin wants that facility in St. Louis. That also puzzled me. Coronin has twenty-two facilities in North America and probably several outside the country. Why would they want another one?"

"How should I know? It's a growing company."

"Yes, but in what areas? Slavery?"

Several people spoke at once. Grant looked over at the group of Coronin representatives and saw none of them saying anything. They watched him, apprehensively, anxiously. He noticed Reed paying attention.

"Quiet, please," Grant shouted. When the hubbub dwindled to stillness, he continued. "It doesn't matter. The fact is, Coronin wanted the facility, and you've always helped them get what they want. Weston and Burnard are their hunting dogs and even though you don't own any stock in them directly, your daughter does. As does Senator Dirkenfeld's son, who is married to her, making a very substantial voting block. I think the connection shows, Senator. You've made connections for them in the Senate, you've arranged for states to accommodate them. You've been in Congress a long time, you're in a good position to ensure federal backing, find suitable banks, make the proper connections in the local governments. A perfectly equitable arrangement, I'm sure."

Reed smiled. "Go on. You amuse me."

"Things didn't go right here. You had a nervous mayor who was terrified of losing the new facility and damaging her political aspirations. Everything that was done seemed logical. Suppressing the accurate reports on the barco in order to guarantee sufficient flow of goods to alarm everyone from Jefferson City to D.C., calling in an outside agent to make the final report to hide any local collusion, then eliminating that agent when her investigation took her in unapproved directions. The entire concept of rigging a federal deportation while guaranteeing a local bank loan for Coronin to occupy that very ground—all of it must have looked perfectly logical."

"So?"

"So you went too far and your people got sloppy. They killed a good agent and failed to find all her records. Everything you've done since has been damage control. But you killed Aaron Voley today and that has guaranteed that you lose all control."

"Proving all these connections," Reed said, "will be impossible."

"That's as good as an admission. But I don't have to

prove all of them, just enough of them to shut down everything you wanted here. There will be no deportation, Mr. Abernathy is cleared of the charges you were setting him up to answer, and the loan to Coronin is off. I count that a good day. The only problem is, I have to be here to save your lives. You had Aaron Voley killed and that has pissed someone off. Someone who is on his way here to kill you."

"I did not have Aaron Voley killed," Reed said.

"Maybe you didn't give the order directly, but the trail can be inferred. By the way, Senator, isn't it a little mercenary to use your own daughter this way?"

Reed frowned.

"Where is she, by the way? You knew, of course, there was an arrest warrant out for her."

"For what charge?" Reed asked.

Grant's eyes flashed angrily. "Oh, a number of charges. But murder will do."

TWENTY-SEVEN

I don't find any of this amusing, Agent," Reed said.

Richard Dirkenfeld laughed sharply. "Really? You should have my perspective—you'd find it hysterical."

"Richard . . ." Senator Dirkenfeld said tightly.

"No, no, Daddy, I don't think I'll go to my room and be quiet." Richard pushed to his feet a bit unsteadily.

"You're drunk, Richard," Reed said.

"Of course I am. I have been since I married your daughter. It's better than not. You know, I don't find it at all surprising that Tess is wanted for murder. Hell, she's threatened me with it often enough." He smiled thinly. "What you so often take for inebriation, gentlemen, is really just plain fear."

"Do you know where she is, Richard?" Grant asked.

"Oh, yes. At least, I did. Home. I don't know if she's still there, with all the police around." He frowned. "She came home early this morning and stayed there all day. She never does that. She finds all sorts of reasons not to be home. Travels a lot for Michael. And others."

"I can't believe this," Tochsin said. "Tess has worked for me since my election."

"Three years," Richard said. "So what? You think that means you know her? I've been married to her for six years, I don't know her."

"Chief Moore," Grant said, "I want that house secured. No one in or out without my say."

"Agent Voczek," Reed said, "you're walking on eggs right now. If you harm my daughter—"

"Threats, Senator? In front of all these witnesses?"

"You have no proof."

Grant stepped very close to him. Reed flinched back, but Grant caught his wrist. "Senator," he said in a tight whisper, "right now I don't need any."

He let Reed go and headed for the foyer.

Police deployed around the Dirkenfeld house quickly and efficiently. Grant admired their evident skill. He went to his car and took off his jacket. He opened the trunk and took out his Browning and slipped it on. He found a small transmitter and its receiver and put them in one vest pocket. He put the nighteyes in his other vest pocket and slammed the trunk. Reva waited on the sidewalk.

"What are you doing?" Reva asked.

"We need to find out if anyone's still home." He handed Reva the receiver. "Where's Richard?"

"Still inside with the other guests."

Grant walked back into Reed's living room and gestured for Richard to come with him. Senator Reed huddled with the three Coronin people. Senator Dirkenfeld scowled at his son and at Grant, but said nothing.

Congressman Tochsin approached Grant. "Agent, just exactly what is this about?"

Grant blinked. "You're kidding."

"No, I—Agent Voczek, I have no idea what any of this is. Abernathy's accusations—I've heard none of this before tonight."

Grant stared at him until the congressman looked away. "And the commodity scrip?"

"That was Tess's idea," Tochsin said. "She said it was common practice and that she could manage the funds without attaching my name to it."

"She used it to finance a very interesting covert operation," Reva said.

"But I didn't know about Coronin or—"

"You were played, Congressman," Grant said. "You have my sympathy. But Tess has killed at least three people I know of, maybe more."

"She's a senator's daughter."

Reva laughed sharply.

"I don't have time right now, Congressman," Grant said. "Please just stay out of the way."

Richard rocked slightly on his feet. He smiled at Tochsin.

"Richard, come with me," Grant said and grabbed his sleeve. "I want you to phone your wife. I want to know if she's still in the house."

"I really would rather not—"

Grant shook him. "I don't care. I want you to phone her, and I want you to explain the situation to her."

Richard paled, but nodded.

"Where's the phone?"

Richard pointed through the opposite door into the library. Grant dragged him along. The phone was on a small table by the bay windows.

Richard tapped the number in slowly.

On the fifth chime it connected.

"Hello?"

"Tess, dear . . ."

"Richard?"

"Yes, it's me. Uh—"

"Where are you?"

"Over at your father's house. I wish you were here. The evening's become most interesting."

"Why are there police outside, Richard?"

"Some sort of threat. Are you—are you all right?"

"What do you mean?"

"Well, it seems that some trouble's come up. There are people here—police and so on—who want to arrest your father."

"Do they?"

"And my father, I think. And you."

"Me?"

"Uh . . . yes."

"Is Agent Voczek there?"

Richard looked up at Grant. Grant nodded. "Yes, he is. Do you want to talk to him?"

"Yes, but not on the phone."

"How, then—?"

"In person, Richard. Have him come up to the house."

"But—"

"I'm not going to hurt him, Richard. With all those police out there? I'd be crazy."

Richard gave Grant a dubious look, but Grant nodded approval. "All right. He'll be over there—when would you like him?"

"As soon as he gets here."

The connection broke.

Richard cleared his throat lightly. "If you want my advice, I wouldn't go."

"Is that the same advice you gave Beth?"

Richard frowned. "That was beneath you, sir."

"Maybe I'll apologize later."

Reva waited in the foyer.

"Go around the perimeter," Grant said as they stepped out the door. "Make sure the police understand that no one gets out."

"And if she kills you?"

Grant gave her a look. "Then I don't care what you do to her."

Grant checked his pistol, reholstered it, and started up the walkway. He saw no lights on in any of the windows. He felt himself tighten up, anxious, and he willed himself to breathe normally.

At the edge of the veranda he looked left and right. No one waited outside that he could see. He stepped up to the door and pressed the bell.

The door opened slightly. A smudge of skin around an eye appeared in the space.

"Agent Voczek?"

"Yes."

"I'll step away from the door and leave it open. Please come in."

"Why don't you come out?"

"Let's not bargain so soon. I haven't made up my mind what to do. Please."

She disappeared. Grant swallowed, took a deep breath, and entered the house.

Within, he saw her dimly at the foot of a broad, bannisterless staircase. He closed the door behind himself, and she gestured for him to follow. At the top of the stairs, the landing opened into a wide platform, backed by tall, geometrically-patterned windows. She went to the left, entering a narrow hallway, and stopped by the first door on her right, waiting. When he reached her, she pushed the door open. Light spilled into the hallway and illuminated half her face and body.

Tess Reed wore black, the kind of practical clothing one would wear for a military operation. Grant noted the pistol at her hip. She gestured for him to enter the room.

The older man—Taraquel—waited within, leaning back against a desk. Dressed similarly, his arms folded across his chest, he gave Tess a dubious look.

"This is not a good idea," he said. He smiled thinly at Grant. "Welcome to the party, Mr. Voczek. May I express my admiration for the way you've fucked everything up?"

"Quiet," Tess said. She went to a chair and sat down, stretching her legs out. "What are you doing, Agent Voczek? Police everywhere, that FBI agent . . . you're becoming a nuisance."

"I thought I already was," Grant said. When she did not respond, he said, "Your father and father-in-law are being arrested for conspiracy to defraud the government. You are being arrested for conspiracy and murder." He shrugged. "I imagine there are more charges, but right now my main concern is arresting you."

She shook her head. "I don't think so. You have no evidence for any of your charges."

"I don't have much, I admit, but I have a witness that you are—were—in charge of the covert lab adjacent to Congressman Tochsin's offices. I have the lab, I have at least one of your people in custody, and now I have you two. I have your presence last night at Aaron Voley's residence—"

"Circumstantial," she interrupted. "I've often been to Aaron's house, on business, with Michael."

"There's more. For the time being, though, I intend to place you under arrest."

"The charge?"

"Murder, attempted murder, conspiracy. But I don't need those charges to put you in protective custody."

She laughed. "Protective custody? Who are you protecting me against?"

"You killed Aaron Voley. You pissed off a friend of his. He's on his way here, now, to kill you. Since he has no warrant and no legal standing as a law officer, it will be murder, but I don't really think he gives a damn. He's coming for vengeance. When he kills you, he'll kill your father, your father-in-law, Congressman Tochsin, and anybody else he can get before he's stopped."

Tess frowned. "Who?" She shook her head. "Why kill Michael? I don't—"

"You mean, Tochsin had nothing to do with Coronin?"

She lost expression. Then her eyes narrowed. "I thought you were looking at Abernathy?"

"Not anymore. I've informed the party next door that he's no longer a suspect. Witness, yes."

"Mitchel? Witness for the federal government?"

"As much a surprise as that may seem, yes. Turns out, he hates being used much more than he hates federals."

Tess stood.

A small beep sounded. Taraquel turned around to study a monitor on the desk. "Someone's just broken into the house," he said. "North wing, ground floor."

Tess scowled. "Who the hell—?"

"Hand over your weapons," Grant said, "and we'll protect you."

Tess drew her pistol. "Like hell." She nodded to Taraquel, who drew his own weapon and left the room.

"Let me guess," she said. "That gypsy—what's his name?—Cozy."

"Have you considered the possibility that you killed the wrong man?"

Tess shook her head. "You miscalculated, Agent Voczek."

Suddenly a shot broke the air. Then another.

Tess looked at the desk. "I think your witness is dead."

"You're sure? Are you mic'd to your man?"

Tess touched a stud on the desk. "Report," she said.

Nothing.

"Fine," Tess said. "Then it's time to leave."

"Why don't you give up? We have Dirkenfeld—"

"You have shit." She grunted. "How easy do you think it will be to make charges against a senator stick?" She shook her head. "Stupid and naïve. I love it."

"Why did you kill her?"

Tess frowned at him. "Who? Oh . . . the other agent. Isn't that obvious? You're here." She waved the pistol. "Let's go."

Grant sighed and went to the door. He opened it enough to peer into the hallway. Empty. He felt her pistol between his shoulder blades and he stumbled out the door.

He began to walk toward the main staircase.

"No," she said. "This way."

He preceded her down the hall, to a back stair that took them down to the kitchen. Grant moved toward the central island, a vague shape in the wan light coming through the windows. He stumbled on something and almost fell, catching himself on the edge of the island.

Tess switched on a flashlight and shined it down on the sprawled body of her partner, Taraquel. Blood spread blackly beneath him.

"Are you here, Cozy?" Grant called.

Tess hissed at him.

"Cozy?" Grant repeated, his heart thundering as he stared at Tess's pistol.

"I'm here, Mr. Voczek," Cozy said very softly. "I got a gun."

Tess's eyes moved in the direction of Cozy's voice. "Put it down, gypsy, and we all get out of here alive."

"I don't think so."

Grant could not see him. He thought the voice came from near the huge refrigerator, but—

Tess swung her weapon around. Grant lunged, ramming her in her chest. Her breath gushed out, followed by a shot.

They hit the floor in a tangle. Grant's head burst into pain from the butt of her pistol. He tried to get his left arm up to block her, and caught her forearm on his elbow.

Her other hand jammed the flashlight into his armpit. He barked sharply to the pain and rolled off her. She snapped to her feet, crouching, aimed into the darkness, and squeezed off two shot.

Grant swung his legs around and knocked her off her feet. She landed on her hip and Cozy fired from somewhere behind Grant.

"Cozy!" Grant shouted. "No! We need her alive!"

"She killed Mr. Voley! She killed Camilla!"

Tess scrambled around the island. Grant rolled to his knees, and pulled out his own weapon. His vision danced with scintilla, his head throbbed.

She appeared, briefly, above the island. Grant fired. In the instant of muzzle flash, she looked surprised. He heard her fall, the sound of a pistol clattering on the floor.

Then the back door opened and closed.

"Cozy," Grant called. "Are you all right?"

No answer came. Grant used the island to climb to his feet.

"Reva," he said, "Tess is out of the house . . ."

He pushed away from the island and staggered into the wall. He found a panel and fumbled with the switches. Lights glared painfully into his eyes. He squinted and looked around the kitchen.

Taraquel stared lifelessly at the ceiling, a hole in his throat.

Across the room, Cozy squatted next to the refrigerator, both hands embracing the pistol propped on his knees. One bullet hole was in the refrigerator. Another was in his shoulder. Tears streamed down his face.

Cozy blankly stared into space as Reva leaned over, examining him. Grant felt clumsy and enraged.

"Bullet doesn't appear to have struck anything vital," she said. "But he certainly needs medical attention."

"Agent . . . ?" a policeman asked from behind.

Grant rounded on the man. "Put out an A.P.B. on Tess Reed," he said. "She may be wounded, certainly armed. And get the paramedics here *now!*"

"They're standing by, Grant," Reva said.

Less than a minute later, the medics brought a gurney into the room. Grant helped them load Cozy, then they took over and strapped him to the gurney.

Grant grabbed one of the paramedics. "He has no CID on him. You put his treatment on the Treasury Department account. He's a material witness. He suddenly 'dies' on the way to the hospital or disappears—"

"Grant," Reva touched his shoulder. "They know."

Grant nodded and watched them wheel Cozy.

"Are you all right?" Reva asked.

Grant shrugged. "Probably not. What about our distinguished suspects?"

"Your Director Koldehn is taking them into custody—*protective* custody for now. Mitchel Abernathy is willing to testify. We have Taraquel." She shook her head. "I don't know. Did we accomplish what we set out to do?"

"I think so." He grunted. "But we found a great deal more that needs doing."

Grant stared at the report on his screen. He still could not grasp it, even though he had written it. So simple, he thought, and lost in so much tangle . . .

Coronin developed, tested, and marketed cutting edge pharmaceuticals faster than any other company in the world. They had enormous markets, both here and overseas. They kept up by bypassing a lot of what they called redundant procedures. Like testing. They went from computer modeling to human tests in one jump. They got their subjects from the barcos. The last several deportations had fed them test subjects no one would follow up on.

Once in a while they needed a specific genetic type, so they found a citizen that matched their profile and replaced him or her with an illegal immigrant or gypsy desperate for citizenship. Reva had stumbled on that in Tamaulipas. It went on all over the country. But mostly they used gypsies. No one really cared, and they had even managed to get the federal government to help with the deliveries.

Lusk had been their code man in Treasury, the one who rewrote the CIDs for the kidnapped victims. According to Tess, they had threatened his family and friends. When he disappeared from D.C., they had panicked and sent in the dogs. Tess was already in St. Louis, preparing the ground for Coronin's newest acquisition. Taraquel and the others arrived to make sure Lusk did not upset anything. For his part, Taraquel had said absolutely nothing since he came to in the back of a police cruiser. Grant wondered how long the man could keep it up. Maybe until someone came to fetch him. It would be interesting to see who that might be.

All this Grant accepted readily enough. He had seen it, guessed much, and understood enough that little of it came as a shock. That and the fact that Paul Kitcher had apparently not trusted his employers. They had set him up in Montreal, then saved him from the wolves and gotten him a position in St. Louis. He had owed them a favor. He had gone along with them, apparently in hopes of reaching his retirement and pulling out completely. But he had kept notes and when Grant finally opened his protected files, he found data going back years on Dirkenfeld, Coronin, and the deportations. It matched the data Beth had acquired.

The surprise was Senator Reed. Reva considered him a bigot, but somehow that seemed to Grant too small a word; too inadequate a description. Without Reed, much of Coronin's program simply could not work.

Senator Parker Reed, Chairman of the Foreign Relations Committee—slaver.

All those trade treaties he had negotiated. All those pieces of protectionist legislation. Everything he had done for almost eighteen years in Congress had allowed him to act as broker for the excess bodies, for the product of their abuse.

He had made the deals and overseen the transactions.

And his daughter had been his wolfhound, his assassin.

The search for her continued, though it was obvious to Grant that she had gotten away. Coronin, he was certain, would find ample employment for her somewhere. He wondered if she would mind living outside the Union.

Grant sent the report and closed his eyes. He was tired. He wanted time off.

The door opened. He looked up at Reva. She grinned and switched on his HD.

"Have you seen this?" she asked.

Congressman Tochsin appeared on the screen.

"—seating a board of inquiry into the conduct of certain members of Congress who have abused their positions and taken advantage of the people. In the wake of the arrests of Senator Dirkenfeld and Senator Reed, I intend to push immediately for a full investigation into the conduct of Coronin Industries and the last decade of deportations of the disenfranchised. We—"

Grant touched his remote and switched it off. "Yes, I saw it earlier. I hope he follows through. At least Coronin can't hide the evidence. That van Cozy took was filled with military-grade material manufactured by Coronin."

"I finally received a report on Tess Reed," Reva said. "I've been trying to get this for days, but it was classified nearly out of *my* reach. She was in Covert Operations, along with Taraquel. Apparently, she was highly decorated. Very good at what she did."

"She's still good at what she does."

"Are you sorry?"

"About what?"

"That you didn't kill her?"

"Am I that transparent?"

"No. It's just . . ."

"I know. Have you received new orders yet?"

"Well, my mission is technically over. I'm heading back to Chicago tomorrow."

"I'll take you to the station."

She smiled. "I'd like that. How about dinner tonight?"

"I'd like that very much."

"Maybe we'll get lucky and see another tagger display." Grant groaned.

His phone chimed. "Agent Voczek."

"This is Chief Moore, Agent Voczek."

"Yes, Madam. How may I help?"

"Would you care to go for a ride with me?"

Grant looked up at Reva. "When did you have in mind?"

"Ten minutes?"

"We'll meet you on Tucker."

"Agent Cassonare? Good. Yes, I'll see you in ten minutes."

Reva frowned. "What now?"

Chief Moore's limousine pulled up at the curb. The door opened, and Reva and Grant got in the back seat. Chief Moore huddled against the opposite door, her face drawn.

"Thank you, Agents," she said.

"We didn't get a chance to thank you—" Reva began.

"Save it. You may not feel like it." Moore scowled and shook her head. "Sometimes I wonder why I don't resign. There are many things a person could do that wouldn't compromise one's conscience."

"What do you mean?" Grant asked.

"This has been an expensive week. Aaron Voley is dead. He will be missed, and not just sentimentally. The public faith in their congressmen is shaken. Not broken, I don't think, but you never know about that. It will be months before we know all the costs and what can't be fixed. And you two are leaving."

"Madam—"

She held up her hand. "I respect the work you did. I'd have to say that it was a net good. But even good has costs. Good is expensive. I wanted you to know just how expensive."

She said no more for the rest of the ride. Grant looked out the window. They headed north, up Highway 70.

The limousine pulled off at the exit outside the barco, then drove up Adelaide and stopped. Moore motioned for them to get out.

Electrical fencing surrounded the barco. Within, quonsets bubbled up in neat rows across from stockades in which crowds of people waited. Trucks loaded groups of gypsies on the far side, near. A hastily-poured spur ran from the loading platform to join up with Interstate 70.

"What in hell is going on?" Reva asked, amazed.

"I don't know . . ." Grant said.

"Did you—? No, you wouldn't have."

He glared at her. "Why would you even ask? This isn't my doing!"

People stood along the footbridge, watching. Their startled expression echoed Grant's own confusion. One of the trucks began its journey from the loading area up the new roadway. As it drew nearer, Grant recognized the stylized caduceus.

"CDC," he said.

Reva nodded. "How—?"

"This has to stop. There's a mistake."

"You won't stop it," Moore said. She stood beside her car. She looked past them, her eyes cold, bitter.

"What do you know about this?" Grant demanded.

She shook her head. "A complete surprise to me. I received the warrant yesterday." She looked skyward for a moment, remembering. "'Due to the unknown nature and transmission vectors of the type X strain *trepona pallidum* present in and around the disenfranchised area, Center for Disease Control has authorization to implement federal quarantine—'"

"But that was an administered disease!" Reva said.

Moore looked at her grimly, then shrugged. "Nothing I can do. CDC has full jurisdiction." She frowned. "You weren't informed?"

"No," Grant said.

"I guess you've been taken out of the loop. Anyway, it's all by-the-rule. I already talked to Judge Thoc Le. His hands are tied. This doesn't have anything to do with your investigation or the events connected to it."

"It does, though," Grant said.

"Not legally."

"I guess," Reva said, "Coronin gets its site after all."

"You didn't really expect them not to, did you?" Moore asked.

"I don't know. I—"

"If CDC has them," Grant said, "maybe they won't be sold out of the country."

"Maybe," Reva said acidly. "What about Cozy?"

"Gone," Moore said. "He left with his girlfriend yesterday, on their way to Chicago."

"Well. At least he got away."

Grant tasted sourness. "At least . . ."

Rycliff met them in the hallway outside their offices. "Ah, Agent Voczek. Agent Cassonare. Have you seen the barco?"

"We just came from there," Grant said.

"What do you make of it? Seems the rats are being removed."

Grant winced. "Yes. Evidently."

"Won't be a permanent solution, but at least for a short while things will be under control."

Grant began to turn away.

"I've been looking for you," Rycliff said. "We've received a notification. D.C. has assigned you here until a suitable replacement for Agent Kitcher can be found."

Grant blinked at him. "How long?"

"They didn't say, sir. My impression was that it is an open-ended assignment."

Grant stared at Rycliff. "You called in the CDC."

Rycliff raised an eyebrow. "Sir?"

Grant sighed. "Never mind. It's not important. Just rats."

"As you say, sir." Rycliff walked away, then paused. "Welcome to St. Louis, sir. I look forward to working with you."

EPILOGUE

T his isn't such a bad city," Reva said.

Grant opened his eyes. Evening light flooded the window, cast orange and gold over everything. He looked at Reva sitting up beside him. A thin sheen of sweat covered her still, and the liquid light contoured her brightly.

"Then maybe you should stay," he said.

"Is that an invitation?"

He looked away.

"Hey," she said. "It's time, don't you think?"

"For what?"

"To let me in. You're the most closed person I've ever met."

"I live on the surface."

"Hell you do. Nobody does. It hurts too much. Except with the right people."

"Are you a 'right people'?"

"I'd like to be."

"That presumes I am. I don't feel very right."

Reva sighed.

Grant got out of bed, started across the room, and stopped, no longer aware of why he moved, where he thought he intended to go.

"I don't understand the question," he said.

"I want to know who you are. That's all."

Grant stared at the bright window. "That all . . . sounds simple. Like directions to a restaurant . . ."

"You don't know, do you?"

"Know what?"

Reva sighed. "Come back to bed. There's time for this later."

He turned. "No. I want an explanation. What does it mean, 'tell me who you are'? People ask it all the time, but—"

"Grant—"

He held up a hand. "When I was a kid, I was the child of an immigrant. People didn't like that. Immigrants are a threat—we're foreigners. So as soon as my father consigned me to the polytech, I stopped being a foreigner. Even if other people still looked at me that way, *I* didn't. *I* stopped being a foreigner. I became whatever was necessary to get along. For my peers, for my teachers—I was good at sports, good at my studies, I pleased everybody. Almost. As much as is possible. When I went through university, I found it convenient to be a chameleon. Be what they want, when they want it, and they leave you alone or help you along. Then I joined federal law enforcement and ended up in Treasury and I found a place where I could be one thing, all the time. I had permission. I'd reached a place where I didn't have to adapt because people might hurt me for what I really am. But it didn't matter. All those things I became before, they're all still me.

"Who am I? Grant Voczek, Special Agent, Resource

Security Division, Treasury Department, Federated States of North America. Every mission I do adds a little more meaning to the title. But for people like you—I don't honestly know what it is you want when you ask who I am. I'm my work. I don't collect old paper currency, I don't give a damn about my genealogy, I'm not terribly interested in history. I'm not political, I have no artistic aspirations, no talents beyond what my job requires, no special obsessions. I have few friends and little desire to make more."

"You can tell me what you aren't forever and it still won't tell me what you are," Reva said.

Grant shook his head. "I just don't know how to answer that."

"Would you like to?"

"I don't know. Is it worth the trouble?"

Reva laughed, startled. "Well . . ."

"I'm sorry—"

"No, no. It's just—you have a way of putting things . . ." She coughed. "Truth?"

He nodded.

"You can't know if it's worth it till you get there."

"Was it worth it for you?"

"Yes."

"I—the truth is, I always measured myself by what others gave me."

"Beth?"

"She was good . . ."

"Maybe you should learn to do that for yourself."

"Maybe."

"But . . . ?"

"My father did that. Measured himself. He didn't seem to need anyone. He didn't need me."

Reva said nothing for a long time. The light faded. Finally, she said, "It's more complicated than that."

"So I always thought."

Later, he thought she asked him to come back to bed. He climbed in next to her and reached out. She took his hand and kissed his fingers, then placed his palm over her heart. He felt his perceptions shift ever so slightly, as if a piece of broken glass had fallen away from his eyes, and from a feeling he could not name he dreamed that long ago he had killed himself and that now, finally, the crime had been discovered and he was being exhumed.

He woke and found himself still wounded and aching, but for the first time in his life wanting to heal.

CHIMERA
AN ISAAC ASIMOV ROBOT MYSTERY
by Mark W. Tiedemann
Cover art by Bruce Jensen
ISBN: 0-7434-1297-4

<u>BOOK 2 OF AN EXCITING TRILOGY!</u>

The Second Law of Robotics states that a robot must obey the orders given it by human beings, except where such orders would conflict with the First Law.

Coren Lanra is the head of security for DyNan Manual Industries. A former Special Service agent, he's never cared for bureaucracy, piracy, or deception. And he *hates* mysteries.

Lanra's troubles begin with the death of Nyom Looms, daughter of DyNan president Rega Looms, during an ill-fated mission to smuggle illegal immigrants from Earth to the colony Nova Levis—all were apparently murdered, but why? The only clue might be contained within the positronic brain of a robot that had accompanied the victims, but it has been deactivated, and Lanra is denied access to its memories.

To make matters even worse, he is soon confronted with a puzzling complication: a possible connection between the murders and twenty babies who were snatched from an orphanage over two decades ago.

With the help of roboticist Derec Avery and Auroran ambassador Ariel Burgess—whom the security chief had aided in exposing an anti-robot conspiracy on Earth a year before—Lanra searches for answers to a twenty-five-year-old mystery . . . and for the identity of a killer, before more lives are lost.

WILD CARDS™
Edited by George R.R. Martin
Illustrations by Mike Zeck
Cover art by Brian Bolland
ISBN: 0-7434-2380-1

When a group of SF's most imaginative writers discovered they shared a secret love of the larger-than-life heroes of the four-color comics and Saturday matinee serials, they gave each other a challenge: What would our world be like if these superhuman heroes and villains had been real flesh-and-blood men and women who lived through this century's most turbulent history?

The alien virus arrived on Earth just after World War II—and the world was never the same. For those who become infected, there are two results: death, or transformation. And depending on the recipient, death is sometimes the preferable outcome. Only a few lucky ones become superhuman "aces" as a side effect of the virus; the rest are turned into horrible, grotesque "jokers." It's a strange and wonderful, terrible and terrifying world where anything can go. A world that, in a twist of fate, could lie just outside your door.

A world of Wild Cards.

Featuring stories by
ROGER ZELAZNY • STEPHEN LEIGH
MELINDA M. SNODGRASS • GEORGE R.R. MARTIN
EDWARD BRYANT • LEANNE C. HARPER
VICTOR MILAN • JOHN J. MILLER • LEWIS SHINER
HOWARD WALDROP • WALTER JON WILLIAMS

WILD CARDS™ II:
ACES HIGH

Edited by George R.R. Martin
Illustrations by Floyd Hughes
Cover art by Brian Bolland

ISBN: 0-7434-2391-7

When a group of SF's most imaginative writers discovered they shared a secret love of the larger-than-life heroes of the four-color comics and Saturday matinee serials, they gave each other a challenge: What would our world be like if these superhuman heroes and villains had been real flesh-and-blood men and women who lived through this century's most turbulent history?

It all began in 1946, when the bizarre, gene-altering "Wild Cards" virus was unleashed in the skies over New York City. A virus that created superpowered Aces and bizarre, disfigured Jokers. Now, thirty years later, the victims face a *new* nightmare. From the far reaches of space comes The Swarm, a deadly menace that could very well destroy the planet. Putting aside their hatred and mistrust, Aces and Jokers must form an uneasy alliance and prepare for a battle they must not lose. . . .

Featuring stories by

ROGER ZELAZNY • GEORGE R.R. MARTIN
MELINDA M. SNODGRASS • WALTER JON WILLIAMS
PAT CADIGAN • VICTOR MILAN • JOHN J. MILLER
LEWIS SHINER • WALTON SIMONS